RUNNING TO CATCH A BUS

Walker Armstrong

Library of Congress Control Number: 2021923716
ISBN: Hardcover   978-1-6698-0052-1
                Softcover   978-1-6698-0053-8
                eBook   978-1-6698-0054-5

Print information available on the last page.

Rev. date: 11/24/2021

To order additional copies of this book, contact:
Xlibris
844-714-8691
www.Xlibris.com
Orders@Xlibris.com
836297

"For Gina"

CHAPTER 1

ANNIE BRYANT WAS bone-tired. She fidgeted in the checkout line at the Gordon Drugstore on a brisk Saturday morning, hoping no one would see her. To conceal her identity, she sought to dress in a radically different way from her normal fastidious manner. Her red hair was loosely pulled back in a scraggly pony tail, covered with a baby blue UNC baseball cap that was worn on the edges from frequent use.

Shading her bloodshot eyes and makeup-free face were a pair of wobbly green and black Wayfarer sunglasses that got slightly askew anytime she quickly turned her head. A hideous violet and lime green warm-up suit completed this impromptu ensemble. It was an impulsive purchase made at Wal-Mart by her and best friend Kim Spenser when they were in a particularly silly mood. Only Kim and a few family members knew she possessed such a repulsive outfit.

Annie was almost home free. She twirled her shopping basket back and forth to reduce her growing state of anxiousness. Her current source of frustration was focused upon an older woman who was digging through her cavernous pocket book for the third time. The lady had mumbled something about looking for an elusive coupon that would enable her to leverage a two-for-one sale on toilet paper.

Annie's basket contained something quite different from toilet paper and Diet Coke. In it was a Cosmopolitan magazine turned face-down; two large bags of Halloween candy; two containers of mascara; a large package of almonds; an eyeliner pen; an energy drink and a partially consumed chocolate candy bar.

She had already taken two large bites out of the candy bar and chased it down with a few generous gulps of the Red Bull with almost no discernible boost in her energy level. The rational part of her brain told her that it would take a little while to get the sugar and caffeine jolt she so desperately needed, but the overwhelming reality creeping into her conscious consideration was that she wasn't feeling very rational today.

It wasn't until she noticed that she had inadvertently sloshed some of the Red Bull on the back of the magazine and on the floor that she halted the mindless, adolescent-like activity. She nervously pawed at the spill with a running shoe trying to disperse the bright red solution, but just seemed to be drawing more attention to her obvious guffaw.

If making a mess wasn't bad enough, she noticed a large smudge of chocolate slathered across her chin as she examined her appearance in the large merciless mirror behind the checkout line. This residual evidence of her momentary lack of self-control triggered an understandable act of self-protective recovery. Pretending to be totally engrossed with the Red Bull spill she bent down to clean up the pinkish fluid with a used tissue from her pocket, hoping to adroitly wipe the smudge off her face on her right sleeve without anyone being the wiser.

Unfortunately, the quick force of squatting down squeezed her carbonated-filled tummy so forcibly that she broke wind. Flush with fresh shame Annie sought a quick route to escape out of the store on all fours so that she wouldn't have to gaze upon snickering eyes.

It was then that Annie realized she had forgotten something. Her teenage daughter Meagan had requested some extra-large eyelashes to compliment the female pirate outfit to she had planned to wear that night at a Halloween Party. If Annie didn't get them, she wouldn't hear the end of it. Without raising her eyes to see who might be gaping at her she got up, pivoted, and quickly scooted over to the cosmetics section.

Upon arriving she tried to rapidly scan the rack, but she was having a hard time reading the prices on the items. She took off her sunglasses so she could more clearly distinguish brands because she was all about finding the cheapest pair the store sold. It was at that moment the thought hit her, *"Oh dear God," please let me get out of here before someone I know walks through the front door!"*

Almost as if on cue the automatic door swung open to her right and her old high school history teacher Phil Mangum strolled in with his wife Dianne. Annie lowered her head and looked the other way, but it was too late.

"Well, if it isn't one of my favorite former students!" barked the old offensive line football coach. "How are you doing, girl?"

"Fine Coach Mangum, hope you are."

"You know, Dianne, she looks almost as pretty as she did when she was in high school." His wife nodded sweetly.

"Hey, you got something on your chin," said the coach so loudly that even someone back in the storeroom could hear him. Annie nodded and tried to remove the rest of the chocolate.

The coach continued his relentless monologue. He scrunched up his oily face and began to look around, and then exclaimed "Good lord, what is that odor? Smells like something up-and-died under one of these shelves."

Embarrassed by her husband's bombastic meanderings, Dianne said "Phil, let's leave Annie alone and go get your prescription." Annie gave an appreciative nod to Dianne. The former student knew that once the Coach got started it was hard to get him to stop, no matter what the subject matter.

"Oh yeah, I gotta' get my blood pressure medicine refilled," complained the overweight man. "Old age ain't for sissies. But the doctor says that this new medicine won't affect my performance in the boudoir." The thought of the hairy, grossly overweight Coach Mangum having sex nearly made the concoction of candy bar and energy drink start to come back up to her mouth. It didn't look like his petite wife was pleased with the prospect either.

Before Annie could excuse herself, she heard the unfortunate words: "Hey, whatcha' got there?" as the Coach peeped into Annie's shopping basket.

Annie tried to distract him by saying "Nothing you would like, Coach." This of course didn't seem to deter his total lack of social propriety.

The coach poked through her items, grinned and then said in his best sardonic tone, "Hmm, looks like a middle-aged woman's survival kit or something. You should be careful of those sweets, because those extra carbs will turn into fat around the old midriff. You don't need to carry around extra weight if you start looking to catch another man, if you catch my drift." He laughed at his own piece of advice grabbing and shaking his gargantuan gut. Neither his wife nor his former pupil found his point a bit humorous.

"Phil, that's enough. I think you've given her all the advice she can handle for the day. Let's go!" commanded the normally sedate woman. He shrugged nonchalantly and told Annie "Okay, well, have a good one," following his wife as she moved with haste towards the back.

Annie breathed a sigh of relief. Coach Mangum had always been a bit of a bore. She was just lucky that her basket didn't contain any feminine products. She looked back to the checkout line. There was only a middle-aged woman and a teenage girl standing at the register so she grabbed the cheapest eyelashes she could find, popped her Wayfarers back on and hurried back to the front of the store so she could get the heck out of Dodge.

As Annie took her place in line, she tried to figure out why she was so tired, but came up empty. The more she thought about it the more anxious she became, making her feel a bit shaky and lightheaded. She wondered if she was sick. Perhaps she had a heart condition, a brain tumor or some mysterious illness that was taking over every cell of her body. It didn't take her long to figure out that this slide into diagnostic melodrama wasn't helping. So, she tried to shake off her obsessive worries like a dog tries to get rid of a pesky flea.

Then, out of nowhere, the real reason why she was so worn out smacked her like a blast of unexpected artic air in her face: Annie was tired of being Annie.

At first, she tried to dismiss this thought as being totally impractical. After all, who in their right mind would try to reinvent themselves at middle-age when such a selfish makeover would create too much chaos and pain in other's lives?

Despite her best efforts, the expanding awareness of her profound fatigue wouldn't be silenced. The more she tried to push it away, the more this singular feeling wrapped around her mind like a rushing torrent, pulling her aware from the shore of logical stability. It seemed useless to deny that she was so fundamentally unhappy, so she gave up and waited for the existential gloom to bury her.

But right before she took the final plunge into the river of middle-aged misery, the twig of a thought snagged her -- Anne believed that she still could muscle her way through the blues. Now that she admitted to herself that she was dissatisfied with her life, she could spend more of her energies on figuring out what to do next.

For example, she could do something different for a living. But that would require more education, or at the very least some sort of apprenticeship with someone that was half her age. Maybe moving somewhere like Atlanta where no one knew her could help her reboot her life from scratch. The only problem with that was she would have to take Meagan with her, and another move would probably send the already extremely moody teen off the deep end.

Annie took a deep breath and told herself, *"This is just the way things are right now. There will be a time when I can figure out a better path. But right now, I have stuff to do."* Her well-meaning self-coaching usually would help her gird up the loins of her mind so she could suck it up and reengage whatever duty lay before her. But today, her Norman Vincent van Peale inner pep talk didn't seem to be helping.

The teen moved out of the way and Annie placed her items on the counter. Out of a sense of exasperation she uttered to herself, "How did I get here?"

"I guess by your cute little car," replied a voice from somewhere in front of her.

Annie was jolted by that unexpected answer. When she shook off the shock, she saw her good friend Tee Blankenship standing by the cash register smiling at her own penchant for cute repartees. Tee was the co-owner of the Gordon Drugstore with Miller, her husband of twenty-four years, and mom to Miller Jr. and Tommy. Of all of Annie's friends Tee was the most unpredictable. She could spin a naughty story that often made her friends howl with guilty delight, and then offer sober analysis for the reasons at a slow business cycle in Gordon at a Chamber of Commerce meeting an hour later. Nothing much phased Tee, even when her friends tried to gently persuade her that attire and hairstyles seemed to be about twenty-five years out of date.

Tee had evidently already added up Annie's purchases and was waiting for her to pay. She looked intently at Annie and asked, "Are you okay sweetie?"

"Eh, yes I'm sorry. What did you say that I owed you?"

"Twenty-six dollars and sixteen cents."

"Here you go," said Annie, handing her a wad of bills and some loose change.

"Annie darlin', you just gave me five dollars and twenty-five cents."

Annie looked right at Tee. She was going to argue the point, but when she looked down and saw that exact amount of money in Tee's hand she plucked the money off the counter, spastically combed through her purse and handed over what she thought was a credit card.

"Ok Annie," patiently replied Tee. "I love Victoria's Secret and so does Miller. But I don't think that their gift card will work at our store." Annie's sunglasses had slid down her nose long enough to reveal that her eyes were now moistening and about to spill out all over the place. Since no one else was in line, Tee stepped around the counter and put her arm around Annie, seeking to say anything that would bring some kind of comfort.

"Annie, what's wrong?" asked Tee.

"Nothing Tee, I'm just tired."

"Are you sure?"

"Yep. But thanks for your concern. I think I will go home and take a nap."

"Do that and I will see you in church tomorrow okay?"

Annie nodded in a reassuring way. Then she quickly handed Tee the right kind of card this time, grabbed the receipt and practically ran out of the store. Tee stood there watching her all the way to the car and then dialed Annie's best friend Kim. When she reached her, she said, "Hey, girl, its Tee. I think something is going on with Annie."

By the time Annie got back to the house, Meagan was in full teenage tilt. Annie could see it coming and almost drove off. Meagan ran right up to the car before it even stopped and as soon as Annie pulled herself out of the Mini-Cooper the tall adolescent lit into her.

"Mom, where have you been? I've called you like nine-million times and you never picked up. Are you deaf or something?"

"Sorry sweetie, I didn't hear it." This was of course a perfectly understandable lie, given only in situations when Momma-hens feel like they are being bombarded by the ceaseless chirpings of their baby chicks.

"What's up?" asked Annie, trying desperately to pick up her energy level.

"What's up?!" retorted Meagan. "I tell you what is up. I have got to get the costume for Lucy's Halloween Party tonight. Don't you remember, or did you forget that too?"

Annie stopped in her tracks as her world-class fatigue was quickly replaced by anger. She spun around and faced Meagan. With her left hand on one hip and her right hand holding up the bag that contained the eyelashes that her daughter "just had to have."

Annie lowered her gaze and said, "I got your eyelashes right here and I will take you to get the outfit this afternoon. Don't push it with me right now!" Meagan of course ignored all the signs that her Mom was on the verge of letting the ungrateful teen get both barrels of her double-ought angst.

"You are always doing things for people at work, at church, even people you don't know that live in this dumpy little town. But when I need one little teeny-tiny thing you ignore me. Why did you have me anyway? Did you need someone to take care of you when you got old? Oh, and here's a newsflash - From the looks of what you're wearing right now, you have become Granny's twin."

That was it. Annie lit into her like a Beagle on a hambone. "Listen, you have no clue what I do for you on a daily basis. If you did maybe, just maybe you would help out a teeny-tiny bit around here. But I can't count on you to do the smallest thing around here, can I little Miss Princess? Oh, by the way, I have no illusions about you taking care of me when I am older because you don't even know how to make toast. And here is a news flash for you: This is a warm up suit that I got on sale so that I could afford to buy your stupid little Pirate-whore outfit for your ridiculous little party!"

"You make me so sick!" screamed Meagan at the top of her lungs. She summarily stomped back in the house yelling irrational sentences sautéed with obscenities.

"I hate you back!!" retorted Annie, all the while shaking her head in mounting disgust.

Normally, Annie would be able to quickly move beyond this kind of argument with her daughter, but not today. This exchange so unnerved her that she unconsciously paced back and forth in the front yard rehearsing other things she might tell her brat when afforded the chance. When she arrived at a more cogent script to share with her daughter about the importance of developing gratitude, she stomped up the front steps, whished through the front door, popped off her shoes and made a bee-line towards Meagan's room.

As she turned the corner, she didn't notice the large pile of dog feces in the middle of the hallway. When her right foot hit the biohazard, she slipped and fell backwards mashing the mess all over her pants and her left hand. The realization of what she fell into evoked a hideous scream that was a mixture of revulsion and sadness. Meagan quickly ran out of her room to see her Mom's legs sprawled out and the evidence of dog stuff pasted all over her mom. She laughed and held her nose.

"Yuck, you are gross!"

"What? Are you kidding me?" replied Annie. "I know you saw this when you went to your room. Why didn't you clean it up?"

"No way, Mom. That is sick!"

Annie jumped up and started towards the teen as if she was going to spread the stuff all over her daughter's face.

Meagan screamed, ran into her bedroom, slammed and locked her door and said, "Stay away from me you crazy lady!" and then started to laugh some more. Annie didn't think the situation was one bit funny.

Covered with dog drippings, Annie yanked off her socks and stomped towards the kitchen. Stuffing her socks under her left armpit she leaned over the sink and turned on the faucet with her right elbow. She washed her hands as quickly as she could, stripped off her clothes to her underwear and moved towards the utility room in a spirit of ongoing resignation. She tossed the soiled suit and socks in the washing machine without any pretreatment, grabbed the box of detergent, dumped a mess of powder in and started a heavy load of wash with only the few items inside. The unique aroma of Tide combined with dog feces was a smell she would soon not forget.

Once she was sure her temperamental washing machine was going to cooperate, she walked back into the kitchen, through the den and eventually into her bedroom. There she noticed the large mountain of unfolded clothes still in the same configuration she left them in when she went out on her excursion earlier that morning.

"It just never ends," she sighed as she looked for something to put on from the large wad of clothes that seemed to be mocking her in the midday sunlight for her obvious lack of homemaking fastidiousness.

Out of the mound she was somehow able to quickly pick out a more sedate pair of light gray sweat pants, white athletic socks, and faded pink tee shirt that read "No shoes, no shirt, no problem" that she got at a Kenny Chesney concert. She quickly put these clothes on and flopped down right in the middle of the multi-colored tepee. Poor, worn-out Annie was about to start crying when the doorbell started ringing.

"What else is going to happen?" she muttered to herself. "If it is those unnerving Girl Scouts selling cookies again, I am going to act like I am blind and I can't sign anything!"

Somehow, she found just enough energy to pull herself out of the mound of clothes and stumbled towards the front door. She was so frustrated that she didn't look through the peep hole to see who was there. She just swung it open and there stood her best friend Kim Spenser dressed in the same hideous warm-up suit Annie had just deposited in the washing machine.

Kim stood there in all of her tacky glory, gave Annie a big cheesy smile, waving her hand in an exaggerated fashion and said, "Hi there! I thought you might need a little more aggravation today, so here I am!"

"Come on in, and while you are at it you can roll on the poop in the floor so we can be just alike!" Annie turned as soon as Kim got a foot in the door, walked back to the den and plopped herself down into her favorite leather chair.

"Oh, that's what that smell is," said Kim as she gingerly entered the domestic war zone. She tried to watch where she was walking while seeking to provide some distracting small talk.

"I see you have been busy this morning," Kim commented as she moved a large stack of newspapers and magazines off the couch to make a place to sit.

"I suppose Tee called you," said Annie in a non-abashed self-pitying tone. "She really ought to mind her own business." Annie slouched further down as she eyed all that she had to do that day.

"Annie, cut it out. She just cares. She was worried about you. That is why she called me and that is why I am here … to save the day!"

"Thank you, Superwoman, but I will be fine."

"Really? You don't look fine and you definitely don't smell fine."

Annie took a quick whiff of herself. "I smell alright. It's the dog crap you catching a whiff of. I hadn't gotten around to getting it up yet. But hey, you are welcome to take care of it since you are here to save the day." Annie stuck her arms straight out and pretended to sail through the air to let Kim know what she thought of her superhero announcement.

Kim gave a spiteful look right back at her best friend. "Nice try, but I am not going to let you mope around this house all day. We are getting out of her for a little bit."

"Kim, I've got too much to do."

"I know, you always do. But I have some gossip to share and I don't have anyone to share it with. It will help me as much as it will help you. Anyway, get your shoes on, unless they have that poop on them and you will need to put something else on your feet. We are going for a walk. Come on!"

Kim snapped up off the couch and spun around. Annie followed slowly behind her picking up a wrinkled dark purple hoodie from the back of the couch and went to the front door to retrieve her discarded running shoes.

Meanwhile Kim made a sharp right out of the den and took a quick hop over the smeared dog's mess. She then looked around to make sure she hadn't stepped in any and knocked on Meagan's bedroom door. Meagan squeezed her door open ever so slightly and spied around the corner to make sure that the coast was clear.

"Hey Kim, is Broom Hilda still here?" asked the nervous girl.

"Yes, and both of us witches are going for a walk. By the way, if you don't have the dog crap cleaned up when we get back, I will tell Tee's son Tommy that you think he is the bomb!"

"Oh my God you wouldn't!" cried out Meagan. One look at the matter-of-fact expression on Kim's face confirmed that she would. "Oh alright, but please bring her back with a better attitude okay?"

The two friends marched out of the house down the driveway and turned left on Briarwood Lane. About a block later they turned left again on Oak Valley Road. They walked above the curb on the left side of the road atop some faded grass until they got on the newly constructed greenway trail, made of crushed rocks and an assortment of recycled material.

Kim walked almost as fast as she talked. Her blistering pace hardly gave Annie time to breathe, much less wallow in her middle-aged funk. Even though they had just got started, the rate at which they were traveling was already making Annie wished she had never agreed to leave the sarcophagus of her leather chair.

"So how is work at the Center?" asked Kim.

"Okay, just all the changes in healthcare make admitting new residents a real headache."

"But at least it is a decent job. My part-time work at the drugstore barely gives me enough money to cover my wine habit!"

"Well, you do drink a lot," smirked Annie.

"Shut up. You would too if you had to play nice all the time for the ladies at NewLight Church. Speaking of that, did you know that Joanne and Billy Phillips are getting a divorce?"

"What? No way! They seemed so, so ..."

"Domestically content?"

Annie sadly nodded.

"Well, it seems that Billy's contentment was being partially fulfilled by some young thing in Asheville. Anyway, Mike has been counseling them but he thinks that Billy is a goner."

Annie thought about her former husband's philandering ways. Her jaw stiffened when she remembered all the times she wasted dragging him to marital therapy while he was still sneaking off for another secret rendezvous with the red-headed skank.

"Men can be such simple-minded pigs!" snarled Annie.

"Yeah, well maybe so," replied Kim as she looked straight ahead.

The walking trail now began to get steeper. Half-way up the hill the gravel path turned into a brick walkway that led into a gated entrance of a new development called Briar Mountain. It contained customized million-dollar mountain chalets; a top-tier private golf course designed by Jack Nicklaus; and a multi-level club house that overlooked a gorgeous view of the Blue Ridge Mountains. The sprawling back porch of the clubhouse provided such a sublime scene that it had been featured in several magazines as one of the best new destinations in the country.

Kim changed her blank expression to a wry smile when she saw the entrance. "Hey, Annie, why don't you find a rich old man to marry and buy one of those little old homes so I can come over and see how the other half lives?"

"The thought has crossed my mind," said Annie grinning back at her.

Right in the middle of their discussion of what it would be like to be rich, two police cars came zipping by them and pulled into the yard of a dilapidated home, protected by a large Pit Bulldog. This snarling protector was tethered to a rusty chain, anchored at the bottom of a twisted pine tree. It was quite ironic that it was juxtaposed right across the street from Gordon's version of Shangri-La.

But it was not alone. All along that side of the road were muddy entrances into more primitive domiciles that were lined up on the hillside, seemingly hanging on for dear life. Compared to the idyllic homes in Briar Mountain, they looked like fodder for some documentary film on poverty in the New South.

"What do you think is going on there?" asked Kim.

"Probably another drug bust," retorted Annie. "It's sad. Those used to be nice little homes. I grew up with kids who lived all up and down this road. Ever since all the companies closed down, they seemed to have slowly deteriorated into worn out shacks. What has happened to my town?"

Kim didn't take much time examining the panoramic display of poverty that had added to her friend's growing despair. She was too busy leading their expedition to get some coffee. In a few moments they turned left at the top of the hill onto Main Street.

As they entered the eastern side of downtown, they saw the familiar faded profile of Teddy Roosevelt on the brick edifice of the old Gordon Tobacco Company building. He was in his Spanish War uniform holding a cigar called "The Country Gentleman." The caption to the right of his toothy grin read "I'm bully for New Canaan Tobacco!" The company had long been closed since it had been bought out by RJR Tobacco back in 1989.

Presently the two-story building housed a gym on the bottom floor named Gordon Fitness, and the offices of a supplement company on the upper floor called Blue Ridge Nutraceuticals. It promoted natural, organically-certified remedies for maladies ranging from memory loss to sub-par sexual performance. The juxtaposition of the two businesses led to a string of off-color jokes.

Right across the street was the Gordon Fire Department. Next door to it was the County Courthouse, Police Department and Town Jail, all crammed into a three story, rose-colored sandstone building that had the look of a nineteenth century Gothic mansion. Beside the Courthouse was the Public Library that bordered Main Street and Broad. It had a more mid-century, modernist feel to it simply because it was the last building constructed downtown.

Back in the driveway of the Fire House stood Chief Andy Foley directing two young rookies on the fine art of fire-engine washing. He spied the women and threw up his hand. Annie returned the courtesy and yelled "Hey, Chief! Looks like you are training some of our town's finest in the essentials!"

"Yep," replied the Chief. "They think it is a waste of time but I call it character development one-oh-one!"

Annie smiled and gave him the thumbs up. She turned back to Kim and said out of the side of her mouth, "He's one to give instructions on character. My dad told me he was back in court last week due to another DUI. I am from this place and I honestly don't know how he has stayed on as chief!"

"Uh-huh," replied Kim, looking disinterested in this piece of Gordon gossip. "Anyway, are you going to Zumba Class this afternoon?" asked Kim.

"I have to. I'm teaching for Suzie."

"I might go," said Kim in a still somewhat distracted manner. She looked back at Blue Ridge Nutraceuticals advertisement on the front of the old Gordon Tobacco Company building. Then she suddenly stopped and grabbed Annie by the arm asking, "Hey, do you think that vitamin BaZing really works?"

Annie looked thrown for a loop. "You mean the male enhancement pill? I have no earthly idea. Why in the world would you ask me that question?"

Kim grinned. "I am for anything that could help Tim along."

Annie shook her head. "That is just plain wrong. Why would you put that picture in my head? Your husband is my pastor for goodness sake!" Kim just shrugged her shoulders and resumed her almost manic pace.

They crossed the street right by Crutchfield's Jewelry Store to Stardust Coffee Shop. "The Dust," as Kim and Annie liked to call it, had previously been so many enterprises that people lost count. Still, it had coffee and pastries that could rival anything you could get in Asheville.

As a customer entered, the cash register and coffee bar were on your immediate right with the rest of the shop crammed full of tile-covered tables, fancy wooden chairs and leather furniture that gave a classy ambiance to the surroundings. On the walls were both pictures from the early days of Gordon interspersed with paintings from local artists. The owners, Fareesh and Tammy Sing, not only wanted to support artists from the town but knew that they had to do everything they could to create a stable business in a town where anything that was new was usually looked upon as strange and unnecessary.

As Kim and Annie came inside Fareesh was making his world-famous Pimento Cheese and Bacon Sandwich, while a teenage girl was helping Tammy crank out several coffee orders.

"Hey, Fareesh, how is business?" asked Kim.

"Better since I started sending out the coupons through that mailer. Good to see you Kim. Who is that strange person with you?"

"Yeah, it is crowded today," said Annie. "I'm happy for you guys, but especially for Tammy since she isn't a foreigner."

"Very funny red-neck lady," replied Fareesh. "Here, please sit as far back as possible so you want disturb my real customers."

"I'm sorry," she said in a fake kind of contemptuous disregard. "I do not understand you because of your weird accent."

Fareesh shook his head and chuckled. He loved Annie. She had introduced Tammy to Fareesh when they were all freshmen at Chapel Hill. Annie had been in their wedding four years later, and was godmother to their three kids. Annie loved them because they stood by her side in good times and bad. And it didn't hurt that they gave her free coffee when no one was looking.

"Oh look, it is our first table!" said Kim grinning as they walked past the ordering station. "Let me go and order for us while you save our seats."

Annie nodded. She sat down and surveyed the surroundings. She only knew a few people in the crowded shop. Despite the uptick in business, she really worried if Fareesh and Tammy's little business would make it to the end of the year.

Kim handed Annie her drink. "Ok, I got you Tammy's Autumn Latte with some cinnamon. Isn't that what you were having the day we met?" quizzed Kim.

"Yes Kimmie!" said Annie in an exasperated fashion.

"You look deep in thought. What is going on?" asked Kim as she peeled the top off her drink and blew on it to cool it down.

"Just thinking how backwards and weird my hometown is."

"Well yeah, but what exactly do you mean?"

Annie took a quick breath as she surveyed the shop. "I was thinking how hard to get old dogs to do new tricks, especially when it comes to food and beverages."

"You talking about your folks?"

"Yeah. Them and everyone else above seventy. Just the other day I tried to get Pops to come over here and get a coffee. You know what he said?"

"No telling."

"He told me, 'Nah baby. I wouldn't know what to order. And if the guys saw me there, they might think that I had gotten a little light in the loafers. I'll stick with my JFG brand.' Can you imagine? He can't seem to pull himself away from his cronies at Larry's Biscuit Shop"

"My parents are the same way girlfriend."

"Well it is wrong. I mean I look around and see how Gordon is dying a slow death and people are worrying about being seen as gay for just trying something new." She took a deep breath and then proclaimed "No wonder people with any sense and style want to move away."

Kim shook her head in agreement. "You are right." Then Kim tried to make eye contact with her friend when she asked "So tell me, what is all the doom and gloom about today? Is it just about the lack of economic development in Gordon?"

"No. Nothing new. I'm just tired of working at everything in my life, that's all."

"Everything?"

"I think that is what I said Kim."

"Is our friendship work to you?"

"Sometimes." Annie leaned in towards Kim as if she was getting ready to lay down some deep wisdom and said, "Who is the one that normally puts together all of our outings?"

Kim thought and countered, "So if I started taking over that responsibility you would be ok?"

"Priceless. You are now making fun of my fatigue. No Kim, it is just one area of my already crowded life. But you wouldn't understand. You have a wonderful husband and an adoring congregation …"

"My husband is far from perfect Annie Pearl, and there are people at NewLight who would fry me for dinner if they had the chance," said Kim without missing a beat. Annie looked off in the distance and didn't see the flash of fear in her friend's eyes. She was too busy enjoying her status as Queen of the Blues.

Kim leaned forward and spoke in a lower tone like an anonymous source that was getting ready to share a big secret … "Annie, all kidding aside your life is all about work: Work at The Center; work raising Meagan; work helping people at church and in the community. You even work at working out! You need some adventure in your life."

Annie laughed. "Are you talking about inserting a man into my crazy existence? No thanks. I don't have a good track record in that area. I'm better off staying at home on weekends watching re-runs of Little House on the Prairie with the dog and the Diva."

"I know you have had your problems, but I get worried when you get like this," commented Kim in an almost mournful way.

"Yeah, I don't know Kimmie. I'm trying to figure out this rut I'm in."

"You mean this most recent rut, right?" said Kim in a corrective tone.

Annie frowned at her pushy friend. "Yeah, whatever preacher's wife. Anyway, I am not sure where it's coming from. I feel like I'm in autopilot traveling at six hundred miles an hour not certain of when or if I'm ever going to land!"

"Well, of course you feel that way. You are all work and no play. That is what I have been trying to tell you. You need to sign up on a dating site and find some young stud and live a little."

Annie put her hand over her mouth and muffled a gasp. "Kim, you are getting as bad as Tee!"

"Oh, I am a lot worse than Tee girl. Tee is more talk than walk."

Annie looked around to see if anyone they knew heard what the pastor's wife was declaring.

"Kim, please be careful. People who hear that kind of stuff will think you are serious."

"Who wants to be careful? And who's to say I'm not!"

"Oh Lord child, you are going to give me a heart attack one day!"

Kim giggled. "Maybe you need a jolt to get that plane of yours to land somewhere and enjoy the scenery. I'm thinking some tropical destination would be good."

"You are right Kim. Not about traveling right now, but about having some more fun. I stuck in a rut, but I am ready to climb out. Got any brilliant ideas?"

"Nothing spectacular yet," smirked Kim. "But give me time darling, give me time." They both laughed and did "cheers" with their coffee cups.

"So, what is Meagan dressing up as for the big party, the daughter of Joan Crawford?"

"You are not funny, and for your information a female Pirate."

"Oooohh, maybe she will meet a younger version of Johnny Depp."

"Kim, you're not helping me one bit. It is not a decent costume. I mean, it is not something you would find in an adult novelty store, but it is not far off. I shouldn't have gotten it for her, but honestly, I am tired of the daily battles with her and just gave in. I guess I am not that great of a Mom."

"You are a good Mom Annie. You just have to do the parenting thing all by yourself. And when parents get tired teenagers are like sharks when they smell blood in the water … they move in for the kill!" Kim clapped her hands so loudly trying to simulate a shark bite that she startled Mabel Billings who was sitting behind Annie trying to grab a morsel of gossip. Mable let out a yelp and spun back around to clean up her coffee spillage.

Annie pretended like she didn't hear her friend's effort at genuine encouragement. "I don't get her Kim. Nothing is easy with that kid. She has this kind of radioactive anger in her that just seems to never stop bubbling over and burning everyone around her. It is as if she is still blaming me for the divorce and everything else that she thinks is wrong with her life. I think she even probably believes I am responsible for global warming too."

Kim snorted and coughed some of her drink on Annie's arm. Annie didn't say anything because Kim quickly wiped her friends' speckled arm and blurted out a child-like "Sorry" before Annie could voice some feigned revulsion. Before they knew it, both busted out in laughter which seemed to lighten Annie's mood a little.

As soon as they both regained composure Kim said, "I think she is a good kid Annie. She's just a very strong-willed person. Just like her Momma."

"I guess so, but I don't remember giving my Mom these kinds of fits."

"Well, didn't you get in trouble with the law when you were a senior in high school? If I recall you and Lori Johnston snuck out of the house with your Daddy's liquor and got drunk. I seem to remember y'all trying to tip some cows and you throwing up in the back of that State Trooper's cruiser."

Kim's statement caused Annie to pause. She turned a little red hoping no one else heard that story. "Ok, I did some stuff, but if I talked to my parents the ways she did I would have gotten my mouth popped. I just don't remember being that disrespectful."

Kim looked at her with the kind incredulity that made Annie drop her gaze to the floor with a guilty smirk slowly sliding across her face.

"Well, it is just different. If you had one you would understand. Anyway, speaking of the little twit I have got to get back and go pick up the outfit. I had Momma makes some alterations so it wouldn't be too revealing."

They stood up from the table and as they were getting ready to leave, Kim spotted a delivery truck at their favorite restaurant Angelo's. She grabbed Annie's right wrist and said excitedly, "Did you hear that Angie finally sold the restaurant? I overheard it was to some strange guy from out of town!"

Annie looked disgusted. "I'm not surprised. He's probably part of some huge conglomerate that has forced Angelo out and now will turn it into a new Target or Bath and Body Works shop. Just one more wonderful landmark that's gone."

Kim shook her head, refusing to let Annie off the hook, "I don't get you. One moment you are talking about the need for change around here and the next you fuss when it happens. It still is a restaurant. There is no way they would put a Target here in downtown. And besides, you love Target! In fact, now that I think about it, you love Bath and Body Works too."

Annie knew her contrived anti-establishment protest didn't fool Kim. She enjoyed retail therapy as much as the next girl. It was she just that she loved that old restaurant and the thought of someone else running it made her feel powerless.

"You don't understand Kim. How would you feel if every week it seemed like someone was bulldozing your memories down, one at a time? Sometimes I look around me and wonder if my childhood was as happy as I remember it. I know change is a part of life, so don't give me that speech. But does everything have to change?"

"You are really in a funk aren't you girl?" said Annie's concerned friend. "I was just going to say that if I was you, I wouldn't feel good if I saw that happen. But then again, I didn't have such a great childhood. So, all this nostalgia doesn't appeal to me. I kind of like change. It keeps me on my toes."

"You are right, I guess. My life sucks so bad right now that I am trying to cling to some memory of past happiness to a least give me hope that it could happen again. I don't know. Sometimes I look around here and see how people are trying to inject life in this old worn-out town and I wonder if it is going to work. I guess I look at myself the same way and think that my best days are already behind me too."

Kim frowned and gently popped her best friend on her hand. "That is the stupidest thing I have ever heard. You are a beautiful, smart, industrious and loyal person. There are so many people around here that admire you. You need to stop this pity party right now!"

"Ok, it's now officially stopped," spoke Annie, moving her hands in syncopated fashion as if she was giving forth some kind of mystical incantation.

In the midst of Annie's nostalgic harangue Kim got another mischievous grin on her face. "Hey … I got an idea. Why don't I get the girls together tonight to review the new food and owner? And it will be my treat!"

"Well I can tell you right now, it won't be good as Angie's food!" declared Annie, hoping to reinstate her status as the protector of the old ways.

"Yes, yes we all know you are the best judge of culinary delights in this cultural center of the Western Hemisphere," sarcastically pined Kim. "But could you please just shut down your inner critic for a few hours and try to just enjoy yourself?"

Annie laughed. She knew she had it coming. "Oh, alright. Anything you want me to do?" she asked sheepishly.

"No darling," said Kim. "Just look beautiful!"

CHAPTER 2

ANNIE DROPPED HER darling little pirate off at Lucy Lowder's. She made sure that little Lucy's Mom Arlene knew where she would be and told her to give her a call if "things got out of hand." Arlene smiled and said, "What can get out of hand with fifteen-year-old silly girls anyway?" Annie nodded and said a little prayer of protection for her naïve friend.

As soon as she said her goodbyes Annie jumped into her turbo-powered, Mini-Cooper and zipped downtown. She drove by Angelo's and noticed a huge crowd around the normally sedate restaurant. *"That's weird,"* she mused to herself. Because of the volume of people at this corner it took her a while to find a parking space.

Eventually she discovered a small slot behind the Gordon Pharmacy that looked like it was custom-made for her car. She jumped out and checked her watch to see that she was about ten minutes late. As she turned the corner from Founders Street onto Main, she tried to put her worries over Meagan into the back of her mind.

The cool October air made her pick up the pace quite a bit. As she walked past Laura's Gift Shop where she saw a reflection of herself that caused her to pause. She made a quick assessment of her appearance. Annie was wearing a deep burgundy sweater and a camel skirt with burgundy pumps that perfectly matched her sweater. She accented the classic look with pearl earrings and necklace her Granny gave her after Meagan was born. As she surveyed her hair, makeup and outfit she thought to herself, *"Looking good girl. Maybe I've got a little more gas left in the love tank!"*

Crossing the street some young lads in a pickup truck honked at her as they passed by and made some cat calls. She blushed, wagged her finger and shouted, "I went to school with your mothers, so watch it boys!"

Once she reached the other side, she slowed down her gait. It was hard for her to do. She was always in a hurry, moving from one accomplished objective to the next assignment on her crowded to do list. Somehow, in the midst of making a living and taking care of everybody, Annie had forgotten what it was like to enjoy just being a woman. With an almost mechanical intensity she leaned her head back, breathed in a deep swath of cool air and began to swing her hips ever so slightly. She started laughing when she thought about what it was once like to be young and trying to learn how to be appealing to the opposite sex. She laughed even harder when she remembered she was just going to hang out with the girls instead of trolling for a man.

As soon as Annie reached Angelo's she noticed how packed it was for 6:30 p.m. on a Friday. Except for a loyal clientele that frequented the restaurant, and the customary procrastinators that went by the drug store for a last-minute purchase, Gordon was usually already rolled up and put to bed. Now, people she didn't even recognize were mingling outside on the sidewalk with drinks in hand making small talk and anxiously waiting for their names to be called. She wedged herself through the door and wondered if any of the gals had gotten there yet. Back in the left corner she spied Kim and Mary Thompson.

Along with Annie, Kim and Tee, Mary was the fourth member of what the women called "The Shopping Squad." She was wife of the town mayor Nolan Thompson and mother to Darla, Rebecca and Taylor.

Mary was not a refined person despite her status. She was a true redhead that was built more like a fire hydrant than a delicate flower of the South. Her sturdy figure reflected her no-nonsense approach to life. Mary could care less who you were or what you had. She was raised on a dairy farm outside of town and liked to say, "I've shoveled enough cow manure to recognize when someone is full of it." People didn't mess with Mary. Even her husband gave her a wide berth when she was fired up.

Annie said hey to several people as she weaved her way through the packed restaurant before finally plopping herself down in the booth.

"Va-voom!" said Mary when Annie approached the table.

"Wow girl!" echoed Kim. "You look great."

"Thanks. I can't remember the last time I got dressed up" said Annie. "I think it was Buddy Tanner's funeral."

"Well it was worth the wait!" commented Mary. "I think you could raise the dead with that outfit."

"You are crazy" replied Annie.

"Speaking of crazy, wait until you get a load of what Tee is wearing" said Mary. "She is in the bathroom, so try not to fall on the floor when she comes back."

Mary wasn't kidding. When Tee rounded the corner, Annie saw what Mary was talking about. Tee was wearing an outfit that could only be described as a dime store inspired representation of *Little Miss Saigon*. Her hair was piled up in an Asian-style bun, pinned up with some kind of audacious costume jewelry. If she was lit up, she could have served as living billboard advertisement for Lao's Chinese Restaurant.

"Greetings Geisha girl," said Annie. She couldn't refuse picking on her good friend, and the jab made her feel less nervous about being around town.

"Ha, ha" replied Tee. "You're just jealous cause you can't make this work for you like I can." Tee looked around and then commandeered a young waiter. "Hey young man, bring us another bottle of the house Pinot Grigio."

"Another?" quizzed Annie. "How long have y'all been here?"

"Long enough to scope the joint" said Mary. "Oh, just so you know, Darrell is here with his newest conquest."

Darrell Eller was a pharmacist at Mack and Tee's store and someone Annie had a brief fling with a couple of years after she moved back home. Handsome, funny and urbane he seemed somewhat out of place in such a small town. He looked a little like a poor woman's Cary Grant, but without the British accent. Women at Shear Ecstasy Beauty Salon made sure to keep the embers of gossip evenly distributed around town regarding Dr. Feel Good's exploits. The gossip didn't bother Darrell. He liked being the talk of the town. Every dog has its day and Darrell considered himself a big dog in a small lot.

Annie snapped her head up with that announcement looking throughout the restaurant to find the scoundrel. Mary pointed to a corner near the bar and there was Mr. Wonderful with some young woman in a small turquoise dress with a generous amount of her cleavage displayed for anyone to inspect.

Annie gasped and said, "Great. This is just what I needed to make a hard day even harder. Is there some place under the table where I can have my glass of wine?!"

"No way" countered Tee. "Don't let that jerk ruin our wonderful outing!"

"You said it sister!" agreed Kim in a somewhat bitter fashion. She grabbed the newly delivered bottle of wine and refreshed her glass.

"Ok preacher's wife," warned Mary. "You need to slow down a bit."

Kim shook her head and replied, "Slow down, I am just getting started!"

Annie sat there trying to get her mind off her troubles. She looked at the newly-designed menus and was impressed. "Goodness. These look like something you would find in New York City."

"Yes, and that isn't that half of it," responded Mary. "The new owner has sunk a lot of money into this place. I was talking with Angie's wife Marta the other day and she told me that the new guy is also cooking here. Angie is helping out until he and Marta decide what to do with their unexpected windfall!"

Annie looked around and confirmed what Mary had reported. Fresh paint, new light fixtures, and beautiful pieces of art portraying life in Italy now decorated the interior of her favorite place to eat. Even the plastic red and white checkered table cloths had been replaced with fine ivory-toned linen ones. She tried to find fault with what she saw, but was secretly impressed.

"I hear he is handsome too," giggled Kim.

"Ok, if you giggle like that once more, I am going to cut you off" warned Annie.

"Oh, leave her alone" said Tee. "It is good to see the preacher's wife have a little fun."

"Good evening ladies!" The girls looked up and saw a man in his sixties standing at attention in a traditional tux. This elegant gentleman was none other than Angie the former owner.

Angelo Lanetti was a character to say the least. He was a second generation Italian-American whose father Luigi immigrated from the Old Country to Asheville as a young stone mason. Luigi tried to get his oldest son to adopt his trade, but the young man told his father he had huge dreams and that he "would make it big one day." He left Gordon to when he was eighteen and moved to New York to try to become a famous singer. When that didn't pan out, he joined the Marines and eventually fought in the Vietnam War.

After the war he traveled a bit and ended up in Italy where he learned how to cook and met his bride. He moved back to town in 1970 with his pregnant wife when his father helped him buy an old diner that he turned into Angelo's Italian Eatery. This quickly became the place to eat and hang out in Gordon. People from all walks of life showed up there to consume tasty food and be entertained by Angelo's jokes and impromptu songs. He was one of the first people in Western North Carolina to install a top-drawer Karaoke machine. Angie was known to do a mean imitation of Tom Jones and loved to sing the song "Delilah."

"And how are the most elegant ladies in Gordon tonight?" asked the gentleman in his Tuscany accent peppered with a Carolina drawl

"Good," replied Annie. "What is this I hear about you selling the best restaurant in the world?"

He smiled as he told Annie and her friends. "I wasn't looking to sell. But Bart showed up and before I knew it, he had me talked into selling the place to him." Stroking his jet-black mustache, he repeated one of his favorite phrases "The Lord has been good to old Angelo."

"We are happy for you and Marta" interrupted Tee as she sought to prevent Annie from ruining their happy mood by cross-examining him. "Here is our big question: Can we count on the same great food at a reasonable price with the new owner in charge?"

"Oh, you are a 'gonna being very pleased, very pleased" responded the gentleman. "Would you permit ol' Angelo the privilege of ordering for you tonight?" Typically, they would not have agreed because each had a favorite dish they rarely deviated from. But curiosity over the new owner/chef got the best of them.

"And the wine is-a-on me" announced the dapper Italian. Tee tried to object but he waved her off just like an Air Boss orders the pilot of an F-14 to not land because he was approaching the carrier too quickly.

"I must respectfully insist. After all I am now a very rich man and you are some of my favorite people in the world." Such charm was impossible to refuse. The girls had often postulated that Angie was probably a real ladies' man back in the day before Marta and the Lord got a hold of him.

"Woo-hoo!" shouted Kim.

"Ok Annie, I take it back. I think we do need to cut her off" responded Tee. She looked at Kim and gave her the universal sign to shut up with her index finger pressed ever-so-slightly against her purple-colored geisha lips.

Within a few minutes freshly-baked bread came to the table accompanied by Caesar salad. This alone could have made a wonderful meal. The women talked while they devoured the hot aromatic bread and crisp tangy salad. Between bites they laughed out loud and said a few "have mercies" as Mary held court about the latest gossip in town.

Then their teenage waiter brought each lady the main course. Tee received Lasagna with meat sauce. The blend of Italian cheeses was married perfectly to the interwoven bed of almost a-dente noodles. This perfectly stacked pie was smothered in a garlic-infused red sauce that was made with a brilliant combination of spicy sausage, tender lamb, hearty beef, spinach and a four-cheese blend that would easily have donned the cover of Southern Living.

Kim got the Lobster Ravioli. Each piece of pasta had a hint of rosemary that was folded into a spinach-based foundation. At the heart of the dish were delicate pieces of Maine lobster bathed in a sherry and saffron-based sauce that made you want to lick your plate when no one was looking. The succulent dish was topped off with exquisite shavings of parmesan cheese atop tender snippets of asparagus that had been grilled with just the right amount of salt, pepper and olive oil.

Mary got the Shrimp Penne. Each crustacean was slightly pink, and deveined from stem to stern. It was linked with pine nuts, Baby Bella mushrooms, pasta, and spinach. The perfectly aged Parmesan and rich chicken broth accented with lemon zest incorporated all of these ingredients into a creamy dream. If shrimp ever had a say in how their lives would end, they would have quickly volunteered for this one-way mission.

Finally, Annie got her favorite -- Chicken Marsala. She was prepared for the worst. Next to her Momma's Macaroni and Cheese this dish was the ultimate comfort food. No matter what she was going through, if she could just have one helping of this food, she felt like she could postpone the blues. Once during her freshman year at Chapel Hill her Mamma brought her a helping of Angelo's specialty because she was homesick. She took a deep breath a placed a generous portion in her mouth.

What happened next was surprising. In that one bite she tasted luxurious combination of the simple flavors of rich butter, sweet wine, roasted garlic, the twang of fresh oregano, pure olive oil and something else that was present but she couldn't quite detect. And the linguine was so tender that it seemed to carry the chicken on a smooth trip from lips, around the mouth, and down her throat to a soft landing in her tummy. Simply biting into a mushroom seemed to release an explosion of flavors that made her not want to drink anything out of the fear that she might dilute the delectable food.

Angelo quietly walked up to the table watching the women as they were diving into their food and asked, "So what do 'ya think?"

"Oh my," said Tee.

"Yeah, oh my," echoed Kim.

Mary just nodded and grinned.

"And how about my sweet little Annie?" questioned Angelo in an almost parental tone. "Does she like her favorite still?"

Annie looked back and smiled. She hesitatingly replied, hoping she would not hurt her old friend's feelings "It is wonderful Angie, just wonderful."

"Great! Senior Bart will be pleased." Then rubbing his hands together with a conquering smile the master of gastro delights changed gears and asked, "Who wants some dessert?"

The ladies initially put their hands up in a surrender-like fashion. But eventually they caved into the sweet insistences of their old friend and agreed to share a large piece of Italian Cream Cake.

When the waiter came back with the cake, Tee got a smile on her face as she spoke to the young man. "Jason," said Tee in the sternest manner she could muster. "Please send the new owner out here. I have a serious complaint!" The other girls looked shocked. Before they could ask a question, Tee hushed them up and sent the confused teen on his way.

In less than a minute a tall man wearing a chef's apron and a red bandana on his head with a cloth draped over his left shoulder quickly strode over to the table. He had the look of frustration written all over his face as he efficiently moved through the crowd to get to his objective. As he got closer, he appeared to be in his forties but had the angular cut of a man who took very good care of himself. His hazel eyes, furrowed brow and neatly groomed goatee reflected the kind of intensity that would be hard to escape. He was all business when he finally arrived at the table.

"Ladies, I understand that there is a problem. How can I help?" said the perturbed chef.

All the women looked to Tee. She cleared her throat and said "My name is Tonya Blankenship, owner of the Gordon Pharmacy. This is Kim Spenser. Her husband Tim is the Pastor of NewLight Community Church. Here is Mary Thompson. She is the classy wife of our mayor. And last but not least, this is Annie Bryant the Admission Director of Oak Valley Rehabilitative Center."

"Nice to meet you all," nodded the exasperated chef. "My name is Bart St. Claire. Now that we have gotten that out of the way, what seems to be the problem?" He now was focusing right into Tee's wide-open eyes.

"Uh, yes," stammered Tee. "Well there isn't really a problem. I guess I brought you to our table under false pretenses."

"Pardon me?" spoke the incredulous owner.

"Well," replied Tee as she did her best to look away from Bart's penetrating glare. "We just wanted to meet you and we felt that you were so busy you wouldn't give us the time of day so I told a little white lie."

Bart looked up to the ceiling and took a large breath. He gathered himself and then said "Look, I am busy. So, if you don't mind, I need to get back to the kitchen."

"I'm sorry" said Tee. "I thought you would like to know some of the more important women here in town. And did I mention that Annie is single?"

"That's nice," replied Bart. "Good evening ladies and please come back to Angelo's." And then Bart disappeared back into the kitchen faster than he arrived. The ladies sat there with mouth's open staring into space as if they had just witnessed a car wreck. Finally, Annie spoke up …

"That was so special Tee. Thanks for that!" Annie took a large swig of wine and slumped back on the leather back of the booth.

"Oh well, nothing ventured nothing gained," retorted Tee. "He is handsome but his Momma evidently didn't teach him proper manners."

"Yeah, handsome and insensitive," said Kim. "Does that sound familiar? He is not what you need right now."

"What I need right now is for my friends to quit trying to fix me up," rejoined Annie.

As soon as she finished that statement the women noticed that there was another guest standing at their table. It was none other than Darrell. This was the last person everyone at the table wanted to see.

"I am sure Annie can take care of herself," said Darrell in a somewhat nervous tone.

Annie looked stunned. All she could do is nod, raise her eyebrows and look away to the front of the restaurant as if she was expecting someone she knew to walk through the door any second.

"I'm sorry to disturb you," said Darrell in an even more nervous manner.

"Not as sorry as we are" countered Mary.

"Well, I just wanted to let Kim know that her prescription is ready." Darrell looked at Kim and all she could do is give the reply, "Gee thanks Darrell. By the way, what time do you need to have your little bimbo back home? Be careful, her Daddy might get mad if you bring her in too late."

Almost on cue, the bimbo started walking up to the table. She flashed her perfect smile and actually stuck her chest out in an almost rehearsed pose as if to say "look here at what I've got." It didn't elicit the envy she hoped would flow out of middle-aged women.

"Hi, my name is Amber and I am a pharmacy intern at the store."

Annie winced. Her ex-lover's new squeeze had the same name as his ex-husband's new bride.

"How many interns have you had at your store by now Darrell, three or four?" Mary was quite proud of her dig into Darrell's not so stellar past with women.

Before Amber could respond, Darrell took her by the arm and abruptly broke in the already dysfunctional situation "Ok, well we have got to be going. Y'all have a nice night." The anxious pharmacist rapidly ushered her out the door as she maintained a confused look on her face.

"Worst mistake of my life!" said Annie in a relieved fashion.

"Amen!" replied Kim. "More wine anyone?"

"Me and Miller would fire him if he wasn't such a good pharmacist" said Tee.

"Seems he likes teaching young things and the ins and outs of pharmacy if you know what I mean," proclaimed an inebriated Kim

The ladies all looked at Kim and busted out laughing as the perky, lit up bundle of boldness. She moved to pour more wine in Annie's glass and ended up splashing some on the table.

"Time to get her home," said Tee in her best mothering voice.

"Yeah," agreed Annie. "I need to get to the Lowder's to see if Meagan has kissed any boys or something like that."

Mary grabbed the check and scooted up to the cash register with Tee and Kim trailing behind, each telling her to give them the bill. Annie moved at a slower pace. She was now thinking about Bart. She tried not to but she couldn't help it. For some reason she was thinking a lot about his hands. They looked like they were strong enough to lift a refrigerator and refined enough to conduct a symphony. And there was also something strangely recognizable about him, but she couldn't put her finger on what it was. It was like that unknown special ingredient in her Chicken Marsala.

Once the bill was settled the ladies said their goodbyes out on the sidewalk. Tee agreed to drive Kim home. She would tell Tim to take his bride to pick up her car after church on Sunday. Mary told everyone she would see them bright and early in her Bible study class at 9:00 a.m. Loud moans were made by all, but especially by the Pastor's wife.

Right after everyone quickly departed, Annie stood motionless by herself in front of the restaurant. The cold wind blew all over her, making her shiver and triggering the self-preserving instinct to get moving. But she stayed there with her feet planted into the cement. She really didn't know why she couldn't get going. Something inside her told her to not leave. She dismissed this as a silly notion.

As she finally moved to her left to walk back to the car, she felt a magnetic pull back towards Angelo's. She tried to figure it out and finally came up with the reasonable justification that she *"had to go back in and apologize to the owner for Tee's behavior."* In a blink of the eye Annie had already moved back into the restaurant and was gingerly opening the door to the kitchen.

What she saw mesmerized her. Instead of the messy chaos that Angelo ran, she was exposed to what seemed to be a streamlined and organized process. Waiters and waitresses were either gathering up meals or moving dirty dishes behind the eastern retaining wall to the brand-new dishwashing station. Both of the Sous Chefs wore bright green bandanas and matching aprons that had a new logo with the eatery's name embroidered on the left breast pocket. Each cook was moving around in a purposeful manner, making sure that that the dishes were well on the way toward completion.

The owner/executive chef was briefly spying on each pan, making some clear and respectful suggestions and opening ovens to guarantee that they neither overcooked any food. Although everyone was working hard, they seemed to be very efficient and actually enjoying the frantic pace. Even the floors looked clean and free of potentially dangerous liquids that could quickly create an unforeseen hazard for any of the fast-moving employees.

Before Annie could speak Bart noticed her and quickly said, "If you have lost your purse or cellphone my Manager can help you locate it."

Annie stood there, mute as a monk during a fast. Bart stepped towards her. "Miss, did you hear me?" Annie nodded yes. Bart turned away and said in a very clear manner, "Then I need you to get out of my kitchen!"

There it was. She received final confirmation that this guy was an ego-maniac. Annie saluted in a derisive fashion and quickly moved out of Angelo's and back into the street. Right in the middle of cursing the new owner out under her breath she got a text. Once she reached her phone what she read from Arlene Lowder and it scared her half-to-death — *"Please come quick. There is a problem with Meagan."*

When Annie got to Arlene's, two police cars were pulled alongside of each other with their lights running at full tilt. Annie thought the worst. In fact, she imagined about twelve different versions of her baby being dead or causing the death of another kid. It is what any self-respecting Momma would do.

She pulled right behind one of the police cars and jumped out of the car leaving her door wide open and the engine still running. Without hesitation she busted through the front door calling out Megan's name. Arlene intercepted her in the kitchen and said, "It's ok Annie, Meagan is not hurt and neither is anyone else."

Annie sucked in another needed breath. *"It is simply amazing how mothers operate on the same emotional wavelength,"* Annie thought to herself. Now that she was slightly more stabilized, she prepped herself for some bad news.

Arlene continued, "But one of the kids saw Meagan and Brittany Phillips smoking pot out behind the back deck. They told my husband and he called the cops. I wouldn't have done this but what are you going to do with a former Army MP Officer?" Todd owned a business doing grading and landscaping. He was used to pushing stuff around and so he typically treated problems with the same blunt force he used in cutting out new highways and driveways.

Annie tried to get a grip, but it was an almost impossible endeavor. "Are you sure it was my daughter?"

"Yes, let me take you to her," said Arlene in as reassuring manner as she could.

Arlene led Annie through the house to the back deck. Two police officers were interviewing both girls while they sat motionless on a bench. When Meagan's eyes met Annie's the teenager immediately dropped her head in humiliation. Annie looked right through her daughter, neither showing compassion nor contempt. She approached the first officer who must have been new to the role because she didn't recognize him and said "I'm Meagan's mother, what are we dealing with?"

The young officer spoke up in an official tone as possible and replied, "Ma'am, when we were called in, we found a few ounces of pot in your daughter's purse. We recovered a small pipe that Meagan had thrown in the woods when Mr. Louder confronted them."

"Ok, ok what is going to be done?" asked Annie as she bit her lower lip and tried not to cry.

"Well, we need to take both of them in and process this," replied the young officer in a by-the-book manner.

Annie sat down beside her daughter on the bench. She knew that all that good food and wine she had just enjoyed was getting ready to come back up.

"Hold on Billy," countered Officer Norm Taylor. Norm was a hometown boy and knew everyone involved. "Why don't we let these kids go home with their parents and let them know when the court date will be?"

"Yes sir, I see what you are saying," said the young man in response to the reasonable suggestion. "But these girls need to understand what a serious deal this is."

"Oh, I think they understand, don't you girls?" asked Officer Taylor. Both girls nodded their heads too afraid to look up.

"But that is not what needs to happen here!" bellowed the young man. Office Taylor took the young man aside. "Listen Billy ... I can appreciate your desire to do things right here. But sometimes if things like this are not handled in the right way, we can end up making them worse for everyone."

"But the law requires … Before he could finish lecturing the elder police officer on procedure Norm leaned in closer and said. "Do you know who Meagan's grandfather is? It is Jake Sawyers." Billy's eyes bulged and he moaned quietly. "That's right knot-head. If you want to get the Judge to have me and you for breakfast then just keep walking down the path you are on.

Officer Taylor turned back to the folks huddled together on the deck, while Billy stood without moving an inch and looking like he had just seen his career pass before his eyes. "So, everyone can go home now. We will be in touch." Norm winked at Annie and ushered everyone towards the side gate that led back to the front yard.

"Thanks Norm," said Annie patting him on the shoulder as she walked by. She saw Arlene and Todd in the driveway on the way to her car and walked up to them. "I am so sorry for all of this. I truly am."

Todd tried to soften his approach a bit. "Look, we have all been teenagers. Dear God, I got into a lot of trouble myself at this age. My old man whooped my tail more than once for this kind of stuff. But they have just got to see that this is not some frivolous thing." Todd looked to Meagan and said "I hope I didn't scare you too bad." Meagan looked the other way.

"Meagan, what do you say to Mr. and Mrs. Louder?" asked a smoldering Annie.

"Sorry" replied the zombie-like teen.

"Annie, please let us know how all this works out. We care. You know that right?" asked Arlene.

Annie nodded. "Sure. Thanks so much Arlene." They hugged and Annie pulled away quickly before she lost her composure.

The ride home was a somber event. Meagan pressed her face against the passenger window while Annie gripped the wheel and muttered things to herself about "not needing to deal with this kind of garbage in her life right now" and other kinds of statements parents make when confronted with major misdeeds by their kids.

Before they came to a complete stop in the driveway, Megan jumped out and ran to the backyard. Annie put the car in park and sat there for a moment trying to gather her wits before speaking to her child. She got out of the car and decided she wasn't going to jump on Meagan, but suggest that they talk on Sunday afternoon about what happened.

She found Meagan on a swing Pops had built for the cute little pixie when she was eight. Annie couldn't help but wish they were back in the days when losing a pet was the toughest thing they faced. She took a deep breath and carefully walked up to her daughter hoping to settle her down.

"I don't see what the big deal is, it is just weed," blared out the teen.

"Pardon me?" responded Annie in a state of disbelief.

"It is not like I killed somebody."

Annie tried not to go-over-the-top but she found herself moving closer to her daughter with very little compassion. "I can't believe my ears!" was her initial statement. That first comment served as a fuse for the upcoming explosion.

"You have broken the law, embarrassed me and involved another child in your illegal activity, and all you can muster up is some kind of weak rationalization for your behavior?"

"Chill, Annie," said Meagan with a smirk on her face.

Annie leapt at her child like a lioness seeking to teach a young cub a lesson about the wild. She stood the shocked girl up with one hand and delivered a sharp and quick slap with the other.

"Damn it, Meagan! You are not going to speak to me that way. I dare you to say another word like that to me again!"

By now Meagan was trembling as her Mother had grabbed her with both hands by her somewhat disheveled pirate outfit. She then continued the all-out assault on teenage disrespect:

"I am sick of your smart mouth. I am sick of your laziness. But what I am most sick of is your ungrateful attitude! You think that there are no consequences for your stupid, stupid choice tonight? Well Missy you are wrong. Starting now, everything you like to do in life is gone. In fact, I think your social life is so gone that you had better plan to stay with me every weekend for the rest of the winter!" Meagan's look of fear shifted to shock.

"No, wait, that sounds like punishment for me. I know, I will have you stay with Granny and Pops on the weekends. Or here is an idea … I will ship you off to live with your Dad and his new wife. Hold on, you hate her guts. On second thought that sounds pretty good. Maybe you two deserve each other!"

"Anything is better than living with you!" screamed Meagan. "You don't have a life and because of that you take your hatred of Dad out on me."

Meagan wrenched herself free, ran back to the car. In a few seconds Annie heard her keys jangling as Meagan unlocked the front door. Annie stood in the backyard still twitching with anger while she heard Meagan slam her bedroom door and start to wail her eyes out.

There is nothing like the brutal precision of an intelligent teen-aged girl who is on a mission to wound a parent. Somehow, they know the exact thing to say that emotionally paralyzes even the brightest of mothers. A woman can have a daughter dead to rights on their misdeeds and get sucker-punched by a timely comment about their parent's shortcomings. The net effect of this strategy is that the real issue gets lost in the smoke of battle while the shell-shocked mom is scrambling around trying to pick up the pieces of her shattered persona.

This particular salvo hit the mark. Meagan was right. Annie always had the sneaking feeling that she didn't have a life. Tonight's cascading series of events simply proved that haunting point. Once Annie focused on this damning perspective about being a failure as a human being, she started the tumble down the rabbit hole of self-disgust and humiliation.

It occurred to Annie that she could work hard, help a lot of people and try to be a decent parent but might never climb out of the rut of middle-aged blahs. She felt doomed to a life of ceaseless obligations. And as far as she could tell, the future looked pretty bleak. Based on her projections, she was probably going to end up with a progressive series of maladies like she saw every day at the Rehab Center. *"Come to think about it,"* the embattled woman thought to herself, *"I have had a dull headache for about a week. I bet I have a tumor or something."*

Based on the preponderance of evidence before her, Annie gave up. She crumpled under the weight of her self-condemnation, sat down on the swing and started to cry. This wasn't the kind of dainty weeping you see heroines do in the movies. It was shrill and messy. It was so loud that their dog Roxie came out from hiding in the small dog house she had been sequestered to since her misdeeds earlier that day. The concerned mongrel's whines turned into howling. So, there they were: three female mammals in pain. The piercing sound of their cries was enough to drive a Baptist preacher to drink.

The next morning Annie dragged Meagan to church, literally. They missed Bible study and were almost late for the 10:30 worship service. Neither one of them had gotten much sleep. Their swollen eyes reflected the kind of stress that can only come from Olympic-grade weeping.

"Good to see you," Annie commented to the Peterson's as she entered the old Winn-Dixie Grocery Store that had been converted to a worship center. As they passed the Welcome Center, she pulled Meagan's ear to her cheek and said "If you don't start acting like you're happy to be here I will spend the rest of the week devising ways to make your life miserable." Meagan believed her. She quickly pasted on a fake smile that could rival her Mom's.

Annie went down the center aisle and found Kim sitting in her usual spot on the front left row. Meagan made a quick move towards the other side where some of her friends were residing. Annie sat down beside Kim who looked to be in a trance of sorts.

"I think I am going to puke," whimpered Kim with a smile on her face.

"I think I am going to scream," countered Annie.

"We make quite a pair huh?" said Kim. The looked at each other and started snickering.

The Praise Band kicked in with an upbeat number that made both women jump. Before they knew it, the service was in full swing. The music reflected a modern but high-quality sound that could have been experienced at a late-night TV show.

In fact, Charlie Downs the worship leader had spent almost twenty years as an arranger and lead saxophone player for a daytime TV show. A near death experience from an overdose on cocaine caused him to re-assess his life. He moved back home to Gordon from LA and started teaching music composition at nearby Briar Community College.

When Tim found out that such a talented man was residing in the community, he pursued Charlie until the burned-out band leader agreed to be a part-time associate for worship. Four years later Charlie led one of the most innovative worship ministries on the East Coast. Tim would tell people that one of the reasons NewLight seemed to connect with hurting people was due to Charlie's leadership. Charlie often told folks that Tim's friendship allowed him to heal and express his talent in ways he never could have imagined.

The upbeat songs neatly modulated to more meditative and sweet songs of personal adoration to a God who pursues messed up people. At the end of the songs a video was played of Media Ministry Director Julie Barton interviewing people at Rockland Mall about their favorite season. As the video ended, Tim stepped up to the platform and read Ecclesiastes 3:1-10. His message was entitled "What Season Are You In?"

Annie didn't remember everything about that message. Maybe her weak memory had something to do with it. It could have been the influence of the Xanax she took at breakfast. But most likely it was about her preoccupation with Meagan's problems.

But there was one statement that stuck. As he was winding down Tim prophetically said the following: "I don't know where you are today. We are so proficient at showing up and looking good on the outside while our hearts are breaking with the weight of the problems we bear. If you are that person take heart. I don't have a quick solution for you. But I do know that whatever problem has you weighed down, remember it is just a season. And the God who made winter is bringing spring right around the corner. Hang in there. Daffodils are going to bloom again."

Annie turned to Kim and with tears in her eyes said, "That was for me." She knew Tim had no clue what was really happening in her heart. She figured God just whispered to him so that Tim could give her a heaping, helping dose of hope, right when she needed it. She closed her eyes during the time of decision and prayed, *"Dear God, help me get through this terrible season."* She opened her eyes, took a deep breath and nodded her head. She was glad she came to church today.

Annie's Standard Operating Procedure after church was to eat lunch at her parent's home. This Sunday she wasn't up for her mother's laser-like probing about what was troubling her youngest child. After pulling into her parent's driveway, she let Meg out and told her, "Tell Granny and Pops I need some time alone today. And Meg, I love you but we are not done talking about what happened last night, ok? I'll be back around three to get you." Meagan nodded and loped towards the front door with a tinge of resentful acquiescence.

Annie left the house, grabbed a double cheeseburger from the local McDonalds. She then inhaled it a slurped down a Diet Coke as she drove next door, picked up a dozen of warm Krispy Kreme doughnuts. She then turned left out of the parking lot and drove towards the Rehab Center.

Another Sunday routine she rarely missed was to go by her workplace and spend time with Pearl Anne Buford. Pearl was a ninety-year old African American lady that had more wisdom in her one-hundred-pound body that a slew of university professors. She was funny too. Nobody could land a sarcastic one-liner like Mama Pearl.

To add to her already vaunted status, Pearl had spent a large part of her life as a nurse for the county and helped a lot of babies come into this world. Three generations had heard her joyful and sassy voice as they took their first breath. She was there when Annie was born and helped Dr. Gordon deliver her. Annie was breach and for a while they thought they would have to do an emergency C-section. But Pearl applied some old midwife magic and Annie popped out pink and smiling. Annie's mom was so grateful that she named her daughter after the luminous lady. To Annie, Pearl Ann was like a bonus mother.

As soon as Annie walked through the double automatic doors the first shift weekend supervising nurse Polly Turner greeted Annie with the question, "Hey, you are early today, aren't you?" Annie nodded and replied, "Yeah, I need a lot of advice today." Annie carried the dozen Krispy Kreme Donuts under her right arm. That was Pearl's fee. Thank God she wasn't diabetic.

Annie made a right turn by her office to the West Wing and found Room 312. When she entered the door, Pearl was reading People Magazine. She looked up from her recliner and said. "Good Lord darling. You are early. You must be in a mess of trouble to come at this time and see old Momma Pearl today! What is going on?"

"Oh, Momma Pearl," said Annie. "I've about had the worst couple of days that a woman can have."

"Is there a man involved?" queried Pearl.

"Uh, yes … no … I don't know." Annie stood there feeling very embarrassed.

Pearl shook her head, "Sweet Jesus, that is what I thought. Sit down child and go ahead and hand me the whole box. This is going to take a while as far as I can tell."

And so, Annie let it all hang out. She talked about how she felt that all she did was work and do stuff for everyone. She mentioned that she thought she was "suffering from depression, a brain tumor or worse." Then she mentioned how "that arrogant jerk" had dismissed her at Angelo's. And of course, she talked about Meagan's drug escapade.

"And then before I knew it, I slapped her Pearl." Annie buried her face in her hands and acted like she was going to cry.

"Good!" replied the old black woman.

"Huh?" replied Annie looking up at Pearl.

"You heard me. Do I stutter?'

"No ma'am" responded a shocked Annie.

Then Pearl sat up, leaned forward and began her lecture. "Let me tell you something. You should have slapped her twice. Once for smoking that junk and then one more time for back-talking you."

Pearl seemed to get more agitated with each thought she expressed. "You young people got it all wrong about parenting. You say 'Aw, the poor babies need to have good self-esteem.' That is horse-crap. What children need are loving doses of reality. You think this cold, hard world is going to give them group hugs every day? No way! This world is going to kick people like that in the teeth and then laugh at them while they bleed. Dr. Spock and all them other doctors can kiss my tail. If he were here right now I'd slap him for good measure!"

"So, I wasn't wrong?" asked Annie.

"Child, do you listen?" replied the perturbed woman. "Don't waste my time, if you ain't gonna' hear me … even though you bring me these delicious doughnuts. And by the way they are especially delicious today and you know how much I appreciate the thought."

"You are right Momma Pearl."

"Don't expect me to disagree. I smacked my kids in the mouth several times, and they turned out all right."

"It is just hard being a single parent and going through all of this stuff" said Annie. She looked at Pearl for some reassurance but the old woman seemed to be somewhere else.

"Now that that is settled, tell me about the man."

"Oh Pearl, I shouldn't have mentioned it. It is nothing."

The old woman starred at Annie for what seemed to be a long time. She leaned back and said, "You say that with your lips, but your eyes tell a different story. You are a terrible liar."

"Ok, I was attracted to him. But I am usually attracted to jerks," sighed the overwhelmed woman.

"How do you know he is a jerk?"

"He told me to get out of his kitchen!" said an exasperated Annie. "Weren't you listening to me?"

"Watch your mouth girl!" spoke the old woman in a blunt manner. "I won't hesitate slapping that mouth if you disrespect me again."

"I'm sorry" replied a humbler Annie.

"See," said the spunky lady in the sweetest of tones. "A little threat helps to lubricate the wheels of understanding. Now, my point was that you had interrupted a working man. Didn't your Momma told you to never do that. Lord God, we got enough sorry men who won't work. Why did you go into the kitchen in the first place?"

"To apologize."

"For what?"

"Oh, Tee asked him to our table under false pretenses to get him to meet me."

"That is why you interrupted a busy man?"

"Well, you had to have been there. Anyway, I tried and he was just rude. He was also rude when he came to our table."

"That is not why you went to see him. You liked him and wanted to talk further but you were not up front. He should have led your dishonest tail out the door. By the way, how good looking was he?"

Annie laughed out loud and shook her head. "He was very good-looking Pearl."

"Uh-huh," nodding her head in sassy approval. "Yes! Did I ever tell you about how I met Edgar? You know we were married for sixty-four years, don't you?"

"I remember," Annie answered. She knew the story but realized that Pearl was on a roll and leaned back for the re-telling of a very familiar tale.

"Well it was 1945. Edgar had just got back from the war and was visiting his Aunt and Uncle who had a farm up Old 19 north. Anyway, my Daddy had the Dairy Business and was making driving up to pick up some milk at their farm. I rode with him and sat in the truck.

Let me tell you child I was a gorgeous, smart young woman and I was bored out of my mind. I was looking forward to getting out of Gordon and going to a black nurse's college in Alabama in a few weeks. I was about to honk the horn to get Daddy going. You know he loved to visit with folks."

Anne smiled. Her Daddy was the same way.

"Anyway, I was sitting there and minding my own business and BAM! Edgar stepped out to the front porch to take a smoke and Lord oh Lord he looked better than my Momma's chocolate cake. Tall, built (she started fanning herself) and sharp as a tack in his Army uniform! I eased out of the truck and acted like I didn't see him. He stood straight up and walked down those steps and said the most amazing thing."

"What?" asked Annie.

"He said 'My name is Edgar James Buford. You are the most beautiful woman I have ever seen in my life. I don't think I will ever look at a Dairy Truck the same since seeing you.'

"Well, we were married two weeks later. We actually sneaked off to Asheville and had my cousin perform the ceremony. It was a long time before Daddy forgave him for that."

"But he did," Annie said grinning.

"Yes baby, Edgar became like a son to Daddy since I was his only child so he didn't have no boy. Did I tell you about our honeymoon?"

"No ma'am."

"Oh child, he was something. Well let me just say that man knew how to love and was that way till the day he died. Have mercy!"

Annie howled so loudly that a nurse making rounds stuck in her head to check in on what first sounded like a scream. "Is everything ok here ladies?"

"Yes Agnes, Pearl is just schooling me on the ways of love."

Agnes laughed. She noticed the box of doughnuts and said "Miss Pearl, you know better than to eat those."

"I will eat anything I want to. When you get to be my age you can tell me what I should eat!"

Agnes knew she had messed up trying to give Pearl advice. She did her best to make a course adjustment by saying "Yes Ma'am. I just know how those things can upset your tummy. I will see you later."

Pearl turned to Annie and whispered. "You know her fat tail don't miss a meal. On top of that from what I can hear she can't keep a man. Stella down the hall told me she is on her third marriage and it ain't doing so well."

Annie knew that story but didn't want to talk about it because she knew Pearl will blab about what she said and Annie had worked hard to get along with all the staff." She did her best to change the subject.

"So, I am going to marry Bart?" sarcastically queried Annie.

"You just might smarty britches. But if you do you are going to have to apologize to me in public at the reception when it happens."

"That is a promise." Annie looked at the old woman and smiled. Pearl returned the heartfelt affection with a loving pat on Annie's left knee.

Suddenly the old woman practically leaped out of her chair, stood up and announced, "Ok, Pearl is done. Girl you wear me out and I need to go to the bathroom because of all of these donuts."

"Ok Pearl. Thanks for everything. You know how much I love you."

"Oh yes baby, Momma Pearl loves you too. Oh, by the way when you looked him in the eyes did you feel the Ju-Ju?"

"What in the world is that?" asked a stunned Annie.

"We will talk about that next week," said the old woman as she walked into her bathroom and closed the door.

CHAPTER 3

THINGS SETTLED DOWN for Annie, at least for a little bit. After the disaster that was Halloween subsided, Meagan ended up having her day in Juvenile Court in mid-November. She got off easy with just having to do six months of community service. Her Mom got her assigned to the Rehab Center. Meagan was learning the lesson of gratitude by cleaning bathrooms, mopping floors and emptying bedpans. Although her sassy attitude was not totally eradicated, it was curbed enough to make her bearable at home.

Thanksgiving rolled around and activities really picked up at the Center. The Holiday Season with the old folks was always fun and hectic. Between coordinating family events for the residents and doing her regular job Annie never seemed to sit still for more than five minutes at work, home or anywhere else.

Her frenzied schedule was even more crammed this year because she had volunteered to be the Chairwoman of the Gordon Christmas Parade. Two nights a week she would hustle home after a full day at work; get Meagan something to eat and started on her homework; and then rush to Town Hall to lead meetings on deciding what floats were going to be part of the parade and how they were going to get some extra cash out of downtown merchants to help provide funding for the seventy-five year tradition

Despite the craziness of her schedule she had developed a rhythm of sorts that gave her a martyr's sense of productivity. She secretly enjoyed others being amazed at her Clydesdale-like resilience and drive. But this superficial sense of control was about to be obliterated one rainy December morning.

The day started out normal. She got up early to do a Pilates Class at gym, came back to the house and wolfed down a protein bar. She practically yelled Meg out of bed, poured a bowl of her daughter's favorite cereal, got a shower and put on the outfit she had laid out the night before. By the time they got out the door they were still running ahead of schedule.

Then Annie turned the ignition in her car. It sputtered and lurched but it never got going.

"Oh, dear Lord not now, not now!" she yelled pounding the steering wheel. Suddenly she recalled the check engine light being on for a few weeks. She sincerely meant to have it taken care of, but that kind of task seems to always get bumped to the back of her list of things to do. Now her procrastination was manifesting into a little crisis that she couldn't postpone. It didn't help that it had begun to rain.

She hastily called her Mom. "Hey it's me. Can you come and pick me and Meg up? My car is dead."

"Oh sweetie, I am hardly dressed."

"Mom, I don't think the Queen is dropping by, so please come get us ok?"

"Oh alright" replied the high-strung Grandmother. She arrived in the driveway in about eleven minutes and the girls piled in the car.

Almost as soon as they started backing up her Mom abruptly stopped the car and said "Oh my gosh. I forgot that I have a doctor's appointment in fifteen minutes!" Annie put her hand on her Mom's forearm as she had done hundreds of times when her Mom panicked over something and replied, "Don't worry. Take me by the bus depot and drop Meg by school on your way to Dr. Schaumburg's. That way we will all get to where we need to be on time." Her Mom nervously nodded her head and Annie sat back thinking to herself, *"It is good that I am so proficient at solving problems."*

In about six minutes they arrived at the Gordon Bus Depot. Annie jumped out and said her goodbyes. She walked up the side walk quickly due to the drizzle and, found the small waiting shelter. She got there just in time for the 7:50 a.m. bus to the south side of town.

Breathing a sigh of relief Annie sat down and started sorting through her papers for the Senior Leadership Meeting that was happening later than morning. It seemed that the new CFO was trying to impress the Director with budget cuts. Annie needed to prepare her plan of defense.

When she had finally found a pen to make some notes on a spreadsheet the phone rang. She looked at the caller id. It was her ex-husband. She let it ring …

Tom was a complex man. He was capable of incredible acts of generosity, moments of incisive analysis and maddening feats of self-destruction. In many ways he was like a priceless work of art that seemed to perpetually be smoldering on the edges of its canvass.

Annie met him when they were sophomores at UNC. He led an Intro to Macro Economics study group that she joined to bring her low D up to at least a respectable C. Back them Tommy was bright, handsome and funny. He had the kind of charisma that made you feel like you were the most important person in the world when you were in his presence.

All the girls in the group had a crush on him, but he focused his attention on Annie. They had one of those on-again, off-again romances that people fall into while in college. After several tries, Tom persuaded Annie to be his wife. They got married right after college. Tom went to Duke Law School while Annie worked as a physical therapist at a hospital in Raleigh. They seemed to be on their way towards a successful partnership.

After passing the bar the Tom got a job at the very prestigious law firm in Charlotte called Tobias, Ashcroft and Bailey. Tom's ambition and optimism knew no bounds. He made certain he was the first to arrive and the last to leave, letting the big wigs knew he was the real deal.

When Meagan was born, he vowed to slow down a bit. But he kept telling Annie that he felt he was on the verge of something big breaking loose in his career. His premonition wasn't far from the truth. He made partner quicker than anyone in the history of the firm, and by the time he was thirty-eight he became Managing Partner mostly due to the early retirement of John Tobias; the illness and death of Philip Ashcroft; and the rampant alcoholism of Meacham Bailey. People in Charlotte started taking notice. Tom was superstar in the making who was just beginning to hit his stride.

But then their world began to unravel when Annie discovered through a series of strange coincidences about Tom's multiple infidelities. The house of cards first began to fall apart when she found a romantic letter in his briefcase while looking for some insurance papers he asked her to sign. The intimate details of the sickening sonnet could not be explained away. Annie served him an ultimatum: "Go to marriage counseling with me or go through a messy divorce." He relented and they went for several months.

Just when she thought they were making progress Tom asked to meet Annie at home one day at lunch. It was there he spilled the beans and told Annie he was in love with his secretary Amber.

Before she could mount a cross-examination using the ideals of duty and integrity to halt him in his tracks, he gave a devastating closing argument. It seemed that Amber was not the first. In fact, he had lost count. The affairs had actually begun one month after they married with the first one occurring with Maggie, one of Annie's bridesmaids. He seemed to feel better getting these things off his chest and told his wife she would "be better off without him." Tom had become the proverbial wolf who chewed his paw off in order to extricate himself from a trap.

All Annie could remember at that moment was screaming obscene things and asking him to leave the house. She had a moving van packed in two days and went back to Gordon, allowing her Dad to take care of all the nasty negotiations of the separation and divorce. Even though it had been six years since everything was settled, she had a hard time letting go the deep bitterness that comes from feeling like you had wasted the best years of your life on a cad …

When Annie finally answered the call, the voice of the scumbag chimed in just long enough to interrupt her trip down misery lane.

"Anne, this is Tom, do you have a minute?"

"No Tom, but go right ahead." Annie started walking away from the depot so that no curious ears could hear her conversation.

"Well, I wanted to talk with you about Christmas plans."

"What about them Tom?" Annie quipped in a clearly impatient manner.

"Now don't get defensive," warned Tom. "I was just going to see if you were flexible this year about Christmas day?"

By now the light mist had now turned into big drops of cold rain. Annie first tried to shield her head with her briefcase, but eventually walked into Stardust Coffee so she could stay dry and watch for the soon-arriving bus. She re-grouped and sought to head her famously verbose ex-spouse off at the pass.

"Tom if you are asking if Meg can come earlier than 5 p.m. you are whistling into the wind."

"Well, I am and why is that the case?"

"Tom, you know why. Our family doesn't get done with Christmas till about four and that barely gives me time to meet you in Statesville to drop Meagan off."

"I understand," said Tom recognizing he was never going to win this argument by competing with Annie's family traditions. Now he tried another tactical approach aimed at seeing if he could leverage any sympathy out of his ex-wife: "This year is going to be a little more hectic with Amber hosting this year and all her family descending down at our house."

"*Bad move counselor,* she thought. That phrase "our house" almost sent Annie in orbit. It was once their house and she believed that although Tom could have afforded another place, the auburn-haired wonder wanted to stick her role as Tom's new bride in Annie's face.

"I could care less about poor little Miss Amber Tom," snarled Annie.

"Well that is not all." Tom measured himself and the dove into an even more controversial subject. "I was not going to mention it but Amber is pregnant and there is a chance that she might lose the baby, so I am trying to reduce her stress."

Annie walked outside into the rain to scream something nasty to her ex when she noticed the 7:50 bus leaving the terminal. "Tom," interrupted Annie as she started to run in her high heels and somewhat snug skirt, "I got to go. Bye!"

She yelled as loud as she could and waved her folder at the driver, but all he did was to go faster as he rounded and made a right onto Oak Valley Road. As she tried to pick up the pace the heel of her left foot grabbed a crevice in the sidewalk and she took a spill, casting her briefcase and papers all across the sidewalk while somehow managing to hold on to her purse.

The poor woman didn't hurt herself too badly. But she got quite wet and a bit scuffed up. Scrambling off the pavement she did her best to quickly gather up her saturated paperwork and insert all the pieces into her briefcase. She also noticed as she stood up that her left heel has snapped off and tried to find it by retracing her steps getting totally soaked in the process.

Once she recovered the bright orange spike, she stood motionless in the middle of Main Street, not knowing if she should go get a cup of coffee or try to hoof it back to the station.

Across the street Bart St. Clair witnessed the ill-advised chase scene. He had parked his forest green colored F-250 pickup truck right in front of Angelo's to wait for a food delivery. On his dashboard were two fresh cups of coffee that was creating a small circle of moisture at the center section of his window shield. Crammed underneath his legs was a bag stuffed with two bagels, some cream cheese, napkins and plastic utensils. Bart had learned that Donnie the delivery guy from Chase Foods always seemed to do a better job when he was bribed by a little breakfast.

Donnie was running late as usual. Instead of getting stoked about the delivery man's tardiness, Bart decided to start in on his breakfast. He had already eaten about all of his plain bagel with the assistance of Frodo his burly English Springer Spaniel who sat on the passenger's side with ears perched, waiting on another morsel.

"Well Fro old buddy" said Bart as he was looking at the disoriented lady. "You want to try to do one good deed today?" Frodo barked and Bart then made a sweeping U-turn so that he could intercept Annie as she walked back to the coffee shop. Even though his turn was near perfect, it still startled the fuming health care executive.

"Pardon me Annie, but would you like a ride?" announced Bart to the wet woman.

"Excuse me but who are you?" asked Annie with the now slightly streaked mascara blurring her vision.

"It is the rude chef from across the street," smiled Bart.

"No thank you!" snapped Annie as she limped towards Stardust. "I have my quota of jack asses today!"

"Funny," said Bart. "But would you please let me make amends for my behavior back in October?"

Annie thought about it. She really needed to get to work and everyone should have at least one chance to correct their mistakes. So, she consented with an "All right." Bart moved Frodo over and quickly wiped the seat down with an old rag by the time Annie came around and opened the door. Despite the preparation, she was quite surprised when she saw the seventy-pound pooch staring her down.

"Oh my," she said trying to regain her composure. "Are you running your own travel service today?"

"Nope, this is Frodo my body guard. You never know when you might need some protection from a dissatisfied customer!" responded Bart in his best effort at deflecting humor. "Where are we off to?"

"Oak Valley Rehab Center," said Annie as she wedged herself as close enough to the door so she could make a quick exit if this knight in shining armor turned out to be a pervert.

"Here," Bart said offering a cup of hot beverage. "It is plain but it's hot."

Annie grabbed it without hesitating. For a brief moment their hands touched and she felt something like an electric surge run from her fingers to her heart. It was so powerful and unexpected that she spilled some coffee on the floor board. Now she felt like a wet fool.

"I'm so sorry," said Annie as she tried to wipe the coffee up with the dirty rag Bart had used to clear off her seat.

"Don't worry," laughed Bart. "You can't get this truck any dirtier than it already is." Annie looked around and recognized that he was right.

For a few minutes they drove in silence. Frodo tried to wiggle over and get a sniff of the new person in his life. Annie looked petrified. Bart kept wrangling him in and said "Give her a break pal. She has had a rough morning."

Bart tried to re-start some conversation by asking what seemed to be an innocent question: "How is your daughter Meagan doing? Is her health ok?" quizzed the semi-stranger.

"Huh?" asked Annie in a confused state. She couldn't remember telling him about her daughter. Maybe Mary or Tee mentioned something to him.

"She is doing well for a cantankerous teenage girl." Annie looked at Bart a little more closely. He had an Atlanta Braves baseball cap on that covered a thick head of hair. He also looked like he hadn't shaved in a few days which made his goatee look coarser. It really was starting to bug her that he looked familiar but she couldn't place him in the right context.

"That's good," he said as he noticed that they had just passed the bus Annie tried to run down. He thought for a moment and then carefully asked her a strange question: "Hey, do you mind if I ask you why you were running to catch that bus?"

At first Annie looked at him as if he had just fell off the turnip truck and hit his head really hard. "Well, senior chef to catch it I suppose. This isn't one of those why did the chicken cross the road jokes or something is it?"

"No" he laughed. "I was just wondering … if I am not mistaken, don't they make rounds about every ten minutes from 7:00 to 8:50 am?"

"Yes" she replied in an irritated manner. "Is there a point to this or are you trying to erase the friendship capital you have built up with your gallant deed?

"Not really. It just reminded me of how hectic my life used to be before I moved here. I was in such a hurry all of the time that being late or getting slowed down seemed to be an unbearable thing. I now think sometimes interruptions and inconveniences are God's way of opening our eyes to unexpected blessings. I forgot that the other month when I snapped at you in my kitchen. Please forgive me for that."

Annie looked away so as not to seem to be phased by Bart's comments. But they dug in deep to where she lived. As she did her best to suppress the fear that comes from being exposed but she felt the surge again, this time climbing around her neck and wrapping around her cheeks. All she could muster was "Not a problem."

They arrived at the Center and Bart drove as close to the covered side walk as possible. "Here you go my lady," said Bart as he waved his arm in a knightly fashion.

"Why thank-you Sir Bart" replied a cautious Annie. She bowed her head to the affectionate dog, patting him on the head and saying "And thank you too noble Frodo" Then she looked up at Bart, winked and said, "By the way, *The Lord of the Rings* is one of my favorites." They locked eyes and the electric warmness that had made her face glow now traveled downward. Embarrassed by her unplanned act of flirtation she opened the door and dismounted. She turned around and waved goodbye before scooting through the front door into the lobby of the Center.

Bart waved and watched her walk through the door. He sat there smiling when Frodo interrupted his train of thought by a short but definitive bark. "Ok, Fro. I know, I know. The last thing I need in my life right now is a feisty, beautiful woman. Besides, she wouldn't know what to do if she knew who I really was."

Diane the receptionist greeted Annie with a "Good Morning" and then asked "Was that Bart St. Clair that just dropped you off?"

"Yes why?"

"Well, I didn't know if you were seeing each other," replied Diane in a probing fashion.

"Diane, we aren't dating. Just having sex now and then. It is a good deal because I get three free meals a week." Annie knew that this would embarrass the prude so much that she would go back to her job and maybe actually do a little work.

Annie took off both her heels and got to her office as fast as she could, leaving outlines of her wet feet as she made the short trip. Once she got there, she quickly unlocked the door, piled her briefcase on one of her wing chairs, chunked her shoes into the trashcan in the corner and dropped her purse on her desk. She looked under her desk and found an old pair of running shoes that she sometimes used to do a little walking around the center when the weather was nice. She squeezed them on without bothering to untie them.

As quickly as she could she went across the hall and got several towels from the laundry storage closet. She cleaned up the spots she left behind with one towel and did her best to dry her hair and clothes with a couple more. She took the final towel and wipe off her face. Grabbing some makeup from her purse she did her best to slap on some foundation, lipstick and a minimal amount of eyeliner. She finally pulled her hair back in a ponytail grabbed the files for meeting and hauled tail to the conference room.

When Annie arrived, she was about two minutes late. Arnold Bickerstaff, the new CFO looked up when she opened the door and shook his head in disdain. Sydney Lawrence, the head of nursing, saw Annie's appearance and seemed a bit concerned. Dr. Bill Gordon who was the Clinical Director and the County Coroner gazed at his watch and sighed. Finally, Stanley Tanner the CEO nodded at Annie and said, "Good Morning Annie, please take a seat at the end there. We were just getting started."

As soon as Annie sat down, Bickerstaff started in: "As I was saying, looking at the bottom line we have to raise our prices for monthly care. If we don't, we could cut staff but that would be like a band aid on a hemorrhaging wound."

"If you cut my staff the quality of care will be dramatically impacted!" announced Sydney.

"The issue of quality of care is an ancillary issue compared to financial viability," countered Bickerstaff. "If you can't pay the bills you won't be able to keep the doors open."

"Well, I am being paid the bare minimum for someone in my position!" barked Dr. Gordon.

"Seems to me Bill you've got a pretty good deal here," interrupted Annie. You take care of old people, which basically means you keep them propped up until they expire. Then when they do, you encourage the family of the deceased to take them to Gordon Funeral Home where you brother makes out like a bandit. Doesn't he pay you a fee for these kinds of referrals?"

"I resent that Annie!" blared Gordon. "You have no idea the complicated nature of my job. All you do is push papers."

Sydney rolled her eyes while Bickerstaff quietly nodded in approval.

"Alright, that's enough folks," said Tanner. "We are not going to insult or attack each other. We are here to solve a problem."

"Look, I know everyone works hard here" replied Bickerstaff, seeking to water-down his Scrooge reputation by showing mock respect. "But Medicare reimbursables are down and my guess is that they are not going to keep up with inflation and the overall expanding costs of healthcare."

"But everyone in this kind of work faces that," retorted Annie. "If we raise prices too much, I'll only be able to house those who are wealthy or worse, we will price ourselves out of business. Or have you considered that possibility?"

Bickerstaff turned towards Annie and stared her down. "This is not a charity ward. It is a business and until you understand that fact you will not come to grips with the stark financial realties we are facing!"

Before Annie could return fire, Tanner held up his hand. "Ok, what we need to do right now is slow down and not panic. I suggest that everyone goes back and looks once again at any legitimate cut that they can make from their departments. We will meet again on Wednesday morning at eight. Then if we have to raise prices, we need to look at a more gradual roll up than hit our clients with a sudden jump in fees. Will that work for everyone?"

All of the leaders in that room nodded. They knew when Stanley Tanner meant business, and anyone who would try to belabor a point after he had made a decision would be in for one of his famous butt-chews.

"Ok, we are done. I will see all of you on Wednesday." As the meeting adjourned and everyone started to meander out the room, Tanner spoke to Annie, "Could you stay behind a few minutes?" All eyes were on the beleaguered woman. It was as if she had just been called into the principal's office because she had been caught righting something nasty in the girl's bathroom. Other than the worried look she got from her friend and colleague Sydney, Bickerstaff and Gordon seemed to express a kind of smug satisfaction at what they thought would happen next for the smart-mouthed woman.

As everyone left Annie moved up to the seat by the door and sat down beside her boss. He got up, closed the door, sat down and took a deep breath. He seemed to be choosing his words very carefully which did not reduce Annie's anxiety.

"Annie are you doing ok?"

"What do you mean?"

"Well, you look like you have been run through the rise cycle at the car wash."

"Oh, well it is a long story but my car died and I got caught in the rain."

"Ok. But I have noticed lately that you have been short-tempered with people and somewhat distracted."

"Are you talking about the exchange with Arnold? I was just standing my ground on what I believe to be true."

"Well, if it was just Arnold, we were talking about I would be ok. He can be a pompous ass sometimes. But you attacked Bill with the comment about his brother and I have heard of similar interactions with other staff."

Annie sat there dumbfounded and a bit scarred. She reviewed in her mind any interaction she had with people and could not come up with a pattern of negativity.

"Was there anything I said this morning untrue?"

Stanley leaned closer and folded his hands. "Look, I know you have been through a lot with your daughter. And being a single parent myself I know a little bit of the unique pressures you are under. But I cannot have you insulting the staff, even when what you are saying is true. You are too valuable to this organization to lose your job over a lack of self-awareness."

There it was. She just received the "Tanner Ultimatum." This was a shot across her bow. She didn't want to wait around for the next salvo. Stanley was neither a hothead nor an arrogant leader. But there was a no-nonsense side to him that left little to be interpreted. She remembered him firing people when they did not immediately comply with his demands. Annie's anxiety now kicked into full-gear and she felt sick to her stomach. She knew he was deadly serious and what he was handing her was a warning, not an empty threat.

"Look, I don't need you to apologize to Arnie but I do need you to make amends with Bob." Annie bit her lower lip to try to divert the energy from flowing to her eyes and making a fool out of herself. She nodded in agreement.

"And I want you to talk to Wanda." Wanda Langley was the HR Director of the Center and someone that Annie had some run-ins with in the past. Everything was black and white with Wanda and she had just as thick a backbone as Annie. Humbling herself in front of this lady was not going to be easy.

"She will give you the number of our EAP contact, or can recommend a good family counselor. I want you to figure this anger thing out, ok?"

"Yes, I can see why you would be concerned. I will take care of that today."

"Good. Call me later and let's set up some time to talk further."

"Thanks for your help Stanley. I will call your office this afternoon and set up the appointment."

"Oh, no rush on that yet. Just take care of the other stuff first."

"I will. Is there anything else?"

"No."

Stanley stood up and Annie followed suit. She gave him a firm handshake, put on her best professional persona and dismissed herself from her boss' presence. It would have been a good exit but her old tennis shoes made an obnoxious squeaking sound as she made a beeline back to her office. Stanley stepped outside of the conference room to identify what he heard. When he saw the source of the sound, he raised his eyebrows in bewilderment.

Annie got back to her office right before the water works let loose. She closed her door and did her best to muffle her sobs. It looked like she was going to have to reapply her makeup for the second time this morning. While she was blowing her nose there was a light rap on her door.

"Annie, this is Syd, can I come in?"

"Uh, sure hang on a second." She made like she was finishing a phone call and said "I will get back with you on that. Someone is at the door. Ok. Bye." She hung up the phone, dabbed her eyes, wiped her nose and smiled. "Come on in,"

Sydney entered the office like she was walking through a mine field. She shut the door and sat down in one of Annie's wing chairs. "Are you ok?" she asked gingerly.

"Sure I am. Why?"

"Annie if you don't want to tell me that is ok. I am worried that's all."

Annie tried to give Sydney a polished-up rendition of her conversation with their boss, but couldn't pull it off. She acted as if she was going to speak but all of the emotions from the previous few hours swept over her again. She rapidly waved her hand in front of her face to ward off the tears but they started to flow.

"Oh Syd, I am worn out. I don't know how much more of all of this I can take."

"Don't say that. You are a tough cookie Annie. This Center would be a mess without you here. Don't let the "Boys Club" intimidate you. If you leave I will too!"

Annie laughed and it helped. Sydney was a warrior for her patients. For as many years as Annie could remember Syd had stood toe-to-toe with doctors and administrators that had seemed to have forgotten that they were dealing with human beings rather than walking Petrie dishes or breathing bills. She also shared the same sense of calling to helping the elderly that Annie did.

"No, don't do that. I will be fine. I just have to go see a shrink about all the stuff going on in my head."

Sydney laughed. "Oh dear God, that will take someone forever to figure all of that out tangled mess!"

Annie stuck her tongue out at her friend. "Yeah, well I could get them to do a two-for-one and let you tag along."

"Oh my, I can just see it now … we would bankrupt the center just due to our overwhelming need for ongoing psychiatric care."

"Well I have to go talk to Wanda and get this set up."

"I will pray for you. I don't like that woman one bit. She is one hard-headed chick!"

"Just like some other women I know" retorted Annie.

Sydney now was the one that stuck her tongue out at her friend. "Maybe so, but I still say she likes telling people what to do."

"Yeah you are right about that one. But that is not all. I have to go and apologize to Bob."

"What?! That man is one of the slackest doctors I have ever met. I can't stand him. He is just on cruise control collecting his check and waiting till the last possible minute to retire. My RNs and CNAs constantly complain to me about how he treats the patients. I have even tried to go to Stanley and give him documentation about this and other stuff and I just get the cold shoulder."

"Well that is because Sydney is no dummy. Bob is a Gordon and they still have a lot of pull around here."

"You know I don't care about that political crap. I tell you what, one of these days I am going to catch him messing up and it will be so bad that our boss will have to get rid of him. I just hope that one of our patients doesn't suffer because of Bob's incompetence."

"I know but I am going to have to find the inner strength to do this."

"What you and I need to do is to go out for a drink tonight after work. My treat."

"I would love to but I have another meeting for the Parade. Why I agreed to do this year I have no earthly idea."

"You are a responsibility addict."

"What is the world is that?"

"You love to be in control because then you can make sure it is done right. I ought to know because I am the same way."

"Is there any cure?"

"If you find it let me know. But hey, on second thought, I kind of like the way I am. I think you the only really screwed up person in this room."

"Get out of here you lunatic!" laughed Annie as she pretended like she was going to throw her stapler at her friend.

"Ok I am going. But seriously, I am in your corner. If you need anything you let me know."

"I will. Love you."

"Of course, you do. Bye." Sydney left Annie's office with the ok sign and a wink. Annie felt strengthened by her visit. She would need it. She looked at the paper work on her desk and for a moment decided she should work through the pile of applications before she would walk down the hall and visit Wanda. But deep down she knew that this was just a delay technique she was playing on herself in order to avoid the inevitable.

Annie got out her mirror from her desk. She made the necessary touch-ups to her makeup to cover up the washed-out look she had from too much stress. Once she completed the refinement she stood up and pulled her shoulders back and said to herself, *"You can do this."* Then, with the resolution of a convicted criminal marching to the firing squad, she began her short walk towards Wanda's office.

She found Wanda looking right at the door when she walked up, as if the steely-eyed HR Director was waiting for her. "Hey Wanda, do you have a minute?"

"Mr. Tanner told me that you would be coming. Please come in and shut the door behind you."

Annie swallowed hard. She was reminded of how her Mom used to lie to her when she went to the pediatrician's office and told her the shots didn't hurt. From all indications this was going to be one of those kinds of visits. The only thing she didn't know at this point was if she had to drop her pants and bend over.

"First, let me say that what we say in this office is under the strictest of confidence. I am not a snitch for our CEO. I am here for every employee, which includes you."

Annie was suspicious. She looked at Wanda and gave her a simple "Ok."

Wanda continued in an almost mechanical way. "Technically we cannot require an employee to get any assistance. And you need to know that if you do choose to get help you do not have to share with a single person what is discussed, including Mr. Tanner."

Annie loosed up a little. "So, I can refuse to go."

"That is right. But I do need to warn you that if you don't and there is not a major change in your behavior Mr. Tanner can fire you without any equivocation or risk on the part of this corporation."

Annie was beginning to understand. It wasn't like a trap was being set for her, but something pretty close. "But if I go and I make improvements I can't be fired," Annie continued, just to make sure she understood what was at stake.

"No, I didn't say that. What I did say is that if you don't go and do not make any changes there will be no room for wrongful termination from your position."

"Well it is good to know where you stand, I guess."

Wanda got up from her desk and sat down right beside Annie and was close enough for them to briefly touch knees. She then handed Annie a single piece of paper that had names and addresses on it.

"This paper is an updated version of what you got in your new Employee's Handbook last fall. I have included names of counselors outside of Gordon in case you want to be as anonymous as possible. I have circled the name of one person in Black Mountain whom I know from personal experience is a wonderful psychologist."

Annie was shocked. There seemed to be a chink in the self-assured armor of the HR lady. Before Annie could thank her Wanda spoke again: "Annie, you and I have had our differences in the past. But I want you to know I always have had a lot of respect for you both as a health care professional and a person. Please take advantage of this opportunity. I have had personal struggles in my own life in the past and found this to be a life-enhancing process." With that Wanda got up and went back behind her desk.

"Thanks Wanda," said a dazed Annie.

"You are welcome. And if there is nothing else, I know that we are both busy. Please let me know if I can be of further assistance. And remember, what was shared here today should be kept in the strictest of confidence." The policy robot reappeared and lowered her gaze back to her computer monitor. But it was too late. Annie knew that there was a caring person behind all that stiffness.

Annie stood up, nodded and left Wanda's office still lightheaded from the shock of having someone offer real help to her that she would have never suspected. When she got back to her office she sat down and called Dr. Marsha Allen's office in Black Mountain. The counselor had an opening for this coming Thursday due to a cancelation. Annie hesitated at first. She didn't know it would be this quick and wasn't so sure that she was ready. But she finally decided to jump in and made the appointment.

Once this was done Annie dove into her other responsibilities. Time flew over the next two hours. She knew she needed to touch base with Bob Gordon but she didn't think she could stand one more intense conversation.

Right as she was picking up her purse to go and grab a quick lunch, she saw Bob sail by her door. Without hesitating she pursued him and caught up with Bob in the parking lot.

"Bob, do you have a minute?"

"No, I am going to my office at the courthouse to make more money," replied the elder doctor in an obviously derisive fashion.

"Ok, I deserve that. But I still want to apologize for this morning."

"Are you apologizing because you are sincerely remorseful for what you insinuated or because Stan required you to do so?"

Annie paused. Her hesitation was long enough to convince Dr. Gordon of her true motivations. "Just what I thought! I know we have to work together but I would appreciate it if you wouldn't waste my time by making this kind of ridiculous small talk." With that Bob turned around and got into his Jaguar and sped off leaving Annie standing motionless in the parking lot.

"Well, that was effective," Annie said out loud to herself. She walked over to her usual parking space to get into her Mini-Cooper and then realized it was still at her house. "Great!" she said as she looked up heavenward. "This has been a hellacious day and it is only lunch!"

The following Sunday afternoon Annie was back sitting with Aunt Pearl. Pearl was polishing off another donut when she looked at Annie and said "How come you never ask me about the Ju-Ju?"

"Oh, I guess I didn't need to know then."

"Do you need to know now?"

Annie blushed and said "Yes ma'am."

"Well, all right then!" Pearl put down the box of donuts and slapped her hands together. She sat up and leaned forward. Pearl then got a curious look on her wrinkled face, like one of those fortune tellers at the Fair. Then she began to give her younger apprentice a crash course on true love.

"The Ju-Ju is the undeniable, deep echo of love. It ain't just attraction. Lord, I can look at a picture of Denzel and get all stirred up. Nah, what I am talking about is something that says to your heart – This is it."

"Do you really believe in all of that romantic love-at-first-sight stuff?"

"Sure I do. But you ain't listening! It is not just attraction. That is why so many people get divorces. They get the "Boom-Booms" for someone and think that they are in love again. That is what happened to your sorry ex-husband. Men are real prone to it because when it comes to true love they are basically stupid."

"The Boom-Booms? How am I supposed to keep up with all this stuff Pearl?" asked Annie in a tone of resignation.

"You are overthinking this. That is why you are such a bitter woman. True love exists my friend. Just because Fool's Gold exists doesn't mean that the real thing won't be in the next creek bed!"

Annie had enough sense to know that Momma Pearl was laying down some real strong wisdom, even if she didn't understand half of what she said.

Pearl shifted in the chair a bit and continued. "Now, let me say that attraction in some ways can come and go. My Edgar could be cutting wood all day and look like a wreck and smell like a mule when he walked into the house. I could be yelling my guts out at him about getting his dirty shoes off my clean floor. But ..."

"But then the Ju-Ju hit you huh?" asked a giddy Annie.

"You got it girl. I'd look into that smiling face and the twinkle in his dark eyes and BAM the Ju-Ju would get me all stuptified. Ju-Ju is what you feel beneath all the imperfections, all the stupid stuff, all the body odors and things that make us all frail people."

Annie thought for a second and said "Are there different kinds of Ju-Ju? I mean when I first looked at Meagan ..." Annie got all misty-eyed.

"Oh child, you are smarter than I have given you credit for," laughed Pearl. "Yes darling. You can feel a different kind of Ju-Ju for your kids or friends. I felt some Ju-Ju when you were born."

Annie blushed and kissed Pearl on the cheek. She recognized she had always had Ju-Ju for Momma Pearl. Then in a snap all of this started to make sense to her.

"When I met Kim, I felt this unexplainable closeness. That was Ju-Ju wasn't it?"

"Yes! Ju-Ju is some deep stuff. If it weren't so then everyone would be your best friend and then actually no one would."

"How do you come up with these things?" asked Annie.

"God Almighty teaches me these things. But a lot of it comes from suffering sometimes too, so it ain't for sissies!"

Annie smiled and then asked "Can you lose Ju-Ju?"

Pearl nodded and said "Yes. But you can get it back because it never totally goes away, it just gets hidden behind fear and worry and anger."

"Did you ever lose your Ju-Ju for Edgar?"

"Oh sure. Several times."

"I simply can't believe that!"

"Really?" responded Pearl. She leaned all the way back in her chair and looked toward the ceiling. "Well let me tell you something only a few people in heaven and earth know. One time I caught Edgar kissing another woman behind our church."

"What?" exclaimed Annie in utter shock. "No way. Uncle Ed was one of the finest men I have ever met!"

"Girl, do you think bad men do all the bad stuff in this world. I take that back about you being smart. You is just ignorant sometimes!"

Annie had forgotten that it was usually a big mistake to question Momma Pearl. "I'm sorry. Please go on."

"Edgar was a fine man but he wasn't always good. No one is. He was good most of the time. Anyway, I caught him kissing Malva Tudder.

She always had an eye for him. Nasty hussy! I warned him about her but he ignored me."

"Why do men do that Pearl?!"

"Your guess is about as good as mine. I think it has something to do with the penis. When it wakes up the brain goes to sleep. Or something like that."

Annie couldn't contain herself again. As she chocked with laughter, she held her hand over her mouth and motioned for Pearl to continue.

"So, when I caught them kissing one night behind the outhouse after Prayer Meeting, I went up side his head and then I tore her up too. It took three deacons and the pastor himself to get me off of them. I think I even tried to bite her on her fat butt. I was out of my mind!"

"You are one fierce chick!" said Annie, bragging on her mentor.

"That's right baby girl. And you know what ... so are you!" Annie and Pearl high-fived.

"Once I calmed down, I told him, 'Don't you show your sorry self back at the house. If you show up, I will shoot you dead.' I then grabbed Teddy and little Marla and dragged them home. Oh my God they started crying and I told them that I would give them some of what their Daddy got if they didn't shut up. It was terrible." Now Pearl's remembered rage was turning into sadness.

Annie was sitting with her mouth wide-open and said "What happened?"

"Well you know what happened. I didn't shoot him and we stayed happily married for over sixty years. But Malva left town. She moved to Statesville and married a preacher I heard."

"Did you get counseling to work through your problems?" asked a concerned Annie.

"Counseling is a modern invention. Back then we reached an understanding."

"But what do you mean by understanding?" asked Annie.

"Edgar understood if he ever pulled that again I would kill him dead and I understood that Edgar understood. Catch up girl. Mercy, how long have we been talking? You better hope I live to be a hundred!"

Annie laughed so hard so she almost fell off the bed. She looked at Pearl and then said, "Do you know it immediately or does it grow on you?"

"Now hold on I almost forgot something," replied Pearl in an abrupt fashion. "The Lord himself will tear my old tail up if I don't mention this. Ju-Ju ain't real if you are committing adultery. It is like drinking cheap liquor. You feel good for a little while and then when you have the hangover from Hades you realize that the fun ain't worth the pain. Momma Pearl isn't endorsing that nonsense. This man ain't married, is he?"

"No. I mean he doesn't wear a ring and he acts like a bachelor" replied Annie.

"Whew, that's good" said the old woman in a relieved manner. "I have been whooped a few times by the Lord and I am too old and my rear is too flat to get a whipping from him now."

Annie built up the courage to confess something. "Well Momma Pearl … I have experienced Ju-Ju!" exclaimed Annie holding up her hands in a Pentecostal manner.

"Ok, now all you need to find out is if he felt it too" said the old guru of love.

Annie felt the air go out of her love balloon. "But how do you do that?"

"I guess I have to teach you everything huh? No wonder so many white people get divorced. You can get a college education but you can stay ignorant about the really important stuff for a long time."

Pearl leaned up and cupped Annie's chin with her left hand and smiled tenderly at her pupil. "Listen up. You pay him a visit at work one day and look him in the eye and say 'I was thinking about you and I just wanted to stop by and say hello.' Then after some brief small talk you suddenly say goodbye."

"That's it?" asked the cynical protégé.

"No. Then you watch for signs. Maybe he returns the favor. Maybe he buys you a gift and brings it to you. The asking out on a date is child's play. Anyone can go out on a date. That is often a man's strategy to woo you to get you into bed. If you are looking for that, just go to a bar and don't waste my time. The wisdom of the Ju-Ju is too important to give to fools!"

"But what is it that I am really looking for?" asked a confused Annie.

"You are looking for trepidation plus desire. When a man feels Ju-Ju he is so worried that he is going to screw it up that he second guesses everything he does and stays that way until he gets confirmation."

"But Uncle Ed was so smooth" said Annie.

"Yes, but he had been to war for three years. He has seen a lot of good men die and he made himself and the Lord a promise: The first woman he met that made him glad that he survived he was going to marry. He was ready to risk being rejected in order to experience true Ju-Ju."

She sat back in her chair smiled and said, "Besides, when he thought he lost me he called me on the phone crying and saying, 'Baby, I just saw a milk truck and I remembered you are the only woman I ever loved. Please, please forgive me. I promise you darlin, you won't regret it." She winked at Annie and laughed.

Pearl sat back in her recliner and folded her arms together proudly stating, "So I forgave that man and he became the greatest husband the world has ever known! Let me tell you the Ju-Ju then became even more powerful."

The smile then faded and she took a deep breath. Two slender tears escaped her eyes as she looked up at the ceiling and said, "Oh it is all up in this room right now. It is like I can feel those strong arms around me and his scruffy beard against my neck. Lord Jesus how I miss that man!"

Annie's heart great heavy as she watched this old saint ache for the presence of her dead husband. She thought about all of this and then said, "So is finding and nurturing Ju-Ju is worth the risk and the pain?"

"Yes baby. A thousand times yes!" said Pearl without a hint of hesitation. The old woman composed herself and lowered her gaze at Annie. "So, what are you going to do now?"

"I guess I am going to start planting some seeds to see if a Ju-Ju tree starts sprouting," replied Annie shaking her head in slight disbelief.

Momma Pearl clapped her hands together and shouted, "Well all right!"

CHAPTER 4

ANNIE WALKED INTO Dr. Marsha Allen's office in Black Mountain. It was actually in a Victorian House on the east side of town which had seemed to have gone through multiple restorations. The bottom floor was a lobby shared by Dr. Allen and a local lawyer, housing a large conference room, a kitchen and his offices. The receptionist/administrative assistant was also shared by both the therapist and the lawyer. This worked out fairly well except for the times when wires got crossed and there was confusion over making appointments or sending out bills. Annie sat down in a rose-colored high back chair and waited.

An older lady walked downstairs with a middle-aged woman. They hugged and the younger lady said, "I will see in a couple of weeks. And enjoy yourself at your daughter's wedding. You deserve it!" The older woman smiled and walked out. Then the younger woman walked up to Annie and announced "Hi, I am Marsha. You must be Annie." Annie nodded. She was taken back a bit because this lady appeared more like someone that would be one of her friends rather than a psychologist. She had long auburn hair and wore a bight flowered blouse with a cream-colored dress that was ankle length. She sported some stylish sandals and had neatly manicured feet. Annie couldn't figure out her age but knew she took very good care of herself.

"Would you like something to drink?" asked Marsha.

"I guess some hot tea would be nice."

"Oh, you and I are going to become fast friends. I am tea lover myself." She turned to the receptionist, "Laura, could you please bring us two peppermint teas?"

"My pleasure," replied the smiling receptionist.

"Thanks darling," said the appreciative counselor.

"Come on up!" Annie followed Marsha up the steps. At the top they turned back towards the front and went to the last door on the right. At the front of the door was an antiqued wooden sign that she flipped indicating that she was "In Session."

Marsha led Annie in and said "have a seat on the couch right there." It was a coffee colored leather couch that had some age on it. But when Annie sat down, she felt like she was being hugged by an old friend. She looked around her and saw what looked to be original art-deco and wooden signs that had wise sayings that were hard to take in all at once. She sniffed and noticed some kind of herbal candle.

"Do you like that aroma?" asked Marsha.

"Yes, it is very soothing."

"A lady from Black Mountain makes these. She claims that the combination encourages openness. I don't know if all that is true, but it sure is fun to imagine."

Annie nodded. She noticed above a desk in the corner there were a slew of diplomas including a BA in Psychology from Davidson, a M.Ed. from University of Florida and a Ph.D. from Baylor in Psychology. She also saw several licenses and certifications from different agencies. This was no ordinary "earth mother" counselor. This woman had multiple layers that intrigued Annie.

"So, Annie, what we are going to do today is a little different. Instead of slowly getting to know each other I want to first ask you one question: Why are you here?"

Annie liked that. She had heard of counselors who developed a long-term relationship with their clients before ever solving a single problem. She didn't need another friend. She needed a therapist who could help her unravel her problems.

"Well, I guess it is about my anger."

"Ok, good." Marsha took up a spiral notebook. "Is it ok if I take notes?"

"Sure."

As Marsha was getting ready to ask another question the receptionist arrived with the tea. "Oh fantastic" replied Marsha. "You are worth a million dollars Laura. I wish I could pay you that much."

"Me too," replied Laura. "Do you want me to shut the door?"

"Yes please." She turned back to Annie and said "On the coffee table in front of you is stuff for your tea." Annie picked out two Splenda packets. Marsha grinned and did the same thing and said "See, simpatico darling!"

Annie leaned back and enjoyed the tea. She was so relaxed that she thought about how nice it would be to take a nap.

"Now, you mentioned anger. How do you act when you are angry?"

Annie thought and said "I guess it is different with different people."

"Give me some examples," said Marsha. Annie noticed that in an almost magically manner she had put on a pair of purple reading glasses. Annie was noticeably staring at her and Marsha notice. "Oh, I have got about a dozen of these to match my mood. Watch out when I am wearing my black ones!"

Annie laughed. "I need several of those."

"I will tell you later about the Drug Store I get them from. So, tell me about the fire in your gut."

"Well with my daughter Meagan I can eventually start yelling. With my ex-husband I try to wound him with words. My Mom I guess I shut her out. People at work I find myself challenging them, especially those I don't respect.

"Ok, that is very helpful. Now, let me ask you about your ex-husband. By the way I have one of those, so don't be shy. Why are so angry with him?"

"Well he cheated on me. I don't even know if that is the right phrase. Maybe I could say he built a parallel universe in which he tried to have sex with as many people as he could and still pretend that he was still a good guy."

"Oh, I am so sorry darling." Marsha let those sincere words of empathy seep into Annie. Suddenly tears started welling up in Annie's eyes. "You are still in a lot of hurt over that aren't you?"

"Yes. Damn-it! I didn't want to get upset!"

"Why not?"

"Well I don't want to be a victim"

"Who said you were a victim?"

"I don't know I just don't want to be a weak person."

"Well, when we are so fundamentally wounded or betrayed, we are initially victims. But to eventually heal we have to get beyond the hurt to a place of abundant wisdom and deepened courage."

"That sure would be nice," said Annie as she reached for some tissues on the coffee table.

Marsha took a sip of her tea. "Ooh, that is so freaking good!" She placed the cup back on the table, tilted her head back and then looked up to the ceiling. She paused for a moment to let her client settle her spirit. Then she shifted gears. "Annie have you ever explained to your ex-husband the effects of his betrayal on your life?"

"Well, yea. I told him what a scumbag he was to cheat on me and how I hated him for making me live a lie."

"That is good. But that is not really what I am asking. What you are talking about is actions or behavior. That is important. But I am asking about something deeper. Let me give you an example: 'Your cheating made me question my beauty'. See what I am talking about?"

Annie took another sip of tea. She leaned back and said "Yes, definitely that and more. I guess … his lying made me question whether or not I could trust a man again."

"Good! Continue."

"Uh, his choice of another woman tore our family apart."

"That is close, dig a little deeper."

Annie sat there for what felt like ten minutes and then it came to her: "When he chose another woman my dream of a having a happy family with him died."

"Yes! That is powerful. You see, unprocessed emotions whether anger, fear, or sadness don't disappear with time. They dissipate throughout our spirits. And then that poison gives our heart a kind of perpetual low-grade fever. Until we clearly identify the source of our pain, we will be treating symptoms rather than causes."

"Oh, gosh," replied Annie like a person suddenly awakened by an alarm. "I am really not over my divorce, am I?"

"Well, you have probably come a long way, but no you are not."

"But, but ..." Annie seemed to be struggling with coming to grips with what she had just learned. "It has been eight years since we separated. How could this happen?"

"Annie, it happens to all of us in some way or another. We all get hurt. I don't mean slightly disappointed. I mean deeply wounded. That is a universal experience for the human species. But if we run from our hurt because of our shame or try to divert it with something else, we delay our healing. Now, you don't need a counselor to heal. Some people figure this out through other means. But the process of healing is pretty much the same for all of us."

"What is the process?"

"Well, there are a lot of ways to define it but because you seem to be a pretty concrete thinker, let me put it this way: First, you have to name the hurt. But as you have seen, this in not as easy as it seems. Then you have to come to terms with how that hurt changed you. For instance, do you feel unworthy of love? Or has fear of additional failure so jammed you up inside that you can open up your heart? Stuff like that. Then you need to let your pain teach you about what is true, real and good. Finally, you need to choose a new path based on what you have learned.

"That sounds like a lot of work."

"Yes, it is. But have you known of anything that was worthwhile and valuable that didn't involve hard work?"

"No." Annie sat there realizing that she had come to the right person. She knew there were no shortcuts. She looked at Marsha and asked, "Do you think there is hope for me? I mean, could I ever love again?"

"Hmmm, this sounds like a loaded question. Is there a man in your life that you are wondering about?"

"That is freaky! How did you know that?"

"It is not important. The fact is that you are scared, aren't you?"

"Oh, dear God yes!"

"Well, before you jump into a new relationship, I want us to work on getting you on a healing path."

"How long will that take?"

"I'm not sure. At the very least you need to make the connection between cause and effect. It's not that you have remained passive. My guess is that the strategies you've employed to deal with the shame, anger and fear haven't worked. That's why you are here sniffing my cool candle and drinking this awesome tea." Marsha took another sip and sat back. "Does that make sense?"

"Yes."

"Good. Now I am going to give you an assignment because I believe that you are the manager of your own healing. What I mean by that is that I can come along side of you and guide you but in the end, you have to take responsibility for yourself."

"That makes sense."

"Ok. Do you own a journal?"

"Yes, I think so."

"I want you to start writing down in that journal what your ex-husband did that hurt you. Then I want you to carefully reflect on how it impacted you. That is all for right now."

"How often should I write? I mean, in the past I tried to do this and I flopped."

"Don't worry about. Do it when you feel inspired to do it. Carry that journal around with you and when you have a moment of clarity jot your ideas down. I don't' need you to write a novel. I want you to slow down and observe what is happening with your feelings and thoughts. Ok?"

Annie relaxed back into the couch. For the first time in a while she experienced the sensation of hope and that helped her to feel empowered in a way that was deeply encouraging.

"Now, I have some paper work for you to fill out. I will leave you in here for the next fifteen minutes to do that and finish your tea. I am going to put on some relaxing music to promote some nice energy in here as you work because some of these questions require a good bit of reflection. When you are done, you can come downstairs and give it to Laura. This is totally confidential so you don't have to worry about anybody else seeing it. By the way, the first session is free. I have to say this to my clients because they are worried about getting their money's worth all up front."

"Wow, thanks. Are you sure about this? I mean, how do you stay in business?"

Marsha smiled and patted Annie on the hand. "Don't worry. Without trying to sound cryptic I do ok because honestly sweetie, when people come to me, they are in need of a lot of help."

Annie laughed and raised her hand.

"Now, when you leave you decide when you want to meet next and set it up with Laura, ok?"

Marsha stood and Annie followed suit. The counselor then opened her arms up. "Give me a hug." Annie complied and after a gentle embrace Marsha grabbed her shoulders and said, "We are going to do some good work together!"

Annie touched her heart and nodded. Marsha winked at her, turned around and left in the same free-spirited way in which she had entered Annie's life. Annie sat back down, blown away by all that transpired in such a short period of time.

Gathering herself she took pen in hand and focused all her energies on the task in front of her. As she listened to the soft acoustic guitar and flute rendition of "Claire de Lune" she relaxed once more. In a way, she felt like she was finally beginning to step up on the path of healing she had been longing to travel for longer than she could remember.

Annie had been working hard for three weeks on her assignment to do some emotional archeology. She had met with Marsha two more times since their initial session. Because the Holidays were in full swing Marsha wanted to get what she called "a psychological turbo-boost" so that they would not lose any momentum before they had to take a two-week break.

This advice had already produced more powerful insights that gave Annie a foothold into how her anger was rooted not so much in injustices as they were in profound loss. These sessions, along with her weekly talks with Momma Pearl, gave Annie the confidence she needed to carefully investigate what was happening in her heart when it came to the mysterious Bart St. Clair.

This is why she had gone to Stardust early Saturday Morning at 7:00 a.m. She was all business on this day because in thirty minutes she would be on the radio getting things ready for the Gordon Christmas Parade. People thought she was crazy for taking on yet another duty. Kim told her that she "was addicted to mania."

Typically, she would stop and chat with Fareesh and Tammy but she didn't' have time. She quickly obtained a $10 Gift Card from Fareesh and placed it in an envelope with a cute card that talked about the unexpected blessings of making a new friend. She carefully inserted the card into a green and red gift bag that also contained a pouch of gourmet liver treats for Frodo that were shaped like T-Bone steaks she purchased the day before at Gordon Pharmacy.

She told her friends that she would see them at the Christmas Parade in a few hours and then darted across the street to the back of Angelo's. Right by the back door was a large drop box that venders could insert food through. She carefully put her bag through the opening and made sure it was upright and somewhat to the left of the slot so a sack of potatoes would not crush her dainty package.

Once this mission was accomplished, she went back across the street to the parking lot beside Stardust and jumped into her newly repaired car. It seemed that she had a bad fuel pump and that purchase would alter some of her plans for Christmas shopping. But she smiled as she thought to herself, *"It might be worth it to have a broken-down car if this new friendship turns into something special!"* As she turned onto Main Street, she then felt a little silly that she was allowing her mind to move ahead to such romantic considerations.

A few minutes later Bart and Frodo pulled up to the delivery door at Angelo's. Bart unlocked the metal monstrosity and saw a few bills, some fresh green peppers he had needed for tonight and Annie's little care package on the concrete floor. He bent down and said, "What do we have here Fro?" He pulled out the card and quickly read it. It was signed "Your new friend, Annie." He grinned, put the gift card in his wallet and then grabbed the doggie treats. Shaking them he said, "Look pal, she got something for you too." Frodo was excited and Bart was impressed. He quickly ripped open the package and threw a treat into the air that his dog quickly inhaled.

Bart then walked back into his office, placed all his stuff on his desk and sat down. As he leaned back, he noticed that Frodo had scooted very close to him, lying ready for another liver snack to be tossed his direction. Bart laughed at his pup and threw the intense canine another treat. He noticed that he felt strangely happy. He still was smiling and then thought to himself, *"I can't remember the last time I felt this good."*

By the time it was 10:00 a.m. a crowd had assembled downtown. This year the number of those gathered looked like it was the largest in a long time. Annie smiled as she stood at the corner of Main and Old Valley Road with her radio/phone in hand making sure everyone was in the right order and ready to go. Despite all the stress associated with putting such an even together she was exhilarated about the parade. It reminded her of what she felt like when she was a kid sitting on her Daddy's shoulders straining to get glimpse of Santa Claus.

The first float to lead the way in the Christmas Parade was the Founder's Float. This depicted a man dressed in a minister's attire standing behind a pulpit with the Bible in one hand and a hammer in the other. Neatly spaced on the rest of this float were people representing different trades.

On this float there were normally descendants of Jeremiah Gordon that were dressed in regular clothes standing on both sides. But this year no one accepted the invitation. Most of the family now lived out of town and Nadine Gordon Chester, the oldest surviving grandchild of Rev. Gordon told Annie that she was "just too tired to participate."

On the back of the float was a person representing Teddy Roosevelt sitting on a Sawyers Mountain High Back Chair, smoking a Country Gentleman. Below at the end of the trailer was the inscription "Nothing is Impossible with God!"

The rest of the floats followed the typical small-town parade progression. There was the VFW float with its ever-decreasing number of participants. The only recent addition was Mike Sawyers who had just gotten back a few months ago from his second tour in Afghanistan with the 82nd Airborne Division. Mike had wanted to join the Green Berets, but a Taliban mortar had cut short his military career. He wore a patch on over his left eye and walked with a slight limp. He was currently looking for more permanent employment while he worked part-time in the Home and Garden section of the Wal-Mart in Asheville. When people recognized Mike, they showered him with cheers. It made him glad to be home.

Next was the award-winning Gordon High School marching band playing a jazzed-up version of "Sana Claus is Coming to Town." The red and gold uniforms looked as if they had been particularly designed for a Christmas Parade. Bill Hunter directed the band from the back of his son Bobby's red Dodge pickup truck. This was going to be Bill's last year as band director. He had been at Gordon High for thirty-five years. Now he spent part of his time in a wheel chair due to severe case of rheumatoid arthritis. But what he lacked in physical mobility he more than made up for in a relentless passion for musical precision. There were no slackers on Mr. Hunter's watch.

They were followed by the Flag Core and Cheerleaders who were tossing out candy to the crowd. This year the girls wore white hose due to the almost freezing temperature that had surprisingly dropped down on the town over the last few days. They didn't look all that happy to be there. Because the cold hair motivated fast movement there were a couple of occasions when they bumped up against the band. One glare from Mr. Hunter sent them back to their rightful spots in the pecking order of importance.

Ingmar Polanski's Dance Studio was right behind the impatient girls. Her husband Bruno was driving in front with his 1965 Shelby Cobra Mustang that had a sound system temporarily mounted in the back seat. It was blaring out "The Dance of the Sugar Plum Fairies" from The Nutcracker. Girls ranging from five to eighteen were doing complicated toe-movements on a surface that wasn't designed for these types of dance shoes, so there were occasional slips and spills.

Although Mrs. Polanski was around sixty, she led the procession and still had some moves, and didn't miss a twirl, leap or bow. Meagan was dancing but seemed somewhat disinterested, even though her grandparents and her Mom were cheering her on. Then right before they turned from Main Street left onto Turner Road, little Terri Dumbar had fallen and started crying. Her Mom Debra was trying to get her to rejoin the ensemble, but eventually had to pick up her and offer warmth and comfort during that chilly morning.

Boy Scout Troop 911 marched in unison behind the little sugar fairies. Old Colonel Silas Thornton was directing his young men in the fine art of precision marching. He was a retired artillery officer who had served in both the Korean and Vietnam wars.

For over forty years he had provided leadership for the Boy Scouts in Gordon. No troop in North Carolina was better-behaved and looked more polished than these young men. Although the crowd snickered a tiny bit at their militaristic cadence, every parent who sent their wide-eyed boy through the rigors of training the "Thornton Way" knew that their son had received an education in duty, honor and country that was priceless.

The Gordon Women's Auxiliary followed the young men. The theme of their float this year was "The Hand That Rocks the Cradle." About ten women portrayed the mothers of some of the civic, religious and business leaders of Gordon. Although it was very well done, people were debating on the sidelines about who each person was supposed to be. Annie struggled with allowing this entry because of that very ambiguity. But since her Mom, her tenth-grade English teacher Donna Evans and her buddy Tee were participating, what could she do?

The Gordon Moose Lodge scooted along behind the refined women of Gordon. Their float didn't have a theme. If it did, it would be called "A Bunch of Old Men Up to No Good." A boom box was playing Louis Armstrong's "When the Saints Go Marching In." That song represented a hilarious irony to say the least.

Case and point: on that float was James Billings who was known to make what the folks called Sawyers Mountain Smoke. People claimed it was the most famous moonshine in North Carolina. Although Big Jimmy had been in trouble with the law most of his adult life, he constantly telling people that he was going "legit" due to the changes in NC distillery laws. Maybe be "The Smoke" would be Gordon's next great export.

Annie thought it would be only apt to have the Gordon Ministerial Association next in this progression. Many of those parsons had chased most of the men of the Moose Lodge for years trying them to convert them. Big Jimmy had gotten saved about four times in the last twenty years. His conversions always seemed to coincide with his arrests.

The theme of this float was "Bringing Gordon to God." What was funny about this presentation was that the first three letters of Gordon had fallen off somewhere back in the line so now it read "Bringing don to God." People laughed when they saw this slip up because Don Phillips was the current Grand Buck of the Moose Lodge. His wife Marge made no bones about how she was praying for Don's conversion for years, so she thought it was another sign from God that her "rascal was going to get right!"

This year Annie added a float from the Oak Valley Rehab Center. Such was one of the few perks of being the Chairwoman of the Christmas Parade! The float was entitled "Celebrating Our Heritage." A few of the staff got to take that fun ride. They were also needed to make some of the handpicked residents stay put.

Annie had Pearl seated on a throne with a big lit up halo sign over her head that read "Momma Pearl." Since many of the residents had been brought into this world by that spunky lady, she got some of the loudest cheers of the day. She ate it up and returned the favor by waving like a beauty queen and launching dozens of kisses out to the crowd. Annie got a little teary-eyed as she saw people react to her second mother. This float was her contribution to Gordon and her clear recognition of one of the area's unsung heroes.

After several other displays and groups passed by, the last presentation of the day was the traditional Santa Float. Dennis Fason had played Santa for long time. But ever since his mishap back ten years ago, people seemed to hold their breath every year since when he and his elves rolled around.

The reasons for this reaction were threefold. First, Dennis had to be pushing seventy. Second his footing was not the steadiest as he stood atop of the high perch of his sleigh slinging candy. Third, Dennis was a recovering alcoholic. That condition had contributed to what people often called "the fall of Santa."

Back in 2000, Dennis was nervous about his presentation of being St. Nick because the newspaper had reported his latest DUI from the previous month. The Gordon News had downsized to a monthly circular, but kept the tradition of reporting the latest arrests and even violations. Some people had threatened to get the ACLU involved pertaining to violation of folk's civil rights or something like that.

In order to soothe his nerves Dennis took more than a few swigs of Big Jimmy's magic mixture back behind the Gordon Furniture building right before the parade began. By the time he reached downtown he was so lit up that his float didn't need any extra illumination. As he reared back to let some candy fly he tumbled over, smashed three of the plastic reindeer and face-planted on the asphalt street. He had to be carried off in an ambulance and went through two different surgeries to reconstruct his face. Ever since then, Santa said Merry Christmas with a slight lisp. Thankfully this year Santa was sober and the parade ended without injury or incident.

By the time clean-up was occurring Annie was full of relief and gratitude. Countless people shared their congratulations at one of the most beautiful and memorable parades ever. As Annie was sipping a "victory Latte" that Tammy had given her, little Tommy Pollard pulled on her sweater. When she looked down, he handed her an envelope with her name on it. She opened it and it read:

> *I request the honor of your presence at 11:30 p.m. tonight in the kitchen of Angelo's. I would like to offer you the first piece of a new dessert I will be featuring next week. Since you are a woman of style and grace (despite a mishap with a shoe on a rainy day) I thought it would be in my best interest to get your feedback on my humble creation. If you are interested, please send my courier back with a "you-betcha."*
>
> *Fondly,*
> *Bart*

Annie laughed and told Bart's little messenger that he could give the nice man a "you-betcha." She spied Bart standing by the front of the restaurant waving at her. Tommy went and found his Dad and crossed the street to give her pursuer an answer. Annie waved and lifted her hot drink to cheer the upcoming date. She walked back to her car and took a deep breath. As she opened the door, she said to herself *"Annie you are getting ready to take a dive into the sea of Ju-Ju. I sure hope you know what you are doing!"*

Annie and Meagan got in her car about 10:45 p.m. that night and headed off to her Mom and Dad's. All the way there Meagan grilled her Mom about the nature of such a late date. She asked how much Annie knew about this stranger.

"Not much," sighed her Mom.

"Well, do you have a will?" asked the sassy teen.

"Why do you want to know that Meg?"

"Because, this guy could be a serial killer and if you die, I want to make sure I am taken care of and I especially want your car."

Annie shook her head and replied, "So good to know how much you really love me sweetie."

Once they arrived at her parent's home Annie's Mom started her own form of interrogation. "Annie, I am glad you are getting out," said the worried mother. "But I have heard some rumors that this man has a sketchy past. Are you sure you want to get involved with someone like that?"

"My point exactly Granny," said the exasperated Meagan.

"Who said anything about getting involved with anyone Mom," replied Annie while staring a hole into her daughter. "We are just having dessert."

"Is that what older people call sex?" asked Megan in a clearly sarcastic manner.

"Shut up Meg," replied Annie.

"See Granny," said Meagan pointing to her Mom as if she caught her in a huge inconsistency. "She gets defensive when anyone questions her about her decision making. But I am supposed to sit there like an obedient nun when she rags on me. I sure hope this is not another embarrassing situation like you know who." There is nothing like a teenager to remind you of your imperfections.

"Ok, that's enough. Both of you can just keep quiet. I am planning to have a nice short meeting with Mr. St. Claire and then plan to pick you up for church tomorrow morning. And if he does kill me, I had already told Kim she could have my car."

"Ok Mom," said the temporarily defeated teen. Meagan then observed the emerald green silk blouse that Annie was wearing. It clung to her shapely figure in an almost seductive manner. Smiling the relentless adolescent changed gears and asked, "Are you wearing a bra under that shirt?"

Annie turned towards the door and hastily exists saying "Good night ladies." She jumped into her vehicle, checked her hair and makeup in the rear-view mirror and leaned back. She liked what she saw and started to back up her car out of the tricky driveway.

But the seeds of doubt and concern that Meg and Lola planted started to sprout. Now she started thinking about what could go wrong in this situation. She wondered out loud, "But what if they are right. What if he is a pervert, or a murderer or worse ... What if he is married? Oh my God, why did I agree to this?" For a brief moment Annie parked her car and picked up her phone to call the restaurant to make up some story about Meg being sick or her dog dying. Then she shook off the paranoia and regained her composure. Gritting her teeth, she put her car back in gear and said "Why does risking your heart always feel so risky?"

When she arrived in the restaurant, she found a place right in front to park. She noticed that employees were laughing as they were heading out the front door. One of the exiting waiters says to her "Annie, Bart told me to tell you to go in and sit at the little table right across from the door in the kitchen and he will be with you shortly."

Annie said "thank you" just in time for him to cut off the lights and lock the front door. There is she is -- in the dark, alone in a restaurant late at night meeting a stranger for dessert. She hoped that she was not going to be the main course for some Hannibal Lecter character. Stranger things have happened. Maybe not in Gordon, but even a small town can attract a weirdo or two. Annie braces herself for the worst and pushes through the swinging doors.

She finds a small table with two chairs, two place settings and a red candle placed on a silk doily in the middle. She takes off her white coat and sits down. In about a minute Bart comes through the back door leading from the storage room, refrigerator and office area. Cupped in both hands are two small plates of a light orange colored pie.

"Good evening," says Bart in a smooth baritone voice as he places the desserts on the table. He was wearing a tweed sport coat, some charcoal pants and an oxford blue shirt that looked crisply pressed. His thick hair was clean and neatly combed and his face was newly shaven with his goatee looking recently groomed. Annie got a whiff of some light cologne that made the package complete.

"You look stunning in that blouse," remarked the smiling man.

"Uh, I am wearing a bra," stammered Annie.

"That is a good thing," said the grinning man.

"Ok, that was embarrassing," said Annie.

"Don't worry about it. Just to be fair I am wearing underwear myself. No bra but some brand-new briefs. I even took a shower and shaved because I knew you were coming." They both laughed and broke the ice in a way that made conversation less stilted.

"So, try this and tell me what you think" said Bart pointing to the delicious looking dessert.

Annie spied it. It was almost an orange sherbet color and had what looked like caramel drizzled all over it forming two hearts on both sides of the pie. She cautiously took her fork and sliced off a small bite. She tasted cream cheese butter, sugar and a hint of lemon. But she couldn't figure out the main ingredient. It was familiar but slightly unrecognizable.

"What do you think?" asked the pensive chef.

"It is incredible, but I can't quite figure out the main ingredient."

"It's sweet potatoes."

"That's it!" said Annie almost shouting. "A sweet potato cheese cake. You are full of surprises. It reminds me of your Chicken Marsala -- familiar but mysterious. Is this a pattern with you?" teased Annie.

"Perhaps. Or maybe I'm just more private than mysterious."

For a moment the tall, strong and somewhat silent man's face looked more like a boy's than a commandant of the kitchen. He looked haunted by an ancient hurt that was too sacred to mention. Annie knew the look. She saw it in her own face more than once when looking into the mirror. Woundedness has a language all its own. She decided to change the subject.

"So, if you are looking for an endorsement you've got it!"

"Thanks," said a grinning Bart. "Maybe I will name it after you."

"Oh gosh, please don't do that! I'm from around here and enough people know too much of my business already. If you are looking for grist for the rumor mill that would be an efficient way to start."

"People have gossiped about you?"

Annie looked into Bart's eyes in the kind of way that elicited a blunt warning. When she saw curiosity rather nosiness, she decided to let him into her life a little bit.

"Yeah." She took a breath and then made a confession. "You know Darrell the pharmacist?"

"Yes ... do you mean you and Darrell had a ..."

"An affair? Yes," stated Annie in a matter-of-fact fashion. "Do you think less of me now?"

Bart leaned forward. He lightly touched Annie's hand. This time she didn't move it away. He looked at her with all the sincerity and compassion he could muster and said in an almost hushed tone like you would use in church, "No Annie. I was just trying to get to know you a little better. I'm sorry if I came across as being invasive or something."

"It's ok," replied Annie. "Being with that jerk was an effort on my part of trying to recapture a sense of being wanted and attractive after a horrible divorce. Let's just chalk it up to the wrong place, wrong time and definitely the wrong person."

"I can't imagine you needing any endorsement of being attractive. You have a classic beauty that is undeniable."

Annie blushed. She hadn't blushed like that in a long, long time. But she wasn't about to lose control. She shook her head and said, "That is nice of you to say, but I think the lighting in here has affected your sight."

"No, you look even more attractive in the daytime." Bart laughed and then said, "You looked especially attractive in the rain the other day."

Annie looked at him incredulously. "Ok, enough of this nonsense. Let's talk about something else. For instance, tell me more about yourself Mr. Mystery."

Bart recognized that even though he was being serious about how attractive Annie was, he needed to follow her lead. He took a bite of the desert and then washed it down with a sip of decaf coffee.

"Not much to tell. I was a partner in a business and had some things happen that caused me to want to quit what I had been doing for a long time. I sold my interest in the business and decided to go to Italy to learn how to cook."

"How did you get from Italy to Gordon?" asked Annie as she polished off her last bite of the cheesecake.

"The same way Angelo did. Well sort of."

"I'm not following you."

"Well, I first went to the *G-Brera* School of Culinary Arts in Como. It is a town about an hour outside of Milan. It was tough, but because I minored in Italian in college, I picked up the language pretty fast. The school was Monday through Thursday. From Friday through Sunday I worked at a little bistro in Milan called La Rosa's. The owner and his wife had been running it forever. They were sort of legends.

Anyway, Rosa ran the dining area. She even had a throne she sat on right beside the bar. Sometimes she would sit there for hours directing people while reading The New Yorker magazine. She liked me because I taught her some English."

"Sounds like my kind of woman," laughed Annie.

"Yeah, as long as you did what she said," countered Bart.

"Like I said my kind of gal," grinned Annie.

"Giorgio was her husband. He ran the kitchen. He was a fiery little guy who loved to correct me. He used to tell me that I was too rigid. He said cooking was thirty percent technique and seventy percent heart.

He told me that if I didn't learn how to let the food speak, I should become a car mechanic."

"Wow, I guess that was tough on your ego. So, what did you do after that?"

"Well it took a year to get through the Institute. I then had built a little credibility with Giorgio and asked him for a letter of reference to take with me to Southern Italy. He refused at first because of the culinary debate that has existed for centuries about whether the North or the South had the best food, wine, etc."

"So, there is a difference?"

"Oh, my Annie, there are some big differences between these folks. This is the kind of thing that starts fist-fights. In a basic sense, every region of every county has different ways of preparing food. If you lived at the coast, you knew various ways to prepare fish. If you lived near grazing lands, you would be proficient in creating great meat dishes. This is a gross oversimplification, but basically true. Even the variations in climate impacts how wines taste."

"That makes sense," affirmed Annie.

"Yeah, we even see this in our own country. For example, ask some New Yorkers about grits and they will often think you are speaking a different language. Ask some Southerners about an Empanada and they would think it would require a visit to the doctor."

"That is funny and true," giggled Annie.

"In Italy, there are even differences in the types of pastas each region prefers. It is not as uniform as people think."

"How did you convince Giorgio?'

"I didn't."

"What did you do?" asked Annie in a concerned manner.

"I got Rosa on my side," said Bart with a sly grin in his face. "We were sitting on their veranda drinking cappuccinos and talking about my past. She looked right at me, shook her fat index finger and blurted out, 'You need to heal your heart. You are very, very sad. Giorgio, I love him, but he's-a-stupid about love. Me, not so much. I believe you should go to Naples. My cousin she's a great cook. No one better to teach you Southern cooking. Maybe you find a beautiful woman like me. I'm a-from Naples. Don't tell my husband but I like it better.' And so, she told him to write me a letter. He did and then I left."

"Did you?"

"Did I what?"

"Find a beautiful woman?" asked Annie in a piercing way.

Bart laughed and then raised his eyebrows as he remembered faces and figures. "There were lots of beautiful women in Naples, no doubt. But that was more of an exquisite diversion. I was focused on learning how to cook, and "little Benita" worked me ragged at her place La casa di Salse."

"What does that mean?"

"Roughly, it means the house of sauces. No one could make her sauces. She almost never shared recipes. Even her chefs were given flavoring pouches to put into certain dishes with very specific instructions. But they never knew exactly what was in them. She ruled everything with an iron fist. Going from Giorgio to Benita was like going from the frying pan into the fire. She especially didn't trust me"

"Why? You got a letter of reference from her cousin?"

"Because of my name. It had French origins. Northern Italians lived next door to the French and so they shared a lot of things, including ways of cooking. Southern Italians often felt that their cooking and ways were purer than the Northern brethren."

"How did you get her to trust you?"

"I saved her grandson's life."

"What?" By now, Annie was hooked. Bart was one of the most fascinating men she had ever met. Her attraction to him had moved beyond the visceral to the intellectual. She knew that she could listen to him for hours.

"He had fallen through a plate glass door at her villa and had sliced his arm very badly. I applied some basic first-aid and kept him from bleeding to death before the ambulance got there. The surgeon said if I hadn't done that he would have died. Anyone could have done what I did, but she felt as if I was an angel from God or something. I went from straniero to figlio in a matter of minutes."

"What?"

"Oh, I am sorry. From foreigner to son."

"Ok. So, did she share with you some of her secrets?"

"Not some, all."

"My goodness! How about my Chicken Marsala? Did it have secret sauce?"

"Yes. Most of my chicken and fish recipes come from Benita. Giorgio really owns my spaghetti and pizza sauces. I created only a few of my own."

Annie was beyond impressed at this point. But she still kept herself outwardly in check. Taking the position of a reporter she shifted the conversation. "But that does not tell me how you got to Gordon."

"Right," answered Bart. "After spending two years with Benita she offered me the option of buying her out. I almost did it. In fact, the papers were drawn up and all I had to do was to sign.

But then something strange happened. I was staying in an apartment she let out that was above her restaurant. The legal agreement for buying her place was spread all over the kitchen table. Every time I tried to sign it; I froze up. I had opened a window one afternoon to get some fresh air and clear my head to make sure I was making a good decision.

It was then that I overheard a conversation. A couple was talking with their tour guide about how much they enjoyed their lunch. The wife's name was Tonya and she said that it reminded her or her hometown's restaurant Angelo's."

"Oh my gosh, that was Tee!" exclaimed Annie. "I remember when she and Miller took that trip. They were standing right outside of your window?"

"Yep and that is not the strangest part," said Bart. "I literally stuck my head out of the window go to hear more and then she said 'I know Angelo is thinking about selling his place in the near future. It would be a shame to lose that great place to eat.' "I closed my window and knew that there had to be some kind of connection."

"This is crazy!" said Annie. "Don't tell me that Benita and Angelo are related!"

"No, not related. Benita trained Angelo."

Annie gasped.

"In fact, she introduced Marta to Angelo. The girls grew up together. When Angelo married Marta, Benita made him an offer to become a partner in the new bistro she had just opened. He refused. He told her that he missed his family and friends back in North Carolina. I don't think that she ever forgave Mario for taking her best friend away."

"So, you contacted Angelo and made him an offer her couldn't refuse," quipped Annie in her best Italian accent.

"That's a pitiful accent, but yes. When he found out where I trained, he was overjoyed because only his youngest son was interested in cooking, but he was way too immature to take over the business."

"I guess you could say that an open window changed your life huh?" asked Annie.

Bart looked above the candlelight into Annie's crystal blue eyes. The synchronistic weight of all these connected decisions made him swallow hard. "More than you will ever know!" said Bart.

CHAPTER 5

"HERE IS THE million-dollar question for today," asked Marsha. "Are you falling in love with the chef?"

Annie sat on the couch squeezing a large calico cat pillow with both arms. "I don't know Marsha. Maybe. Oh, dear God, am I ready for this?"

"I don't know, are you?"

"I hate it when you do that! I just want you to tell me if I am crazy or premature or something."

"I know dear, but only you can answer that question."

"But do you think I still need to heal more before I go into another relationship?"

"That is a better question. I think you have come a long way. How do you feel about your journey so far?"

Annie put down the pillow, scrunched up her knees and leaned forward with her hands gripped together. "Oh gosh I don't know. I'm not as angry as I was a couple months ago. But I still haven't shared with Tom what I have needed to about the affairs and stuff."

"Why do you think you have been procrastinating on that?"

"Probably because I am worried it would bring up some very painful things and would end in a nasty argument."

"I can understand that. And what would happen if those feelings come up again or if this tough conversation ends in an argument?"

"Ok, you are doing that psychologist stuff we me again aren't you?"

"Yes, I am very sneaky." Marsha sat very still and waited for Annie answer.

"Well, bringing those things up would make me feel powerless. And I guess getting into an argument would make our situation worse."

"Is there anything other than powerlessness you feel?"

Annie looked frustrated again. "Isn't feeling powerless enough?"

Marsha seemed to understand Annie's sense of being stuck. "Let me ask it another way ... why just not simply you say you are angry and upset that this cycle of never getting to the heart of the matter keeps popping up. That is a lot different from being powerless."

"But it is how I feel Marsha!"

"Obviously. But it is your sense of powerlessness coming from others?"

"Yes, because of what people have done to me, especially my ex."

Marsha let those words settle for what seemed to Annie to be an indeterminable amount of time. Then she spoke the next two sentences very carefully: "What if that is really true? Where does that leave you?"

"It is like being in prison with an unknown sentence," Annie blurted out. She then bowed her head in defeat with that statement of utter resignation.

"Yes, Annie. That is what it feels like. I have been there myself. But what if there is a way out of the prison?"

"What is it Marsha? Seriously. I am not kidding."

"What if you have the key?"

Annie shifted her mood. She stared straight into her therapist's eyes and said, "I think that is a cruel statement Marsha. I feel like you are making light of my struggles and you are going to give me psychological bromides that don't help me a bit."

Marsha nodded. "I hear you. Not my intention, but you are actually closer to the real root of your problem than you can possibly imagine. What do you know about shame?"

Annie raised her eyebrows and relaxed a bit. "I guess is it feeling bad about yourself because of what you've done or how people have mistreated you."

"A lot of people think that way. You are not alone. But the first thing you described is guilt. We should and need to feel guilt when we do wrong. The second thing you mentioned is being wounded or rejected by others which really hurts. But shame is not about what you've done or even how others have treated you. It is how you see yourself."

Annie slowly nodded. "Ok, I think I get you, tell me more."

A broad smile broke across Marsha's face. "Look at you asking those clarifying questions. Who's the therapist now?"

Annie smiled back. "But what does this have to do with my procrastination over talking to Tom or pursing another relationship?"

"Your prison is self-imposed. You are afraid of confrontation and risking because you feel that your ex-husband's infidelities were a reflection of what was lacking in you. That's why you can't investigate a new relationship. You don't want to be exposed again as being someone invariably broken, insufficient or incapable of having mutually beneficial relationships."

This seemed to be digging deep into Annie's heart. She seemed to be both comforted and challenged all at once. She struggled for words but couldn't articulate what she was feeling.

Marsha shifted gears again. "I know your faith is key to your life. So, I feel that it is ok for us to broach this subject. I am no expert, and I still have a long to go. But think with me for a moment about God's grace offered to us in Christ. I think it not only ushers us into forgiveness we need to assuage our guilt, it allows us to accept ourselves as we are and receive God's help to move us to where we need to be. Grace addresses both guilt and shame."

Annie started nodding her head as if some of the fog in her heart was clearing up a bit.

Marsha continued. "Until we experience forgiveness, we can never truly offer it to others. And until we see that God loves us completely just as we are, we will never feel that we are enough. You are enough Annie, with or without a man. Clinging to shame does not protect you or even helps you, it poisons you. But until you really believe that in the deepest part of yourself, you are going to always be giving people power over you they are not intended to have."

Marsha's last few words did more than strike a chord. They released an entire new musical movement. Like the last few pesky pieces of a puzzle Annie saw how her cyclical anger, cynicism and anxiety fit into place with what Marsha was saying about shame. It was as if she was standing on Mt. Mitchell with her eyes closed expecting to see the signs of Spring only to discover as she cracked them open to be surprised by the vast patchwork of red, yellow and orange leaves of Fall.

"I, I know this is true. I just had no idea how my shame was driving everything," said Annie Marsha nodded back in a very sober manner. "That is what is so insidious about it. It often feels like we are being honest or responsible about our shortcomings by belittling and punishing ourselves, but in reality, we are digging ourselves deeper into a big fat hole. Sad thing is some people never get out of it."

Annie now understood how that could happen. In fact, at that very moment it occurred to her that she had been living a large part of her life for the past few years from the bottom of a self-imposed mud pit. But despite this incredible revelation, she still seemed somewhat perturbed. "Ok, I think I get it. So, I shouldn't really care how Tom responds to all of this? I mean, it is unreasonable to expect an apology or something?"

"Great question Annie!" said Marsha. The psychologist then put down her notebook on the coffee table between them leaned forward and then said, "Are you looking for freedom from your shame, or some kind of vindication that makes Tom the ultimate villain and you the ever-suffering victim?"

"What do you mean?" Annie reluctantly responded.

"Who do you want directing your life? And even more importantly, how do you want to live your life from this point forward?"

"I want to direct my own life. And I want to be at peace," said Annie as she tapped emphatically with each spoken word at the center mark of her chest.

"Then if that is true, you have to shift from this cyclical pursuit of getting some kind of psychological justice to feel better about yourself and stake a new claim on your life that moves away from bitterness and shame."

Annie nodded again. She now knew she was ready to talk to Tom.

Marsha noticed Annie's new focus. Leveraging that moment, she shifted her attention again and said, "Now, just for fun let's talk about that mysterious man you seem to be falling for."

"Oh, good gosh! I don't know if I can do that" replied Annie as she looked up to the ceiling.

Marsha saw the consternation on her client's face. "Ok, let's try this from a different angle. If you were to get romantically involved with someone again, what would you now be looking for in a man?"

That question seemed to connect to Annie. She looked at Marsha and said "Honesty, kindness, intelligence, physically attractive are a few things that come to mind."

Marsha nodded. "Well he sounds like he is smoking hot, very bright and he was humble enough to apologize for being rude. But do you think Bart is dishonest?"

These words pierced Annie's heart. Her eyes opened wide and she whispered "Yes."

"Why do you believe that?"

"Well, when you look at him and talk to him … I mean he is the total package. Why would this kind of man be here in Gordon of all places? Something doesn't fit! It is almost like a dream. And Marsha I am too old to dream."

"Oh, horse hockey! You are not. We should never stop dreaming. When you do you are in a really bad place. No, your real issue is that you just don't want to be hurt again like you were with Tom."

Annie responded to the counselor's challenge with bitter and focused energy: "Well it is the same thing for me Marsha!"

Marsha didn't say anything. She let Annie sit there, trembling with fear and anger. In a few seconds Annie calmed down a bit. "I'm so sorry Marsha. I know you are just trying to help me. I guess I am kind of answering my own question here with the way I'm responding to you."

"Don't apologize sweetie. You are making progress. Do you feel like taking break right now?"

"No, I want to continue." Marsha touched Annie on her right arm. "Ok. I don't want you to misunderstand what I am saying. It is normal and very healthy to not want to be betrayed the way you were with Tom. I would worry about you if you didn't feel that way. But unless you figure out how to balance this healthy concern with being intelligently open to new things, you will never be able to heal. And that would be the bigger tragedy."

"Ok, this is scary but I think I am ready."

"I knew you were. So, here is my suggestion with Bart at this stage of the game. In order to protect yourself while probing more about who he really is I recommend you let him into your life a little, and then observe."

"What do you mean a little?"

"Well, tell him about a mistake you have made and what you have learned from it."

"And then?"

"If he is the kind of person you should move forward with, he will return the favor. If not, I would suggest that you look for an exit as quickly as possible."

"Yeah, really! I was thinking about doing that right now."

"That is fine as long that you are doing that based on what is in front of you rather than what it behind you."

Annie sat in her office at the Convalescent Center, trying to figure out what to do next about Bart. Marsha's words were still ringing true from their previous session, but she felt frozen in place because she feared making a big mistake. When she thought about their unconventional late-night date, she thought of his smile, his intense hazel eyes, his strong hands and his compelling voice. It appeared that he was her dream man.

But "it appeared" was the operative phrase. As compelling as his story was, it had gaps. It was these missing pieces in his surreptitious journey to Gordon that both intrigued and frightened her. There was no doubt she felt an almost overwhelming attraction to him. She knew he was attracted to her. But she was not ready to weather another profound disappointment in the relationship department. And the gaps in his story not only gave her substantial pause, it almost caused her to make an abrupt and supremely self-protective decision to cut off further interaction with the mysterious man.

But Annie needed to get back to work, so she refocused on the spreadsheet she was putting together for the next Manager's Meeting. It was then she heard a tap on her office door. She felt a little unnerved by the interruption and responded in a frustrated tone, "Come on in."

When the door swung open there stood Bart. He was dressed in jeans and a Duke football sweatshirt that looked old but well kept. She couldn't help but smile and think *"I knew there was something wrong with him!"*

Those unfamiliar with the intense rivalry between UNC and Duke probably don't realize that there are only approximately eight miles that separate these storied universities. Put Ohio State and Michigan next door to each other and you would begin to get the feel of the perpetual tension that exists between followers of the Tar Heels and the Blue Devils. It would only take one visit to the Dean Smith Center when these rivals are locked in one of their epic basketball battles for a novitiate to recognize that there is no love lost between these two programs.

Annie smiled and said "Aha, I have found a big chink in your armor!" as she pointed to her UNC diploma that was placed proudly above her desk.

Bart looked and said in a somewhat sarcastic manner. "I see. Well this revelation will require further contemplation on my part pertaining to any further romantic interactions."

"You mean you've got to think about whether you want to date a Tar Heel?" Annie shook her head and then provided a conversational counter-punch, "Just like a Duke grad. Making simple things sound complicated."

Bart narrowed his eyes and leaned forward, "Just like a Carolina grad to take complicated things and make them look simple." Both of them stared each other down for about ten seconds and then broke out in tension-relieving laughter.

"Well now that we got that out of the way," sighed Bart, "I was wondering if you could slice out some time this afternoon to take a walk with me and Frodo at the park?"

"You mean would I be willing to venture out on a peripatetic excursion in which we will explore the possibilities of further romantic interactions?" said Annie in the snobbiest accent she could muster.

"Yeah, I reckon to would be something like that" responded Bart in his best Southern red-neck twang.

"Sure" said Annie smiling. She made a quick phone call to the Nurse Manager to let her know she would be out for a little while, forwarded her phone to voicemail and then promptly marched herself out of her office with residents and staff looking amazed as she headed out the door with a man no one knew.

Once they arrived at the park, they walked to the left towards the small lake that was surrounded by an asphalt walking trail, benches and a smattering of dogwood and cherry blossom trees. Frodo took off towards the Canadian Geese to see if he could acquire a fat snack.

As Annie and Bart started on the path, Bart began the conversation by saying, "Listen, I had a great time the other night."

"Me too!" said Annie wondering where this introductory statement would lead.

"Yeah, well I've been thinking and I know you must have a bunch of questions twirling about in your mind about my past."

Annie nodded. She was a bit surprised that he would cut right to the heart of the matter.

"Anyway, I promise that I will never lie to you. But like you I've got some ghosts in my closet that rattle their chains quite a bit and it is very hard for me to talk about them."

"You don't mean you are a serial killer, do you?"

"No," said Bart smiling. "I just have some pain that I am still working through. I am sure you can understand."

"Ok, can we make an agreement to ask each other any kind of question, but the other person can graciously choose not to answer?" proposed Annie.

"That sounds great," said a relieved Bart. "I feel like something special is happening between us and I don't want to blow it. But I also don't want to let my heart go and then have you turn out the lights on me when you learn more about me."

"I understand" said Annie gently patting Bart on the back of his left shoulder. "Can I start with a question?"

"Sure" said Bart in a nervous manner.

"Were you ever married?"

"Yes, once."

"Divorced?"

"No, my wife passed away."

Annie slowed down her brisk pace. "I'm sorry Bart. That must have been hard."

"Yeah, it was somewhat unexpected. I don't want to get into the details right now. But I will later."

"That is ok," said Annie in a gentle manner. "Do you have any kids?"

"Well, kind of." Bart stopped and looked across to the swing set on the west side of the park. "My wife died when she was eight months pregnant with our first child. We couldn't save the baby."

Now Annie was getting a better picture of this man to whom she was increasingly attracted. "Oh, gosh," she said with an almost immediate tear in her voice. "I don't know what to say."

"Well that is a very insightful thing to say, especially for a Carolina grad."

"Touché," said Annie recognizing that she should shift the inquiry to less painful topics.

A few seconds passed by with complete silence between them. In order to work off some nervous energy, Annie picked up the pace a little in her gait and then asked, "What did you major in at Duke?"

"Biology," replied the still distant chef.

They traveled a few more paces and rounded the corner to head back towards the parking lot. Suddenly Annie halted and looked at Bart. "I think I know who you are!" she said in an astonished manner.

Bart had the look of a boxer who was up against the ropes waiting for a body-blow that would send him crashing to the canvass. He braced himself with a false smile and said, "Really who?"

"Aren't you the wide receiver that ran in a reverse against us in the last seconds of the game in 1994 at Keenan Stadium to beat us?"

Bart laughed in a nervous manner and said "Yes, that was the highlight of my football career."

"So, you went to Duke on a football scholarship?"

"No, I was offered one, but actually went on an Angier B. Duke Scholarship."

"Oh yeah, that is almost as prestigious as the Morehead scholarship at Carolina" quipped the faithful fan.

"Whatever you say Annie," sighed Bart, knowing that he would never win this kind of argument.

"But I don't remember you playing after that season. What happened?"

"Well, I blew out my knee the following year at spring practice and never could get back to playing form."

Annie grinned, looked Bart over and said, "Your playing form looks pretty good to me."

Bart was flustered by the unexpected compliment. All he could muster at that moment was "Why, thanks!"

Now Annie couldn't resist taking advantage of the conversational momentum she had established. She pushed the envelope a little further by asking, "So, what did you end up doing with the biology degree?"

"I went to medical school at Yale. When I finished there, I did my residency at Johns Hopkins in Cardio-Thoracic Surgery. Then I was fortunate enough to after that to do a fellowship at Stanford. That is where I met Sue. She was finishing up her residency there in Pediatrics. I thought I would end up teaching or practicing medicine in Northern California since that is where she was from. But I got an opportunity to come back to North Carolina and start my own practice with a few classmates."

Annie was trying to take it all in. She realized that the man that she was falling for was more mysterious than she imagined. Sometimes additional information makes things muddier. It is a lot like going spelunking into one cavern and finding eight additional portals that you could take. She couldn't decide what to ask next: "Why did you quit medicine?" or "Where did you practice?"

Bart interrupted her inner dialogue to say, "Hey, look at the time. I need to get to the restaurant to move the crew along. Why don't we go out later next week for a more traditional date?"

Annie shook off her worries long enough to say "Sure, just let me know when so that I can make arrangements for Meagan."

Bart agreed to the terms of reconnection and drove Annie back to the Center. After saying their goodbyes Annie watched Bart drive off and wondered to herself why romance had to be so complicated.

That week went by quickly. Whether it was the rush of the holidays or the constant frenetic energy required to keep up with a teenage girl Annie had lost track of the time.

When Bart finally called to confirm their next date, Annie realized that she hadn't set up something for Meagan. In defense of Annie he did call on a Thursday night at around 9:00 p.m. and propose that they go out on Sunday night. Because this was a school night, she wasn't sure that it would work. Her hesitancy caused Bart to wonder if the logistical challenges were worth the effort.

"Hey, if this isn't going to work for you, we can reschedule" replied the somewhat frustrated suitor.

"No, I want to do it I just have forgotten about how I was going to take care of Meg." Annie thought for a couple of seconds and then proposed another possible solution: "Why don't you come over to my house for dinner on Sunday night? It won't be the caliber of your food, but I am not a bad cook."

"I don't want to put you out."

"That is not a problem. You would be helping me out because of what is going on with all of the holiday stuff and the fact that I need to get the princess in bed at a decent hour."

Bart realized that he had not thought about what it was like to be a single Mom with all of the responsibilities of work and home constantly dumped on you with almost no reprieve. "Can I bring anything?" said the now recalcitrant man.

"Why don't you bring the wine?" replied Annie relieved to know that she could see Bart and keep track of her wild, blossoming young lady at the same time.

"Consider it done. Do you have idea if I should bring red or white?"

"Probably red. But surprise me. I will drink anything you bring!"

Bart laughed and said, "I will bring something special that I promise you will like."

WALKER ARMSTRONG

"I am sure you will," said Annie with a fluttering heart.

She hung up the phone and took a deep breath. He daughter noticed her Mom's frazzled state and asked, "Is that your new fling Mom?"

"Hush Meg! I don't want to hear your saucy mouth right now, ok?"

"Geez-Louise Mom you are more nervous than a priest in a whore-house!"

"Meagan-Ann!" countered the shocked mother. "Where in the world did you hear that kind of stuff?"

"From Tommy Miller" said Meagan in an un-repentant manner. "I think that it is funny."

"I love Tommy but I don't want you hanging out with him. He is sixteen and has been in a lot of trouble," said Annie in her most authoritative tone.

"Whatever!" replied Meagan in the dismissive manner that would enrage the most placid of parents.

Annie stood staring at her teenage misfit. She felt angry and scared at the same time. She imagined Meagan pregnant and living with Tommy in a rat-infested apartment across the railroad tracks where all kinds of illegal and immoral activity occurred. No one ever warned her that raising a teenager in the twenty-first century was this hard. She found herself entertaining Momma Pearl's advice of "smacking a smart mouth first and then asking questions later."

"Listen, I am the boss here, not you and I can make your life more miserable than you can ever imagine. You had better wise up and quit being so disrespectful."

"Ok, Mom, I get it," said Meagan realizing that she wasn't ready for a battle of wills with her Mom right at this moment.

Annie nodded her head and then said, "And by the way, that was Bart and he is coming over to our house for dinner Sunday night."

"Oh my God Mom, you have got to be kidding me!"

"No and you will be respectful or I will have you come with me every day afterschool to clean up more bedpans at the Center, instead of just three times a week."

Meagan ignored the threat. She now focused in on her Mom's judgment in men. "You hardly know this guy and you are bringing him to our house? What is next? Are you going to marry him and move me to a convent or something?"

"I am thinking about the convent already," quipped Annie.

"And I heard that this guy was in trouble with the law. Don't bring him here until you know more about him. I don't want to end up on the Channel Three news as another one of his victims!"

"Where did you that information?" asked Annie in a nervous way.

"Never mind. Let's just say that he has a past and you need to be very careful!"

Upon hearing this unexpected version of Bart's past Annie started the worn-out habit of second-guessing herself. She wondered if there was something sinister in Bart's past that she would discover after it was too late and they were married. The more she thought about it, the tighter her stomach got.

"Why do you need to date anyway?" asked Meagan in an aggravated fashion.

"Because I am lonely and I like being with a person that finds me fascinating and attractive, that's why!"

"Isn't that what got you into trouble with Duane?" Meagan looked at her Mom and recognized that she had crossed the line once again. She tried to re-direct her Mom's anger by asking, "You have friends, don't you? Spend time with them."

"Meagan, we are not going to talk about this any further."

"Well, if you are expecting me to eat with y'all that night you can forget it!"

"I don't want you to," said Annie in an equally dismissive manner. "Besides, you had better be respectful or I am going to …"

"I know, I know," said the tired teen. "You will make my life miserable."

"You got it!" responded her mother in a matter-of-fact fashion.

"I just wanted to voice my official disapproval of this relationship," commented Meagan.

"Duly noted," responded Annie. "Now, I am going to need your help this weekend to clean up the house. I don't want him to think that we are slobs or something like that." Meagan nodded in a kind of

WALKER ARMSTRONG

protesting resignation that made Annie think that her daughter might find a way to have the last word in this discussion. Annie made herself a mental note: *"Keep an eye on that kid."*

When Sunday night rolled around Annie was a nervous wreck. Meagan had agreed to eat with Annie and Bart. Now Annie was wondering if that was such a good idea. She got dressed, did her hair and put on her makeup in stages as she cooked and put the last few touches on her decorations. In the oven was her Mom's recipe for potato casserole that was simple but very tasty. Awaiting insertion into the stove were fresh green beans that were seasoned with salt, pepper, oregano and olive oil.

For the main course she decided to cook bone-in rib eye steaks. As long as she didn't burn them, she felt safe in the preparation. Annie used her Dad's homemade steak rub that was a legend among family and friends. She cooked in a little ahead of time, letting then sit before re-warming them in the oven. It wasn't the ideal way to prepare the steaks but she didn't want to smell like charcoal when she greeted Bart at the door. For dessert, she had thawed out a New York Cheesecake that Angelo had made her for her last birthday. All-in-all she felt ready.

Bart was right on time when the doorbell rang at 7:00 p.m. She had just finished applying her lip gloss and tapped on Meagan's door in route to greeting her handsome new friend. She was wearing a white turtle neck with a Christmas sweater that was red with white snowflakes and black pants with black alligator shoes that had a silver buckle. It was very conservative attire but she was dressing somewhat defensively because she knew that anything she wore would be publicly picked apart by her number one fashion critic Meagan.

As she opened the door, she noticed that Bart had on a white turtle neck, a tan sport coat, a red sweater and black dress pants with black loafers. They simultaneously noticed the copycat outfits and laughed so hard that they both almost fell down onto the front porch.

As they stood side-by-side Bart commented, "We look like we should be on The Osmond Family Christmas Special."

Annie responded, "Or Andy Williams!"

This unexpected fashion snafu helped to make a somewhat awkward situation more palatable. Annie guided Bart into the den and had him sit on her prized leather chair. It was a deep red high-back reproduction of a Windsor chair that she stumbled upon in a local auction. Bart sat down and Annie noticed that it fit him to a tee. She asked if he would like anything to drink and he declined for the time being.

Annie pulled the potato casserole out of the oven, turned the oven to broil and inserted the green beans and set the timer for two minutes on her microwave. She walked back into the den and asked Bart to tell her about the wine he brought.

He sat forward cradling the bottle and with excitement noted, "This is 2006 Audrey Pinot Noir from the Scott Paul Winery in Oregon. It is named after Audrey Hepburn because of its graceful and elegant bouquet. It reminded me of you."

Annie couldn't help but beam a little when she said, "Audrey Hepburn is my favorite actress of all time!"

"Well then, why don't we sample a bit? I like it slightly chilled so I stuck it in the frig for a while, hoping that by the time I got to your place it would be just right."

Annie motioned Bart with her right index finger in a "come-hither" fashion to follow her into the kitchen. As they entered, she pulled the green beans out of the over, tossed them and reinserted and set the timer for another two minutes. She then handed Bart a wine opener and pulled out two wine glasses from her cabinet. Bart was momentarily distracted as he noticed Annie's shapely figure and almost dropped the bottle. He quickly regained his composure and opened the wine in a quick flourish. He poured about three sips in both glasses and offered Annie the first taste.

She gently sipped and was immediately taken with the smoothness of the wine. She looked at Bart and said "If I had a piece of dark chocolate with this, you might have to leave while I had my own little moment."

Before she knew it, Bart pulled out a Dark Chocolate Godiva candy bar from his coat pocket. When Annie saw it, she almost choked on her second sip. "You are full of surprises Bart, full of surprises!"

She then pulled out the green beans and laid them on the top of the stove with the potato casserole. Next, she took the steaks that had been cooked at medium rare, turned down the oven to 175° and set the timer for two minutes. Without missing a beat, she placed some crescent rolls in a toaster oven and flipped it on. Bart noticed how on top of things Annie was and commented, "Have you ever thought about becoming a chef?"

"No way!" replied Annie. "I couldn't take the criticism. And you need to reserve judgment until after you have eaten my food."

Annie pardoned herself for a minute and quickly walked back to Meagan's room. She tapped on the door firmly and announced, "Meg, dinner is ready."

"Coming mother," replied the daughter in a saccharine sweet manner. *That didn't sound like Meg* thought Annie. She felt a strange gnawing in her stomach. She wondered what the kid was up to. Annie prayed a prayer under her breath as she walked back to the kitchen, "Dear God, please don't let her ruin a nice evening!"

When she got back to the kitchen, she pulled out the warmed steaks and kept an eagle eye on the bread. Bart was smiling at her and asked, "How do you do it? How do you get so many things done at once?"

"Lots of practice my dear man. Lots of practice," laughed Annie as she took her last sip of her wine.

Just as Annie was getting ready to start the plating process Meagan walked in. She was wearing some jeans with holes in both knees, flip-flops and a tee shirt that read "Resist All Authority." Annie took one look and rather than make a scene she simply said, "Thanks for dressing up for the occasion sweetie!" Before she could introduce her daughter to Bart, Meagan walked right up to him and said, "Meagan Ann Bryant. I suppose you are Bart."

Bart smiled politely, "Yes, it is nice to see you again ... I mean it is nice to meet you." Meagan looked at Bart and then turned towards her Mom and made a face as if to say *"He's a real winner Mom!"*

Annie directed both Bart and Meagan to take a seat and lit the Advent Wreath at the center of the kitchen table. Since it was past the third Sunday in December, she lit three. Surrounding the candles was an arrangement of artificial holly leaves and bright red berries. They perfectly matched her Christmas china that had an almost identical border with male cardinals in the middle. Annie quickly delivered everyone their plates, poured wine in glasses and sat down. She held out her hands and bowed her head. Meagan offered her hand to Bart like a limp dead fish. He clearly got the message that she wasn't all that excited for him to be there.

After giving thanks the trio dug into the hearty meal. Bart was the first to speak and said with sincere conviction. "Annie, this steak is incredible. How did you season it?"

"Ah," replied the smiling host. "It is a family secret."

"Speaking of secrets," interrupted Meagan, "Mom tells me you were once a Doctor. Why did you quit?"

Annie froze with a bit of casserole about to enter her mouth. She couldn't even look up from her plate partially out of fear and a little out of exasperation with her only child.

"Well," replied Bart as he neatly wiped his mouth. "I was very sad because of the death of my wife and child. And I never seemed to be able recapture my love for medicine. So, I sold my part of the practice to my partners and moved to Italy."

"I hope that there wasn't any problem with the law or something" said Meagan in an almost ruthless tone.

"Meagan Ann, I think that is enough!" said in her Mom locking eyes with the teen-aged interrogator.

Once again, Meagan ignored her Mom and kept pressing the issue. "So, how did your wife and daughter die?"

Before Annie could say anything, else Bart waved her off. He looked straight into Meagan's eyes. Suddenly Meagan felt uncomfortable. It was little like a child teasing a tiger behind the cage only to find the animal a few inches from their face. Bart took a silent deep breath and said "My wife took her own life. By the time I found her too much time had passed and we couldn't save her or my daughter."

Meagan looked stunned. Her anger and mistrust felt out of place. She knew from the look she received from Bart that she had reached the limits of his patience. When she shifted her gaze to her Mom Annie said, "Come with me for a moment." The two got up from the table and the quickly traveled to the den.

Annie spun her daughter around and grabbed her by the right elbow and pulled her close. "I warned you, didn't I?" said the furious woman. "Now, starting next Monday you are going to not only pull cleanup duty at the Center, you are going to work at the kitchen helping Louise cook on Monday, Wednesday and Friday nights. If you say another disrespectful thing, I will shut down your social life to such a degree that your friends will wonder what happened to you."

Meagan thought about saying something, but knew better. She nodded and then Annie said, "Now march yourself back into the kitchen and apologize to Bart and then excuse yourself from the table. You can eat later or not eat at all. I really don't care. You got me?"

Meagan knew she was in deep trouble. She bowed her head and walked back into the kitchen in front of her mother. She looked at Bart and said "I'm sorry," in the same way a prisoner would humble them self to avoid time in solitary confinement. She looked back at Annie and said "May I be excused from the table?" "Yes," replied her stone-faced mother. Then the young girl made a hasty exit and Annie sat back down.

Annie gathered herself and said "Bart I don't know what to say. I am so sorry for her behavior."

Bart shook his head and said, "No need to apologize. I think I understand what this was all about. She is just being protective of you. I was going to eventually tell you about it anyway."

"Let's change the subject," said Annie in as gracious manner as she could. "More wine?"

"Yes! I probably should have brought another bottle."

Annie laughed and said "Maybe you can prescribe one a day for me in order to deal with a smart-mouthed teenage girl."

"Well, I think that might be able to be arrange that. But I am sure you will work it out," said Bart as he took a bite of the green beans. "Mmmm, great balance of herbs with olive oil!"

The two adults then shifted the conversation to safer subjects like the parade or the unfortunate decline of Gordon. After dinner was finished Bart volunteered to clean up but Annie declined and had him retire to the den as she fetched a piece of cheesecake and a cup of coffee. She then got her dessert and coffee and joined him.

As they were enjoying Angelo's special treat a car pulled in her drive way and beeped the horn. This startled Annie. She got up and went to the front door and saw Tommy Miller in a red 2005 Mustang GT waving at her. She walked back to Meagan's room and opened the door.

The once androgynous looking teen had now transformed herself from a much older looking vixen with the addition of lots of makeup, a pair of tight jeans and even tighter sweater. Annie closed the door behind her and asked "Why is Tommy here Meagan?"

"Well, we are going out with some other kids. Didn't I mention that to you?"

Annie really thought she was going to kill her kid now. "Not only did you not mention this, you are most certainly not going anywhere tonight, especially with Tommy!"

"I thought that you and the Doctor would want some private time together," responded Meagan in a pseudo-considerate manner.

"You stay right here and I will let Tommy know he needs to go back home and after Bart leaves you and I are going to have another little chat!" Annie turned away to deal with Meagan's would-be date. Meagan marched around Annie and stood in blocked her at the front door.

"Mom, you are embarrassing me. I will tell Tommy," said Meagan as she turned and opened the front door. Before Annie could grab a hold of her daughter Meagan slammed the glass screen door. Annie tried to grab the handle but missed with her palm absorbing the full brunt of the swinging door.

The glass shattered making a large popping noise. Annie looked down and a large triangular piece of the door was wedged into her open hand. She instinctively pulled the piece out and blood spurted against the wall. Annie felt weak in the knees and sat down on the floor. The last thing she remembered was noticing that she had forgotten to dust the light fixture in the foyer as she looked up right before passing out.

When Annie woke up, she was in her leather chair in the den. Meagan had a streaked face with smudged mascara generously spread all over her cheeks from plenty of tears. "Mommy, are you ok?" asked her trembling child. Annie was about to answer her when she noticed Bart sitting on the leather ottoman with a pair of horned-rimmed glasses holding her injured hand. On the left side of his glasses was some type of attached magnifier that he was using as he was closely examining her hand.

Annie looked down to see that Bart was finishing up delicately stitching up her gashed hand. On the floor were some bloody towels and a few cotton swabs. Her hand was stained with betadine and blood. On the end table was a spent syringe, a pair of forceps placed on a napkin and beside that another napkin with a few small shards of bloody fragments of broken glass. She felt faint again and leaned back to regain her composure.

"We're going to need to take you to the hospital to make sure that I got all of the glass out of the wound and get you a shot of antibiotics just to be safe" said Bart in a somewhat of an authoritative manner. Bart then looked up from his glasses and said, "Meagan was an excellent assistant."

Annie looked over at her daughter and said "That doesn't mean that you are out of the dog house young lady."

"I know Mommy, I was very scarred. There was a lot of blood. I'm sorry Mums." Meagan started to cry and placed her head against her Mom's knee.

Annie stroked her daughter's head and said "You ought to be you little stinker! I'm ok, just a little woozy." She turned towards Bart and asked "Where did you get all this stuff from?"

"Oh, you never know when you might be able to help a beautiful woman out with a gash on her hand" quipped Bart.

Bart stood up and then said, "Ok, are you strong enough to stand up and walk to my truck?"

"Yeah, I think so" said the still disoriented woman.

Meagan helped Bart as they supported both arms and walked Annie out the front door and gently placed her on the passenger's side of Bart's truck. Meagan sat beside her Mom and held her injured hand up to keep it clean. Bart jumped in and before they knew it, they pulled up to the front door of the Emergency Room at Gordon Memorial Hospital.

Bart walked in and got a wheelchair. He came back to the truck and gently placed a protesting Annie in it with Meagan's assistance. Without hesitating, he pushed her through the door and pulled right up to the Triage Nurse's station. There were only a few folks scattered in the waiting area so Bart took charge and announced to the young woman. "My name is Dr. St. Claire and I have a patient that needs immediate attention. She has received a nasty laceration to her left hand and I am not sure the degree of nerve or ligament damage she incurred." The young nurse nodded her head without looking up.

Bart understood Emergency Room protocol but didn't like the nurse's attitude. "I said now!" thundered the tall man. This pronouncement not only got the nurse off her feet but was loud enough to get one of physicians from out back. It turned out to be the head of Emergency Medicine Nolan Bright. Nolan and Annie graduated from Gordon High together. After sizing up the man the man that was making all the fuss, he recognized Annie in the wheelchair.

"Annie, what in the world happened to you?'" quizzed the Nolan.

"Oh, I had a little accident with the front door," said a lightheaded Annie.

Nolan knelt down, unbandaged her hand and examined the wound. "Wow!" he exclaimed. "These sutures look like that they have been done by a plastic surgeon." He looked up at Bart and said "You must be the loudmouth I heard back in Triage Four."

Bart nodded, somewhat embarrassed and replied, "Yeah I apologize. I just wanted to make sure she was taken care of."

"She will be. I suggest you and Meagan have a seat in the waiting area and I will see to it personally that we get an x-ray and have a closer look at this nasty cut. By the way, that is very nice work you did. Where do you practice?"

"I don't anymore," said Bart trying to deflect further questions. He had been through enough interrogation already and he just wanted to be left alone.

WALKER ARMSTRONG

"What a shame, you are very talented" said Dr. Bright looking intently into the mysterious doctor's face. Nolan then shifted his focus and told the triage nurse at the front desk. "Lou Ann, please take Annie to Triage One and call Radiology and have someone get down here to take some pictures of that hand ok?"

The nurse nodded and moved Bart out of her way and then pushed Annie through some double doors. Bart looked at Nolan and them said, "I appreciate you giving her this attention and again I am sorry for the disruption."

Nolan grinned and said "I guess we doctors can act like real jack-asses when we want something done stat, huh?"

Bart knew he had been put in his place. He shook Dr. Bright's hand and then guided Meagan over to the waiting area. They found two seats near the TV perched on the wall in the western corner of the room. It was playing a re-run of some familiar sitcom from the 70's.

Right across from them a Hispanic family was speaking Spanish in hushed tones. Bart supposed that with the worried look on the older woman's face and her constant pointing towards her chest that maybe her husband was in a room with the ominous symptoms of myocardial infarction. Behind them was a young man about twenty years of age holding a pack of ice on a swollen hand. He had the makings of a shiner on his right eye and his pupils betrayed the picture of someone who had been ramped up on something other than testosterone. To his right was a young couple that holding each other very tightly trying not to lose their composure. Bart looked at the blood on the woman's pants and guessed miscarriage.

He sighed and looked up at one of the flashing fluorescent lights and remembered one of his professors at Yale telling then that "If you are passionate about medicine you can't just shut off your diagnostic engine just because you are off duty." He was not comforted by the resurrection of this obsessive part of his personality that he thought he had buried with his wife and child.

After a few moments of silence Meagan spoke up. "Thanks for helping my Mom. She really likes you. But I don't trust you."

"Yeah, I picked up on that."

"Well she is a good person and I really don't want anyone to hurt her."

Bart looked at Meagan with compassion and said, "No one wants to be hurt Meagan. And I care about your Mom too."

"I'm sorry about your family dying and stuff. But I won't apologize for trying to find out the truth. My mom was really hurt by my Dad. But she still wants to find someone. I think she trusts people too easily."

"I guess you don't trust as easily as your Mom does, huh?"

"Nope," replied the frank teen.

"Me neither," said the somewhat rattled ex-doctor. "That way you don't get hurt as easy."

Meagan looked up from the worn-out People magazine she was flipping through with a little bit of shock. She shook her head in agreement and said, "Exactly!"

Inside Triage One Annie had already put on a gown. Her hand was really starting to throb and she wondered how long it would take to find out the seriousness of her injury. Nolan Bright stood at the closed curtain and said, "Knock, knock, are you decent?"

Annie smiled and said "I haven't been decent for a long time Nolan. Come in."

The doctor walked in and pulled up a stool that had rollers close to her bedside. He had a new nurse with him who was carrying a tray. "I'm going to give you a shot of antibiotics and I also brought another for pain if you need it."

"Ah, a knight in shining armor!" exclaimed Annie. "Yes, please give me something for pain. This thing really hurts." Nolan called a nurse in and she adroitly gave the antibiotic in Annie's right arm.

Nolan then tapped Annie's left arm and said, "Now, we can give the pain shot in your here or in your backside, which do you prefer?"

"Right, nice try Doc," smirked Annie. "You always wanted to see me naked since we were in high school. I think I will take the arm." Nolan nodded at the nurse and she prepped Annie's left shoulder for the pain shot and quickly plunged the needle into her shoulder.

"Ouch!" yelped Annie. "That hurt a lot more than the other one!"

"Well," commented the amused doctor. "There is a lot more cushion on your behind."

WALKER ARMSTRONG

"You're not winning any fans here Nolan with that comment!" retorted Annie. "I hope you don't talk to your wife that way."

Nolan grinned and then switched roles to a more clinical one. "That should help for a couple of hours. I will also proscribe some more pain pills for you because unfortunately this cut is going to hurt for a while."

"Thanks. How long do you think it will take?" asked a very tired Annie.

"The x-ray tech in on her way down. I think we can get some pictures and let you know within the hour if anything else needs to be done. But from the looks of it, your new friend did a bang-up job. Where did you find him?"

"Oh, we met at Angelo's. He is the new owner. He used to be a surgeon somewhere in North Carolina. Then when his wife and daughter died, he quit practicing medicine."

"So that's the story huh?" said Nolan as he kept looking at her hand from various angles. "Very interesting."

"What do you mean Nolan? Spill the beans right now or I will tell your wife that you were fresh with me," winked Annie.

The perturbed doctor looked at Annie and blushed. Everyone from Gordon knew he had always had a crush on Annie since grade school but never had the guts to ask her out.

He cleared his throat and said, "I'm just wondering what could make such a skilled doctor walk away from medicine. Most doctors I know would have simply thrown themselves into their work after something like that rather than just up and quit."

This comment made Annie pause. "I don't know Nolan. He is just a nice guy who is trying to rebuild his life. There are a lot of people out there who are just trying to pick up the pieces."

"Ok, point taken. Just be careful ok?"

"Gee whiz, everyone around here thinks I am an idiot or something! I am a forty-five-year-old woman. I think I am perfectly capable of figuring this stuff out."

"Yes Ma'am!" Nolan laughed as he stood up with his hands in surrender-like fashion. He turned back to the nurse assisting him and asked, "Liz, please check on the tech for me ok?" "Yes sir" responded the nurse. She parted the curtain and was gone in a blink. Nolan turned back to Annie and put his hand on her shoulder "I will check in on you in a bit." He stripped off his gloves, deposited them in a container, and looked back at his old friend and smiled.

Annie smiled and said "Thanks Nolan!" The doctor left her alone and she closed her eyes as she began to feel the pain medicine take effect. Right before she fell asleep, she heard the squeaking of rubber wheels on polished concrete floor. She looked up and a young man was pulling a portable X-Ray machine.

Miss Bryant, I am Norrell. I will be taking some pictures of your hand ok. Are you feeling alright?"

"Yes, thank you. I am just ready to get out of this place."

"Well, that is why I am here. If you can sit up, I will prop up the bed a bit and get this knocked out for you."

Annie liked his take charge attitude. He was true to his word and in a few moments, he had taken several pictures without aggravating her injury. When he was finished, he told her "You take care and the doctor will be back in a little bit with the results." Then, the energetic tech left about as fast as he entered her room.

"Thanks," said Annie to the back of his head. She sat back and realized she hadn't asked him to put her bed back so she could closer her eyes for a little bit. She saw a re-run of Judge Judy was on the little TV mounted to the top corner of the wall. She wasn't a fan of legal shows because they reminded her of how much she disliked lawyers.

At this point Annie really wanted to change the channel, so she started moving around a lot looking around for the remote. In her effort to find it she inadvertently bumped her injured hand against the rail. "Ouch" she yelled. She quickly gathered up her blanket with her right hand and bit into it so as to prevent any loud obscenity from bursting forth from mouth. Tears welled up in her eyes as she leaned back and tried to occupy her mind with something while holding her throbbing hand up in the air.

The only thing that seemed to remedy her preoccupation with pain was to think about Nolan's questions regarding Bart's background. She didn't want to consider his probing questions at first. She had just begun to drop her guard a little bit and the idea of being let down again would bring a kind of pain to her heart that would rival the aching wound in her hand.

But there was just no way of getting around Nolan's inexorable logic. There had to be more to Bart's story than just the horrible tragedy of losing his family. Bart didn't strike her as someone who would quit when the chips were down. Nor did he remotely seem like a person who would give up the engrossing challenges of literally holding people's lives in your hands for the more mundane routine of making homemade pasta.

Her restless questions were interrupted by a voice. "Hey, can we come in?" She opened her eyes and saw Bart and Meagan were standing outside the room.

"Sure, come on in. But I've got to warn you that I have been given some really good drugs, so there is no telling what I might say."

Bart led the way in and Meagan, still embarrassed about the argument that led to her Mom's accident, hid behind the larger man just in case Annie was still upset with her.

"So, what do you know so far?" asked a concerned Bart.

"Nothing yet" sighed Annie. "They took some x-rays a few minutes ago and Nolan is going to come back when they have the results."

"Your hand is really hurting isn't it?" asked Bart as he pointed to Annie's unorthodox methodology for reducing the throbbing ache.

"Yeah. It hurts like a you know what!"

"Like a bitch Mom?" asked Meagan who was standing at the foot of the bed with her head still down.

"Yes Meg." She knew her child was scared. "Come on over here and give me a kiss." The teen smiled and complied. The both seemed to be comforted by the simple show of mutual affection.

"I'm not mad at you baby. It was an accident, ok?" reassured Annie. She stroked her daughter with her good hand. Meagan countenance took on the appearance of a sweet child.

Bart took Annie's injured limb and gently placed it across her chest. He then raised the bed a little more. "This is a more realistic way to reduce the pounding in your hand." Annie nodded in appreciation. "It was Meagan's idea to come back here. She was really worried about you."

"Yeah, I was worried that they were going to put you into surgery and I wouldn't get to see you. That and I got tired of staying in the waiting room with all those scary and smelly people."

Annie and Bart laughed. Meagan was a little put off by their mirth at her expense. She was serious.

As their laughter subsided Dr. Bright walked in with the X-rays in hand. "I have the double cheeseburger and fries you ordered."

"If I ate anything right now, I think you would see it all over this shiny floor" said an increasingly wobbly Annie.

"Well how about I just show you the pictures of your hand instead" replied the doctor. He flipped on a switch and slapped up three pictures on the wall. "Here is the great news. First, no trace of glass or any foreign object has been left behind in your hand. You did a superior job Doctor!"

Bart nodded. He was scanning all of the pictures looking for something else.

"You also don't have any break or fracture in your hand or fingers" continued Nolan. "But right here is something that concerns me a little" as he pointed to the middle of her hand with his silver ballpoint pen.

"Are you talking about the median nerve Dr. Bright?" asked Bart.

"Yes, Bart" replied Nolan. "The cut was deep and I think we might need to check this further for any peripheral damage." Annie and Meagan were both uncharacteristically quiet. "Did you give her any numbing agent when you were cleaning the wound?"

"Well the cut was deep and I had to probe a good bit so I gave her two different injections of lidocaine."

"That is what I thought" said Dr. Bright. He walked over to the left side of Annie bed and picked up her hand. "I am going to touch your hand with the tip of this pen. I want you to close your eyes and each time I touch you let me know if you have feeling, very little feeling or no feeling." Dr. Bright started with her thumb, moved to her index finger, then to her ring finger and then finally to different areas on her palm. Her answers ran the gambit from feeling to no feeling.

Dr. Bright placed the pen back in his jacket and stood erect with his arms draped across his chest. "Alright, here is the deal. With the amount of lidocaine that Bart had to give you I am unsure if there is going to be any permanent nerve damage."

"Per … permanent damage?" stuttered Annie?

"Now don't panic" countered Nolan. "Some of this numbness you feel right now could be caused by that medicine. In that case, as you heal you will notice a progression whereby feeling or some feeling will return to different parts of your hand."

"Some feeling?" replied a worried Meagan. "Is my Mom going to be a cripple?" Meagan's eyes got moist as she grabbed her mother's blanket-covered foot.

"Ok, young lady. Let's not jump to conclusions. I think once we let this heal and get the stitches out our best route is to schedule you a visit with a neurologist friend of mine over in Asheville. He has all the state-of-the-art equipment to do never tests that will give us a clearer indication of what is going on."

"You mean like an EMG?" asked Bart.

"Exactly" replied Dr. Bright. Nolan turned to Annie and said, "What Bart is talking about is a test called an electromyography. It measures the impulse between stimulation and reaction. It is not a lot of fun because they have to stick very small needles in the muscles of your hand to send a very slight electrical current through to see what is going on. But it is very accurate when it comes to pinpointing if and where the damage may lie."

Annie looked in shock. Bart tried to console her by saying. "You don't need to worry right now about this. We just need to get the scripts from Doctor Bright and then get you home where you can get some rest."

"Dr. St. Claire is right dear." He reached in his coat pocket and pulled out a handful of packaged pills and handed them to Bart. Here is some pain medication that can help get you through the night until you can have your prescription filled." Dr. Bright then walked over to the table beside him and very quickly wrote out two prescriptions. One of these is for pain and another is an antibiotic. Get these filled tomorrow."

"I will take care of it, Nolan" replied Bart as he stuck the pills and the papers in the right pocket of his slacks. "Should she work tomorrow?"

"No, I would rather you rest Annie and then see if you feel like it on Tuesday."

"But I have a lot of work to do" said Annie trying to muster up her best form of protest.

"I think they can survive one day at The Center without you."

Annie agreed in a sheepish manner because she was starting to feel nauseated again.

Dr. Bright leaned over her bed and said, "The doctor I am referring you to is Stanley Rayno. He is the best around. His secretary will call you to schedule an appointment."

"But what if all the feeling comes back to my hand?" asked Annie.

"Well then you can cancel the appointment. But that is the only condition. Don't make me hunt you down and embarrass you in front of all your workmates!"

"Ok Nolan. Good gracious, between you and Bart I don't stand a chance, do I?"

Nolan smiled and then winked at Bart. "Of course not! We doctors have to stick together, especially when dealing with stubborn patients like you!"

With that, Dr. Bright dismissed himself. He was almost immediately replaced by a nurse with all kinds of discharge papers. Once Annie took care of the paperwork Bart went to get a wheelchair. Meagan stayed behind and helped her Mom get dressed.

"I appreciate your help sweetie," Annie said as she gingerly slid her hand through her blood-stained turtleneck.

"No problem Mommy. I am sorry for all of this. I don't know what gets into me sometimes. I say and do stuff before I think I guess."

"We all do Meg. The real issue is do we learn from our mistakes."

"Yeah, you're right."

"I'm what?"

"Very funny Mom. Hey, while we are at it, I just want to say ... I mean I think that ..."

"Is anything wrong honey?"

"No. What I meant to say is that Bart is an ok guy. That's all."

Annie placed her forehead against Meg's. "Thanks. I think he is a pretty good guy too. And he can sew a pretty mean stitch too."

Meagan nodded. The word stitch made the thin scar on her chest itch a little. Instinctively she reached up and scratched it as she had done a thousand times before.

CHAPTER 6

ANNIE'S HAND HEALED up nicely. She marveled at what little swelling occurred from her cut. After she had the stitches removed, she almost totally forgot how traumatic the injury was. Occasionally it itched, was still somewhat numb and if she bumped into something, she was reminded that the healing process was not quite complete. But all-in-all she had little deleterious effects from the ordeal.

A few days after Bart took out her stitches, she went to Dr. Rayno's office to have the nerve conduction test done. Unfortunately, there seemed to be some slight damage from the accident, but not enough to warrant surgery. Dr. Rayno told Annie, "This might clear up on its own, but my guess is that you might have some numbness in your thumb and index fingers the rest of your life. If it gets worse let me know and we can decide what to do next." Annie accepted his prognosis and knew it could have been a lot worse.

Bart had been with her almost every single day since the accident. He was very firm with her when she thought that the directions she received from both doctors were optional. He was also patient with her when she worried out loud about the long-term effects of the mishap. Annie couldn't imagine going through the ordeal without his calming presence.

There was no doubt about it – Annie was falling in love with Bart. It was uncanny how he seemed to have answers to questions she had yet to fully articulate. Her worries about Bart's past slowly faded into fascination with the man who seemed to have so many hidden talents. She noticed that with each visit or phone conversation he smiled or laughed more often. Annie knew he appreciated her zany sense of humor and overall zest for life. She valued his dry wit and stable persona.

Occasionally someone close to her would ask a question about Bart that she didn't have an immediate answer for, but these inquires about his past seemed to bounce off her heart like bullets off Superman's chest. Even Meagan's jabs or sarcastic comments didn't aggravate her as much as they did a few weeks back. Folks at work frequently commented on how pretty she looked and how happy she seemed. Just the other day Momma Pearl looked at her during lunchtime at the Center and said, "Lawd, baby, you got the Ju-Ju all over you!" No one close to her uttered the infamous four-letter word, but the evidence was undeniable.

One night, Annie while she was chatting on the phone with Bart, she decided to take a risk. "Hey, I was wondering."

"Uh-oh, that usually means some kind of challenge for me" sighed Bart.

"Don't be silly. Anyway, every year my Mom and Dad put on a Christmas Eve Party for family and friends. My sister Jan and her family will be there and so will a lot of folks. I was wondering if you would like to attend."

There was a brief pause. It was one of those awkward moments of silence where a person wishes they could retract what they have just spoken. Bart ended Annie's agony in a few seconds when he spoke. "I haven't met your parents yet. Do you think this is best venue for our first meeting?"

Annie could tell Bart was nervous. She tried to make him feel better by saying "Oh, they are just ordinary folks who love to have a good time."

"Annie, from what I understand your Dad is a former Marine officer and has been a judge in this county for about forty years. Your Mom is head of the Women's Auxiliary, and has her fingers in about another half-dozen community organizations. I would hardly call them Ma and Pa Kettle."

Bart's hesitancy now concerned Annie. "Well, if you don't want to go don't worry about it."

"No, I didn't say that I would not go. I am just nervous that is all."

"You mean a big, strong man who used to do heart transplants is worried about some country folks like my parents?"

"Yes. By the way, does your Dad own any guns?"

"Several."

"Great!" Bart flopped down on his couch and pointed an invisible pistol to his head.

"Just be grateful you are meeting them with a bunch of people around. Daddy would never shoot you in front of all those folks. Too many witnesses."

"You are not helping Annie" replied the anxious suitor. Bart took a deep breath and said. "Ok, I will go."

"Fantastic!" exclaimed Annie. "Oh, and did I mention that we have to give Momma Pearl a ride?"

"You mean your Godmother; the woman who helped bring you into the world and the person you were named after?"

"The same."

"This just keeps getting better and better."

Bart decided to ask Angelo if he could borrow his Lexus LS 430 so that he could escort his passengers in style. When Angie knew of the challenges that were facing Bart, he was more than happy to lend his new friend the vehicle. "If you-a-gonna drive Miss Pearl around you better make her comfortable" said the wise restaurateur. Bart was grateful. The only decision he had left now was the amount of Scotch he was going to consume before picking up his sweetheart and the spiritual matriarch of the town.

Bart and Annie arrived at The Center at 6:32 p.m. When Annie picked her up at the door she said "My Gosh Pearl, you look stunning!"

"You are two minutes late! Does this man of yours know how to be on time?"

"That is my fault Pearl. I had to change my dress when I saw how he was all spiffed up. You sure look gorgeous!"

"I know I do sweetie," replied Pearl in a sassy manner. "I am sure some of the older men folk will want to ask me to dance or something but I ain't that easy. But if I get some of your Daddy's punch in me, I can't promise anything."

Bart opened the front passenger door for Pearl. He introduced himself and gently shook her extended hand. "My, my" said Pearl in a

WALKER ARMSTRONG

coy manner. "You sure are a handsome man. I can see why Annie has got the Ju-Ju for you!"

"The what?" replied Bart.

"I'll explain later," said Annie as she shot Pearl a look as if to beg her not to say any more.

As they left the Center, Pearl spoke up "I hope that dwarf Larry ain't going to be there. That man gives me the creeps. I feel like he checking me out and Pearl don't do that."

Bart laughed out loud. It was the kind of unintentional burst that was a lot like what happens when someone burps unexpectantly. He immediately felt embarrassed, especially when he caught Pearl staring him down.

"Anyway," Pearl continued, "is May-Belle Stuart going to be there?"

"I think so," replied Annie. "You are not going to cause a scene, are you?"

Bart looked confused. Annie turned toward Bart and said in a somewhat hushed tone, "They had a dispute over a jam recipe at the fair about forty years ago."

"It was forty-two years ago and that witch stole my recipe and got the blue ribbon" said a disgusted Pearl. "There she was in her chiffon dress and her fancy hair acting all fake and surprised. That made me so mad. So, I got her back. I dumped my first-place chicken pie all over her dress. She didn't enter any jams in the fair after I set her straight."

Bart muffled his laughter this time. He quickly wiped the smirk off his face and said, "It seems to me that you are quite the formidable foe."

Pearl looked back at Annie with a little incredulity and then said to Bart, "If you mean that I am not someone to be messed with, you are right!"

Bart got the message. He looked at Annie in the rear-view mirror with the reaction that a little boy would have right before getting a whooping. Annie recognized the reaction and leaned back and giggled.

Annie gave Bart clear directions, making him feel a little less nervous. In about ten minutes they arrived. There were already too many cars to count up and down the street. The whole scene looked like something out of a Norman Rockwell painting.

It started with the old sixty-foot Magnolia tree on the front of their property. It had a Moravian Star on top with multiple strands of colored lights wrapped from all the way down to the bottom branch. Each year for the past six years Jake hired a friend of his to use his crew and his cherry picker to put on the lights. It was so perfectly lit that people from all around the area would drive by to see this perennial favorite.

In the middle of their spacious front yard was a life-sized version of the birth of Christ with a shed, lit figures, a troth and hay. A few years back someone stole the baby Jesus, so Jake designed a way to bolt each figure down. Above the scene was a suspended star that changed colors from white to yellow and then to blue.

The roofline was outlined by some more of those old fashioned large colored Christmas lights. On the top ridge of the roof was a sleigh with some reindeer. Right beside the chimney was a plastic Santa that looked like he was climbing in with one had holding a bag of toys with the other. This was the second Santa Jake had purchased because the first melted one year due to becoming overheated when Jake forgot to turn it off that Christmas Eve. When they awoke the next morning, they found Santa drooped over into the chimney as if he had too much punch the night before and was spilling his guts down the chute.

When guests arrived, they were greeted at the front door by Larry Barber in an elf outfit. He was a midget, but didn't mind being typed-cast in this role. First, because he was proud of his unique stature (he was the only midget in Gordon) and second because Jake was his first cousin.

Larry had run his Biscuit Shop for over thirty years and it had made him a very decent living. Some people said that Jake helped Larry get it off the ground with a personal loan. Jake never admitted nor denied that question. But Larry would jump up and slug you in the chin if you ever even thought about saying something bad about Jake. Not that anyone would. Everyone in Gordon loved Jake, even the criminals.

Larry knew he could always count on Jake. In fact, he had gotten Larry out of a fix with the police over some kind of domestic dispute with his third wife Wanda. It seemed that little guy had a magical way with some of the larger ladies in the county, and Wanda had caught him and another portly woman at the Mellow Mushroom in Asheville. Wanda laid quite the beating on this other woman, and Larry got Jake's help in bailing out his wife.

Jake later served as Wanda's attorney and helped her plea down to the lesser charge of disturbing the peace rather than be hammered by the possibility of large fines and maybe a little jail time if she had been convicted of assault. Then after the dust settled from that affair, he represented Larry in his divorce from Wanda. Larry was often quoted by the townsfolk that "it took a lot of biscuits to cover the costs of three divorces." But if the truth be told, he would have never survived without his friend's counsel. Larry owed Jake in a lot of ways. Besides, the elf outfit was Larry's idea in the first place. He thought that the ladies really liked it.

Once you were greeted by Larry you would find Jake and Lola dressed up like Santa and Mrs. Claus taking people's coats or directing them to the huge spread of food that was laid out in the living room. When Annie was a teen her parent's behavior (along with cousin Larry prancing around in the Elf attire) would create a great deal of embarrassment for her. Now that she was a middle-aged woman she reveled in her parent's child-like enjoyment of the season.

Although there was more food at this party than you can imagine, most of the men congregated around a huge china serving bowl to sample Jake's Christmas Cheer. Jake had a secret recipe that he would never give away. It was delicious and the punch behind the drink was not felt until after the second or third cup. Many an attendee had to be quietly escorted home due to unexpected expressions of holiday gaiety.

At some point in the party they played a version of "Dirty Santa." Everyone brought a gag gift that wasn't worth more than ten bucks, and everyone drew a number that was correlated to a specific gift. The rule was that you could only switch off your gift two times before you had to keep what you got. Sometimes parents had to hide the innocent eyes of their children when an adult-themed gift was opened. More discussions were stimulated about the "birds and the bees" as a result of these parties than all of the heroic efforts middle and high school science teachers made in trying to warn curious teens about the dangers of pre-marital sex.

The grand finale every year was the Reindeer Races. Jake had built six wooden versions of the famous creatures that stood about knee high. They were differentiated by felt saddles made up of the six colors of red, blue, green, yellow, purple and orange. He has also created two large dice that was color-coded according to the different reindeers. Lola has sown several pads representing the race path. They set up a course throughout the house so that a usual race would last about five minutes.

Lola was the "mistress of ceremonies." That meant that she rolled the dice and called each race. Jake was the "bank." He collected all the money, usually had Annie help him record the one-dollar bets and distribute the winnings. It could get very loud when around seventy or so adults and kids were screaming for their horse to win. No neighbor ever called the police because the Chief of Police Billy Winston never missed a chance to guard Jake's punch bowl. Eventually by around ten o'clock cabs were called, goodbye kisses were given and everyone had enough time to get back to their homes to put the kids to bed in preparation for Santa's arrival.

Bart stopped the car in front of the house and helped Pearl get to the front walk. He then jumped back into the car and drove off looking for a safe place to park the nice ride.

Annie led her Godmother up the front walk and to the front door. She opened it for Pearl who was immediately greeted by Larry the Elf. "Well hello lovely lady," said Larry. Pearl pushed him out of the way and quickly countered, "Don't start with me shorty! Where is the punch bowl?"

Annie bent down and gave Larry a kiss. "Hey sweetie" said the somewhat perturbed Elf. "Where is this is the infamous Bart?"

"He is out parking the car. Please be nice to him Larry."

"I will, I will. But he had better treat my little Annie right. I know how to make people disappear!"

Annie shook her finger at the little man and said, "Now Larry. I don't think you are anyone to throw stones in the relationship department, are you?"

WALKER ARMSTRONG

Larry threw up his hand in humble acknowledgment and said, "So true, so true. I will give him the old Gordon Greeting when we meet!" Annie shook her head in disbelief and went to the kitchen to find her mother.

The small kitchen was crammed with people carrying empty trays in and quickly reloading them to take them out to the Living Room. Lola spied her youngest child and scooted over in her tightly-fitted Mrs. Claus outfit to give Annie a hug.

"Good Lord Momma, don't you think you have outgrown that thing?"

"Well, I would quit wearing it but your Daddy just won't let me. "It's because it shows off your ample boobies," said a slightly exasperated daughter.

"You better believe it!" bellowed a voice from behind her. She turned around to find her beloved father. Jake was a stout man who had clear blue eyes, square chin and a flat top haircut from the 1950's. He was wearing his Santa attire without the hat and had pulled down his white beard so he could consume an egg roll. "You need to stay out of such affairs baby sis!"

"Hey Daddy," replied Annie. The old man kissed her on the check and gave her a big bear hug. "Where is this gentleman friend of yours?"

"Right here sir," replied Bart as he slid beside Annie. "It is nice to meet you Judge Sawyers." Bart shook the old man's hand but soon discovered Jake still possessed the grip of a famished Ball Python.

"Oh, just call me Jake," grinned Annie's father as he recognized that Bart flinched a little when their hands met. "But you better by God and his Son Jesus Christ call me Judge if you ever are in my courtroom. Ho! Ho! Ho!" Bart got the message.

"John Barrow Sawyers!" shouted Lola. "You be nice to Annie's guest." She placed her hand on Bart's stiff back and said, "Ignore him. His bark is worse than his bite." But Bart wasn't about to believe this polite deflection.

In response to his wife's sarcastic rebuke Jake stuck out both his hands in gripper fashion and said "Grrrr" as he chased his wife out of the kitchen with her half-hearted objections trailing behind them.

"Well, you have met the folks before you have had a stiff drink. Sorry about that!"

"Who's said I haven't already?" replied a smirking Bart.

"Why Dr. St. Claire, I am utterly and confoundedly shocked!" said Annie in her best imitation of her mother's debutante drawl. "Seriously, what do you think of all of this?" Annie asked in her normal voice.

"This is probably the largest assembly of audacious Christmas sweaters I have ever witnessed!" announced Bart in his Kentucky Colonel accent. "I can see that this is not going to be a normal party by any stretch of the imagination."

"It never is!" came a voice right behind him. Annie looked around her beau and saw her sister Jan. They both screamed and hugged each other as if it had been a year and a day since they last laid eyes on one another.

"Bart, this is my much older sister Jan." Bart immediately noticed the family resemblance in the eyes and mouth. But Jan was about three inches taller a little leaner than her voluptuous sister.

"Annie Pearl you know better than saying that kind of thing to someone. I should have drowned you in the tub when we were kids."

"You would have become an only child to the Adams Family," retorted Annie.

"Well put baby sis. I now formally retract my earlier statement … if it so pleases the court."

"Ooo-rah" said Annie raising the punch glass her mother had put down earlier when she went to hug her.

"Bart, have you had any of my Daddy's magic elixir?" asked Jan. "It is essential medicine for anyone who is going to stay at this party for more than ten minutes."

"No ma'am."

"Well, Annie dear why don't you go fix him a plate of food and I will take him to the male wildebeest watering hole."

"You ok with that handsome?" asked Annie.

"It doesn't feel like I have a choice," replied the overwhelmed chef.

"You don't!" laughed Jan as she swung her arm inside his and practically dragged him through the kitchen doorway.

As they meandered towards the dining room, Jan leaned over towards Bart and whispered, "You know my sister has fallen hard for you, don't you?"

Bart felt a little uncomfortable, but nodded in the affirmative". "The feeling is mutual."

Jan squeezed his arm and said, "That is such good news because I would hate to see something bad happen to such an erudite and handsome man as yourself."

Bart swallowed hard. He hadn't been under this kind of scrutiny in a long time. "It seems that a lot of people possess the same sentiment about Annie that you have just expressed."

"Well she is a special someone to a lot of people, but especially to our family. We Sawyer's tend to stick together. It has something to do with our Scottish blood. The Old Man especially has a real protective feel for her since Mom almost died having Annie. He calls her nicknames like "Baby Sis" and "Bonnie Lass." I really thought he was going to kill poor Tom when he found out about the man's infamous misdeeds. Oh, look here we are."

They were standing outside the door to the already crowded dining room. "You have yourself a drink. It looks like you might need it. Baby Sis will be by in a shake with your food. Bye now." Jan sashayed off leaving the dismayed doctor in the wake of her staccato warnings. She made a couple of swift turns and found her father in his study. She closed the door behind her.

"What did your recon reveal eldest daughter of mine?" spoke the Santa behind the large cherry desk.

"I am happy to report that the subject has been sufficiently warned."

"Outstanding! And what is your general impression of the man?"

"I liked him Daddy."

"Well then. Now we wait and see. Here is your drink my dear. A job well done!" Jake handed her a glass of Glen Livet, neat of course.

"Semper Fi Daddy" growled Jan with a wide grin on her face as she took a sip."

"Ooo-rah baby girl!"

Bart meanwhile was trying to blend into the wallpaper hoping he could sneak out, find Annie and go stand outside to stand beside the plastic baby Jesus for some kind of cheap comfort. He noticed Momma Pearl at the punch bowl holding court. He stepped close enough to hear Pearl say, "Charlie Griffin. Don't argue with me about Joe Montana. He was the best that ever was. I helped the doctor circumcise you, so don't act like you are Mr. Macho!" The other men hooted so loud that the whole house heard the uproar. Charlie turned red and walked away. Nobody really liked Charlie all that much, so insulting him wasn't that big of a deal.

Pearl looked around and saw Bart. She motioned him to come forward like an elementary school teacher calling a cognitively challenged boy to do a math problem on the blackboard. He knew he was stepping into potential problem. So, he took a deep breath and grabbed the cup of punch that Pearl had already extended to him.

"What about you Mr. Duke? What is your opinion about who is the greatest quarterback of all times?" barked the old lady. "Didn't you play ball in college?"

"Yes ma'am" replied Bart in a very low-keyed manner. "I guess it all depends on how you measure greatness."

The other men grunted in agreement. "You sound like a politician," said Pearl shaking her head as she helped herself to another helping of punch.

"Well, Joe Montana was a great quarterback. He possessed great instinct, incredible vision, superior foot work and rarely threw a bad pass."

"That's what I am saying! Did you hear that boys?" asked Pearl.

Bart continued. "But he played for Joe Walsh, one of the smartest and most innovative coaches of all time. And it didn't hurt that he got the throw to a guy named Jerry Rice." The other men who had been beaten down by Pearl roused to life again with all sorts of affirmations.

"Oh, my goodness!" exclaimed Pearl. "And just when I was getting to like you a little bit!"

"Just let me finish," Bart said in a respective tone towards Pearl.

"Case and point: I think if Steve Young had gotten to play earlier, he would have done as much or maybe more than Joe did. Young was one of the best athletes to play that position. He made All-Pro, won an MVP and a Super Bowl and was inducted in the Hall of Fame all after following Montana. What I am trying to say is that no one does it alone. In some ways I think Montana was a bit overrated because he had a lot of help. Football is a team sport when it is all said and done."

By now Bart noticed Annie standing in the back of the room with his food and a very worried look upon her face. Pearl looked hard at Bart as if she was getting ready to rip into him and then suddenly grinned. "The young fella' makes some good points. Steve Young was an amazing athlete. And not bad looking neither. But I could also make an argument that Jerry Rice wouldn't have been the player he became if Joe hadn't been his quarterback when he first came into the league."

Bart grinned at Pearl. He had never met anyone like this feisty, bright lady. He now knew in some part why she was such an important part of Annie's life. He raised his cup and said, "Here is to the woman of a man's dreams – Momma Pearl!"

"Here, here," said a few of the semi-sloshed gentlemen.

Pearl acknowledged the praise like a blushing teen-age girl who has just been asked out on a date by the cutest guy in school. "Aw Bart," she cooed. "You make an old mare feel like a young filly. I think I might be getting used to you after all."

As the conversation blended into several less controversial topics Annie took Bart back towards the kitchen. She motioned for him to stoop down and then unexpectedly pecked him on the cheek. Then she said, "Great recovery back there. You earned some real valuable respect points from Momma Pearl. And she is one hard cookie to crack!"

"Good. I was beginning to wonder if I would survive the night."

"Oh, don't worry about Daddy and Jan. If I get you into Pearl and Lola's good graces they will be like putty in my hands. Don't let them fool you. My Mom is the real power behind the throne around here!"

Back in the kitchen Lola was bending Tee's ear about what project they should be lining up for the Women's Auxiliary in the spring when

Annie and Bart arrived. Annie preceded to tell her Mom about what had just occurred in the dining room.

"Well aren't you something!" declared Lola. She hugged Bart around the waist and said "You stick with me and my little Pearl here. If we like you everyone else will follow suit."

"That's the truth!" said Tee taking a big hunk out of a spicy chicken wing.

Annie laughed at Tee and looked out the kitchen window. The ladies were talking about whether to start Dirty Santa now or later when Annie saw someone walking up the side driveway that created some concern.

"Mom," she quietly queried, "that isn't Barney Trapani is it?"

"Well I think so honey," replied Lola in her typical preoccupied manner.

Now normally this wouldn't be a problem. It seemed that Barney was known and liked by a lot of people. But he was the husband of the same woman whom Larry was fooling around with when the big brawl happened at the Mellow Mushroom. Barney had promised if he had gotten Larry alone, he was "going to cut him down to size," and for a midget that meant that not much would be left after the slicing was done.

The reality of her snafu of inviting Barney hit Lola square in the forehead. Jake walked in and shouted "Lola let's get this party rolling and do Dirty Santa!" All she could muster up was "Jake come with me to the door right now!" Annie, Lola and Jake hurried to the door. But it was too late. Larry and Barney were outside sizing each other up.

"Jake please do something!" plead a mortified Lola.

"Aw baby," growled Jake. "There ain't no backing down in the little feller and Barney hates Larry something awful. What in the Sam Hill were you thinking inviting Barry to the party?"

Before Lola could answer Larry jumped onto Barney and they started rolling around in the front yard. There is nothing quite as simultaneously scary and funny as a midget and a fat guy trying to beat the stew out of each other. For one thing, Midgets don't fight fare. When you think about it why should they? And for another you worry about large middle-aged men who smoke light a train, eat like a horse and get no exercise keeling over with a sudden heart attack. Who needs Circus de Sole when you got this kind of activity going on?

In a matter of seconds, the attendees poured outside and were laughing, cheering and even a few of the men were taking side bets as to who would win. Barney got the upper hand when he tossed Larry a good distance into the Manger Scene. But that just made the midget mad. Larry ripped Joseph off his stand and used him as a battering ram to thump Barney in the gut.

"Oh shoot" said a frustrated Jake. "I knew I should have used one-inch bolts on that sucker!"

By now the women were getting seriously offended and downright hysterical. Several of the men stepped in and separated the two. When the ruckus finally settled down both were bent over breathing pretty heavily. Even though they said some menacing things to each other, everyone knew that the fight was over.

The Chief of Police stepped in and said in a somewhat parental tone, "Now boys, both of you are fine fellas. You need to put the past behind you and shake hands and let's bet back to the best party of the year. Otherwise y'all are going to tick me off and I will have to get one of my men to come over here and arrest you and put your butts in jail. Well, what is it going to be?"

Larry and Barney looked at each other and mumbled some things under their breaths. Finally, Larry stuck out his hand first and said "I'm sorry for everything Barney. I should never have tried to fool around with your wife. Please forgive me."

"Well," stammered the stocky Italian, "she was always a bit strange in the head. To tell the truth, I wasn't the kind of husband I should have been. Please forgive me for calling you a Hervé Villechaize wanna be."

"Who is that?" Lola asked Jake

"You know," replied Jake. He was that little feller that played Tattoo on *Fantasy Island*."

"Oh," responded Lola. "I think Larry is much more handsome than him."

Jake looked at his wife's backside and commented "You have put on a few pounds back there lately. Should I be worried?" Lola smacked him on the arm and shook her head as she moved back into the house. Larry and Barney followed behind her chatting and laughing like they were old buddies. Bart looked at Annie with a blank stare. She took him by the arm and said, "I told you that you would not want to miss my parent's Christmas Party, didn't I?"

After the commotion died down Lola conducted the Dirty Santa portion of the festivities. When the first gag gift was open people started hollering and it was like the whole midget/jealous husband fiasco never happened. Bart ended up with the prized fake vomit that had been around so long that it was starting to smell like the real thing.

Annie got a cute ornament of two hearts that were surrounded by a small holly wreath. She lost it once in all the trading but eventually got it back and kept it. She felt like it was a sign of something special. When people saw her obvious joy over obtaining the somewhat cheap ornament people started kidding with her about her determination to land that prize. She looked at Bart in a moment of vulnerability and grinned. He grinned back.

This was of course followed by the Reindeer Races. There was a bit of controversy that occurred when the Sheriff won three consecutive races. Cries of cronyism and political corruption were hurled back and forth because both friends were up for re-election next fall. Finally, the Judge made his twelve-year old grandson Grant the Grand Rules Official and that seemed to quell the argument.

By the time Annie, Bart and Pearl piled into the Angelo's Lexus everyone seemed to be in a festive outlook. Even Barney volunteered to give Larry and a few others who had too much punch a ride home. Annie tried to stay and help her Mom clean up but Lola reminded her that Pearl needed to get back to the rest home. Southern women are famous for that kind of stylish martyrdom. It gives them the kind of secret power that causes people to admire them and speak well of their robust hospitality long after the party is over.

When they pulled out of her folk's driveway Annie's mind seemed a million miles away. She checked on a sleeping Momma Pearl and then stared out the rear window as she watched her Daddy reattach Joseph to his rightful location. She hadn't felt this peaceful in a long, long time.

Bart noticed this and said, "Is the party always this urbane?"

Annie looked back at him and replied, "Well there was year that Sheriff Billy got drunk and drove around the neighborhood flashing his blue lights and yelling Merry Christmas over his bullhorn. That made the papers. But he still got re-elected the next year because he ran against Charlie Griffin."

"And no one likes Charlie," chimed in Bart.

"Very good Sir Bart! You will become a Gordon-nite soon with trenchant analysis like that!" Annie leaned back and said "I hope you weren't too shocked by everything."

"Not a bit. Everyone treated me very nicely and that was the most entertaining Christmas Party I have ever attended!" exclaimed Bart.

"Well it means a lot to me that you and Pearl were there." Annie touched Bart's right forearm. Their eyes met and both of them felt the surge of unexpected passion.

This romantic electricity was short circuited as a voice from the back of the van rang out "I had a large time too!" Annie looked to see Pearl holding a fist full of cash. "I did pretty good at the Reindeer Races. Maybe I will try my luck soon at Vegas."

Annie and Bart laughed together at the bombastic ninety-year-old woman. Bart thought if he could break down what was in her blood and concoct an energy drink from her genetic properties, he could make a mint.

The three carried on their conversation about the unusual events of the party when they finally pulled back up to the Center. Then Pearl surprised both Annie and Bart by saying "Mr. Duke, could you escort me back to my room. I am feeling a little wobbly and I am not sure Annie can handle me if I should slip."

Bart looked at Annie and she winked at him and said "Go ahead. If you give me the keys to the Lexus."

Pearl waited this time for Bart to help her out of the van. They walked slowly back to the front door and Bart rang the security bell to get an attendant to open up. As they walked past the front desk Nellie

Graham the shift supervisor noted Pearl's attire and her handsome escort and commented "Now Pearl you know you can't have any overnight guests in your room."

"He would be so lucky. Nah, this is Annie's beau Dr. Bart St. Claire. Bart this is Nellie Graham one of the nosiest humans on the planet."

"I love you too Pearl," chuckled Nellie.

Bart steadied Pearl as she leaned a little too far when they rounded the corner. "My goodness," said Pearl. "You must still work out. Your arm feels so big and strong. It reminds me of my dear departed husband Edgar. Now that was a man if there ever was one!"

Bart grinned and said, "He had to be to keep up with you."

Pearl ignored the compliment. She stopped by the door into her room, straightened herself up and leaned forward to make sure he was going to get the message she was intent on delivering. "Listen. The reason I asked you to take me to my room wasn't because I needed the help. I wanted to tell you something I see about you that worries me"

Bart swallowed hard. He now knew what some of his former patients felt like when he was about to deliver some bad news. He shook his head and dropped his hands by his side.

"I think you are a decent man. You ain't no playboy or shyster. But you are very troubled person Bart. All I know about you comes from Annie. But I can read people in ways you can't imagine. And what I read about you is that you are a runner."

Bart tried to hide his fear by asking "What do you mean Pearl?"

She narrowed her eyes and said, "You see, right there you are being dishonest. Don't mess with me boy. These old eyes have seen more troubles than I can remember. So, you can cut the crap and get real. You know you are a runner."

"Go on," said the sober former surgeon.

"Well I am worried that something is going to happen and then whoosh, you will up and vanish and leave my Annie heartbroken. That will not do."

"What do you think I should do?" said Bart in a humble and transparent manner.

Pearl smiled ever so sweetly and put Bart's troubled face into her wrinkled hands. "You make peace with your past darling," spoke the prophetess of Gordon, "or you will never be at home anywhere."

"I don't know how Pearl. I honestly don't know how."

"That's because you are trying to do it with your head rather than your heart. Are you a praying man son?"

Bart sighed and felt the cynicism start to well up in his soul. "I used to be," commented the now distant man. "But like you said, I've seen too much to believe in a personal deity that fixes problems like a fast order cook fixes a hamburger."

"I don't believe that neither," replied Pearl in a blunt manner. "What I am talking about is bowing your hurting and proud heart before the Lord God and asking him for wisdom."

"No, I don't think I have prayed like that in a long time."

"Well until you do you are a hazard to yourself and everyone around you!" said Pearl in an almost confrontational fashion.

Now Bart was getting a little aggravated. This woman had no clue about what he had endured and the mistakes he had made, and he wasn't in the mood for any homespun spirituality, no matter how sincere it might be.

Right about the time he was getting ready to give her a polite goodnight Pearl pulled his face down and kissed him on the cheek. She looked him in the eyes and said, "Son forgiveness is a gift. You don't wait to ask for it when you feel worthy enough, and you should never wait to give it when the other person has made everything ok. It is always an act of faith to let mercy step in front of justice."

Bart look startled when he heard these words. He knew Pearl was right. He just didn't think he would ever be able to follow the path that would lead to real peace. Too much water had flowed under his bridge and too many dreams had been washed away by the torrents of tragedy.

"Well thanks Pearl. It has been nice to get to know you a little bit."

"The same to you Dr. St. Claire. Now go and take my Annie home. She can't wait to get you alone you know!"

Bart slightly bowed to the elderly sage and then hurriedly left the center. As he was walking up the sidewalk his head was down filled with the weight of Pearl's incisive words … *It is always an act of faith to let mercy step in front of justice.* Indeed!

When he looked up, he saw Annie in the sedan smiling at him. He opened the passenger door and asked, "Don't you want me to drive?"

"No way!" chirped Annie. "I haven't driven a car this nice in a long time1"

Bart jumped in a put on his seatbelt. She stuck the car in gear and hit the gas. It had more horsepower than she anticipated and she almost the Center Van.

"Woops," said an embarrassed Annie. "Hey, how did it go in there?"

"What do you mean?" asked Bart in the same habitually deflective way Pearl had just rebuked him for.

"You know, what did Mama Pearl want to tell you?"

"Oh that. Not much. She was just thanking me for the night and told me to treat you right."

Annie looked at Bart almost the same way Pearl had just a few minutes earlier. She thought carefully and then told Bart. "It's ok if you don't want to tell me everything she said. Talking with her is like conversing with a living x-ray machine. She doesn't pull any punches."

"I gathered that but I know it is also part of her charm."

"Is that what you call it? I think she can be quite bossy and opinionated but I love dearly and would do anything for her."

"Evidently the feeling is mutual," said Bart as he looked towards the exit downtown. He realized was so wrapped up in everything that happened that he forgot to call Angelo to see how the restaurant fared without him there. He was trying to think about anything that would move his mind off the subject of God, forgiveness and other uncomfortable issues.

When they arrived at Annie's house the front porch light was on. Annie's sister Jan's car was in the driveway. Jan took Meagan and her kids back to Annie's house before the party shut down. Jan was planning to spend the night with her younger sister and catch up with all that was happening, especially in the romance department. When Annie parked the Lexus Bart got out and walked her to the front door.

Annie looked at Bart who seemed to be buried under a mess of worry. "What's wrong Bart?

"Oh nothing, just thinking about some of the stuff Pearl said."

"Don't let her bother you."

"She didn't."

Annie pulled closer to Bart. This definitely shifted his focus. She looked up at him and said. "You know I am getting used to you being around. You are a pretty ok guy for an ex-doctor turned chef."

In a moment all the burdens of the past that had been dug up by that little old lady evaporated and Bart realized how truly beautiful Annie looked. All he could say is "You are something else, you know it?"

She pressed her finger up against his lips. He got the message. He slowly bent down and gently kissed her waiting mouth. He pulled back after a few seconds. When he opened his eyes, he saw the earnest and sweet desire of a woman who had not been truly kissed in a long time. He reproached a second time and their lips merged into a smooth and ever-intensifying motion of passion ignited. He didn't know how long the second kiss lasted, but by the time they both came up for a breath he noticed that they were pressed so tightly together that their dark jackets looked as if they were one garment.

"Oh, my goodness," said Annie in a breathless hush.

"Yeah, oh my goodness" replied Bart. "That is the best first kiss I have ever had in my life!"

Annie giggled. As both of them were contemplating a third kiss the front porch lights flashed on and off. "It looks like I am past my curfew" said the frustrated woman.

"Well, I got to go and check on Frodo" said a swerving Bart. "I sure he has torn up the apartment. I will call you in the morning before you go to church ok?"

"That would be fabulous. Hey, why don't you go with me tomorrow?"

Bart looked down at his feet. He shuffled around a bit and then said, "I can't tomorrow but I promise I will come with soon."

Annie didn't know why but she somehow understood. She smiled at him and said goodnight. He waved at her like a goofy teenage boy and trotted back to the car. Annie walked into her house and quickly entered the kitchen so she could watch him drive off.

Jan was standing right behind her. "I thought you would appreciate Dad's old intimidation strategy for moving hot blooded boys off of our trails."

Annie would normally glare at her nosy big sister but she was feeling too fine to let such trivial matters mess up her awesome mood. "You didn't bother me sis."

Jan took one look at Annie and said, "Oh my gosh! Did you just get kissed on your own front porch by a yummy eligible bachelor?" Annie nodded and both women let out a simultaneous squeal that got Meagan to run into the kitchen and see what was happening.

"Meg," said her aunt with great pride, "your Mom just got her first kiss from Bart!"

"Gross!" said Meagan. "That is too much information. I think I have a little throw up in the back of my throat."

Jan and Annie ignored the grumpy teen. Jan said to her baby sister "Since I already have my pajamas on and am ready for bed why don't you do the same so we can sit and talk like we used to when we were kids." Annie agreed and literally trotted back to her bedroom. In a few moments so she was all ready for the "girl chat." Jan made some hot chocolate and they retreated back to Annie's bedroom.

As Jan's kids Grant and Phillip played video games in the den, Meg was totally engrossed in some teenage drama with a friend. The two middle-aged women sat cross-legged on Annie's king-sized sleigh bed and renewed an old tradition that kept them close during the topsy-turvy days of first dates and first loves.

"So," said an anxious Jan, "tell me about Mr. Mysterious."

"I don't know where to start." Annie then took a deep breath and did her best to summarize her whirlwind romance. "He went to Duke on an academic scholarship and played football there until he got hurt. Went to medical school and became a heart surgeon. Was married but his wife committed suicide and was eight months pregnant and the child didn't survive. He was devastated so he sold his part of the practice and moved to Italy to learn how to cook. There he worked with a lady that knew Angelo and he found out from her that Angelo wanted to sell the restaurant. So, he contacted Angie, bought the place and moved here about six months ago. Oh, and he has the neatest dog named Frodo. You know how I love Tolkien."

Jan looked puzzled. Annie picked up on this and asked "What's wrong Sissy?"

"Nothing really. Did he tell you where his practice was located?"

Annie got ready to answer the question and said "Now that I think about it, we never talked about exactly where. I knew it was somewhere here in the state. Why do you ask?"

"No particular reason. I just know that for a guy who has committed so much time to becoming a heart surgeon and had an established practice it just doesn't make a lot of sense why he would leave that even after going through something terrible like what you mentioned."

Annie shook her head in frustration. "This is just like you Jan to pick things apart that you don't understand. You are so much like Dad!"

Jan knew where this was heading. She and Annie were about as close as sisters could be but they had some intense fights growing up. Jan looked at Annie and carefully chose her words, "I am not questioning his story. He seems like a real nice guy and I can tell that he cares for you. I am just cautious when it comes to your feelings. I don't want you to get hurt."

Annie could tell that Jan was really trying not to give into her suspicious nature. She knew her first reaction to Jan's question was a bit of a reflex. She took a deep breath and said "I know you don't. I am just really happy. My life has been in such an utter state of shambles. For over seven years that this feels like the first real light of hope I have had about a relationship in a long time."

Jan rubbed Annie's leg like she used to when her baby sister would cry in her crib. With all the sincerity she could muster she replied "I see it and I am excited for you. I just have wondered if anyone asks you the kind of questions I do."

Annie knew that this was a kind way of Jan reminding Annie of her tendency to be somewhat impulsive about big decisions. Annie couldn't get too mad because this was true. Jan had been with Annie through the best of times and worst of times. Annie gathered herself and said, "I haven't done a huge amount of due diligence on Bart. But he has told me things he wouldn't have if he was just trying to impress me. I can't explain it but I do trust him."

"That's a good sign," said Jan in an encouraging manner. Seeing her sister a little deflated she changed the subject and asked "What is your favorite thing about him?"

Annie said "Well before tonight I would say that I really like his intelligence, his sense of humor, his eyes, the fact that he is a better cook than me and that he has this really neat servant's heart. But now I would have to add the fact that he is best kisser I have ever had in my life!"

This confession won the protective older sister over to the degree that she started giggling. Jan winked at Annie and said "I wonder what else he is good at?" The middle-aged women started laughing so loud that Meagan pounded on the door and asked them to quiet down.

Annie placed her chin between her elbows and sighed. She looked at her big sister and said, "I can't explain it Jan but it feels like I have known him a long time."

CHAPTER 7

THE NEXT TWO months flew by as Annie and Bart's relationship moved from romantic curiosity to something more serious. They couldn't believe how much joy and passion they had discovered in being together. They tried to be sober and careful, but it would be akin to telling a malnourished child not to eat too much at a sumptuous banquet. Each delectable course of new disclosure gave way to child-like revelry.

Family and friends sought to warn them that things were moving "way too fast." This cautious perspective was not merely genuine concern over Annie being deeply hurt if the romance didn't pan out. Some of her buddies from the Shopping Gang were also jealous of how a lot of Annie's attention and affection had been transferred to this nice stranger. Annie understood. She was probably more shocked than anyone about how much of her relational energies had now been focused on Bart.

Lola was particularly worried. She had seen very little of her daughter since Bart came on the scene, and had tried to ask her youngest a few questions about how things were going. The typical response she got was short and upbeat. Lola decided to take a more indirect approach in trying to get to the bottom of what was going on. Annie's birthday was coming up in March and it was a tradition for her and Lola to go to Asheville for some shopping and a nice leisurely lunch. She would find a way during that appointment to dig deeper.

Annie was sipping on a Carmel Frappuccino at a local Starbuck's in Asheville as her mother was droning on about all of her responsibilities in Gordon. It was obvious that Annie's mind was elsewhere when her mother asked for the second time, "Honey, what do you where do you think we should have the Spring Fling this year? Annie did you hear me?"

"I'm sorry Mom. Uh, I don't see why you can't use the Civic Center again."

"But I just told you that the Cub Scouts have already reserved it for the Derby Race Day. Child, sometimes I just don't know about you anymore."

"What do you mean Mom?"

"Well, it just seems that every time I try to talk with you about anything you are not all there, or you're in an all-fired hurry to get somewhere."

"Mom, you are exaggerating."

"Ok then, never mind."

Annie knew that this was her mom's way of saying her feelings were hurt. Within a few seconds Lola would start pouting.

"Alright, I know I have been a little preoccupied lately."

"A little? Annie, outside of asking me to spend time with Meagan you have hardly said ten words to me in the last few weeks."

"Well, we have talked a bunch today."

"Yes, but there have been several times today when you have seemed to be on another planet. Are you thinking about Bart?"

"Here we go. I know you have been itching to talk about this. So, what do you want to know?"

"Now you are being disrespectful and I don't deserve that!"

Once again Annie realized that she was fighting a losing battle. "I'm sorry Mom. You are right. To be honest I am worried."

Lola quickly got reengaged. "What are you worried about?"

"I am happy as I have ever been in my life and yet …"

"Do you wonder if it is for real?"

"Yes. Silly isn't it?"

"No actually I am relieved."

"Why?"

"Annie Pearl there is no human being on this whole-wide-world that wants you to be happy more than me. But I have been sick to my stomach over this thing with Bart."

"Do you think he is not good enough for me?"

"No, that would be what your Daddy would say. My worry is about how fast all of this happened and how we still know so little about Bart. For instance, where was he born and who are his parents?"

"He was born in Gastonia and his parents are deceased. He is an only child and has some aunts, uncles and cousins that still live in Gaston County. Does that help?"

"Some. But getting that information out of you was like pulling some wisdom teeth."

"You're right. But I do already know a lot about him. I probably could fill a book with all the stuff I have discovered about this man. It is just that I am now forty-five and I feel like I don't have time to waste. What if Bart is not all that he appears to be?"

"None of us are what we appear to be when we are head-over-heels in love Baby Sis. That is why me, your Daddy, Jan and some of your other friends are worried that you are going to crash and burn if this doesn't work out. And darling I am getting too old to go through another emotional tsunami."

"Are you talking about what happened with Darrell?"

"Honey, I am talking about Tom, Darrell and a host of other heartbreaks. A mother absorbs all of these throughout their child's life. Do you hurt when you see Meg sad?"

"Well of course I do Mom. What a crazy question!"

"Then just imagine if it was Meagan who went through what you did. How would you feel after all of that devastation if she fell in love with someone who seems too good to be true?"

That question seemed to hit Annie hard. "I guess I would be as worried as you are."

Lola tilted her head and raised her eyebrows as only a mother would when her wisdom had been vindicated. "Please don't misunderstand me. I am not saying that you shouldn't see Bart honey. If he is the right man for you, I will lead the dance line at your wedding. Just be a little more careful ok?"

"I will Mommy."

That one word made a broad smile spread across Lola's face. "Now, on your next date I want you to wear those ear rings I bought you today. They accentuate your beautiful eyes!"

Annie was running around her house like a chicken that had its head chopped off. She was a nervous wreck. *It couldn't have been about going out on a date with Bart* she kept telling herself.

Maybe it was the reverberation that was echoing in her heart from the chat she had with her Mom the previous day. She knew she needed to ask Bart some more probing questions. She just wasn't sure how she was going to pull it off.

It probably it also had to do with how difficult Meagan had been the last week. After almost two months of parental bliss, "Moody Meagan" had reappeared with a vengeance. She wanted to see if she could parse her daughter's emotional state to discover what was bothering her before she left

"Meg," Annie shouted from the kitchen. "Could you please come here for a second."

The teen appeared with in a moment. "Yeah, what do you want?"

"No need for a bad attitude," countered Annie. "I was just wondering what was going on with you. You have seemed really mad this week."

"I have a lot of struggles in school right now, but you don't care!"

"I don't mind staying at home and talking with you if you could be a little clearer."

"Never mind Mom," was all she got out of her only child.

Annie put her hand on her daughter's shoulder. "I am always here for you. You know that don't you?"

"Whatever Mom," said Meagan turning her head away in a not-so-subtle form of disrespect.

"Meg, I am far from perfect but you know that I am totally committed to your welfare. But that is not what this about. Are you jealous of Bart?"

Meagan sneered at her Mom and said "Yeah right."

Annie didn't let up, but for some strange reason she didn't seem mad. "I have more joy in my life that I have had in a very long time. It would seem that if you loved me like you claim to, this would make you somewhat happy." Annie paused long enough to catch her daughter's glimpse. "Why aren't you happy for me Meg?"

Meg looked shocked. Normally this kind of confrontation would end in a shouting match. Her mom wasn't taking the bait. In fact, she never has seen her mom this resolute and clear-headed.

"It's just, since he came into the scene, we don't spend any time together anymore" replied Meagan in a calmer fashion.

"Well, I've got to take you for a checkup with the doctor in Charlotte. Why don't we make a day of it and do a little shopping?"

Meagan was out of ammunition. All she could do was to respond meekly, "That would be cool."

"In the meantime, said Annie in a little firmer tone, "Don't give Granny a hard time while we are gone or the deal with shopping is off."

"No prob Mom." Meagan smiled and gave her mother a kiss and practically skipped back to her room. The doorbell rang almost simultaneously with the cessation of the shockingly sedate conversation. Annie went to the door and let her mom in.

"How is it going?" asked Lola.

"Ok. Meg and I have reached an understanding about her attitude. If she gives you a hard time tonight be sure to tell me. We have worked out a deal about shopping on Monday that is contingent on her not being a pain in the butt."

"Oh, I can handle that girl." Lola looked into the refrigerator.

"Don't worry about cooking. I have the delivery guy from Angelo's coming by with some food for both of you."

"I wish you wouldn't do that. You younger folks eat out too much. I could have whipped up something for me and my grandbaby!"

"Well, now you can rent a movie and relax."

"You know I don't know how to operate that thing. Beside I am worried that I might accidentally rent something inappropriate like I did last time. I had no idea that they put that kind of filth on TV these days."

"Mom, Meagan knows how to operate the cable box. Just try to talk to her a little. She seems like she is going through something right now."

The doorbell interrupted their debate about modern life. When Annie came to the door Bart could tell that everything was far from being "ok."

"What's going on?" asked the concerned man.

"Just the usual teen-age drama!" huffed Annie.

Bart walked cautiously behind her as she fetched her overcoat from the kitchen. He saw Lola sitting at the table and greeted her with a warm "hello."

"Hey Bart," replied the already exhausted grandmother. She was not looking forward to hearing Meagan's rift on the problems with Annie dating Bart. It seemed that this was all that anyone ever wanted to talk about anymore.

Bart sensed the tension and tried to do some damage assessment. "If we just need to go pick up a pizza and be here tonight, that is ok with me," said Bart in the most supportive manner he could.

"No way," said the re-focused Lola. "You guys go and have a good time tonight. I will stay and try to tame the little tiger. I have already been through this teenage drama two times with Annie and Jan. If fact, Annie was a bigger pain in the butt than Meagan!"

"Really?" grinned Bart. "I want to hear more."

Annie grabbed Bart's arm and started pulling him toward the door. She waved at her Mom and said "Thanks for coming Mom. I love you."

"I love you too baby girl. Please be careful. There is a lot of construction going on this side of I-40. Oh, and Bart, have Annie tell you about her date with Roger Crews when she was fifteen."

"We will Lola and I will certainly get some information on Senior Crews" replied a quickly moving Bart.

Once that got in the truck Bart looked at Annie and said, "Well?"

"Well what?" replied Annie in a mocking way.

"I want to hear all about Roger," replied Bart as he moved his eyebrows up and down in a risqué manner.

"Ok I was fourteen and in ninth grade. This absolutely gorgeous guy named Roger Crews was a senior. He was a captain of everything and Class President and he wanted to take me out."

"Mmmm, I am already feeling jealous" said a sarcastic Bart.

WALKER ARMSTRONG

"Yeah, well anyway he had even had come to the house and asked my Dad if we could date."

"What did Jake say?"

"What do you think? He was polite but gave Roger a firm no. Dad told him what he told me a number of times: 'Annie can go out on a one-on-one date when she turns sixteen. But if you and Annie want to hang out with a group of friends that will be fine.' Roger was nice about it but I was mad as a wet hen."

"I would agree with your Dad," replied Bart in a very mature tone.

"Typical male response!" said Annie staring a hole into her man.

"Well, I bet he was up to no good, wasn't he?"

"That's beside the point," replied Annie hoping to keep Bart on the point she was trying to make.

"Ah-ha!" said Bart triumphantly.

"Like I was saying, Dad was trying to invoke his parental authority with no discussion and no compromise."

"So, what did you do?"

Annie started shaking her head and smiling. "Now I see Mom's perspective. How does she do that?"

"Huh?" said Bart missing the point once again.

"Never mind" said Annie regaining her focus. "I decided to sneak out one Friday night to go with Bart to a late showing of *Rocky Horror Picture Show* at the Tyner Drive-In. I actually crept down into the basement like a ninja on a mission and crawled through the transom window."

"You didn't!" replied Bart in a pseudo-shocked manner.

"Very funny! Anyway, I thought I had pulled off a major caper. I thought I was a woman and should make my own decisions. Anyway, we were sitting there enjoying the movie like a couple when Roger made his move."

Bart started shaking his head as if he knew the routine. "I knew it!" he said like a detective who had a hunch about a suspect and then found incontrovertible evidence.

Annie pretended to ignore him. She continued. "One moment he was sitting on his side of the car, the next he was on me like a possum on a June bug. He was slurping and grabbing and begging and groaning and I thought I was a goner. Then out of nowhere Dad opens the door and pull's Mr. Hormone out of the car. I jumped out quick enough to see Daddy pin Roger up against the car and say to him 'When I say no I mean no. You got me!'

"Whew, I am sure your Dad can be intimidating when he wants to be!" said Bart smiling at her father's bold move.

"Yeah, my Daddy was a former Marine and from what I was told he was a rounder before my Mom got a hold of him."

Bart, now fully invested in the story, asked "So what happened?"

"Well, I would like to say that I quit sneaking out but that would be a lie."

"What?" said an incredulous Bart.

Annie giggled and gave an "oh-well" kind of shrug.

Bart now was on the offensive. "You mean to tell me that after all of that you didn't learn your lesson?" he asked Annie slightly popping the steering wheel with the pronunciation of each word.

Annie tried to regain control of the conversation. She looked straight ahead and said, "I guess not but I was trying to make a point."

"What kind of point?"

"I was trying to let my Dad know that I was mature enough to make my own decisions." Annie then froze. She realized that even though Meagan was immature and impulsive she was trying to do the same thing with Annie.

"What are you thinking right now," asked Bart?

"I just realized that I am going to have to shift gears with Meg," replied Annie as if she had just received a new map for getting to a desired location.

"I am totally clueless once again," said a frustrated Bart.

"I know you are darling, but I love you anyway."

"You what?" said Bart almost swerving off the road.

"Oh my gosh, that just slipped out!" Annie now felt at a disadvantage. She really wanted Bart to say it first. Because she had uttered those famous three words there was no going back. She swallowed hard and looked over at the wide-eyed driver before taking the leap again, "I love you Bart."

"What a relief! I thought I was the only one that felt that way." Bart suddenly took the upcoming exit off of I-40. He quickly reached the top of the ramp, turned right, wheeled right into a service station parking lot and came to an abrupt stop. He quickly slipped over to Annie, pulled her close, looked into her eyes and said "I love you too Annie!

They laughed out loud at the same time and then passionately kissed. It was a kiss of deep relief and solemn confirmation. When they finished Bart looked at Annie and asked "Does this remind you of the drive-in?"

Annie laughed and said, "No sweetheart. You are much better kisser than Roger!"

Bart and Annie ended up having a fantastic date. It amazed Annie that she could know someone so profoundly in just a few months. Just when she thought they had reached a slow-down point of their relationship they were able to take it to a deeper level of intimacy. Annie's heart was filled with gratitude and she felt that she was finally able to trust again.

The next night she took Kim out to dinner at Angelo's. It had been a while since they had spent some one-on-one time together and so there was a lot of catching up to do.

Annie arrived at Angelo's that night around 6:30 p.m. Kim was already there seated at the table all of them sat at that fateful night she was first introduced to the brooding chef.

"Greetings stranger!" said Kim in her most cheerful tone as she reached across the table and hugged her adopted sister's neck.

"Hey my friend!" replied Annie. "I noticed that you got started without me," smirked Annie pointing to the already opened bottle of house Pinot Grigio. "Has Bart come to the table yet?"

"Oh, he is the one that reserved the table for us and he gave us this bottle of wine on the house." Kim grabbed the bottle and expertly poured Annie a glass of wine. It seemed that she had a lot of practice in doing this. Annie made a mental note of it and planned to discretely ask her friend more pointed exploratory questions about this.

"I have so many questions to ask you!" burst forth Kim.

Annie took her first sip. It was just what her palate needed. "I can only imagine. Where would you like to start?"

"How about are you two deeply in love?"

Annie blushed a little and then pretended to speak in a hushed tone. "More than I can possibly explain."

Kim lifted her glass and shouted "Woo-hoo!" A few people turned around to see what all the celebration was about and Kim waved at them saying "Don't mind us, we are just celebrating true love!"

Annie put her left hand to cover her brow and said "Calm down Kimberly, you are going to get people to start talking."

"It is too late for that sister. People have been talking since your first sweet potato cheesecake date!"

Now Annie was in a bit of shock. They had tried to be private about their affair. It seemed that those efforts had evidently been a waste of energy. She looked at Kim and said "How could people know about this?"

"Well, a few of us figured it out pretty quickly" replied Kim. "But why do you think I had all of us come here last fall for dinner?"

"You mean you wanted me to meet Bart?" asked Annie. She felt a little woozy. She knew that the wine could not work on her that fast.

"Yes darling. And might I add that I am a sneaky and a really good cupid. Wouldn't you agree?"

Annie sat at the table motionless. Before she could ask another question Bart suddenly appeared at their table. "Greetings to the two loveliest ladies in Gordon!"

Kim liked his style. "Oh Mister' Bart, you say the most adorable things" cooed Kim in her best Scarlett O'Hara imitation.

Bart knelt down and grabbed Annie's right hand. His kissed it gently. She did her utmost to protest his public display of affection. "Bart" she spoke in the quietest way she could. "People will see that."

"Frankly my dear I don't give a damn," responded Bart in a pretty good Rhett Butler. He winked at Annie, stood up and said "What can

I interest you ladies in tonight? Would you like one of our specials, or would you like for me to pick for you?"

Kim spoke up before Annie could say anything, "Why don't you pick for us Bart?"

"Consider it done! Ma'am" spoke Bart like a Sargent taking order from a Colonel. "I will make sure one of our waiters brings you some fresh bread. I will be by later to check on you. He smiled at Annie and then went to another table to greet some guests.

"My, my" said Kim. "He sure is smitten with you! What have you done to this poor man?"

"Nothing" said a recovering Annie. "We just have a mutual admiration society."

"Whatever you call it, you both seem to be very happy. And that makes me very happy. Cheers!"

Annie needed that kind of affirmation. She lifted her glass and said "Thanks sweetie! You will never know how much your support means to me."

"I know what you have been through and I know how rare it seems to find someone so suited for you. I don't care what other people say!" replied Kim.

"Are other people saying mean things? asked a somewhat concerned Annie.

"It doesn't matter girl" retorted Kim.

"I want to know what are they saying and who is saying it Kim" said Annie in an aggravated and very serious fashion.

Kim could tell from the look on Annie's face that she would not be deterred until she found out what people were talking about. Kim leaned forward and said quietly "Well, a few ladies from the church have said that they think Bart is hiding something. I have spoken to them and have told them that they need to be careful of gossip."

"Is one of them Ruth Phipps?" asked Annie. Kim nodded yes. Annie threw down her napkin in disgust.

Ruth was the owner of Gordon's Ladies Emporium. It was the finest clothing shop for women in the county. Ruth had opened it up fifteen years ago after her husband Tony had made a killing on a Golf Course development that he built up towards Asheville. Once it was established, he sold it to investors from California and now spends most of his time either day trading stocks or working on new real estate projects.

Tony and Ruth had met when they were attending Living Truth Bible College that was located in Cary, NC. They got married right after graduation and went to Japan as missionaries. After serving there for two years they came back to Gordon when Tony's dad Russell unexpectantly died from a heart attack.

Since Tony was the oldest of three boys, his mom Elizabeth asked him to consider running the family construction business. Acquaintances of the family said that he negotiated a deal with his mother that if he ran, he would have complete control of the business. Because they were cut from the same cloth, she knew he would make them a lot of money. Her other sons, who had both worked for their dad since they graduated from high school, disagreed. Eventually, both left the business and the youngest son Philip hadn't talked with Tony for ten years, despite living five minutes from him.

Both Tony and Ruth were heavily involved at NewLight Community Church. Tony was an elder and chairman of the Building and Grounds Committee. Ruth led a very popular ladies' Bible Study called "Digging into the Word." You could even say that Ruth had a following of sorts, especially among the younger women. If the truth be told, Ruth enjoyed being in the limelight and especially savored being a person other people came to for counsel and advice.

The Phipps were one of the four founding families of the church. They started NewLight when they felt that their home church Sawyers Grove Methodist was becoming too liberal after having two successive pastors that were more than just a little progressive in their thinking.

In fact, Ruth was chairwoman of the Pastoral Search Committee that called Tim. During the first year that Tim and Kim were serving at NewLight, Tony and Ruth took the young couple under their wings and got them settled into the community. It wasn't unusual to see the two couples together out in the community. Tim was grateful for their help, but Kim was always suspicious of Ruth's motives.

Annie knew Tony because they grew up in church and school together. She attended Tony and Ruth's wedding that was held at Ruth's home church in Raleigh. Annie's first impression of Ruth wasn't that solid. The reason for this distrust had to do with how Ruth treated out of town guests that were from Gordon.

During the reception Annie discovered that Ruth had gotten all of her family and friends that traveled from out of town heavily discounted hotel rates while never informing the folks from Gordon about that opportunity. She was all smiles and warmest of greetings when she met people from Tony's hometown, but Annie felt that such sweetness was saccharine at best and manipulative at worst. It was all of these kinds of memories that was fueling Annie's sudden disgust.

"So, what exactly did Miss Nosy Britches say Kim," asked Annie poised to pounce.

"I know you don't like her but she has been a big supporter of me and Tim since we came to Gordon," replied Kim in a superficially defensive manner.

"Cut the crap Kim. I know you don't like her either. Don't worry, I am not going to confront her or anything. I just want to know what I am dealing with."

Kim took a breath and said, "Best to my recollection she said something along the lines of: 'Annie seems to have a real problem with being impulsive in the romance department, doesn't she?' Annie's face seemed to get tight with anger as Kim continued.

"I corrected her and told her that you were being level-headed about it all, but she said she was just worried that you were going to make another mistake like you did with Darrell." Kim winced a bit because she was pretty sure what was coming next. And she was right.

"That self-righteous busy-body!" quipped Annie. "Who does she think that she is butting into my life? Did she say anything else?"

"Oh gosh, why are you making me do this?" said Kim. Kim wanted to change the subject but the wine worked on her like truth serum. She bit her lower lip and sheepishly continued, "She did say something about Meagan smoking pot and how you should stay close to home and keep an eye on her rather than going out with a man who had a suspicious past."

Annie looked like she was going to explode. She closed her eyes and sought to calm down. When she opened them back up, she saw Kim waiting for an eruption of sorts. What Kim got was something very different.

"Well, she might have a point about Meagan. I am really working on how to shift my gears with her to help her make the transition from a child to a young woman. It is hard. I agree in theory with Ruth about our kids being our first priority. But she has no idea what it is like to be a single parent. I know her kids are all-stars and have never even inhaled second hand smoke of any kind. But I am pretty much alone in trying to teach Meagan some scruples without a father around to help me."

"I know, I know" replied Kim. "Don't get mad I am on your side, remember?"

Annie smiled at her entrapped friend and said "I know you are. I am sorry that I got you to spill the beans. I am just very protective over my relationship with Bart. He is the best thing that has happened to me since Meg was born!" Annie started to cry a little. She got mad because she didn't want anyone else to see her, so she quickly wiped her face and took a more generous sip of wine this time. She cleared her throat and said, "So how are you and your terrific husband doing?"

Kim looked away for a moment and then reengaged. What Annie saw startled her. "Ok I guess Annie."

"Please don't tell me you guys are having problems."

"Ok, I won't tell you" replied Kim, nervously laughing while pouring herself another glass of wine.

"Dear Lord, what is going on?" asked a rattled Annie.

"Tim is a good man Annie, but he takes me for granted. He is the consummate pastor. He is a great preacher and always available for his flock when they have a need. But the time he spends with me seems obligatory. Like this is what he is supposed to do to be a godly man. To tell the truth I am sick of the church and sick of our lives!"

Annie did her best to regain her composure but her efforts weren't working very well. "Kim, does Tim know this?"

"I suppose deep down he does. But Tim thinks that I will just keep my head down and try to make it work. I went to see a counselor about a year ago but it didn't really help me because they didn't understand the pressures of ministry. Everybody claims that they know you are human, but they don't treat you that way. You can never get mad. You can never say a bad word. And if certain people knew I drank wine they would probably have conniption fit and say I am an alcoholic. Honestly Annie if it weren't for you and the girls, I would have probably already left him."

"Are you an alcoholic Kim?" asked Annie in the most compassionate way she could muster.

"What if I am?" snapped Kim. "Would that de-legitimize everything I have just said?"

Annie never saw this side of Kim. She was beyond angry. She was seething with a kind of bitterness that takes years to develop. She reached out and grabbed her friend's hand and said, "Not one bit. I am just worried and you know that I won't judge you or abandon you if you were."

"Are you sure you won't judge or abandon me Annie?" replied a somber Kim. "You have no idea about the struggles I have been going through. Everyone has their limits you know."

Kim's rapid conversion from anger to a kind of numb resignation bothered Annie. She wondered how she could have not noticed the deep pain and despondency that Kim had been struggling with for a long time. She really didn't know what to do. Although they quickly changed subjects and even told each other some funny stories, Annie felt dogged by her worries for her best friend. Over the next several few days these worries would change into shock, and her friend's strange little prophecy would come close to being fulfilled.

On Monday, Annie got Meagan into the car early in the morning. They had an 8:30 a.m. appointment in Charlotte to do a follow up visit for her heart health. After her aortic replacement that she underwent at five, she went about every few months for evaluation. Then she went yearly until she was ten. Since she was ten years old the yearly visits now were less often. She was due for a checkup, because it had been a while and the practice wanted to see if the growing pains of adolescence had made an impact on her heart.

When the doctor's office called Annie last month to schedule a routine checkup she reluctantly agreed. A few times she almost rescheduled. She knew Meg needed to be seen. She just didn't relish that much face time with her unruly daughter. Now Annie was excited because she wanted to take this opportunity of to talk with Meg. And going sixty-five miles per hour made it tough for her daughter to run away.

They first went by Larry's Biscuit Shop to get some breakfast. Larry and his new girlfriend Leticia were busy as bees. Leticia was helping the cooks crank out some orders and Larry was standing on his custom stool and manning the cash register. Annie grabbed their food, said some quick hellos and then left so she could get on the bypass and merge onto I-40 as quickly as they could.

Once they started cruising on the interstate, Annie cleared her throat and said, "Meg I have to apologize to you for something."

Meagan looked shocked and spoke through the bite she had just taken of her pork tenderloin biscuit, "About what Mom?"

"Well, I realize that I have come at you the wrong way about some of your struggles. I know you are growing up and I shouldn't try to hammer you with automatic limitations of your freedom."

"I don't get what you are saying," said the dazed teen.

"I need to give you more freedom not less. But what that means is that I also have to be plainer about the connection between choices and consequences."

"I still don't get it Mom. Is this some information you got from a new parenting book or something? Oh, I know. Your counselor has told you how to handle me now."

"Not really. But she has helped. It has just occurred to me that you need to start learning about what it means to be an adult. So instead of trying to give you unrealistic boundaries and then almost expecting you to fail, I want to widen the road a bit. This means that from now on I want to help you to see the consequences for the choices you make."

"Sounds to me like the same old stuff Mom." Meagan rolled her eyes and took another bite of biscuit.

"Ok," said Annie as she paused and regrouped. "The law of choices and consequences works for everyone at some level. If you work hard at school you make better grades, right?"

"I suppose," said Meagan.

"If you don't, you get worse grades and eventually that limits the kinds of colleges you can apply to and even makes it harder for you to break the bad habit of laziness."

"Are you worried I am going to end up pregnant living at the Sattler Arms Hotel or something?"

"No. Is there something you need to tell me?"

Meagan grinned. "Don't worry. I am still a virgin … at least for the time being."

Annie felt rattled. She ignored the comment and changed the subject. "Now, let's take the issue of pot."

Meagan let out a huff and blurted out, "Here we go. "I thought your new ideas were going to lead to this discussion, I told you that it was just one-time Mom. Geez, when are you going to let it go?"

"Just be patient with me. I really don't want to argue with you. But it is important for you to understand this stuff. There are some adults that don't and they are constantly moving from one crisis to another."

"This applies to you too huh?"

"Yes."

"Well what about the deal with Darrell?"

This is where Annie would typically lose her temper and try to overpower her daughter. She paused and then said, "That is a good example Meg. Dating Darrell was a choice I made. Instead of being cautious I jumped in without learning more about him as a person. The consequence is that I was treated more like a plaything than an individual. When the dust settled after he started seeing someone else behind my back people questioned my decision-making process."

"So, how do you know that you aren't doing the same thing with Bart?"

"Good question," said Annie in a surprisingly non-defensive manner. "Bart and I took it a lot slower early on. There were a lot of conversations over the phone and even emails before we started officially dating on a regular basis. It is also a more mature relationship because it is not based on having fun or being attracted to each other. We do have fun and we are attracted to each other, but I would say that we are first and foremost wonderful friends."

"What are you going to do if you discover something about his character that is bad?" asked Meagan in a spirit of cross-examination. Annie thought to herself *"This kid could have a great future as a litigator."*

Annie gathered herself again and then said, "I suppose I would have to re-assess our relationship at that point. The honest truth is that there are times you think you are making sound decisions in one situation and then discover later through additional information that it was a bad choice. Making good choices is not a fail-proof way to avoid pain. But it sure helps in avoiding less pain."

Meagan didn't immediately reply. She sat back and seemed deep in thought. "This makes sense. So how does this apply to pot?"

"I am glad you asked. Instead of laying down the law and promising the kind of severe punishment that is hard to carry out, I am going to give you a scenario of good and bad consequences."

"Sounds like a bad deal for me regardless of what you call it."

"Not necessarily. First here are the bad consequences. If it is revealed that you are smoking pot again, I will no longer permit you to hang out with whoever you were with when it happened. I will also regularly have you tested over a period of six months at unpredictable times."

"You are a Nazi in an Anne Taylor dress!"

Annie laughed but kept on task. "Then, if you refuse to be tested or if you are caught again, I would increase the amount of testing and then have you go through counseling for at least six months."

"Mom, this is ridiculous!"

"I am not finished. If you are caught again after that or if you refuse to go to counseling, I will believe that you have a bigger problem than I anticipated and will send you to an off-site rehab program."

"You mean like one of those Boot Camps I have seen on TV?"

"I would only send you to a place that has a proven track record at helping addicts."

"This is like some Kurt Vonnegut novel or something," said Meagan as she stared out the window.

"Wow, I am impressed that you have expanded your reading beyond *Us* magazine!" But the key here Meg is that as the parent I set what I believe to be fair boundaries. It is your choice what you are going to do with them. And it is only fair to you that you know them in advance."

"What are the good consequences for not smoking pot?" asked the blown away teen.

"The main one is trust. The result is that I will give you more freedom not less. Some of your friends will say stuff like 'I can't believe that your Mom lets you do that!' You will in turn respond, 'It is because she trusts me.' And then you will start learning that freedom and responsibility go hand-in-hand. This will put you ahead of many of your peers in the journey of growing up."

"I like the freedom thing." She thought a bit more and said, "Does this apply to everything like dating and other issues?"

"Yep" replied Annie in a matter-of-fact way. "You see this is not about punishment but discipline. Punishment is reserved for people who just don't get it. Discipline is something that successful people will eventually apply to their own lives in order to create more freedom and opportunity."

Annie and Meagan continue to have maybe one of the best conversations in the history of their relationship. Typically, there would be long stretches of silence or even the occasional argument if they were travelling together in the car. But now they both felt that this conversation of mutual respect was uplifting and stress-free.

Before they knew it, they were parking at the doctor's office and Meagan was finding a seat in the waiting room while her Mom checked in. Within about five minutes they were called back by a nurse, weighed in and were placed in Examination Room Three.

The first person to see them was a Physician Assistant named Paula. Paula had been with the practice a long time and was on board when Meg had her surgery. She was an upbeat lady that knew how to make anyone feel comfortable. She specialized in explaining complicated conditions and procedures in a way that made a patient and their family feel empowered.

Paula greeted Annie and Meagan with a huge hug, and pulled out a candy cane stick for Meg. This piece of candy always seemed to help Meg calm down when blood was taken or a procedure was performed.

"Am I going to get stuck today?" asked a now nervous Meagan.

"I'm afraid so sweetie" replied the wise PA. "That's why I brought you this" pointing to the red and white stick of candy.

"Can I have one of those too?" joked Annie.

"Sure" replied Paula as she whipped out another treat. "Now Meagan I am going to take some blood, listen to your heart, get your blood pressure and then get a sonogram of your heart muscle before Dr. Vance sees you."

"Would you heat up that gel stuff?" asked Meagan. The last time I was here they forgot and that goo was so dang cold!"

Paula laughed and then said "No problem. Ok pull up your gown and let me listen to your ticker."

Megan pulled up her shirt. Annie noticed that her daughter was starting to blossom some more and that she had obviously outgrown her current bra. This embarrassed Annie terribly and made her feel like an out of touch Mom.

Paula finished and made the comment that "You will have no problem wearing a bikini young lady. Dr. St. Claire did a marvelous job. Your scar is barely recognizable."

Meagan and Annie both gasped at the same time. Annie regained her composure first and said, "What was his name?"

"Dr. Ian St. Claire" replied Paula. "Is there a problem?"

"No. It is just that we know another St. Claire that used to be surgeon.

"Well, I am sure he is not the same person" said Paula. You two sit tight and the sonographer will be in shortly. It is great to see both of you. You have come a long ways sweetie!"

As soon as Paula closed the door Megan spoke up, "Mom, you don't think that it is Bart, do you?"

"No" said Annie trying to hide her panic.

"What will you do if it is? If it is him that would be so gross!"

Annie looked away for a second and then there was a tap on the door. The sonographer walked in. Megan knew the drill. She lay down on the table, pulled up her gown and loosened her bra. The technician pulled the machine close, sat on a stool and applied the warm gel on Meg's chest. She then made a series of sweeping circular moves as she occasionally clicked on a mouse that sat on a compact space attached to what looked like a really fat computer screen. In a few minutes the young lady was finished and handed the teen a fresh towel to clean up with when she sat up. "The doctor will be in here soon," said the sonographer in soothing manner.

When she left Meg looked at her Mom and asked "Are you going to mention the Dr. St. Claire deal to him?"

"I don't know, but I sure don't want you to say anything ok?"

"I won't if you do. But if you don't then I am going to ask him. This is so freaky!"

Within a few moments Dr. Sid Vance walked through the door. He was a handsome gentleman in his early fifties that was a very meticulous, deliberate physician who was always immaculately dressed. Dr. Vance made Megan feel cared for with his calm and careful manner. He had a girl Meg's age so Annie believed that was why he took such a special interest in her daughter.

"Good morning ladies!" announced Dr. Vance. "I was looking at your chart and pictures and everything seems to be outstanding!" Meg looked at her Mom and motioned in a way that indicated she wanted her Mom to say something and Annie shook her head in disagreement.

"So, let me listen to your heart if you don't mind. I know Paula did it but I just want to make sure myself." Meagan hesitated a little since she was becoming more mature, but Annie winked at her to make her feel more at ease.

About every four seconds he asked Meg to take a deep breath and would nod with each beat he heard. After moving from front to back on her upper body, he looked up and winked at her saying "You can put your clothes back on in a minute. I know it is kind of icky to let an old dude put a cold instrument to your chest. I bet my daughter Emily wouldn't even let me do it to her."

Dr. Vance sat moved away from the table on his stool with rollers. He spun around to talk to Annie giving Meagan enough privacy to take off her gown and put her shirt back on.

"I can say with excitement that the valve seems to be working perfectly. No abnormal heart rhythm and the pictures reveal a heart working the way it should for a healthy teen age girl. We will get the blood work back in a couple of days and if there is any abnormality, I will call you. Do either of you have any questions?"

"I do!" announced Meagan. "I know you were sick the day I was operated on. Who was the surgeon who did the work?'

"Well, you were very fortunate. Dr. Ian St. Claire was available and stepped in for me. He was a world-renowned guy in the valve replacement area. And he was practically a plastic surgeon when it came to closing people up. Your scar seems to be almost invisible now. Amazing work."

Annie gave Meg the hush sign with her finger and butted in, "You said used to, did he die?'

"No" replied Dr. Vance. "He went through some horrible personal problems and then had a routine oblation procedure go terribly wrong on him and a patient died. He ended up leaving medicine and no one really knows where he ended up."

"I know someone but his name is Bart St. Claire" replied Annie in a hopeful way. "I guess it is not the same guy, … is it?"

"Bart you say," said the doctor stroking his chin. "Ian used to be called that until he went to Medical School at Yale. His full name is Ian Bartlett St. Claire. He got his middle name from his mother's family. That's why they called him Bart. Do you know him? I would love to chat and catch up."

Annie got up abruptly and shook the doctor's hand saying "No, the person I know is a chef. Thanks for your help and we will be in touch."

Dr. Vance looked a little confused but accepted Annie's quick response. The three of them exchanged good-byes and they followed him out of the room to the front desk to check out.

There were no words exchanged between Annie and Meagan from the time they left the office until they left downtown Charlotte and went south to go to a couple of shops and grab a bite to eat.

Finally, Meg broke the ice. "It has got to be him Mom. You know it. What are you going to do?"

Annie looked to be in a different world. She recalled seeing Bart in his surgical suit and cap after Meg's surgery. He didn't have a goatee back then and was wearing glasses when he debriefed Annie and Tom about their daughter's condition. She now knew why she thought she recognized him.

"How could I have been so stupid?"

"What are you talking about Mom?" Meagan looked worried.

Annie mustered up her best smile and said. "Don't sweat it sweetie. Let's go have some fun and I will figure out how I will handle the doctor ok?"

"He has no idea what is going to hit him does he Mommy?

Annie lowered her head and gripped the steering wheel with great ferocity. "No Miss Meagan he does not!"

CHAPTER 8

THE SMOLDERING EMBERS of Annie's rage did not dissipate the rest of that day. In fact, they spread to the degree that the noxious smoke from the growing fire of her anger clouded her vision about everything and everyone.

Meagan first noticed it when her mom was uncharacteristically surly with the sandwich maker at one of their favorite sandwich shops. He had put mayonnaise on her turkey, bacon and lettuce sandwich when Annie was abundantly clear she did not want any. After reaming the young man out the manager came by their booth and offered to make her another sandwich. Annie ignored the manager's bid to foster good will. She snapped up out of her seat, grabbed her pocketbook and announced to him, "No, we are leaving and I will never be back again!" Before he could respond she walked out. Meagan quickly got up and hurried out the door with her sloshing drink and partially-eaten sandwich in hand.

Then an hour later Annie stormed out of a clothing store in a real snit when her question about a particular pair of jeans they were looking for was totally ignored by a gum-chomping, twenty-something employee. Meagan was put off by the salesperson's behavior too. "Yeah, he was a real jerk," she agreed as they practically were sailing by the stores on their way to get a cup of coffee. But her mom's frustration didn't disappear with her daughter's feeble effort at calming Annie down. She seemed to ignore Meagan's attempt to what Meagan said when she pronounced "These young kids know nothing about true customer service. I am better off ordering your stuff online!"

At some point Meagan thought her Mom would snap out of it. But Annie seemed to be locked down in an almost unconscious state of irritation. It didn't matter what they were doing or where they were, Annie found something to complain about. These rapid-fire ejaculations of condemnation seemed to send Annie deeper into the vortex of her sulfurous indignation. Eventually Annie threw up her hands and told Meagan," I can't put up with this anymore. We are going home." Meagan didn't say anything. She knew it would be pointless.

For a few minutes there was a lull in Annie's emotional firestorm. They got back on I-77 and then on I-40 without speaking a word to each other. About half-way home Annie tried to apologize to her daughter.

"Meg," I, I … Annie got so choked up she couldn't speak.

"It's ok Mommy. I know you are upset."

Annie shook her head and quickly wiped his eyes with her sleeve. Her mind was ablaze with both self-recriminations about her poor decision-making and bitter invectives she was planning on spewing all over Bart.

She gritted her teeth and tried to "suck it up" the way her Dad taught her when she was a little girl and she skinned her knee or didn't get invited to a party. Annie hated losing control of her emotions like this. She didn't want Meg growing up thinking that when things got tough women were supposed to fall to pieces.

She tried to shift her attention onto a couple of projects she needed to wrap up at work. When this didn't work, she turned up the radio, but no matter what station she picked, every song that was playing seemed to be talking about love. No distraction seemed to ease her boiling wound.

Meagan saw what was happening and took over radio duty, finding a classical station that was featuring some kind of Mozart festival. Annie knew that Megan hated that kind of "funeral music." She smiled at her daughter.

"You and I make a good team don't we darling!"

"Yes, Mommy we do."

"Who needs a stupid man anyway, right?"

Meagan didn't answer. She was afraid to. She wanted her Mom to be ok. She gave her best cheerleader grin to the fragile woman and then looked back out the passenger window. They traveled the rest of the way back to Gordon in almost complete silence.

When they arrived home, they retreated to their respective safe zones. They spoke briefly a little later when they ate some leftover homemade chicken noodle soup while watching some news and a full episode of Wheel of Fortune. Meagan went back to her room and Annie fell asleep on the couch only to be startled awake later by the dog barking at her around midnight. She took the pooch out the front door in her pajamas and bare feet, not caring about the cold or her appearance.

By the time she got to bed she didn't bother pulling down the comforter. Neither did she remove all of her decorative pillows. She simply carved a spot out for herself of the right side of the bed and pulled her grandmothers quilt over her and went to sleep.

When Tuesday rolled around Annie was on a mission to take care of her looming problem. In her rush to get ready, she said very few words to Meg as they hurried through breakfast and then jumped into the car.

Finally, as Annie was driving her to school her baby girl spoke up and said, "Mom, are you going to say something to Bart?" Annie looked at Meg with such sober intention that Meg suddenly felt like a shipwrecked soul doing backstrokes over the Marianas Trench. All she could muster in response to the stare was "Sorry for asking."

After Annie dropped Meg off at Middle School, she made a beeline for Angelo's. She knew that Bart would be there by himself and she didn't want nosy ears picking up on a single syllable she was going to utter. She pulled up to the back and parked alongside of Bart's truck. It didn't take her long to whip out the key that Bart had given to her and opened the heavy door.

Bart heard the beep on the security system and got up from his desk smiling as he and Frodo went to greet their favorite person. He had no clue what was getting ready to happen.

"Hey good looking!" piped up Bart.

"We need to talk," responded Annie without making eye contact. She brushed by him and marched straight into his office. Annie stood in the office waiting for Bart to sit down. He did and asked "What's up darling?" She stood with her face down tapping her right foot.

"Do you know where me and Meg went yesterday?"

"Yeah I think you said she had a doctor's appointment."

"She had a heart check-up in Charlotte Bart."

For a split second it didn't hit him. Maybe it was because he believed that the old Ian had died. Or maybe his love for Annie had finally allowed him the sweet luxury of opening up his heart without a worry about the consequences. Whatever the reason he genuinely felt confused. And then the truth grabbed him by the throat.

"Oh," said the guilty man.

"Oh?" shouted Annie. "Is that the best the world-renowned surgeon can do? Can you possibly even imagine what I am feeling right now?"

"No, I can't Annie," sighed Bart. He immediately started making his plans in that brilliant mind to find the least painful exit strategy out of the relationship and even out of Gordon.

"Well, let me tell you. I trusted you with my heart. A lot of my family and friends warned me not to, but good old naïve Annie jumped right in and fell in love. Now I wonder how much of this was real because I wonder how real you are."

Bart sat almost completely motionless as he leaned back and prepared to take more of the much-deserved verbal whipping. "That makes perfect sense. I would feel the same way."

"What is wrong with you?" asked Annie in utter frustration. She shook her head and violently flailed her arms around to emphasize her anger with the man who was now breaking her heart. She took a breath to make sure she wouldn't start crying and lose her superior offensive position in the argument. But in fact, it wasn't much of an argument at all. It was like taking target practice with a Howitzer at an indoor shooting range.

When she realized that he wasn't going to argue with her she decided to cut the cord. She pulled off the key to the restaurant and threw it at him. "I am done. I don't want to see you or hear from you ever again!" Then Annie spun around and quickly exited with her pride somewhat intact.

Once she reached her car she jumped in, turned on the ignition and got ready to put the car in reverse. Then the waves of grief started pounding on the shore of her devastated heart. She started to sob and then wail. She kept repeating the phrase "Why God, why?" as she pounded the dashboard.

After a few seconds she regained some emotional self-control and backed out of the parking lot and jammed the car into first gear. She hauled down Main Street so fast and so recklessly that it caused Fareesh to step out of Stardust's and look with worry as he saw his friend speed off.

By the time Annie reached the Center she had decided to pretend that nothing was wrong. She quickly re-applied her makeup and walked in the center greeting everyone she saw in the main lobby. She made a right turn by the nurses' station and walked into her office and closed the door. Laying down her briefcase and pocketbook she powered-up her computer to pull up her appointment and tasks she had scheduled for today.

When her Outlook popped up, she noticed a message from Joanne Hartsell the Assistant Principal of Gordon Middle School. The short message read "We Need to Talk About Meagan ASAP!"

At first Annie decided for the sake of emotional self-preservation she would wait to read the message after lunch. If there was an emergency they would call. Just then her phone went off and she recognized it was coming from the school. Annie closed her eyes and said, "Oh dear God, how bad can this day get?"

She mustered up her remaining emotional resilience and answered "Hello, this is Annie Bryant."

"Annie, this is Joanne at the Middle School. Did you get my email?"

"I just got into the office and was reading it when you called. Is everything alright?"

"I am afraid not."

"What is going on Joanne?"

"Well, I was looking out my office window waiting for a parent to show up with a package so I could meet them outside and help them get on their way. I saw you drop Meagan off. The problem is that she didn't come into the building. I saw her make a phone call. She kept standing outside until someone picked her up. I think it was Tommy

Blankenship. They took off and so I sent you an email as quickly as I could.

"This doesn't make sense Joanne."

"I can imagine how you might feel. But to be honest there have been some rumors that the two have been spending a lot of time together. This concerns me because Tommy was caught a few months ago selling some pot. Did Tee mention this to you?"

Annie started shaking a little. She recalled telling her friends last fall about Meg's run in with the law. Tee acted surprised but promised she would keep Meg in her prayers. Now Annie was wondering how many people were hiding difficult truths from her.

"No, she didn't Joanne" commented Annie in an exasperated voice.

"Well, we have a school official out looking for them. I will let you know if we find them, ok? I am so sorry about this. We still need to meet and talk sometime about Meagan's slide in academic performance. Do you want to schedule it now or later?"

"Definitely later," whispered Annie trying her best to keep her composure. "Thanks for your phone call. Goodbye." Annie hung up before she heard Joanne say goodbye. She hit the speed dial number for Tee and waited."

"Hey girl," Tee replied. "What are you up to this fine morning?"

"Oh, I don't know how fine it is Tee. It seems that your son Tommy just picked up my daughter at the Middle School a few minutes ago."

There was a long pause of silence on the other end of the phone. "Tee, are you still there?" questioned Annie. "Yeah," replied Tee in a voice of resignation. "I will be right over to your office." Tee hung up and Annie wondered how much her friend knew. She was never drawn to conspiracy theories but now she felt like questioning everything she knew to be true.

Tee got to the Center in around five minutes. When she walked into Annie's office her face reflected one of familiar panic. She didn't sit down but told Annie "Let's go. I think I might know where they could be." Tee took one look at Annie and she knew that she had better be honest with her friend right now if she had any chance of retaining her friendship.

The two got into Tee's diesel Mercedes and puttered off. Tee looked straight ahead and started as best as she could to enlighten Annie while turning north onto the bypass. "Miller and I were suspicious of Tommy about a year ago … Phone calls in the middle of the night; people dropping by the house that we didn't know; catching him in silly lies about where he had been and stuff like that."

Annie glared at Tee because she could almost guess what was coming next. Tee pretended not to notice and knew she had better get to the bottom line quickly.

"Anyway, Miller found a bong under Tommy's bed in his old suitcase one night when Tommy went to a football game last fall. Miller texted him and said something along the lines that he should "get your sorry ass home now." Tommy complied quickly because his Daddy never talks like that. Miller met him at the door and jerked him inside. I just knew he was going to beat him half-to-death"

Annie showed not even an ounce of empathy.

"When I tried to intervene, Miller looked at me like a wild animal. I backed off."

"He should have beaten him" replied Annie as she shook her head in disgust.

"Well, Miller slammed Tommy into the couch and then stood there just trembling with rage. Both Tommy and I were scared. Miller calmed down and asked him how long he had been smoking and where he got it from. Tommy didn't answer. That's when Miller slapped him."

Tee's lower lip started quivering as her tears started spattering the steering wheel and the front of her blouse. "Oh Annie, he hit him so hard that I thought he broke that child's face. Miller stood him up and then said 'Boy if you don't tell me the truth I will beat you senseless!' I knew where this was coming from."

Annie suddenly got a lump in her throat. She remembered too. About thirty years ago Miller's twin brother Michael overdosed on cocaine. Miller was disconsolate. He felt his parents were too easy on Mike and their enablement led to his brother's downfall. To this day Miller can't talk about Mike. But he did name Tommy after his beloved twin – Michael Thomas Blankenship.

As Tommy grew, he started to look and act a lot like his deceased uncle. Everyone commented on it but Miller. Annie knew that Miller worried about his youngest son. She also knew that if he had could beat this impulse out of Tommy, he would do it without blinking.

Tee gathered herself again. "Right before I thought it was going to end very badly Tommy started crying. Miller picked him up in those old burly arms and started crying too. He then slipped up and said 'I don't want to lose you Mikey!' Tommy looked over at me. He knew what was going on. He patted his big Daddy on the head and said, 'Don't worry Pop I am not going to do it again.'"

Tee wiped her face on her sleeve and smeared makeup all over it. She didn't care. "Miller calmed down and then told Tommy he couldn't use his car for the rest of the year. He also got drug tested a few times. Miller and I thought it was over."

Annie looked straight at Tee and said, "Why didn't you tell me, especially when I had all that trouble with Meg?"

Tee shook her head in humble agreement. "You are right. You should be mad as hell. But Miller made me swear I wouldn't tell a soul. When I told him about Meg he went straight to Tommy and asked him if he knew anything. Tommy lied to us Annie."

"How did you find this out?" asked Annie in a calmer fashion.

"We discovered this right before Tommy was arrested back in January. I found a notebook with names, the symbol for ounces and money amounts in columns. Meagan's name appeared about four times in the notebook."

"Four times? Oh my God Tee! What is wrong with you?"

"You don't understand. I didn't want Meg to get arrested Annie. When Miller saw the notebook, he got so furious that he told the Chief of Police. They followed Tommy for about three weeks before they caught him red-handed in a deal."

Annie bent over like she was going to get sick, "Oh my God, O my God. You should have told me Tee." Annie started crying again. Tee tried to reach out and console her but Annie recoiled at her friend's touch.

"No matter what happens you had better keep your boy away from my kid or I swear to God I will take my Dad's shotgun and shoot him Tee!" screamed Annie. Although Tee would step in front of her son if this was attempted, she understood Annie's rage at her son. Tee then took the exit to Sawyer's Mountain Park.

Annie looked around and said, "Is this where he does his deals?"

"This is where he was arrested. Look Annie I know you are mad at me and my son, but let's just be calm about this ok?"

Annie looked at Tee as if she had just stepped off of a space ship with three heads and a ray gun announcing peaceful intentions. "No, you look" growled Annie. "My kid is fourteen, yours is almost seventeen. I am not making excuses for my kid. I promise you she will be dealt with. But I will deal with Tommy any way I see fit including calling the police on him for taking a minor off of school property!"

Tee recognized she was fighting a losing battle. She now wished that she had told Miller where she was going and why when she left the store in such a hurry. As the rounded to the top of the park they saw Tommy and Meg sitting on his Mustang talking.

"Dear Lord!" blurted Meg. "There are our Moms. We are so dead!"

"Hey don't worry about it" said Tommy in his coolest voice. "Your Mom likes me. I'll just explain that you were real upset about your family problems and needed someone to talk to. Just let me handle it."

Meagan looked at him and said, "It is your funeral."

Tommy slid off the hood and waived at the quickly approaching Mercedes. Annie was the first to jump out. She moved rapidly towards the car. Tommy grinned and stuck out his hand to Annie "Hey Mrs. Bryant."

Annie grabbed his hand and twisted around his back, slamming him against the hood of his car. "Ouch" yelled Tommy. "Meg, tell your Mom to calm down!" Meg didn't utter a sound but prayed that her Mom would not do worse to her.

"Young man, you have no clue how much trouble you are in!" barked Annie. She released his arm but Tommy stayed on the hood of the car waiting to see if she was going to pull any more martial arts move on him. Annie walked over to Megan and said, "Get off this car right now!" Meg swiftly complied.

Tee spoke up and said "Tommy, how could you?!" She couldn't bear to look at him. She stared at the ground hoping there would that some kind of sincere remorse would flow from his heart and out his lips.

"We weren't doing anything wrong. Geez, why do you have to be such a loser?"

Annie lurched at him and said, "Shut your face! You are lucky to have such a kind-hearted mother. But I bet your Dad won't be as nice huh?" Tommy looked over to his Mom in a very frightened fashion. "You are not going to tell Dad are you Mom?"

Tee shook her head in disgust and then said "I have made a lot of mistakes with you but I won't make that one. You bet I am going to tell your Dad!"

Annie pulled her cell phone from her pocketbook and dialed her Dad's number. He picked up on the second ring. "Hey daughter, what can I do for you?"

"Dad," said Annie in an exhausted tone, "would you please come and pick up me and Meg at Sawyers Mountain Park? I will explain later. Thanks." Annie turned back to Tee and said "Y'all go back to town. I will wait on Dad here. It won't take him long."

Tee nodded and then motioned her son to get into the car. They took off in a puff of black smoke, leaving Annie and Meg overlooking the town of Gordon below. As they stood speechless in an empty parking lot, Meg tried to say something. "Mom, I just want to say ..."

Annie put up her hand to silence her daughter then she looked straight at her. "We are going straight to school and talk with Mrs. Hartsell first. It seems you aren't doing very well in school and I want to find out more. Then we are going straight to your pediatrician's office and I am going to get you tested for drugs. If you have been doing anything it will come out and I will make good my promise to you that we spoke of yesterday."

"I'm sorry Mom," said Meagan. She knew that Annie was going to drop the hammer of judgment on her and that there was nothing she could do about it.

Annie didn't even look at her daughter as she prophesied "I promise you, you are going to be sorrier than your little brain can ever dream."

Jake pulled up to the ladies right after Annie spoke this foreboding injunction to Meg. They both got into the car without speaking a word or making a sound. Jake drove off knowing that something big was happening. He didn't ask because he had been around long enough to know that if he needed to be involved, he would be recruited.

After the grueling visits to the school and doctor Annie and Meagan got home totally exhausted. Neither spoke to the other from the time they left the pediatrician's office till they arrived back at the house. Meagan went through the door first, ran into her bedroom, closed the door and started crying.

Annie ignored her daughter's familiar cries of shallow grief. Annie felt that she could barely put one foot in front of the other. She stumbled into her bedroom and collapsed on her bed. Sensing that old familiar feeling of mind-numbing anxiety she reached to her nightstand on the right and grabbed the bottle of Xanax. She popped one pill in her mouth and, without the aid of any water, chewed it up ignoring the bitter taste that lathered her tongue.

After a few minutes she looked at the clock on the nightstand to her left and saw that it was 5:30 p.m. The voice of duty momentarily took hold and urged her to go to the kitchen to fix some dinner. But the more overwhelming sense of apathy trumped the calmer voice of duty. After making what she hoped was the last major decision of her stress-filled day she closed her eyes and fell into a deep slumber.

The next thing she remembered was waking up to the dog's barking. She sat straight up in bed and looked to her left. It was 8:32 p.m.

"What has happened to the time?" questioned Annie groggily. She got up to check on Meagan and the doorbell rang. The dog started barking again. Meagan moaned from her bedroom, "Mom, are you going to get that?" Annie thought of a lot of things she could say but was too tired to show any level of wit at this stage in the game.

Annie slid in her socks to the front door and looked through the peephole. There stood Tim and Kim Spenser with a picnic basket. She opened the door and said in a slightly slurred manner, "Is this your Meals on Wheels ministry for tonight?"

They smiled and Tim replied, "We thought we would visit the backslidden folks of the church and your name was on the top of the list!" He hoped that his dry sense of humor wouldn't be met with anger. Annie gave them her best fake smile and opened the door.

Tim took the basket into the kitchen and laid it on the counter. Kim followed Annie into the den and sat on the couch as Annie flopped down into her favorite leather chair. Tim soon joined the ladies and sat beside Kim on the couch.

For about thirty seconds nothing was said. Tim decided to jump in and tell their friend the purpose of their late visit. "We're here tonight Annie because we know you have had the day from hell. Bart came by and talked with me, and Tee spent some time with Kim this afternoon. We tried to reach you by phone but your Dad called us back to tell us that you evidently left your phone in his car. We decided to make up some food for you with the hopes you were up for a visit. I really don't know what to say other than that."

"Well Pastor," uttered Annie, "neither do I."

Kim looked at Annie and said, "I've brought my pajamas because I am going to spend the night with you."

"That's really not necessary Kim. Unless you are here to prevent me from killing my kid, I really don't see the reason why you would volunteer for such petrifying duty?"

Kim winked at Annie and said "Scary is my middle name!"

"Whatever. I am too tired to argue with you" said Annie looking at the ceiling while trying not to cry.

Tim took the lead again and said "Well, I am going to leave you girls to figure out all the world's problems. Annie, I am keeping you in my prayers." Tim stood up and went over to the slouching Annie and gave her a kiss on top of the head. He walked back to his wife and gave her a peck on the lips and said "Call me if you need me."

"Thanks Tim" said a washed-out Annie.

Tim left the house and the sound of his car driving off prompted Annie to break the silence. "You got a good man there Kim. Better hold on to him because there are not that many around."

Kim bowed her head. She knew Annie was right. "Well thanks, but we are not here to talk about me but about you. How are you holding up?"

Annie laughed. She starred straight at Kim with her eyes welling up with tears and said, "By a thread sweetie, by a thread." Kim looked at her and could tell she was speaking the truth. She didn't know what to say or do.

As she was struggling with this dilemma Meagan walked in and announced "Mom I am starving. What do we have to eat around here?" Annie didn't say anything. The last thing on her mind right that second was worrying about what her kid had to eat. She knew that her parental instinct should kick in, but she wasn't feeling very empathic or noble at this moment. It was hard to feel hatred towards the fruit of your womb.

Kim spoke to Meagan and said "Tim and I brought a Chicken Casserole, a salad, some fresh bread and banana pudding. It's in the kitchen." Meagan loved Kim's Chicken Casserole, so any excuse not being around her angry Mom was a welcomed diversion. Annie marveled at how Meagan could remotely be hungry after the day they had been through. It occurred to her that maybe this was what it was like for a prisoner the night before they were to be executed.

"Is there any wine in the house?" asked Kim interrupting Annie's maudlin fantasy.

"There is a nice bottle of unopened Pinot Grigio in the refrigerator."

Kim got up without saying anything and in about a minute quickly produced two large glasses of white wine.

"You are quite handy with my old wine opener" said Annie as she took her glass from Kim's hand.

Kim nodded in agreement and replied "Yeah, being a pastor's wife gives you a lot of reasons to drink."

"What do you have to worry about girl? People love you and Tim."

Kim looked back towards the kitchen as if she didn't want to make eye-contact at that moment. "I think people love Tim and put up

WALKER ARMSTRONG

with me" she said peering over the back of the couch as if something important was happening right behind her. "Anyway, my problems aren't why I am here. We can talk about that another day."

"You here to fix me?"

"Nope. I am here to listen and love. I am in no position to give advice."

"Well cheers," said Annie as she took a big gulp of wine. "That is the first real helpful thing I have heard all day."

Kim took a big swig herself. "Yeah, well I am good for something other than just being really fabulous eye-candy!" The women both laughed. They each individually needed some frivolity at the moment, but for very different reasons.

Annie walked into Dr. Marsha's office the next day at four in the afternoon. She had called earlier that morning and told Marsha that she needed to meet with her ASAP. Marsha recognized the shaky timbre in Annie's voice and decided to shift some things around so that they could meet. Once they confirmed the time Marsha said, "Don't worry about checking in. Just walk upstairs and knock on my door." And that is exactly what the distraught woman did.

Marsha greeted her with a hug and pointed at the coffee table where a cup of hot tea was waiting on Annie. "I took the liberty of making you some tea. You don't have to drink it if you don't want it."

"No, I do. I could use some soothing right now."

Annie sat down and gingerly picked up the cup with shaking hands. She took a little sip, placed it back on the table and leaned back on the couch.

Marsha looked at her and said. "Something big has happened. What is going on dear?"

"Too much."

"Ok, start wherever you would like and we will see if we have time to talk about it all today."

"Well it's over with me and Bart!"

"Oh my, that is big. Tell me how you came to this huge decision?"

Annie went on to tell her about the revelation of Bart as the surgeon who performed Meagan's heart surgery over ten years ago. Then she shared how he didn't offer a defense about his lack of honesty and "just sat there like a frog on a log while my heart broke right before him."

"So, you are mad because he didn't tell you that he was her doctor?"

"Well, yeah. I mean that is being dishonest and you know how I feel about dishonesty!"

"I think so. But why do you think that this type of dishonesty bothered you so much?"

"What do you mean? Dishonesty is dishonesty, right?"

"Is it?"

Annie felt anger well up in her. "Of course it is!"

"Well, have you ever not offered the whole story of a situation to save someone's feelings or even protect them from further hurt?"

"I suppose so."

"And have you ever not given all of the information you could because it made you look bad?"

"Sure."

"And you still don't think that is different from lying about being unfaithful in a relationship or spinning some fables on a resume?"

Annie sat there for a few seconds. "Well, now that you put it that way, I guess there are different kinds of dishonesty. But you make it sound like it is not that big of a deal!"

"No, I didn't say that. I am just trying to get to the bottom of why you have dumped all this toxic anger on Bart. Was he unfaithful to you?"

"No."

"Did he lie about who he is?"

"No … well maybe a little."

"Ok. So, he was dishonest about being the person who performed her surgery. Did he do a good job operating on Meagan?"

"Yes, he probably saved her life. And he paid a lot of attention to the scar on her chest so she wouldn't be embarrassed wearing a bathing suit one day."

"Did you thank him for that?"

"Well yeah, back then I did,"

"But what about when you let him have it yesterday?"

"No, because I was too mad."

"Interesting. Let me see if I understand: Instead of letting your gratitude over his top-notch performance as Meagan's heart surgeon balance out your concern over a possible pattern of dishonesty, you just totally ignored the good that he did."

"You are making this my fault?"

"You seem really focused on blame here. Do you have any idea what is causing your crusade to find someone to punish in this situation?"

"Marsha, I don't think you understand. I mean, I lived through all that pain with Tom and I vowed never to go through it again."

"No, I do understand it. I just don't see the connection," replied Marsha as she took a long sip of her tea.

"Well, I will not be lied to again."

"Ok, you are saying that Tom's serial unfaithfulness and Bart's omission of the total truth of his identity is the same thing?"

"Why do you do this to me?" shouted Annie as she buried her head in her hands. She sat there for what seemed like a long time and then sat up and looked back at the counselor to find she was still waiting on an answer.

"They are not the same thing, but I am trying to prevent being cheated on again from happening."

"And what is your plan for preventing that?"

"I guess if I a find a man lying to me that I am dating, then I will cut him loose."

"That makes sense."

"Thank you!" said an exasperated Annie.

"But …"

"Oh, dear Lord!" cried Annie acting as if she would pull out her hair.

Marsha kept pressing on. "But we just determined that there are different types of lies. Should those different types of lies warrant different responses?"

"I guess so."

"I would agree with you." Marsha then took her hands and pointed back towards her left ear like a runway worker helps a pilot back up a plane. "Let's take a step back once more: When you talked with Bart, were you in attack mode or information gathering mode?"

Annie got a sad look on her face. "I guess attack mode."

"And what does that remind you of?

Annie looked confused. She and Bart had never had an argument since they had been dating. As she was reviewing past conversations the real truth punched her in the gut. "Oh no ... this is just like the arguments I have had with Tom."

"And is Bart Tom?"

"No. Not by a long shot."

"And still you treated a man you deeply love ... a good, decent but imperfect man the same way you have treated your ex-husband who repeatedly cheated on you. Why do you suppose you did that?"

"I don't know Marsha. I guess I am really screwed up!"

"No dear. You just haven't totally closed the door of a past marriage that ended very badly."

"So, how do I do that?"

"Annie," she said in a tender manner, "You still have to talk with Tom, share the fundamental way he wounded you, how you struggled to overcome your shame. Then, you have to put it behind you. If you don't you won't ever able to have a healthy relationship with a man because deep down you will always wondering when and if the proverbial other shoe will drop."

Annie sat there staring into space. No one had ever such a clear connection between not taking charge over her past pain and her penchant to get very angry with people who let her down.

"This is hard. I guess some part of me still hates Tom."

"There you go" reassured Marsha. "And remember ... the energy of that hate doesn't disappear with time. It dissipates. I would even say that in a way, it lurks around like a big tiger hiding in the jungle waiting to pounce the next time you are hurt. Have you done that recently?"

"Yeah, all day yesterday, and some this morning."

WALKER ARMSTRONG

Annie knew Marsha had discovered the "mother lode" of where her anger was originating. Still, her first response was to sit up and prepare a verbal counter-punch. The only problem was she couldn't utter a sound. The truth of the deal was starring her square in the face. She couldn't avoid the plain simplicity of the fact that her hatred for Tom had helped her to create a strategy for resolving conflicts based on the negative energy of stored anger. Now her choice was if she was willing to do something about it.

Marsha didn't let up. "Look, this is why I keep telling you that you need to tell him two things. First, you need to share the impact of what his betrayal did to you. He knows what he did was wrong. But he may not know what it really did to you."

"And the second thing?"

"You need to tell him that you forgive him. Now, let me tell you what that means to me. The word forgiveness literally means to release. I don't think this is as magical as some people claim. I think it happens in stages. The first step is releasing the natural desire for payback or vengeance."

"You mean, don't hire a hit man?" Annie quipped without missing a beat.

Marsha smiled. "Yes, and that anytime you imagine really wicked stuff happening to him, say a little prayer like 'God I give these feelings to you about Tom. I don't have time for rage and hate.' Makes sense?"

"That's hard but I get that. Anything else?" replied Annie secretly hoping that was it.

"Well, if he asks for forgiveness, you open the door for him to rebuild trust at whatever is appropriate for your relationship at this stage of journey." Marsha waited for Annie's pushback.

Annie looked down at the gnarly pine floors that seemed to have one-hundred years of polyurethane piled on top of each other. Then she did something unexpected. Her head snapped up and with a look of peaceful resolution she said "I am ready to do that Marsha!"

"Wow! I am blown away by you girl!' The veteran counselor leaned back in her chair, stunned by her client's surge of strength in midst of dire heartache.

Annie smiled. It felt good to be moving in the right direction. She looked at Marsha and saw the counselor slightly raise her eyebrows, seemingly looking for something else.

"What?" asked Annie. "Is there more?"

"Yes, but maybe we can talk more next time."

"No, I want to keep going. What do I need to do? Do I need to forgive Bart and Meagan and anyone else on a list?"

"Sure, but do you think there is someone else you need to forgive?"

"Marsha, just please tell me," Annie begged in an exhausted voice.

"You need to forgive Annie," Marsha replied staring into Annie's eyes with a kind of relentless compassion that was impossible to ignore.

"Come again?" retorted Annie as if she was clueless. The only problem was that her counselor sat there quietly still staring into her client's eyes.

"Well, I do need to ask a lot of people to forgive me, that's for sure," said Annie, hoping that would let her off the hook.

Marsha didn't budge. She in fact leaned forward and said, "I'm not talking with you about those situations. You need to forgive yourself for the whole Darrell mess."

Once again Marsha had hit the proverbial nail on the head. Annie hadn't thought about how her affair with Darrell had impacted her relationship with Bart, but it had. She opened up her heart a little more and sincerely asked her counselor, "How does all of this work?"

Marsha closed her eyes and opened up her hands as if she was by herself in a state of deep meditation. "Because you are a person of faith, I will put it this way: Forgiving yourself finds its source in allowing the forgiveness you have asked from God to wrap around your soul like a warm blanket on a wintry evening. The more you become convinced of the deep warmth of God's love for you through the gift of his forgiveness, the more you can let go of your past failures. Then, you can live free and don't constantly live on the edge of allowing the weight of shame and guilt keep you emotionally unbalanced."

"I think I understand," said Annie in a semi-agreeable fashion. "But ow does that work in how I relate to others?"

"What I have learned from my own past is that when you don't forgive yourself you place yourself on a kind of tightrope," said Marsha.

Marsha then opened her eyes, got up out of her chair and stood on top of the coffee table. Annie laughed and clapped her hands in glee. "You see," said Marsha wobbling back and forth. "If you're on a tightrope, any imbalance on your part, even any unpredictable shift in the wind can send you toppling down towards the ground." She then slipped a little and Annie's tea went hurling on the floor and spilled on Annie's feet. Both of the women screamed and then chortled. Marsha carefully dismounted and handed Annie a couple of tissues.

"I still don't quite get it. I am sorry, just slow I guess," replied Annie in

But Marsha didn't give up. "Ok, look at it like this: The same thing happens with people who don't enjoy and appreciate the grace of forgiveness. They are constantly trying to walk safely while carrying all this weight. One little thing can knock them off balance and they end up falling into the habit of lashing out at others."

"I get it now!" rejoiced Annie. "You are saying that forgiving myself is a like getting off a tightrope? I like the sound of that. What is the benefit of forgiving others?"

"I think it resembles not having to carry around a loaded gun with you any longer because you have gotten rid of the paranoia of being hurt. I mean, imagine if you had a loaded gun with you 24/7. Because you are looking for an offence or a threat, you will eventually find one. Once you start shooting people you get a reputation as an unsafe person."

"Ok, I think I've shot like ten people already this week!" replied Annie.

"Yes, and think of how many you have shot in the last year!" laughed Marsha. Annie stuck her tongue out at her counselor, but knew she was right. There was no way to estimate.

"People who haven't forgiven themselves are so worried about being hurt that getting close to them in nearly impossible. Think about trying to be the friend to a person who has a pistol by their side all the time."

"Good gosh, is that how I appear to people?"

"Sometimes."

Marsha held out her hand at Annie, pretending it was a pistol. "When we refuse to forgive, we become unsafe people. The problem is that if you ever let someone down that is unsafe, the punishment will far exceed the crime. A lot of fundamentalism in religion takes on this approach to relationships."

Annie knew that the advice Marsha was giving golden. This wise woman was not only professionally adept, she exuded deep wisdom. "How did you get so smart about all of this stuff?" quizzed Annie.

Marsha leaned in and whispered, "I will tell you a secret if you can keep it to yourself?"

"Ok" Annie whispered back. She was beginning to pick up on Marsha's exquisite form of sarcasm and waited for the punch line.

"I have screwed up so many times in my life that I figured if I was ever really going to help others, I would have to get a few things straight myself. Now, let's put together a plan for you so you can make some substantial progress in making forgiveness a way of life."

"Ok Doc, I am ready!"

CHAPTER 9

ANNIE SPENT THE next three weeks trying to figure out a way to talk to Bart. Like many wounded lovers she second-guessed her decision to end their relationship. The weight of unanswered questions and the ache of regret over how she behaved made her wonder if she had done the right thing. A few times this strain had been so unbearable that she had picked up the phone to call, but at the last second hit the end button of her cell to circumvent her impending embarrassment.

She also did her best to avoid any place where she could run into him. For instance, she hadn't visited Angelo's since the breakup. Several friends had invited her to go, but she couldn't muster up the strength to put on a show of the kind of effervescent aplomb that was one of her winsome trademarks. This time the shell of her heart couldn't take the strain of diverting energy to camouflage her unmistakable sadness.

Beyond the unique stress that came from regret she also found herself disappointed in Bart. Deep down Annie had hoped that he would push through all of the obstacles that hostility and fear created, and refuse to leave her presence until they fell together in each other's arms in exhausted relief. As much as she hated to admit it, she wished he would act like the knight in shining armor that she once believed him to be.

But after the third week of not hearing from him she knew that her searing words and his misjudgment combined to create what seemed to be an impenetrable gulf between them. Annie sought to assure herself of better days ahead by comforting herself with the fatalistic idiom: "Things always work out for the best." The only problem with this philosophy was that Annie wasn't all that convinced that it was true.

So, she tried to keep her mind off of her heartache by focusing on Meagan. Since her daughter had skipped school with Tommy, Annie had laid down the law. For the past three weeks the school bus had dropped off Meagan every day at the Center. From 3:30 p.m. to 6:30 p.m. Meagan cleaned out bedpans, swept the floors and helped the ladies in the kitchen prepare the meals for the residents.

When they finally got home every night after eating at the Center Meagan had to do her homework in front of her Mom. Meagan hated this but Annie told her that when she got a better report on the next grading period, she would release Meg from fulfilling such stringent procedures.

But "Queen Annie's reign of terror" didn't stop there. She totally shut down Meg's social life and limited her interactions with kids at the church youth group meeting on Wednesday evenings. If that wasn't enough to sober her up, Meg's cell phone was confiscated every night at 9:00 p.m. sharp, no matter what kind of "important conversations" were happening at the moment. Each time Meagan tried to complain Annie looked straight at her and said, "It can get a lot worse if you push it." Meagan believed her. She had never seen her Mom so ready to do whatever it takes to help her daughter get the picture of the importance of being a trustworthy person,

But the most amazing thing about this was not merely Meagan's compliance but the visible shift in her overall attitude. The unruly teenager secretly liked having more structure in her life. It took some pressure off of having to figure everything out. The result was she seemed to be a lot more at peace with herself.

Another unexpected benefit from Meagan's sentence was that the teen gained a whole new level of respect for Annie. She saw that the staff valued Annie's leadership and how the residents really loved her Mom. Meagan knew that if her Mom quit tomorrow that she would be truly missed. This caused Meagan to be less sassy and more proactive when it came to helping out around the house. Annie noticed all of this and wondered if she should hire Tommy to sneak her kid off of school property about every few months so she could inject some more discipline into her strong-willed daughter's life.

As Meagan began to settle down Annie decided on the Monday morning of the third week of not hearing from Bart to take care of some previous business by finally calling Tom. She knew that she should have a done it earlier, but she wanted to impose the changes in Meagan's lifestyle and get her own emotional upheaval under control before talking with her ex. She picked a time when she thought he might not be in court or with a client and called his cell number. She was surprised when he picked up after the first ring.

"Hey Annie, I was just getting ready to call you" replied a surprised Tom.

"Well, that's good. Do you have a minute?" asked a nervous Annie.

"Sure. You sound worried. What's wrong?"

Annie leaned back in her office chair and closed her eyes. "Has Meagan mentioned to you in your conversations about getting into trouble?"

"No" Tom said tightening his grip on his own office chair. "She hasn't been caught smoking pot again I hope."

"No, but she snuck away from school with Tee and Miller Blankenship's son Tommy"

Tom was now getting irritated. "How long ago did this happen?"

Annie realized that this could be the point that the discussion could quickly turn ugly. She didn't know what to do but tell him the truth. "Tom I should have called you earlier but I didn't. I had a lot of stuff going on in my life at the time. But that is no excuse. It happened almost a month ago." Annie cringed, waiting for some kind of explosion.

There was several seconds of silence over the phone. Annie was scared to say anything because she knew that interrupting Tom's deliberation could result in a very bitter rebuttal, and when Tom argued he pulled no punches. Maybe that is what made him such a good lawyer.

Then he spoke up. In a surprisingly quiet and reserved tone he said "Ok, what did you do as a result of her behavior?"

Annie relaxed a little and gave him the lowdown of all the corrective actions she had taken. She reported that these efforts had seemed to have made a difference with Meg.

"Sounds like to me that you have things under control," replied a calm Tom. "How can I help?"

Annie couldn't believe her ears. She was at a loss of words for a few seconds. When she recovered, she said, "Well, I know Meg is coming to see you this coming weekend so I wanted to let you know the kind of restrictions I put on her. You obviously can choose to do nothing or keep in place what I have done. It is up to you."

"Well, I appreciate that," said Tom. "I think we will keep up the phone plan that you have got going. That sounds like a good idea."

"Thanks Tom. Listen, I want to apologize to you for not keeping you more up to date with Meg. I know you love her, and to be honest you have always been a better Dad than I have given you credit for. Please forgive me for not involving you more in her life."

Now Tom was the one blown away. He tried to form a witty response but all he could say was "Wow, thank you it means a lot that you think that."

"You are welcome," said Annie in a gracious and warm manner. "And while we are at it, I have something else to share with you."

Tom braced himself. He thought for a moment that Annie had pulled a bait and switch with him like she used to. When they were married, she would soften him up with a compliment or an apology, and then hammer him with a criticism that would usually be the spark for a knock-down argument. "Ok" he said cautiously.

"You and I have had a lot of problems in the past. I have been deeply hurt. But I realize that maybe the real reason why I haven't included you in on both the good and bad things that were going on with Meg is that I still harbored some resentment, well let's be honest, I hated you a bunch."

"Uh-huh" said Tom waiting for the boulder to drop upon his head.

"Anyway, I have been seeing a therapist for several; months now and she has really helped me."

"That good Annie. I have been doing the same thing."

"Really? Has it provided any insights?"

"I can't even begin to tell you how much it has helped me deal with stuff in my life. I knew I was messed up, but I really didn't know how much." Tom laughed out loud. Annie remembered how that laugh used

WALKER ARMSTRONG

to calm her nerves and make the hair on the back of her neck perk up. No one had a laugh like Tom.

"Well, I am sure your therapist has given you homework at times. I was given mine early on and I have been procrastinating for a while. It is really hard for me to talk about stuff that happened between us, but I know for all of our sakes I need to. Do you feel like listening? If you don't I understand."

"That is totally scary. I was calling you for the same reason."

"Oh my goodness!" exclaimed Annie. This was not what she expected. She nervously laughed and said "It seems like this might be a good time after all." Annie took such a deep and quivering breath that Tom knew what she was getting ready to share something that had some deep roots to it.

Annie continued, "I guess the main reason I didn't want to talk is that we used to have some hellacious arguments and I just don't want to do that anymore."

"Me neither."

"Good. Now if at any point you feel I am being unfair or too intense you can stop me and we can talk later. Does that sound good to you?"

"Sure."

"Ok, here goes. I was first told to let you know the impact of what your unfaithfulness did to me."

There was silence over the phone once again. Annie worried that the call had dropped. "Tom?"

"I'm still here, just listening."

"So, there are is a lot here, but after thinking about it I have boiled it down to just two big things."

"Well, that is a bit of a relief" commented Tom. Annie didn't know if he was being sarcastic or just nervous. She chose to choose the later interpretation.

"First, I felt like you thought I was unattractive and that really rocked my self-confidence as a woman."

"I could see how you would feel that way."

Annie couldn't believe how peaceful Tom seemed. She tried her best to stay on track. "Well, it still occasionally reaches up and grabs me by the throat and makes it difficult to be in another relationship."

"Can I address that or do you want me to wait until you are finished?" Tom asked in what seemed to be a very respectful manner.

"Uh, I guess you can talk about what I have just said."

"Annie, I am so sorry. My infidelities were never based on believing you were unattractive. You are a very attractive woman. It was always based on my pitiful need to be affirmed."

Annie was shocked. She expected Tom to be argumentative and even demeaning as he had in the past. She sat there dumbfounded not knowing what to say next.

"Annie … did you hear me?"

"Yes, I am sorry. I was getting ready for one of your famous rebuttals and I was a bit shocked by your kind response."

"Yeah, I guess when you don't want to deal with a big problem a person tends to put up a smokescreen to divert attention away from their misdeeds. I did that a lot."

"You were good at it," laughed Annie.

"No question about that. What is the second thing?"

"Oh, uh the second thing is that when I could no longer live with you because of your infidelities, we got a divorce. And getting a divorce was the death of a dream."

"What dream are you talking about Annie?"

"It was the dream of having a happy marriage. You know, the dream of living together the rest of our lives; of raising Meagan and enjoying our grandchildren. Stuff like that."

"Yeah, that was a big loss. I didn't realize that myself until all the dust settled from our divorce. One night I thought about taking Meagan to a new Disney movie that had just come out. I actually went to her bedroom and she wasn't there. It was the loneliest feeling I have ever had in my life."

Annie sat there soaking in what Tom had just said. "I never really thought about what you lost Tom. I guess I believed since you were free of me you could go out and live any way you chose to."

"Yeah well, I guess when you are unhappy with yourself you can never be free until you find peace."

"Have you found peace Tom?"

"Most days I think so. I still have a ways to go. You don't resolve bad habits and destructive behavior overnight, but I have really made some progress."

"That's good." Annie felt a strange twinge of anger. She wondered why Tom couldn't have been this self-aware during their marriage. Before she let herself go too far down that path she asked, "So why were you going to call me?"

"You wouldn't believe it if I told you."

"Try me."

"My therapist told me a while back to call you and to ask you to share with me how my unfaithfulness hurt you."

Annie gasped.

"Yeah, kind of weird huh?"

"Why didn't you call me Tommy?"

Tom smiled. Annie was the only person he allowed to call him by that name, especially after his mother died.

"Probably the same reason you didn't. I was worried we would get in a huge argument. I knew you hated my guts and I didn't blame you for that."

"It was that obvious huh?"

Tom started laughing again. "Yes indeed. I guess when you hear your ex-wife say "I hope you burn forever in the hottest regions of hell" it is a clue that there might be a problem with seeking to have a civil conversation."

Annie laughed. She knew she shouldn't but she couldn't help it. 'I am sorry Tom. I know I said that and a lot of other horrible things."

"Listen, don't apologize. I would have done the same thing if I were in your shoes."

"Well, I appreciate that but my therapist showed me that hate is never a constructive emotion, no matter what the cause."

"I can see that. And there is something else."

"What?"

"The other reason I didn't call was that it created all kinds of anxiety in me when I thought about facing the consequences of my terrible actions. The guilt was overwhelming."

"I didn't know that."

"Yeah, once the divorce was final Amber and I went through this difficult time. I didn't think it was going to work out. I knew I needed to talk to someone so I found this psychologist in Charlotte who was amazing. He helped me to see how guilt and shame was driving my life."

"That's powerful. Do you think you and Amber are going to make it now?"

"I think so Annie. I appreciate you asking. I know she is not your favorite person and I understand why."

Annie felt a flood of peace come over her. She was proud of herself for being sincere when she asked about Tom's relationship to the woman who helped to break up her marriage. She was then reminded of the second big thing she needed to tell Tom.

"Tommy, I want you to know that I forgive you of everything, and I wish you and I hope things work out for you and Amber."

Tom didn't know what to do. He could tell that Annie was being sincere. As he leaned back in his chair, he recalled Annie's tears and her heartbreak over his numerous infidelities. A tear started rolling down his right cheek and he quickly brushed it away, even though he was all alone in his office. He cleared his throat a couple of times and spoke:

"Annie I really don't know what to say. I know that I have apologized to you many times, but the only way I know how to respond to your graciousness is to say that I am truly, truly sorry for all the stupid and wrong things I have done. I don't know if this will mean anything to you but it was never because of you. You are a kind, bright and beautiful woman. It was because of my ego and other junk I am still unwrapping and dealing with now. But you didn't deserve such treatment from me, and doing this stuff to you will always be the greatest regret of my life. Thank you for forgiving me."

Annie was startled by the profound humility in Tom's voice. He almost sounded like a different person. Suddenly she felt like the scales had fallen from her eyes and she was able to see him as he was – a decent man who had let an unchecked ego and deeply hidden insecurities get the best of him. Finally, she felt free. Free from the chains that she had first placed around his guilty neck but later wrapped up her own heart. These chains made it almost impossible for her to trust again.

"You are most welcome Tom," she said sighing in relief. "I promise to keep you updated more regularly on Meg, ok?"

"That sounds great," said Tom. "I will call you later in the week about when and where to pick up Meg." There was another pause and then he said "Annie ..." Tom's voice began to crack with overwhelming gratitude, and before the healing floods of forgiveness could overcome him, he quickly ended the conversation by saying "God bless you!"

Annie heard the rapid beep of Tom's line going dead. She took a deep breath and shook her head in amazement. She wondered why it took her so long to realize that forgiving someone was not letting them off the hook. It was freeing yourself from the exhausting work of trying to make someone pay for an indeterminable debt that could never be settled. Despite her longing to be with Bart and her worries over Meagan, she knew right at that moment that she was in a good place.

Ruth Phipps was on a mission. She had walked out of the Gordon's Ladies Emporium and had left young Leslie Harding in charge to mind the store while she went across the street for a cup of coffee with her pastor Tim Spenser at Stardust's. It was around three in the afternoon, so she figured that they could sit in the back corner of the shop and have practically complete privacy. They would need it. The information she was getting ready to share with Tim would change his life forever.

When she walked into Stardust's she noticed Tim chatting with Fareesh. She nodded at Fareesh and then motioned for Tim to join her at a booth near the restrooms. He shrugged at Fareesh and followed her wondering what all the fuss was about. Tim knew that when Ruth needed to talk about something there was no stopping her.

He sat down with his fresh cup of coffee with a big smile on his face and asked, "So what couldn't wait until church council tonight Ruth?"

Ruth wasn't smiling. Her facial expression was a mixture of anger, worry and determination. She leaned forward, looked straight at Tim and said, "I am very troubled and heartbroken at what I am getting ready to tell you Pastor. I have been sick on my stomach about this for days. Both Tony and I have been praying about it for a while and I have waited until the right time to tell you this."

Tim's smile quickly shifted to a look of real concern. This didn't sound good to him and he wondered what would be his course of pastoral intervention as a result of this conversation. "Go on Ruth," he coaxed. "Tell me what is troubling you so."

Ruth leaned as close as she could and lowered her voice. "There is no easy was to say this so I am going to come right out and share the truth with you – your wife has been having an affair with Darrell Eller."

Tim laughed out so loudly that Fareesh looked back to see what all the commotion was about. When Tim finished shaking his head, he noticed that Ruth had not changed her expression one iota. He looked at her again and said, "What in the world are you talking about?"

Ruth continued. "My suspicions about it started late last summer. I went to the Drug Store one day and noticed them chatting in a very friendly way to each other by the vitamin section of the store. I didn't think too much of that until a few days later I noticed them standing outside the Drug Store doing the same thing. You know my store is right next to the drug store."

Tim just nodded and tried to swallow the big sip he had just taken from his cup of coffee.

"Anyway, I decided to start taking a log of how many times I saw them around each other." Ruth swiftly pulled out a little red spiral notebook out of her purse and placed it as Exhibit A on the table. Opening to about the third page she pointed to a column that had a number on it and in an almost a prosecutorial fashion commented, "By October 31st I had seen or heard about them being together thirty-one times!"

By this point in the conversation Tim was getting angry. "Look," he fumed, "that can easily be explained by the fact that she has been working there for a while. To extrapolate that into an affair is ridiculous!"

"I thought you would say that." For a moment it looked like Ruth was so sad that she might cry, but she wiped any form of empathy off her face and rejoined her mission to tell the truth come hell or high water. "You remember last November when you were gone to speak at that men's weekend conference in Louisville?"

"Yeah, why?" said a still aggravated Tim.

"Well, you know that your wife didn't go to her mother's house in Greenville that weekend like she told everybody she was going to."

Tim looked hard at Ruth. He was usually somewhat careful about what he would say around her. Now he knew why. Ruth was a morally upright person but she lacked boundaries. She believed that her passion to do right gave her ample moral capital and a platform to weigh in on the deeds of others. His mentor in ministry Charles Caudle warned him about such individuals when he used to tell him, "Beware of people who seem to enjoy revealing the sins of others. They feast on the heartaches of people like a wolf devours unsuspecting lambs."

Just before he was to light in on her about the dangers of gossip Ruth pulled out a photo from her purse and placed in on the table. It was a picture of Kim and Darrell locked in a passionate embrace on the lighted porch of what looked like a restaurant. Tim tried to respond about the quality of the photo, but the identity of the lovers was just too obvious. Now his anger was turning to nausea.

"That picture was taken at the Albemarle Café by April Knorstrom. She and her husband Phil had gone to see her parents and had taken them to dinner. I guess those two thought their little tryst was safe since they were almost a couple of hours from home."

Tim didn't move an inch or change his expression while he stared at the photograph.

Ruth continued her presentation. "Anyway, April made Phil and her parents get into their car and follow them. Since this was her Pastor's wife, she wanted to be sure before she told anybody about what they had seen. So, they followed the two of them to a bed and breakfast inn close by. I've got pictures of that if you need further proof."

Tim didn't say anything. He looked straight through Ruth as if she wasn't there. Suddenly, he got up from the table and spilled his coffee all over the floor. He thought about cleaning it up but he was getting so light-headed that he knew he needed to get some fresh air and fast.

He stumbled through the shop and busted through the door muttering "No, dear God please no!"

Ruth followed close behind. When she caught up with Tim outside, she found him bent over trying to catch his breath. Ruth put her arm on his shoulder and said in a saccharine manner "Oh Pastor, I can't imagine what you are going through right now. Is there anything me or Tony can do to help you through this awful time?"

Tim couldn't look at Ruth. He composed himself, stood erect and then spoke to her in a very measured way, "Please keep this to yourself. I mean tell whomever you have talked with that I don't want this getting out before I have had a chance to deal with it."

Ruth nodded and said "Of course we will." But that was a lie. She had not kept it quiet, nor was she planning to. In her mind, anyone who has sinned so egregiously deserved to be talked about. She had already chatted with several of the influential women in town including Mary Thompson one of Kim's closest friends and wife to the mayor. Plans were already in the works to deal with this problem.

Tim mumbled something about having to go home and walked towards the parking lot to his car. But before he got into his vehicle Ruth had already called her husband.

"Tony, it's me."

"How did it go?"

"Well, he is in shock."

"That is to be expected. Did you tell him the Elders wanted to meet with him tonight?"

"I tried to but you will probably have to call him later. Listen, I need to call some of the ladies to set up a ministry time with Kim."

"Ok, well this is a terrible situation. I don't see how he is going to be able to stay in the church."

"You are right dear and I think unless his adulterating wife does not come clean and repent I am sure that their marriage is in the toilet!"

"No doubt. Well, I will see you at church tonight."

"Ok, bye."

Ruth didn't miss a beat She quickly dialed Mary Thompson and impatiently waited for an answer.

WALKER ARMSTRONG

Mary picks up the line and says, "Hey Ruth, did you talk to Tim?"

"Yes Mary and he is a mess!"

"I am so sick about all of this. I can't believe Kim would do such a thing. Just when you think you know someone that go off and do something despicable."

"I know. This totally disgusts me and Tony too. That is why I want you to call some of Kim's friends. I think while Tim meets with the Elders it would be good for us to go by their house and have a talk with Kim. But don't call Annie. I am sure because of her past with Darrell she won't be any good to us tonight."

"But Annie is Kim's best friend Ruth."

"Exactly and I think she is a fine person and all that but I don't think Annie has the same level of moral conviction that you and I do. We need to have a clear, united message to Kim that this is a serious problem and she needs to get right with the Lord."

"Well, I just want to see her marriage restored. But I don't know if there is any way she can rebuild her ruined reputation."

"I agree Mary. And Tony and I think that Tim's ministry here is almost surely spent. It's such a shame too. He is one of the best preachers I have ever heard!"

"Ok I will call you back when I have contacted all the ladies in the church I think can help."

"Please be in prayer. We need to be ready for the attacks of Satan if Kim does not take this well."

"Amen sister!"

Tim Spenser sat in his driveway for a long time. He didn't know how he was going to talk with his wife. His mind raced back and forth between stilted conversations and strange happenstances that now seemed to be illuminated in the light the revelation of her affair. All of those moments of awkward distance between them and her unexplainable disappearances when he couldn't reach her now made perfect sense.

But this retroactive knowledge didn't aid him in his desperate attempt to find some level ground on which he could stand. Tim was struggling. His heart was torn by the opposing emotional poles of grief and rage. He loved Kim but part of him was tempted to make a public spectacle of her and have her driven out of town and out of his life. He entertained even more sinister fantasies about what he could do to Darrell. Other random thoughts popped in and out of his head at such a rapid rate that he felt paralyzed. He truly didn't know how he was going to talk with his wife.

Despite his feelings of panic and inadequacy he was thankful that he was well-trained in pastoral counseling. It reminded him to not overreact and automatically burn bridges that later he would want to try to rebuild. This, coupled with his experience of helping several couples carefully navigate the emotional rubble that infidelity brings, enabled him to have a thin slice of hope about this trauma. He tried to remember some names of solid marriage therapists he and Kim could see, but the flashes of Kim and Darrell together made it difficult for him to maintain any semblance of rational stability.

Kim kept watching Tim from her kitchen window. She knew something was wrong with him. The thought that he might have somehow discovered her affair with Darrell flashed across her conscious consideration. But she dismissed this as highly improbable.

She believed this for several reasons. First, she had broken it off with Darrell almost two months ago and had never mentioned the affair to a single human soul. Second, they had been very discrete in their liaisons. There were no incriminating emails to speak of and they never spent any time together in Gordon. All of their rendezvous were carefully planned out of town, much like commandos create secret missions into enemy territory.

Even their phone calls and texts always sounded clinical. They had a code that aided in their ongoing deception. Darrell would call and tell Kim that "her prescription was ready." Kim would respond and phone the pharmacy asking for "some medical advice." When this happened, they found a way to talk on public phones and plan a meeting.

Once Kim dismissed this worry about Tim discovering her affair, she decided to walk out on the front porch to see if she could get his attention. When she did Tim saw her waving at him and waived back.

He got out of the car and started shuffling towards the house not making eye contact with his wife.

"What is wrong honey?" asked Kim in a concerned fashion.

"We will talk about it in the house" Tim responded in a robotic like way as he walked past her with his head still looking downward. Kim knew something was terribly amiss and this awareness caused old anxieties to bubble up once again.

Tim sat down at the kitchen table. Kim sat down beside him and put her hand on his left forearm and tried to look up at his downwardly dejected face. "What in the world is going on Tim?"

Tim looked up and asked "Do you love me Kim?"

"Of course, why do you ask?" replied Kim.

"Well, what I am getting ready to tell you will test our love and determine what will happen with our marriage," said Tim in an ominous manner as his eyes began to fill with tears.

Kim immediately thought he was going to confess that he had an affair. She was always suspicious of his relationship with Lanelle Johnson. Lanelle was the former Miss Gordon and First Runner Up in the Miss North Carolina Pageant back in 1991. She was gorgeous, talented, charismatic and always seemed to beam in Tim's presence. She chaired the Visitation Committee and served with all of the other main leaders at NewLight on the Church Council. It was also a well-known fact that her marriage to Ted had been on shaky ground for years.

In a way, Kim had hoped that this was true to assuage her guilt over her affair with Darrell. That way, they could both confess and then re-dedicate their marriage to God. Maybe Tim could even get out of the ministry. Before she could extend this fantasy further, Tim interrupted her train of thought.

"I know about your affair with Darrell," Tim replied in a matter-of-fact fashion while nervously tapping his right forefinger on the table.

Kim looked like she had been hit square-on by a semi-truck. "Please don't insult my intelligence by denying it because I've seen pictures," said Tim now staring at her with the kind of controlled rage she had never seen before.

Kim looked down and then nodded. Tim thought that her admission would make him feel better but it didn't. "I don't know what to say to you," said Kim still trying to catch her breath.

"I know that I am far from a perfect husband," said Tim desperately trying to be respectful. "But I have never been unfaithful to you and I have tried my best to be a good husband. Can you tell me why this happened?"

"I guess I had gotten bored with our lives and always felt that I wasn't a good minister's wife and …"

"Did I ever say that to you?" replied Tim in a clearly angry manner.

"No, not really," said a petulant Kim.

"So, you choose to have an affair with the biggest rake in three counties to make you feel better about yourself?" Tim was no on a roll and he wasn't about to let Kim off the hook that easily.

"I know, I know. I was a damn fool. I came to my senses about two months ago and broke it off. I'm so sorry Tim, I am so sorry!" Kim erupted in the kind of explosive grief that Tim had seen in many congregants who has made a mess of their lives and didn't know what to do.

For a moment he felt a surge of sympathy for his bride. Somewhere in the midst of all of this hurt he knew she was a good person who had lost her way. But then his pride started taking the lead, and it drowned out the sweeter instincts that were just beginning to surface.

"Do you have any idea how embarrassing this is for me? Obviously, people already know about it. I don't know how I can stay at the church now. You have ruined it for me. All the hard work just washed down the drain because you wanted to have fun!" Tim shook his head in disgust.

"Who knows Tim? How did they find out?" asked Annie in a petrified manner.

"Does it really matter now Kim?" Tim looked at his disheveled wife and then somewhat out of respect told her, "Ruth and Tony Phipps … Phil and April Knorstrom … God knows who else."

Kim started to feel sick and decided to run to the bathroom. She got there just in time to spill her guts on the floor and in the toilet.

WALKER ARMSTRONG

Tim sat stuck at the kitchen table trying to figure out if he wanted to stay married.

As he was analyzing the shattered mess of his life the cell phone rang. He looked and it was Tony Phipps. He didn't answer. He figured that Tony wanted to get together and have an impromptu elders meeting. Tim knew that this was just the start of endless meetings and conversations over very sensitive and private matters that he was going to be forced to discuss. He wondered if there was any room for him in the bathroom.

Tim sat motionless at the table waiting for Kim to get her act together. He heard her flush the toilet and run the sink water. She walked back to the bedroom and evidently made a phone call because he heard her mumble a few phrases. By the time she came back to the kitchen Tim had pulled out a bottle of Scotch from the top left cabinet his dad had given him "in case of ministerial emergencies."

Tim never drank. He didn't want to debate with people about whether or not ministers should drink, so he just chose not to imbibe. He thought tee-totalers in his church were a bit weird and superficial. He never really cared for the taste of alcohol, but right at this moment he felt he was due. He was already on his second glass when Kim reappeared.

"I just got off the phone with Annie and told her we needed to talk," said Kim noticing that her husband was pouring down the liquor like he was consuming a sport's drink after a softball game.

"You two going to compare notes about your common lover?" said Tim in a sardonic manner.

That arrow went deep. Tim knew how close Kim and Annie were, and his statement burrowed down to reveal the damage that was likely to occur once this affair came to light. Kim knew that she could lose her best friend and her husband all in one fell swoop and the thought of that was unbearable.

"I deserve that," said a recalcitrant Kim. "I just want Annie to hear it from me before she hears it from someone else."

"I wish you had been that considerate of me" said Tim as he finished his second glass and poured his third, placing the bottle behind him back on the kitchen counter.

Kim was at a loss of words again. "Are you going to be ok?" she asked Tim, hoping that he knew she still loved him.

Something gave way inside of Tim. All of the self-control he had tried so hard to apply to his wounded heart immediately left him. He flashed a glance that made Kim step back out of self-preservation. In one smooth and violent movement he leaped up and tossed the kitchen table against the wall. A leaf popped off at the hinges while the centerpiece of flowers he had given her three days earlier commemorating the anniversary of their first date shattered into dozens of tiny shards. Although he was able to still hang onto the glass the Scotch itself was flung against the wall making a sudden mess of the once neat kitchen.

"Ok?" he snarled. "Sure Kim, I'm ok. Just go and spend some girl time with Annie. Maybe by the time you get back everything will be cleaned up and back to normal"

Then Tim made a grandiose gesture with his hand and then pointed to his head. "Wait. Here is a better idea – I won't be here when you come back so you better get your stuff and go to your mom's or Darrell's or whoever will have your sorry ass. But don't come back here, do you understand me?"

Kim knew her normally gentle husband was on the edge. She nodded and quickly left the house. He sat back down and found the bottle once more. After pouring himself a refresher he picked up his cell phone and called Tony. Tony answered on the first ring.

"Hey brother, how are you?" asked Tony feigning a profound level of concern.

"Not good Tony," responded Tim. "I need you to do a favor for me."

"Anything Tim" said Tony in an almost over-anxious fashion.

"I will not be at Church Council tonight. You will find a copy of the meeting agenda on my desk. Feel free to lead the meeting any way you see fit."

"Will do Tim," said Tony. There was silence on the phone and then Tony spoke up. "Tim, I have asked the elders to have an emergency meeting with you tonight. Are you up for it?"

"No Tony, not right now. But I will get back to you because I am sure you guys will want to find out what I am going to do" said Tim in such a sarcastic way that Tony was sure to get the message to not push the issue.

"Well, we are here for you" said Tony in his most reassuring voice. "Let me know whenever you are ready to meet." Tony took a breath and then changed gears. "Now Tim, with all that has happened do you think it wise to preach this coming Sunday?"

Tim knew exactly what this was about. It was Tony's adroit way of trying to do damage control. Tim wasn't in the mood for this kind of political posturing. He lowered his voice to for emphasis and said, "Tony, if I don't think that I can handle my duties I will let you and the board know. But unless you have facts to prove that I am unfit, I suggest you let me handle it my way, ok?"

Normally most decent folk would let sleeping dogs lie, but Tony was the kind of person who thought he would never get bit. He pressed the point further: "That will work for now Pastor, but you know that our Bylaws state in a situation like this we can have a vote of confidence and temporarily suspend you from your duties with a simple majority vote. I really don't want it to come down to that, but I thought you needed to know all of our options."

Tim gritted his teeth. Tony was a smooth operator, but Tim wasn't going to just disappear because he and his Kim were having problems. "I am well aware of all of our options Tony" said Tim in a thinly guised business-like manner.

"Good. I am sure we will talk over the next few days" said Tony in almost pastoral way. "By the way, is there any chance that Kim is going to be there tonight? My wife and some of the ladies want to minister to her."

Tim sat silent for a moment and said "I don't know where she will be Tony but I will send her the message whenever I see her again. Have a good night." Tim hung up his cell not waiting for a response. He leaned back and took another drink, this time out of the bottle. He looked outside. The sun was quickly fading beyond the tree line and the kitchen was almost dark. He buried his face in his hands and asked out loud, "Dear God where are you?"

Annie was more than just concerned for Kim. Her best friend had called her crying and mumbling over the phone a few minutes earlier. Annie could barely pick out understandable phrases but she knew from what she heard that Kim and Tim's marriage was in trouble. Kim asked if she could come by and Annie heartedly agreed.

After getting off the phone with her frantic friend Annie dialed her mom and asked her if she could drop off Meg at her home. She told her mom that "I will explain later, but I wouldn't be asking if it wasn't really important." Lola reluctantly agreed.

When they pulled up a few minutes later Lola greeted them at the front door in her housecoat and slippers. She made the universal sign with to be quiet and ushered them inside.

"Your daddy is asleep in his recliner. I don't want to wake him" whispered Lola as she guided them into the guest bedroom. "Meg, I was getting myself a sweet tea. Do you want some? It is decaffeinated.

"Sure Granny" replied Meagan grinning at her grandmother.

As soon as Lola got out of earshot Meagan turned to Annie and whispered "Ok Mom, spill the beans. Why am I here? I am tired and I've got school tomorrow."

"I know honey. But if I tell you why, can I ask you to be a grown-up and not mention it to a soul?

"Yes ma'am."

"I think Kim and Tim are having marital problems and Kim needs my support right now. She is embarrassed I think and she wouldn't want you hearing whatever she needs to tell me."

"Thank you. Don't worry, I won't tell Granny."

Annie kissed her daughter on the cheek and then quickly moved to the front door, shouting out a good-bye to her mother. She ran to her car and cranked up the engine, much like a racecar driver at Le Mans who was trying to catch up with the competition. Annie wanted to get there before Kim so she could prepare herself for the coming storm. It was times like these that her speedy little car came in handy.

Once she arrived back at her house she rushed into the kitchen, opened up a bottle of wine and poured two glasses. She placed one on the coffee table beside her leather chair and the other on the larger coffee table beside the couch.

Annie tried to sit down in her chair and take a deep breath. The only problem was that she was filled with such an abundant helping of nervous energy she couldn't sit still. She got back up rearranged the pillows on the couch twice. Looking around she noticed that the room seemed too dark and depressing, so she proceeded to turn on all the lights in the den. Once she turned on the lights, she saw that it had been over a week since she last dusted. She ran into the kitchen and grabbed a dust cloth and some cleaner and went to work.

Before Annie could clean and redecorate the whole house a voice spoke up behind her causing her yell and do a 180°turn in midair.

"Sorry to scare you. It looks like you need some help." Kim stood in front of her almost unrecognizable. She was wearing no makeup and had jeans and a tee shirt on from a summer youth camp from three years ago that had the remnants of past painting projects dappled all over. Her hair was soaking wet and combed straight back and her eyes were swollen from hard crying.

As soon as Annie saw her, she grabbed her and hugged Kim real tight. Kim started crying all over again and Annie led her to the couch. She handed Kim a glass and decided to grab hers and sit right down beside her disheveled friend.

Each time Kim tried to speak she lost her composure. "It's ok sweetie, take your time" said Annie in a reassuring way.

Finally, Kim spoke up. "I don't know where to start. I had made a really stupid mistake several months ago that I thought was behind me. But today it has come back with a vengeance. I really don't know if my marriage is going to survive. And to be honest I'm also scared that if I tell you what it is you will leave me too."

Annie smiled and said "That will never happen. So, tell me what is going on."

Kim folded her hands together, closed her eyes and bowed her head as if she was going to pray. Swallowing hard she turned towards Annie. "Last summer the church was really going through a growth spurt. Tim was tickled and was very busy. I was seeing less and less of him and when we were together his mind seemed to be elsewhere."

"I remember that."

"Right in the middle of all of that we had gone to see a fertility specialist."

"You are kidding me," replied Annie shocked that she didn't know such an important bit of information.

"I don't tell you everything dear. Anyway, we had been trying for about a year and I couldn't get pregnant. After some tests the doctor said I had a bad case of endometriosis and Tim's sperm count was fluctuating all over the place. The doctor suggested we both go on some medication. If that didn't work the next step was in-vitro fertilization."

"Oh, I didn't know Kimmie. I am so sorry."

"Thanks. Well Tim just seemed to shut down. He said he wasn't going to take any medicine and had personal convictions about why he didn't like the in-vitro process. I tried to talk with him about it but he would either change the subject or get mad. After being denied the chance to talk things out I just quit trying. He got even busier and by that time it seemed that we were more like partners in a business than husband and wife."

"Why didn't you say anything to me about this?"

"I guess I was ashamed."

Annie reached her arm around Kim and tried to hug her but Kim shrugged it off. She was determined to keep talking.

"You need to sit tight, there is more."

Annie nodded and sat back.

"When I was probably at the lowest point of my life a single guy here in town started paying attention to me. At first, it seemed pretty innocent. We joked a lot where we worked and I found myself starting to look forward to our conversations."

"Wait, so you work with this guy?" The only person she could think of at the drug store that was single was Mark During, a pimpled-faced teenager who delivered prescriptions.

"Yeah, but don't worry it's not Mark."

Annie tried to not look too relieved, but she was.

"Then one day he asked me if I would like to ride with him to Asheville to pick up some supplies for his business. I shouldn't have but I did. We grabbed some lunch and ate it at Sawyers State Park. Right before we got up to leave, he kissed me. My first response was to pull away but it had been so long since I had been kissed in a passionate way that I gave in. Before I knew it, we were in a full-blown affair."

"I can understand how that happens Kim," said Annie. "You know my past and I always appreciated how you never judged me for my mistake with Darrell."

Kim looked at her friend and nodded. "I knew it was wrong. But it felt like the only good thing in my life. I never fell in love or anything like that. I just felt like I was pretty and important in his eyes and in the short-term that made me feel good."

"But you are both of those things girl," said Kim's supportive friend.

"Thanks, but I didn't feel that way. I guess Tim assumed he never needed to tell me that." Kim stopped for a moment and acted like she caught herself saying something inappropriate. "But I am not justifying any of this, ok. There wasn't a moment when I didn't know deep down I was wrong."

"You don't have to defend yourself Kim. You are with me, remember?"

Kim continued her confession. "It took a lot of energy to keep it quiet. Or at least we thought we were keeping it quiet. We got really intricate and fancy with code phrases and texts to cover up our affair. But underneath all of the fun I was filled with fear. I knew this guy was a player and I was just another notch on his gun and that the party would eventually end."

"So what happened?" asked Annie.

"Tim preached a sermon one Sunday in January about the trap of deception. Do you remember?"

Annie thought for a second and then she recalled Kim knelling at the altar during the time of invitation after Tim's powerful message. She remembered that there were a lot of people that responded to this message. At their church they invited people to receive prayer or counseling following the sermon. This was a way to help folks nail down a commitment or just receive care regarding a problem. On that particular Sunday Annie remembered Kim being really upset.

"Yeah, I remember that you cried a lot" replied Annie trying to read between the lines

"It was that Sunday I decided to cut it off. I called the guy that afternoon. I told him that I loved my husband and that being with him was the biggest mistake of my life. He tried to get me to meet with him, but I hung up on him and I never turned back."

"Good for you Kim!" said Annie with a broad smile on her face.

Kim looked off and became very serious. "That decision seemed to open up all kind of insights about my life. I went and started meeting with a counselor. Well actually, I still am. The counselor is Marsha Annie."

"Oh, well that is kind of weird, but that makes me feel better. She is awesome. Just one more thing we share together huh?"

Kim nodded in a very sad way. "Yeah, unfortunately that's not all. Anyway, the next few weeks were like a spiritual spring cleaning. I sensed a closeness to God that I haven't experienced since we first came to Gordon. Even my relationship with Tim became sweet and enjoyable once again. I couldn't believe how good things were going. This might sound weird but I haven't had that kind of peace in my life in a long, long time."

"So why all of the sadness now?" asked Annie in a somewhat confused state.

"Ruth Phipps met with Tim this afternoon at Stardust and told him she knew about my affair."

"How did she know about it?"

Kim started turning a little pale as she sought to relay this information. Tim's angry words had not lost their sting. She allowed herself to settle down some and said, "Evidently she had been taking notes and pictures since she noticed something going on between us."

Annie sat back and let out an "Oh Lord help us all." She immediately knew that this was no longer a private issue between a husband and wife. If Ruth was involved then lines were going to be drawn and relationships were going to be damaged.

"This is not good Kim," said Annie.

"I know, but that is not the worst of it" said Kim as the anxiety in her heart was now reaching an emotional crescendo. Kim gripped the arm of the couch and said, "Annie the person I was involved with was Darrell Eller."

Annie was so stunned that she said "Oh dear God no Kim. Please tell me that this isn't true."

"It is," said Kim as her tears began to flow once more. "Now you know why I was worried about our relationship."

Annie stood up. She really didn't know why. She wasn't going to confront her friend. It just felt like the right thing to do. Kim looked at Annie, got her purse and stood up.

"It's ok Annie. I understand. I think it is terrible too."

For a moment Annie didn't look at her best friend. Kim moved hurriedly out of the house before Annie could respond. Annie really didn't know what to say. She was feeling so many emotions that all she could do at that moment was to stand frozen in place like a rookie guard at Buckingham Palace.

Then something inside of Annie switched on. Nothing had been resolved or figured out. Annie simply knew that Kim was in deep weeds and if she didn't reach out to her Kim would soon disappear. She ran after Kim until she caught her on the driveway, grabbed her on the arm and spun her around.

Kim seemed startled as if she expected her ex-best friend to slug her across the jaw. But the look on Annie's face surprised Kim. It wasn't rage or contempt she perceived, but compassion.

Annie grabbed Kim and hugged her. At first Kim was like a limp ragdoll. But after a few seconds she finally gripped Annie so tightly that it nearly squeezed the breath out of her.

"I am not going to leave you Kim," said Annie as she cried with her broken friend. "Besides, who am I going to go and buy gaudy workout clothes with?"

Kim pulled away and looked at Annie. "How can you be like this after what I just told you?"

Annie looked up towards the stars and then back down into her friend's face. "Kim, I never loved Darrell. I fell into the same trap you did."

"But don't you think I am terrible for hooking up with him after all that happened between you two?"

"No, just I'm just sad for you and I really think he is a scumbag now."

Kim laughed. Then Annie started laughing. Before they knew it both of them collapsed on the driveway and started laughing so hard they couldn't catch their breath.

When Kim finally gained some composure, she stood up. Then she helped Annie to her feet and asked "So, what now?"

"I guess we go inside drink some more wine, pray, cry, laugh and do whatever we need to do to make sure you are going to be ok."

"I love you Annie"

"Love you too dear!"

As they walked arm in arm back towards the front door Annie suddenly turned to Kim and said, "Can I ask you a personal question about Darrell?"

"I don't see why I shouldn't. I have no pride now anyway!"

"Well, did he ever tell you that *looking into your eyes made him feel like he had just stirred from a long sleep to find himself lying in a field of daisies?*"

Kim screamed and then laughed. "Oh my God! You have got to be kidding me. Yes!"

"Shoot! And I thought I was really special!" said Annie as she winked at Kim.

Both women started howling again, almost falling through the front door as they went back into the brightly lit house.

CHAPTER 10

T HE ALARM CLOCK'S buzz startled Annie out of a deep dream early Sunday morning. The frazzled woman slapped the off button quickly so as to not wake up her slumbering friend who was sleeping on a blow-up mattress beside her. Kim had stayed with Annie and Meagan for several days while trying to figure out where she would live.

As Annie lay in the bed, she stared at the ceiling trying to get her bearings. The emotional vestiges of a dream she awoke from had left an indelible mark, and she was doing her best to make sense of it. This was the third time in that many nights she dreamed the exact same thing. Something inside of her told her to quit avoiding the message of this persistent dream. She hoped that Kim and Meagan would stay asleep while she did her best to figure out what was happening.

From what she could remember of this haunting vision, she was riding on a horse galloping in the woods behind a pack of hounds in hot pursuit of some kind of animal. At some point she lost track of the hounds and came upon a fork in the road. Without any hesitation she took the left path. She traveled a bit and came upon a large, foreboding castle. It was heavily fortified with medieval soldiers armed with cross bows, cannons pointing out of every crevice and countless Mastiff's that patrolled around the castle looking for intruders.

Annie dismounted her horse. She waited by the edge of the woods until a supply cart of sorts rode by. When no one was looking she jumped into the back and hid herself under a cloak of hay. In a few seconds she heard a draw bridge open and felt the click of boards rebounding off of wooden wheels. The cart reached its destination and Annie lay there motionless while men unloaded all the supplies, leaving her huddled in a corner.

When the voices ceased Annie peaked between clumps of hay and noticed no one around. She slowly slid out of the cart so as not to attract attention and found a narrow alley in which to hide. Stooping low behind a large barrel filled with water she saw knights with chained dogs ramble by her. While she was trying to figure out what do next, she noticed a bright red door at the front of what looked to be a chapel. Looking left and right several times she saw that the coast was clear. She then scurried across the cobblestone road and entered the church.

As soon as she entered the chapel, she was immediately a washed with a sense of sacred awe. The wooden pews were filled with individuals draped in hooded cloaks. The sound of Gregorian chants circled upwards towards the cathedral ceiling as a priest stood at the altar with his back toward the congregants. He was swinging an amber and gold colored incense lamp in perfect rhythm to the ethereal song that these monk-like figures were singing.

On both sides exquisite stained-glass windows lined the walls. She stood in the back and noticed that each window seemed to depict a parable told by Jesus in the Gospels. Behind the altar was the largest stained artwork. It looked like the story of the Prodigal Son. As she started to walk down the aisle the picture of the figure that portrayed the repentant wayfarer came into clearer focus. It was Bart. At that moment she knew he was somewhere in the small crowd. The only thing she knew to do was to pull off the hood of each person that was seated until she found her lover.

One at a time she gently pulled back each hood. Instead of finding men with a tonsure hairdo she discovered all kinds of people from every race and tribe she could imagine. The further she went towards the front, the more she began to recognize some of the people she was uncloaking: a corrupt politician; a defrocked TV evangelist; a famous actor; a burned-out rock star and many others.

In the last few rows, she was even more surprised to find people she knew: Miller Blankenship, Momma Pearl, Kim Spenser and even her dad. At the front she saw a man seated up against the left corner of the left pew. She looked down and seated beside him was Frodo, Bart's

Springer Spaniel. Annie ran over to the figure and pulled back his cloak. Before she could see the face of her beloved, she awakened.

"What in the world does this mean?" Annie mumbled to herself.

Just then Kim woke up and said "Are you talking in your sleep again?"

"Huh?" replied Annie.

"I have been awake every night this week and heard you singing some gibberish. The other night I determined to write it down."

"So, what did I say?" said a curious Annie. Kim rolled over and grabbed her purse. She pulled out a folded sheet of paper and read:

"Gratia Dei liberat fractus amore."

"Weird!" replied Annie. "That is what I heard the monks in my dream sing in the church. What the heck does it mean?"

Kim smiled. "I looked it up yesterday. It is Latin for *the grace of God frees broken love*. I don't know what is going on, but for some reason I think that message is for me. At least I hope it is. What were you dreaming about?"

Annie was too tired to explain. She told Kim "We'll talk about it later. Let's make some breakfast since you are up."

The two friends meandered into the kitchen. In a few minutes they whipped up scrambled eggs with cheese, grits, link sausage, toast, coffee and some freshly squeezed orange juice. Both of them were so famished that they didn't even leave a single piece of toast for the sleeping teenager. Annie noticed this and said, "Oh well, she can eat some cereal."

Between bites and gulps they giggled like two adolescent girls. They really didn't know why they were acting so silly. Based on the circumstances they were facing both of them should have been at the very least discouraged. But somehow the primal need to de-stress gave them the ability to postpone all serious contemplation and enjoy the moment.

After breakfast the stuffed ladies reclined in the den. Annie was complaining about how badly out of shape she was as she rubbed her warm belly when Kim changed the subject.

"So," commented Kim. "When are you going to actually talk to Bart?

Annie sat up from her prone position on the couch. This very subject had been on her mind since she awoke from the dream. She looked at Kim and said "I guess after church if I can find him."

Kim nodded her head in an affirming manner. "I think that is a great idea. What are you going to say to him?"

"I think the first thing I will do is to apologize for my behavior. And then I will ask him why he felt it was necessary to not let me know that he was the person who saved Meagan's life."

Kim caught Annie's eye and replied, "Maybe you ought to thank him for doing that very thing."

"I did when he came out in his entire surgical garb and knelt down and told me and Tom what happened." Annie remembered the feeling she experienced when Bart told them that they had "lost Meagan three times on the table." Despite how rotten Meagan had been lately she could not imagine life without her. The thought of it sent a muted shiver down Annie's spine.

Kim wouldn't let up. "Maybe you should thank him again," she retorted in a sarcastic tone. Annie stuck her tongue out at Kim to register her frustration at her friend's painfully accurate assessment of her need for more humility. Kim playfully returned the favor.

Annie got up from the couch and stretched. "Well, I better get ready for church."

"I won't be going today" said Kim as she pulled a blanket up to her chin. "In fact, I may never go back. I'm sure by now that good old Ruth has gathered a posse for my hanging."

"Don't worry about her. I've got your back. Maybe folks who have never made some big mistakes in their lives will side with her self-righteous ways. But there are enough of us banged up people who have made plenty of mistakes that will stand by you, ok?"

Kim stood up and hugged Annie around the neck. "I am more grateful for our friendship than you can possibly know."

"You should be," laughed Annie. "Friends like me are hard to find."

Annie was late for church. She noticed when she pulled into the parking lot that it was crowded. She found a spot after circling around a bit. It was unusually cold for a March morning, so she walked briskly to the building from her remote location. It occurred to her as she was weaving around all the cars that the packed parking lot must be an indicator that people were curious about what they had already heard about Kim and Tim. Ruth and Tony must have been busy marshaling the troops.

Annie slipped into the back of the Worship Center and stood against the wall right next to the main doors. She looked around the stuffed auditorium for an empty seat, but couldn't find one beside anyone she liked. It was very different from the sanctuary in her dream. NewLight's sanctuary (if you wanted to call it that) used to be a grocery store. They converted this building and the one adjacent to it into worship, education and office space. It was sparsely decorated, but clean and neat in appearance.

What it lacked in aesthetics it made up for in performance. The music was top drawer. Annie listened to the Praise Team lead a modern arrangement of "On Christ the Solid Rock I Stand." All across the building people had their hands raised and their eyes closed. Despite the utilitarian look of the facility, Annie felt as reverent as she would have if she had been seated in a candle-lit sanctuary in Italy like the one in her dream. She had hoped somehow that God's love would envelop the congregation. But she was afraid that hidden agendas and politics would rule the day.

When the song ended Tony Phipps walked up onto the platform. He had a very serious look on his face and was carrying a plain manila folder. Annie quickly scanned the audience and could not find Tim. On the front center row, the rest of the Elder Team was sitting together. Annie recognized what was happening. This show of solidarity probably meant that Tim was either going to be asked to step aside or that he had already resigned. Annie's hope for a safe place for Kim and Tim to work out their problems evaporated as quickly as water on asphalt in the scorching summer's heat.

Tony pulled out a couple of sheets of paper from the folder and placed it on the clear plex-glass pulpit. He leaned forward and began to speak:

"Sometimes in the life of a church we have to deal with tough things. This is one of those times. Because this is a matter for our church members with sincere humility, I want to ask that all non-members please leave quietly."

Only a few people got up and left. It was clear to Tony that a lot of the people present were not going to budge. He looked back down at his papers and continued.

"Over a period of a few weeks it has come to the attention of several leaders in this church that a member in our fellowship has been involved in an extra-marital affair. Because this person is a leader in our church, we feel that in order to protect church unity and promote the life of holiness that our Lord expects of us we are forced to deal with this in public. The Scripture gives us precedent for doing this. That is why I am sad to report that ..."

As if on cue, the main doors swung open before Tony could reveal the identity of the person involved. Tim strode down the center aisle with a determined look on his face. Almost immediately there were gasps and all types of conversations initiated by Tim's sudden appearance.

Tony tried to recapture control by saying "Hello Pastor, we are glad you are here." But Tim seemed to ignore that initial greeting and walked right up to the pulpit. He then briefly acknowledged Tony's presence and said, "I will take it from here Tony."

At first Tony looked like he was going to object, but he could tell that the majority of the expressions on the faces of members that they were relieved to see their pastor. Ruth made a motion for Tony to stay on the platform but he didn't catch her gesture. He removed himself from the stage and sat down on the front row with the other elders with folded arms and unmistakable anger written all over his face.

Tim looked across the entire audience. He noticed some who were crying, others who were stone-faced and some who looked confused and worried. Tim bowed his head and prayed a silent prayer for strength. When he looked up, he had tears in his eyes. He swallowed and then began to share his heart:

"For the past three days I have been up in the mountains in a cabin provided by a friend. I took only my Bible and my journal with me. Risking your possible evaluation of me being spiritually prideful I want to tell you that I have had nothing to eat and only water to drink during that time. I have poured out my heart to the Lord literally day and night asking for his strength and wisdom." Tim looked down and wiped his eyes and nose with a handkerchief from his back pocket.

"I had some important decisions to make about my marriage, my job here at the church and even my own faith. I expected to receive instruction about these issues but what I got instead was a revelation of my own problems. You see I have a confession to make."

Some of the power brokers in the church looked confused. They expected him to resign for personal reasons or make some opaque statement in reference to Kim's unfaithfulness. Without saying a word Tim looked straight at the elders and at then at Ruth and some of her followers and said, "I have had a mistress for over four years."

When he spoke these nine words it was as if someone had thrown a switch that sent an electrical current through every single body in the Worship Center. Not a single soul sat unaffected by this unexpected confession. People had their heads bowed, others looked shocked and a few people appeared angry as if they had personally been betrayed.

"My mistress took me away from my wife on weeknights and weekends. She was relentless in her demands and I was all too willing to heed her siren call because of how being with her made me feel. I tried to break it off several times but was unsuccessful. It perhaps has cost me my marriage and job as your pastor. But my mistress is not who or what you might expect. My mistress is this church."

If people were not already confused this blew their minds. Ruth and others began to shake their heads in disagreement, but this did not deter Tim from speaking. It only emboldened him.

"Some of you know what I am talking about. Others are clueless and a few of you think that I am trying to blow smoke and deflect you from the real issue. So please let me try to explain. I am not saying that ministry in and of itself is the problem. Neither am I blaming any of you.

What I am saying is that my own obsession to be seen as a successful minister caused me to forget my crucial mission as a husband to love my wife like Christ loves the church. Kim is an amazing person and has gone without my true affection and attention for a long, long time.

We have both refused to address this serious gap in our lives and as a result are now teetering on the precipice of divorce."

Tim began to lose some composure as his voice trembled under the weight of a heavy heart.

"Because of this, I am asking for a two month leave of absence from my pastoral duties while I work on my marriage. I have no idea if we will make it. But not to give it my full attention would be a travesty." This statement created more under the radar conversations. Tim looked back at the Elder Team and some of them started nodding their heads in affirmation, while Tony another elder sat with no expression on their faces.

"I know some of you are wondering about details like pay and benefits. I have sent a list of suggestions to the entire Elder Team and have opened the door for their ideas so that we can come to a quick agreement that would be fair to both the church and our family. Next Wednesday NewLight is scheduled to have a quarterly business meeting. I think it would be appropriate for the entire church to vote on a plan that the elders will offer to deal with this time of waiting and transition."

Once again Tim almost lost his composure. He bowed his head and gripped the pulpit like a man suffering from a sudden heart attack. He looked back up with a blotched, tear-stained face and said with a quivering voice, "I would ask you to not gossip or offer conjecture regarding who has done what or who is at fault. I love the people that make up NewLight. I love this community. But I love my wife more!"

Tim could no longer restrain himself. He leaned on the pulpit and started weeping. He tried to shake it off but the grief in his heart was now on full display. Without a cue one woman stood and began applauding. Others quickly joined her. People also started shouting "We love you Tim" and "We love Kim too!" The Elder Team sat still at first until Barry Tompkins stood and joined in the applause. Eventually, only out of sheer embarrassment, the remaining handful of people who hadn't stood reluctantly joined this spontaneous show of love. In the end, everyone stood except Ruth Phipps.

Annie leaned against the back wall with tears flowing down both cheeks. She wore a huge smile as she recalled all of the conversations she and Kim had over the last week. There wasn't a doubt in her mind that Tim and Kim were going to make it. She made eye contact with Tim and blew him a kiss of support and respect. Tim recognized this and smiled for the first time in days.

It was going to take a lot of courage for Annie to go and talk to Bart. But she knew if she didn't do it now, she probably would never talk with him again. After church Annie drove straight over to Angelo's and parked in the back. Bart had lived in a small studio apartment above the restaurant since he moved to Gordon. Annie had forgotten to give him back the key to his place when she broke up with him. When she didn't see his truck, she decided to go up the steel staircase to see if she could wedge a note in the door.

For a while Annie stood at the bottom of the steps. Finally getting the gumption she needed she climbed up the rusty steps onto the landing and peered into the window of the front door. What she saw shocked her: The apartment was empty. It wasn't merely empty. It looked like it had been scrubbed clean of any evidence that Bart had ever lived there. She jostled the front door and discovered it was unlocked.

Annie entered the main room with trepidation. As she scanned the place, a sinking feeling began to rise up from her stomach to her throat -- She knew Bart was gone. Annie felt like crying but didn't seem to have the energy to muster up one single tear. She turned to leave and out of the corner of her right eye she noticed one box that was placed on the corner of the kitchen counter right beside the refrigerator. When she approached the box, she noticed that it was neatly packed with plates, cups and some of Bart's favorite chef knives that were wrapped up in a worn black cloth.

"Bart will be back for these," she said out loud. A little hope sprang up in her heart when she made that statement. She looked for a piece of paper in her pocketbook to write a message on and realized she left her notepad at home. Her small bit of hope seemed to be slowly smothering under the burden of this silly little logistical challenge.

Finally, a folded piece of what looked like to be really nice stationary caught her eye. It had fallen down between the counter space and the refrigerator. She reached down and pinched one edge of it and slowly dragged it out. Annie looked carefully at the pearl-colored envelope. At the center of the back were the monogram letters SSB. She opened it to find a letter with some beautiful handwriting:

Dearest Ian,

By the time you have read this the hydrocodone I have taken had done its job and I am dead. I am sure that our child is dead also. Perhaps this sounds too brutal, but the plain truth of it is that I could no longer live a lie. Nor did I want to subject a child to your gruesome fantasy world where you are the medical savior and everyone else plays a supporting role in your sick play.

I am sure that my past struggles with depression will be the fodder for your explanation to our family and friends for what will be called my sick and irrational choice. But they have not lived the mirage like I have. Years of suppressing my needs and never being taken seriously have created a yawning vacuum in my soul that I can no longer fill with alcohol or social clubs.

The saddest part of all of this is that I know we were once very much in love and yes, even happy. But your constant pursuit of recognition for your brilliance with a scalpel has bled my heart dry. This felt like my only choice. I won't ask you to forgive me. But I do ask that you would cremate both mine and our child's ashes. It is the very least you can do.

Sue

Annie's hand trembled as she put the note back on the counter space. Bart's choice to remain silent while she shot arrows of heart-ripping accusations at him now made sense in light of this fully unveiled calamity. She wished that she could hold Bart in her arms and tell him that he was a fine man. She wanted to assure him that his mistakes in his marriage weren't the cause of his former wife's decision to end her life and the life of their innocent child.

At that moment a lot of things fell into place for Annie. The very thing about Bart that caused her the greatest angst was no longer a mystery. She now knew that his reticence to be fully truthful was a telltale sign of what happens when a soul can't seem to process a horrendous catastrophe.

"It is so easy to judge people," Annie said out loud. Her pronouncement echoed in the bare room reminding her of how the ghosts from her past had served as a merciless judge and jury over her life. Almost instantaneously her self-righteous indignation over Bart's lack of transparency began to melt with the piercing revelation of this heart-wrenching ordeal.

Annie then made a bold move. She took out a pen from her pocketbook. On the back of Sue's suicide note she wrote the following: *Gratia Dei liberat fractus amore. Love, Annie.*

She hoped that this note would not offend her lost love. It was a big risk, but it was worth it if she could help this good man mend his broken heart. Annie said a prayer and walked out of the apartment, down the stairs and got into her car. She had no clue what was going to happen next. People who live by the impulse of the mysterious breeze of grace rarely do.

By the time Bart got back to his apartment he was very tired. He had moved all of his stuff into the old Sawyers farm house on Highway 16. He bought it for a song, and had already started some renovation work. His plan was to ask Annie to marry him and have them restore it. It seemed like a perfect fresh start that they both needed, and it didn't hurt that she had once told him it was "the most charming place in the county."

After Annie broke up with him, he decided to just keep it as an investment property. The old familiar pattern of packing up, winding down and closing some deals began for Bart as a default mode to protect himself from further pain.

A week after Annie ended their relationship Bart contacted a friend he had met in Italy, an entrepreneur was Bill Trainer. A while back Bill was traveling with his wife Nancy in Italy and had enjoyed Bart's cooking at La casa di Salse. They got to know Bart and Bill told Bart that he owned several restaurants in California. He offered Bart a job at his trendy place called Italian Bam in LA. Bart declined but kept all of Bill contact information.

After drinking several glasses of Scotch one night he called Bill and told him he was ready for a change. Bill jumped at the chance to land this incredible chef. Bill and his wife had just bought a vineyard just 40 miles north of the Golden Gate City. Bill desperately needed a chef to re-open a restaurant on the property. This sounded like just the very thing the sad man needed. He bought a one-way ticket to San Francisco, California online that night. Bart then had talked with Angelo the next day and told him of his plans. He would find another buyer for the place, but in the meantime, he told Angelo that he and his son could run the restaurant for a while until a deal was made.

But the day before he was to leave a child of one of his cooks walked up from behind when he was giving some last-minute instructions and goodbyes. She was about four years old and looked a lot like what he thought his daughter would look like if she had survived. She had picked a flower, one of the first of the season, and handed it to the preoccupied chef. He almost put it aside but stooped down and thanked little Audrey. She smiled and gave him a kiss on the cheek. "I am glad you are here!" said the little doll. "You are the best boss my Daddy has ever had."

Bart stood and held the flower for a moment. He missed Annie desperately. But something else suddenly occurred to him. He had not only fallen in love with a mesmerizing woman he had fallen in love with a town. If he left, he didn't think his heart would ever recover. Right then he decided to stay and find some way to work Annie out of his heart. He called Bill and told him he was tired of running from his past. He was ready to settle down.

Now as Bart came to pick up the last few things from his apartment he stood there for a moment for some final thoughts. He was kind of glad he was leaving this apartment. There were too many haunting memories from that place that were now added to the gallery of ghosts that he carried around with him wherever he went. He took a deep breath and went into the kitchen.

There he noticed the famous note on the counter. He didn't know why he kept it. Maybe it was some form of penance he practiced by which he was reminded why he didn't deserve to be happy again. The other day he thought he had lost it and was both sad and relieved. Seeing it resurface made him feel a little deflated.

When he grabbed the note to put it into the box, he noticed Annie's message on the back. He read the Latin phrase and gasped. It was a gasp of resurrected faith. This surge of emotions reminded of times when his patients had a huge look of relief on their faces when they found out they didn't need open heart surgery. Bart now knew he had not lost Annie. He grabbed the box and sailed down the steps. Frodo whined as he slid into the door when his master jerked the truck into gear and did a violent U-turn.

Annie was looking out the bay window of her kitchen when she saw Bart wheel into her driveway. He stopped his truck so abruptly that it frightened Annie a bit. At that moment she wasn't so sure it was a good idea to write the note. She walked to the door and prepared herself for the verbal barrage that was going to happen.

As soon as Annie opened the front door Bart busted through, grabbed her and gave her a passionate kiss. She fell limp, relieved to feel his all-encompassing embrace again. Both blurted out, "I love you" almost at the same time and then started laughing. Annie had forgotten how much she and Bart laughed together.

"Can we go sit down outside and talk?" asked Annie. "I am feeling a little lightheaded."

"Sure."

They walked out to the back deck and collapsed into two Adirondack chairs Jake had built. Bart had a look of deep contentment that Annie had never seen before. He grabbed her hand and closed his eyes. She followed suit. Then Bart said to Annie "There are some things I need to explain to you."

"Please do," replied Annie as she opened her eyes and turned towards him.

"I didn't tell you about being Meagan's surgeon because I believed that you would automatically question my motives for seeing you."

"That makes sense," said a supportive Annie.

"I didn't realize who you were until Angelo told me a little of your background. Then, when we started falling in love, I kept postponing telling you the whole story. I'm sorry."

"I forgive you Bart and I want you to forgive me for being so hateful towards you."

"You don't need to do that."

"I appreciate it but I do need to apologize to you. My bitterness wasn't about you. It was about my refusal to forgive Tom. I didn't realize how all of that hate had poisoned my life till I almost lost you."

"You are never going to lose me sweetheart – that is if you still want this broken-down dude."

"More than you know" replied Annie as she leaned forward and gave Bart a soft, wet kiss."

Bart took a deep breath. "You sure know how to make a man feel all stuptified!"

Annie giggled. "You have been around Momma Pearl too much! The feeling is mutual."

Bart leaned back and then got a serious look on his face. "Well, do you think you have forgiven Tom now?"

"Oh yes!" said Annie excitedly. "We talked the other day and had the most wonderful conversation. It was healing for both of us. I am so relieved."

"That great. I wish I could have done that with Sue." Bart's voice trailed off as he looked down at the ground.

"Bart, I hope me reading that note was not the wrong thing to do."

"No, it is actually a huge relief that you know all about that now. There are days when it feels like it happened to somebody else."

"But it didn't"

"Yeah, that has been a big part of the problem. I thought that I had washed away all that pain until you came along."

"Was our relationship painful?"

"Never. Just the exact opposite. I hadn't been this happy in a long time and it scared me."

"Why would something this good scare you?"

"I guess because of that very reason. It was so good I doubted that it was real at first. I had come to believe that my best days were behind me and the best I could do was to work, survive and not hurt anyone. When I was with you, I was waiting for it to blow up. When it didn't, I wanted to do whatever it took to protect it."

Annie was beginning to see where Bart was coming from. She touched his shoulder and said, "I felt the same way. But you could have trusted me with that information. It would have been a little weird but you saved my daughter's life. How could I stay mad at you for not telling me everything?"

"But there is more," said Bart trying to prepare Annie for more tough truth about his past.

Annie didn't overreact this time. She remained calm and said "Tell me about it."

"When I lost Sue and the baby I started drinking heavily. At first it didn't affect my work. But after a while I started missing patient appointments and staff meetings. People at the practice did their best to cover for me at first. That is until one day I went into surgery hung over from my previous binge."

"What happened?"

"It was a routine by-pass procedure. My patient was a guy about my age whose family members on both sides had a history of heart disease. We caught his disease early. He was a fit guy who took good care of himself. He only had two blocked arteries, so we didn't have to put him on the by-pass machinery.

Anyway, my chief nurse saw me getting sick before the surgery. She tried to wave me off, but I cussed her out and stumbled into the surgical room. I was still buzzing from the night before. My head was really pounding and I was dizzy from being severely dehydrated. Despite that, the surgery seemed to go ok, but I had inadvertently nicked an artery. A day later he had lost four units of blood and was fading. One of my partners went back in fixed my mess.

We thought this guy was out of the woods but he got septic and then died three days later. It devastated his family. He had two kids and a loving wife. His name was James Fonville. He was an Elementary School Principal, a deacon in his church and a soccer coach. You might have remembered the funeral. It was all over the news."

"I am sorry but I don't."

"Anyway, the partners had a meeting with me and read me the riot act. If I hadn't helped to make all of them wealthy people, they would have probably reported me to the State Medical Board. I was so sorry for what I did that I sold my part the practice and vowed never to do surgery with these hands ever again, I guess you know the rest of the story."

Annie sat up from the chair and said "Ok, you made some mistakes, some pretty bad ones. But you had helped a lot of people. Why walk away from something you invested all that time, effort and money to become? Do you ever miss it, I mean saving people's lives?"

Bart knew where Annie was coming from. He looked up at the sky and replied, "Sometimes. But losing Sue and the baby really laid me low. I was so low that I started questioning everything. I knew deep down that I didn't cause their deaths, but I still couldn't get rid of the guilt. I tried to drink it away but that only caused more problems. When my recklessness cost a man his life, I knew that I had lost the passion to do the job. That is why I walked away."

"And now?" asked Annie pensively. "Do you want to walk away from me?"

Bart grabbed Annie's hand again and looked into her eyes. "At first I did. Not because of anything you said or did. I just didn't want to hurt anyone and I didn't want to be hurt anymore. Does that make sense to you?"

"Yes darling," said Annie as she kissed his cheek. "I can't imagine the pain you have been through. After reading the letter I felt ashamed for my outburst."

Bart shook his head. "There is nothing to be ashamed about. I am the one that needs to ask for forgiveness. And I made a commitment the other week to stay in Gordon even if you never spoke to me again. I am tired of running."

Annie got out of her chair and knelt down beside Bart. Taking his face in her hands she said, "Ian Bartlett St. Claire, you are one of the finest men I have ever met in my life. What you have just told me doesn't make me love you or respect you less. It makes me love and respect you more."

Annie then sat down on the deck with her legs crossed, "You remember that day you gave me a ride to work?"

"You bet! That was the day me and Frodo realized you were something special."

"Well, you made a comment about my frantic pace of life. You questioned why I would run after a bus in the rain when another one was going to come around in a few minutes."

"Oh yeah, that was pretty arrogant of me."

"No, it wasn't. That conversation changed my life. I took a hard look at myself and I realized that my busyness was my strategy for not dealing with old wounds. You helped me to face some deep pain that I needed to take care of."

"I don't know what to say. I can't believe I could help anyone with what kind of mess I have made of my life."

Annie continued. "Now let me return the favor if I can."

"I am all ears," said Bart grinning at the love of his life.

"You have been trying for years to run from tragedy, the kind that can wreck a life."

The broad smile quickly disappeared. Bart looked out towards the budding trees and said "You're right about that."

"But this type of pain is not the kind you run from. It is so profound and deep that it is a part of you. You could no more get rid of this pain than you could cut out your own heart and keep on living."

"I guess I never thought of it that way."

"Bart, the only way to make peace with it is to forgive Sue for taking doing what she did. And you then need to forgive yourself for being a selfish and reckless person."

Tears began to fill Bart's eyes. These simple truths seemed to be coaxing him out of his self-imposed solitary confinement.

"I want to. Will you help me Annie?"

Annie pulled Bart up from his chair. She looked straight at him and said "I think we should help each other. Have you taken a look at my mess lately?"

Bart nodded in agreement. "Yeah," he smirked. "Your life is pretty screwed up in some ways."

Annie smacked Bart in the arm and replied, "Hey, you don't have to agree with me so quickly." Bart grinned back at Annie.

She placed her head on his left shoulder and patted him on the bottom saying, "Now that we have all that heavy lifting of burdens out of the way, let's go get Meagan and take her over to Mom and Dad's. They could use a little teenage angst to liven up their dull lives!"

Bart wrapped his left arm around Annie's waist and said "I could use a little diversion myself."

"On the way there I need to tell you all that is going on with Tim and Kim."

CHAPTER 11

VERY FEW PEOPLE ever saw Tim Spenser mad. He had an all-American look about him and the kind of Boy Scout manners that seemed to naturally disarm upset people. He was the type of guy you wanted around to solve a problem because no matter what you threw at him, he never lost his cool. Tim's unflappable nature was a great asset when he was counseling warring couples or taking a potentially volatile church business meeting and turning it into an opportunity for substantial dialogue.

But at this moment he was not his normal self. After his confession of his love for Kim at the Sunday morning worship service he spent the next two hours trying to find her. Yet, nothing he did seemed to work. At first, he had left her a kind message on her cell phone, but she hadn't returned his phone call. Then, he tried texting but she still didn't respond. He had gone as far as to drive by all of her friend's homes and he favorite restaurants to see if she was there, but he couldn't find any sign of her.

As a last ditch effort he went by Stardust's remembering all the times Kim and Annie had spent there lounging about with the favorite drink. When he walked in he recognized she was missing. Now his anxiety was at full pitch. This put him on edge.

When he didn't find her he bought a coffee and sat outside to breathe in the cool spring air with the hopes that he could somehow settle his nerves. But his worry and the caffeine in his drink proved to be a volatile concoction stirring up the cortisol in his brain and flushing that dangerous hormone throughout his whole body. That was when he thought he saw Kim's car parked across the street at the Gordon Pharmacy.

If Tim had more closely inspected the gray Honda Accord, he would have known it was not Kim's vehicle. But visions of Kim and

Darrell having a passionate rendezvous in the storage area drove him to walk right past the car and through the doors of the drug store with no concern for thinking more carefully.

Little did he know that Tony and Ruth Phipps were inside doing the same thing. A few minutes earlier Ruth had spied what she thought was Kim's car as they passed the drug store on their way home. She had told Tony, "We need to deal with this before it becomes any worse."

"Ok dear, but I still think you need to get in touch with her and set up a time to chat," he said as he reluctantly parked the Ford Explorer a few spaces ahead of the grey Honda. Ruth got out and slammed the door. She walked rapidly until she noticed that Tony was following behind her at a very slow pace.

"Do I have to be the one with all the gumption in this family Tony?" she barked at him. "I swear, sometimes I wonder if it wasn't for me what you would really be doing."

"Living somewhere in the mountains in peace," muttered Tony.

"What's that?"

"Nothing dear."

Ruth walked through the automatic doors looking for Kim and Darrell while Tony stopped by the magazine stand to secretly scan the most recent version of the Sports Illustrated Swim Suit edition.

Tim followed behind them about twenty seconds later. He didn't see anyone because he was making a beeline for the storage area when he saw Darrell speaking with a patient at the consultation window. Unfortunately Darrell did not see Tim until it was too late. Before he knew it Tim had brushed the young woman aside and grabbed Darrell by the lapel of his lab coat. In one violent motion he jerked Darrell through the window, tossing him onto his back. This whack of the pharmacist's back hitting the concrete floor made such a loud noise that one of the store associates peered around the corner to if a large item fell from one of the shelves.

When the young woman who was brushed aside saw this transpire, she let out a shrill scream that turned everyone's head in the store. Poor Darrell had the look of sheer terror written all over his face.

"Tim … Tim listen to me … I want to apolo …"

The enraged minister interrupted Darrell's faux apology with a crushing right to the jaw. Tim didn't stop there. He began to pummel the pharmacist's face with a flurry of alternating punches. Darrell tried to resist, but Tim had both knees pinning Darrell's arms to the floor. All of this was purely academic because by the fourth or fifth punch Darrell was unconscious. But Tim didn't care.

The only thing that saved Darrell from getting more seriously injured was that Tony Phipps had sought to intervene by grabbing Tim around the neck and wrestling him away from the unconscious Casanova. This stopped Tim long enough to divert his anger. Tim didn't know who seized him around the neck. He just instinctively reached back over his left shoulder and grabbed his invisible assailant by the hair, flipping him into the diaper section of the store. Tim then jumped on top of the mysterious attacker with his bloody right hand cocked and ready to fire when he noticed it was Tony. Tim then stood up and pointed at Tony and said "Don't ever get involved in my personal affairs again!"

He pivoted away and headed towards the front door. Ruth initially tried to stand in his way by the checkout section.

"You are surely going to be fired now Tim!" she said shaking standing with her hands propped upon her hips.

Tim moved towards Ruth with his teeth barred like a rapid dog. "You shut your face! Fire me if you like but get out of my way." Before Ruth could give him another piece of her mind Tim gave her one look that stopped her sermonizing. Ruth was known by most to be emotionally-arrogant. but no one would ever call her stupid. So she let him pass by.

Tim trotted across the street and jumped into his car. As he mashed the accelerator and headed towards the bypass his neo-cortex began to inform his limbic system that his acts of aggression were going to have serious consequences. Tim shook his head and tried to slough it off by reminding the reasonable section of his brain that "these people had it coming," but deep down he knew better. Tim not only had just made a complicated situation more entangled, he wasn't even sure if Darrell was still alive.

Right as he was making his turn onto the bypass his phone rang. He looked down and saw Kim's name. At first he was going to ignore it but on the fourth buzz he picked up.

"Yeah, what do you want?" snarled the perturbed man.

Kim was taken aback by this response because Annie had already phoned her and told her what had happened in the church service. Tim's humble and sweet message he had left on Kim's cell phone added to the tender shoot of hope that was just budding again from her pruned soul. The man she was talking to now hardly sounded like the same person.

"Well, uh, I" stuttered Kim. "I was just returning your phone calls."

"Where have you been?" asked her still angry husband.

"I had to go to Asheville to pick up my phone. I had left it last night at the pizza pub when Annie and I went out to dinner." Kim measured herself to make sure that she didn't antagonize her already perturbed husband. "Is everything all right?"

Tim now understood why he wasn't able to reach Kim. Embarrassment began to creep in and he felt really foolish about what had just happened. "No Kim everything is not all right."

"Where are you Tim?" asked Kim.

"I'm on the bypass heading I don't where. I screwed up really bad. I won't be surprised if the police won't be coming after me soon."

A thought ran across Kim's mind that Tim might have just killed Darrell. Instead of making that inquiry, she asked, "Are you near Sawyer's State Park?"

"Yeah," replied Tim.

Kim's protective nature now kicked in. "Listen Tim. Just go there and park the car. I am only a few minutes away. I will be there as soon as I can. Please promise me you will be there and that you won't do anything stupid."

"Ok," said the frightened man.

"Tim," said Kim in her most reassuring manner. "We can get through this, I promise. I love you more that I can say."

By now Tim was crying. He felt silly and out of control. He entertained the idea of continuing to drive west until he reached California. But the calming sound of Kim's voice connected to the more logical part of his mind and he concurred with a simple "Ok. I love you too."

Tim was such an emotional wreck that he missed the exit for the park and had to drive several miles down the highway before he could turn around. As a result of this error Kim got to the park before Tim did. This gave her time to give Annie a call. Her best friend answered laughing with a male voice in the background.

"Annie?"

"Hey Kim. What are you doing?"

"Is Bart there?

"Yes."

"So, from the sound of things your talk with him went well?"

"Oh yes. I have so much to tell you."

"I am happy for you. But I want you to say a prayer for Tim."

"What's wrong?"

"Evidently there was some kind of confrontation with Darrell and Tim is convinced that the police will be coming for him. Annie I am worried that he killed him."

"Kim, let's not jump to that conclusion. Do you know where he is?"

"I am at the park and we are meeting together. I don't know why he isn't here. I am really scared Annie."

"What can Bart and I do?"

"Nothing. Just pray and I will call you back when I know what is going on."

"Ok sweetie, please call back soon."

Tim drove up as the conversation was ending and parked beside Kim's Honda. "Annie I've got to go" she said in a hurried manner and then hung up her phone. She got out as soon as he cut off the engine of his car.

Tim slowly poured himself out of his vehicle. His normally ruddy complexion had turned pale. His walk was unsteady as if he had just awakened from an all-night bender. All he could utter to his concerned wife was a faint "Hey."

Kim approached him in a gentle manner. She wanted to run into his arms and give him a passionate embrace. But she discerned that at this stage such an action would be a bit presumptuous. Walking up to Tim she returned his simple greeting by repeating, "Hey."

They stood there for a moment, not knowing who should speak not what they should say. Finally Kim broke the ice. "So, what happened that makes you feel you are going to be arrested?"

"I went to the drug store and found Darrell. I beat him unconscious, and when Tony Phipps tried to break it up I flipped him into some display shelves. If that wasn't enough, I threatened Ruth when she tried to confront me on my way out of the door." Tim leaned back on the hood of Kim's car. He looked as if he was going to be sick. "I have sure made a bad situation worse Kim. I hurt him badly. I don't know if he is still alive. I am so sorry."

Kim reached up and moved his chin back towards her gaze. "No Timothy, I am the one that should be sorry. If I hadn't been so stupid none of this would be happening."

Tim looked at her and smiled a little. "You are right. You were pretty stupid." They both laughed for a moment and that seemed to lessen the tension a bit.

Tim looked across the mountains and sighed. "I have no idea what is going to happen. Everything is falling down around me."

"I don't either. But let's not get ahead of ourselves. I am sure he is fine."

"I hope so Kim. What he did was wrong but he didn't deserve me hurting him like this. I just got all angry and upset when I tried to call you and you didn't answer."

"But I was in Asheville picking up my phone."

I know, dear God I know that now but not at first. I drove all over the place to try and find you but you were nowhere to be seen. And then I saw this grey Honda at the drug store and I thought …" Tim lowered his head again and started crying.

Kim gently grasped Tim by his broad shoulders. "Honey please don't do this. I am the one that should feel badly. You are a good man and a good husband."

"Yeah, well not anymore." Tim pulled away from Kim a little as if being around him was not a wise thing for her to be doing at this juncture. "You need to start thinking about yourself. I can't see this ending good for me. Even if Darrell is ok I am sure he will press charges."

"Maybe not" said Kim doing her best to inject some much needed optimism into the deteriorating situation.

"Well, if he doesn't I am sure the Phipps will. I think I messed up Tony pretty badly. He was holding his head like it really hurt. I guarantee you that he and Ruth will have me thrown under the jail."

"Tim I am not going anywhere ... that is if you will still have me."

Tim placed his left hand on Kim's shoulder. "Listen. All this stuff that happened between you and Darrell, well ... I mean it wasn't your fault entirely. I let the church get in the way of our relationship. I didn't mean for it to happen. But I guess that my ego and insecurity drove me to constantly seek the approval of others. I am sorry for neglecting you Kim."

Tears started flowing out of both of Kim's eyes. She stepped away and tried to regain her composure, but she couldn't. Her tears were a powerful mixture of regret and relief. She was sorry for hurting her husband and simultaneously comforted by the fact that somehow he still loved her. She felt very unworthy of such love, but she wasn't about to turn away from this incredible gift.

Tim walked up to her and gently took Kim into his arms. She buried her face into his chest and let loose the hounds of remorse. Tim didn't say anything. He placed his chin on her head and gently wrapped his blood-stained hand around the back of her head. They stood in this position for a while. Tim didn't let her go until the crashing torrents of Kim's sorrow ceased.

When Kim finished crying she wiped her face with her unzipped warm up jacket. Tim offered her a handkerchief and she made thorough use of it. She offered the cloth back to him.

"No thanks you can keep it now." They both laughed again. He reached out to pat Kim on the shoulder with his right hand when he noticed that his it was really throbbing. He pulled it back and examined the clear evidence that he had worked hard at teaching Darrell a lesson. It was then that he saw that it was black and blue and already swollen.

"Well that is great," said Tim shaking his head in disgust.

Kim looked at it and said, "Oh my gosh honey, we need to go to the Emergency Room. That thing looks broken."

Tim nodded. In a millisecond Kim went from repentant woman to assertive wife. She pointed at her car and said, "I want you to get into my car right now and I will drive up the hospital. We will come and pick up your car later. Don't argue with me ok?"

Tim wasn't about to argue. There was no doubt that his hand was messed up. But beyond that medical fact was the comforting reassurance that Kim really cared about him. It had been a while since he was on the receiving end of this kind of sweet compassion and he liked it. Besides, he was starting to feel a little lightheaded and he knew that all of his adrenalin was starting to wear off and that hand was going to hurt worse.

Tim complied and got in Kim's car. It didn't take her long to get to the hospital. Tim noticed that there two police cars parked by the Emergency Room entrance. When they walked in Tim saw two deputies he recognized from the Gordon Police Department. They were taking notes as they were talking with Tony and Ruth Phipps. Tony had an ice-pack against his head and Ruth seemed to be very animated.

Kim either didn't see this or chose to ignore it. She had already reached the information desk and was checking her husband in. Tim walked by and didn't make eye contact with the Phipps. He sat down in the left corner right beside the TV set that was playing a rerun of The People's Court. As soon as the officers saw Tim they walked up to have a chat. Tim knew what was going to happen next.

"Hey Pastor Tim," said Office Danny Turnhill. Officer Eddie Blanton slightly nodded and pulled out his notepad.

"Hey guys," replied Tim. "I guess you are here to arrest me or something like that."

"Let's not get ahead of ourselves" replied Danny. "It looks like you got a messed up hand. Did that happen in the fight?"

"Yes. I am guilty of beating the crap out of Darrell and chunking Tony into the wall. I will be happy to come along with y'all as soon as I get this thing checked out."

"You are in some serious trouble Rev. Spenser" said Officer Blanton in a very matter-of-fact manner. "The list of your offences goes beyond just beating the crap out of a pharmacist."

Office Turnhill looked aggravated with the younger man. He peered over his shoulder and said, "Eddie, why don't you finish taking the Phipps' statement. I will handle Tim on my own." The young man walked away mumbling something under his breath. Turnhill looked back at Tim and said, "The exuberance of youth is the fountainhead of most impulsive judgments."

"Is that Cicero?" asked Tim rubbing his arm.

"I can't remember" replied Danny. "I read it in an old Reader's Digest when I was sitting on the toilet last week."

Tim laughed heartily and for a moment it took his mind off the pain. Kim walked up and sat down beside her husband. "The nurse told me that they can get you back in triage soon" said Kim as she patted Tim on the back.

Danny resumed his interrogation. "So Tim," he said pulling out his own pad. "What happened at the drug store?"

"Well, I went in looking for Darrell. We had a problem of a very personal nature," said Tim looking down trying his best not to make his wife feel any worse.

Danny nodded and said, "Yeah I was told about the affair by the Phipps. So why did you decide to yank him through the window and commence to beating him about the head and shoulders? You are a smart guy. Didn't you know that was kind of illegal?"

Tim leaned forward and said, "I wasn't really thinking. But I am willing to face whatever charges Darrell presses against me. Is he ok?"

"Yeah, but I think you broke his nose and he might need to have some surgery."

"Dear Lord," replied Tim.

"Oh, don't worry, Darrell ain't going to press charges," replied the officer. "But those two," pointing to the Phipps, "are another deal altogether. What happened with Tony?"

"I was on top of Darrell and then someone grabbed me around the neck and started choking me" said Tim. "I took a hold of his hair and flipped him into the wall."

"Did you hit him?"

"No, I just told him to stay out of my life … or something like that."

"Ok, and were you threatening to Ruth?"

"Not really. I mean I told her to shut up and get out of my way but I didn't threaten her with any physical harm."

Danny nodded again. "That is the same testimony given by a couple of bystanders. Of course Ruth and Tony had you acting in a lot more menacing way towards them."

"I can imagine," said Tim. "But what I told you is the truth. And like I said, I will deal with whatever I am guilty of. I feel badly about Darrell, but I will never apologize for what I did and said to the Phipps."

"I suspect you won't, considering the circumstances and the people involved" said Danny as he inserted his small notebook back into his shirt pocket. "But just in case I need you any further please stick around here. I want to call the chief and ask him what he wants me to do. I still might have to take you downtown."

"I won't be going anywhere for a while" said Tim waving his right hand.

Danny turned and walked towards the Phipps to help his partner finish that line of questioning. Tim looked around and saw Bart and Annie come in through the front doors. Kim motioned for them to join her and Tim. She turned to Tim and said, "I called Annie as soon as I saw Ruth and Tony. They are here for moral support."

Tim rolled his eyes a little and then said "Well, I am sure the news will be out soon enough. I guess a few more witnesses won't matter in the long run."

Kim looked a little embarrassed when Tim made that comment. Even though she knew that both Annie and Bart could keep a confidence, none of this barrage of crazy happenings would have occurred if she had just exhibited some self–control. She got up and gave Annie a big hug. Bart walked over and sat down beside Tim. "Hey friend" said Bart in a concerned fashion. "Can I take a look at that?"

"Why not," said the exhausted pastor.

Bart gently pulled up Tim's hand by the wrist. He turned the hand to the left and right and asked Tim to make a fist. Tim tried but winced in agony. Bart shook his head and said, "Yep that hand looks broken. The degree of damage won't be known until they get some x-rays. But don't be surprised if they will have to do some surgery."

"Oh no," gasped Kim. "This is terrible. I am so sorry Tim." Then the waterworks started again. Annie put her arm around Kim and said, "Don't worry sweetie. This hospital is known for its great orthopedic surgeons. We use them all the time for our patients needing joint replacements and the like. Tim will be in good hands."

Kim seemed to understand, but it didn't stop her from crying a little more. She took out Tim's handkerchief from her purse and wiped whatever remaining makeup she had left on her face off. Tim just leaned back and stared back at the front desk. Bart didn't know what to say so he picked up a People magazine and acted like he was interested in an article about a starlet's recent plastic surgery. Kim got up to go to the restroom and asked if Annie would check on the status of when Tim could be seen. Annie agreed and quickly walked up to the front desk. After finding out that it wouldn't be long, she started back towards the corner of the Emergency Room.

"I guess birds of a feather flock together huh?" said Ruth loud enough for the whole room to hear her.

"Excuse me?" said Annie flashing a look of disdain towards Ruth.

"You heard me," replied Ruth. "It is such a tragedy that women in this town fall for the manipulative ways of that corrupt man. But I guess if a person is spiritually weak, they are capable of falling for anything."

Annie flew hot. She walked right up to Ruth, even though Tony was only a few feet from them giving his version of events to the two police officers. Annie pointed her finger straight at Ruth's face and said, "You really like having the dirt on people, don't you? I think it gives you some kind of cheap thrill."

The police officers both glanced back to make sure that there wasn't going to be a cat fight right there in the Emergency Room. Tony seemed content to keep looking the other direction.

Ruth now became very uncomfortable. She tried to counter this challenge by saying, "I am not the one guilty of sexual sin. The damage that women like you and Kim do, to communities, churches and families is hard to fathom. Now, after today, Tim will have to leave the church. This is such a tragedy … such a preventable tragedy!"

"I am not fooled by your use of empathic language Ruth" said Annie moving her finger ever-closer, almost touching Ruth's nose. "I think you are what Jesus called a blind guide. You love being listened to and having influence over weak-minded people. But deep down you are filled with all kinds of sick stuff."

Ruth was shaken by that comment. She turned to her husband for moral support. Tony pretended not to have heard the justified reprimand. He was turned in the opposite direction, still holding the ice-pack to his head and was explaining to the officers how he was accosted by the raving lunatic.

When Ruth saw that her husband was oblivious to her plight she sat up straight and said, "I think if you really care for your friend you will advise her to leave town. After this Wednesday night Tim will be out of a job. I think she will be lucky if her marriage survives."

"We will see about that Ruth," said Annie in a defiant manner. "There are a lot more people in this town that don't think you and your husband are as spiritual as you believe yourselves to be! I think that you're in for a big shock." With that comment, Annie walked off leaving Ruth sitting with her mouth wide open.

Annie got back to the "sinner's corner" and found everyone staring at her with respect and astonishment. No one had ever challenged Ruth like that. Kim stood up and gave her friend a hug. "Thanks Annie," said Kim with a grin on her face. "You are my hero!"

Bart leaned over and gave his sweetheart a peck on the cheek after she sat down. "Mine too," said Bart winking at Tim.

"I appreciate what you said Annie," responded Tim. "But I was planning on sending a letter of resignation before the meeting. It is really of no use to fight anything now. Especially after what I did at the drug store."

Annie patted Tim on the knee. "You will do no such thing Pastor!" replied his good friend. "You just plan to be there on Wednesday. We are not just going to let mean, manipulative people win. To give in to people like the Phipps right now would be bad for everyone. I am not going to let them run you out of town like they did the last minister. Besides, if we can't stand beside each other during rough times, we ought to close the doors."

Tim was overwhelmed by such gracious loyalty and support. He grabbed Kim's hand with his good hand and bowed his head. Annie smiled at Bart and then looked over to Ruth. She gave her the kind of stare-down that is reserved for gladiators who were getting ready to join in mortal combat. There was no way Annie was going to let that woman and her band of religious suck-ups prevail.

The parking lot of the church was packed on Wednesday night. Annie was not surprised. She knew that Ruth would be busy the previous few days putting together a formidable cadre of zealots set on firing Tim. This fact caused Annie to get on the phone and speak personally to everyone thought had been helped to by Tim. She was determined that if Ruth and Tony were going to try to use brute force to remove Tim, she would be sure that this naked display of power would be exposed.

When Annie walked in with Tim and Kim she recognized the animated conversations that were already occurring and that there was a good chance things could get nasty. Almost all of the folks noticed when the three of them walked down the aisle. They were hard to miss. Tim had a large cast on his right arm that was supported by a sling. He had just gotten out of the hospital late Tuesday afternoon after undergoing surgery. He was still a bit woozy, so Kim walked on his right side trying to prop him up as best she could. Annie led both of them to the front row of the center aisle. She was ready for whatever Ruth and her minions threw their way. They sat down and people began to find their seats, still chatting about what they felt should happen next.

The meeting commenced with Elder Barry Tompkins leading in prayer:

"Dear Lord, we are in a tough place right now. Help the full truth to be seen so that we don't make a bad decision. I ask that honesty, love and grace would govern what everyone says tonight, and that somehow the unity of the church will be preserved. In Christ's name, Amen."

When he finished Elder John Baskin read the minutes from the last meeting. Then some general business was covered like calendar issues and funding for a youth mission trip to Peru. After making a few corrections he asked for a vote to accept the minutes as read. It was unanimous and then John sat down.

Tony Phipps took the stage next. He was wearing a neck brace, not because he was truly injured but to accentuate the message that Tim Spencer was unfit for ministry. He looked across the building and saw more than 400 people assembled. This large of a turnout surprised and intimidated him. He swallowed hard and began his speech. "Folks, in a crowd like this there could be the chance that some people here are not members. Let me remind you that when it comes time to vote, only members of good standing can participate. So, if you are not a member let me not only remind you of this fact, let me also remind you will not be allowed to speak on behalf of any position on the issue at hand."

Tony once again looked across the auditorium. He saw that on the center isle of the front row sat Tim, Kim and Annie. Annie looked up at Tony and made eye contact. She gave him the clear message that she was ready to go to war with him and anyone else that sought to dismiss her friends. Tony then looked to Ruth for support. She urged him onward and then looked over to Annie, Tim and Kim and let them know she was also ready for a fight.

Tony began his introduction. "Dear precious members of NewLight. We are gathered here to deal with a heartbreaking and difficult situation. Recent revelations of the behavior of both our Pastor and his wife have led us to the inevitable position we are in tonight. For the past two weeks the Elder Team has met a total of four times. During these long sessions, we have heard testimony from several witnesses about descriptions of immoral and violent behavior. We have prayed and discussed about all of our options. As a result of these discussions, even as late as last night,

WALKER ARMSTRONG

we have come to the conclusion that it would be in the best interest of the church to ask for Pastor Tim's resignation."

As soon as those words left the mouth of Tony a few people shouted out things like "That is so wrong" or "We don't want you to leave Pastor Tim!" Tony could see that the meeting could get quickly out of hand. "Listen dear brothers and sisters" he responded. "We don't want anyone shouting out messages, no matter how well-intentioned. As soon as we hear the testimony from these individuals I promise you that we will open the floor for discussion and questions."

Tony then motioned to his wife to come forward. "My dear wife will come and be the first witness of these tragic events. You all know what a dedicated woman of God she is and how she is looked to by many of you ladies as an example of what it means to be a servant of Lord. I am grateful that she is my partner and the mother to our three outstanding children. Ruth will you please come and share with us what you know?

Ruth Phipps was already on the stage before Tony finished his introduction. She was dressed immaculately in a high collared, long-sleeved ruffled shirt and a black and white herringbone skirt that went to her knees. She wore a large black belt that had a silver buckle that neatly tied the shirt to the skirt. Her shoes matched her belt so as to give the message of both propriety and style. Her hair was pulled back into a bun and her makeup looked as if she had been a model for one of the women's kiosk stores at the mall. No one could ever say that Ruth's appearance lacked in style.

Ruth carried her New American Standard Bible Study Bible that was almost the size of a large phone book. She opened it and read from 2 Timothy 3:16-17. She made it a point to emphasize how God's word was profitable for rebuking. She closed her Bible and laid it aside.

"My brothers and sisters" she said with trembling voice, "we are here tonight because two of our members, yes even more importantly two of our leaders are guilty of sin." Unlike her husband she never really looked at the audience to read them. She gazed straight ahead like a Panzer tank moving towards its objective.

"We do not do this lightly," she said as she cleared her throat. "But we are certain of the facts. And the facts that I am to share about tonight have to do with Kim Spenser's affair with Darrell Eller."

Ruth spent the next seven minutes describing in detail what she and three other women in the community observed for a period of about three months. She used as the crown jewel of her deposition about how Kim and Darrell's affair was finally confirmed when church members saw then together in Albemarle.

She concluded this presentation by saying, "It grieves my heart to no end to be privy to these things. It has kept me up at nights with worry for the marriage of this dear couple and for the reputation of our church." Then with a quiver in her voice she said, "I humbly believe that in order to somehow preserve their marriage and protect the unity of the church we should ask Tim to resign."

Ruth then bowed her head and walked off to a few handclaps, some Amens, and a lot of indistinguishable whispers. Tony chose not to correct the show of support for this position. This double standard was duly noted by more than a few people in the audience. If someone wondered if there the meeting was going to be contentious, they had little doubt now.

Tony then asked Tonya Billips to come forward. She was the young lady standing by the Consultation Window at the drug store who had witnessed Tim's assault of Darrell Eller. She was briefer than Ruth and somewhat clinical in her description of what took place. At times her presentation seemed so caned that several wondered if she had been coached. Annie leaned over to Kim and whispered, "Isn't that the same dress Ruth had in her display window at her shop?" Kim nodded affirmatively. Just when Annie thought she could think less of Ruth than she already did, something like this would occur and cause her downgrade Ruth's character even further.

Tonya finished her damning testimony and then sat down beside Ruth. Ruth patted her on the thigh and one could easily see she told her "Good job." Tony asked Ralph Mako another elder to come and lead the impending discussion. Ralph, the local District Attorney, was famous for putting away criminals with cold, hard efficiency. Rumor had it that he was going to challenge Jake Sawyers at the next election for Superior Court Judge of the county. He would not allow any nonsense and would probably make it very difficult for anyone to speak their mind.

Ralph started out by saying, "I am the Chair of this meeting. As the Chair, I will not put up with any shenanigans. There are wireless microphones placed throughout the Worship Center. If you have a question to ask or wish to make a statement you must raise your hand. I will then recognize you. You cannot speak until that happens. Then, you are to state your full name loudly and clearly. If at any time I deem you out of order I will have the microphone taken from you and you will not be allowed to speak the rest of this meeting. And I must also tell you that if too many act out of order I will cut it the discussion short and we call for a vote. I will not let this serious issue degenerate into a popularity contest."

Annie then raised her hand. A microphone was taken to her and she said. "Mr. Chairman, my name is Annie Bryant." Ralph nodded in approval and Annie continued. "My brothers and sisters, I am not here to question the facts as they have been presented. Neither do I want to question the motives of those who have spoken thus far. What I want to talk about has to do with whether or not we are being fair and open about all that has transpired."

"Is there a question or questions contained in statement Miss Bryant?"

"Yes Mr. Chairman there are" replied Annie. "My first question is this: How many meetings did Tim attend of the four mentioned?"

Tony stood up and had a mike already at his disposal. "Annie there were four and Rev. Spenser did not come to any."

Annie looked at the Chair and asked "May I ask him another question Mr. Mako?" Ralph Mako nodded. Looking at Tony she asked, "How many did Tim know about Tony?"

Tony's face got red. He knew exactly where she was going with her line of questioning. "I asked him to come to one and he refused. In fact, he was very clear and plain about wanting to handle this on his own."

Tim looked at the Prosecutor and shook his head. Annie looked at Ralph and asked, "May I have Tim answer that charge?"

"It is not a charge Miss Bryant and this is not a court of law," replied Mako in a very stern manner. "Reverend Spenser is free to answer any questions that pertain to him."

Annie handed Tim the mike. He turned to the audience and said, "I never said that." Murmurs began to swell with that plain statement.

"Settle down folks" said Mako. "I was not kidding about my earlier comment. Please continue Pastor."

Tim nodded and picked back up where he had first addressed the issue. "I called Tony right after Kim and I first talked about our problems. I asked him to lead the meeting that Wednesday night because I didn't feel that I could carry on at that moment.

It was then that Tony revealed to me that he had called a special elder's meeting to, and I quote, 'deal with the issue.' I was really bothered by that. I was so upset because I thought that such a meeting was premature. I told him that I wasn't able to come that night, but I would be in touch. I never heard back from him, so I didn't know about these other meetings."

Ralph Mako then took the lead before Annie could ask a follow-up question. "Tony," said the DA, "Does my memory serve me correctly when I say that you had communicated to the rest of the Elder Team that Tim refused to meet with us at all?"

Now Tony was in a fix. No one, including him, wanted to get on Ralph Mako's bad side. Tony paused and then said, "It was my impression that this was how he felt." Several people nodded in agreement since anyone can misunderstand someone else, especially in an emotionally charged situation.

But Annie did not let that slide. She asked for the microphone back from Tim and then turned back to the Judge. "Mr. Chairman, may I ask Tony another question?" Mako nodded and smiled. He thought to himself that Annie had missed her calling. He knew exactly where she was headed and how poor, stupid old Tony had fallen into a noose that was quickly closing.

"Tony," said Annie. "Did you ever inform Tim about the other meetings?"

"No Annie," replied an angry Tony. "I did not because I thought that he was in a bad state of mind and that he wouldn't meet with us?"

"Ok Tony. I see where you are coming from" said Annie with a wry smile on her face. "Tony, were you aware that in our Church Constitution that it states specifically in Article Nine, Section Three, Item D that, quote *Since the Senior Pastor plays a crucial role on our Elder Team, he cannot miss more than one meeting a quarter of the monthly meetings. If due to illness or other special circumstance he can no longer carry out that requirement he is to meet with the Chair and Co-Chair of the Elder Team and reach a temporary arrangement until a more permanent solution is rendered. Until this condition is met no additional Elder's Meetings can be scheduled.*

Tony stood dazed at this undeniable fact. He looked towards Ralph Mako for support but found none. Annie placed the paper behind her on her seat and turned square up towards Tony and asked "Did you and Barry Tompkins have that kind of meeting with Tim?"

"No we did not Annie" said Tony.

Turning back to Ralph Mako Annie said, "Mr. Chairman I declare a point of order."

"What is your point of order Miss Bryant?" asked Mako.

"Mr. Chairman, because the Elder Team did not comply with the wise provision as stated in our Constitution, any formal recommendation that they make here tonight will null and void."

Ralph Mako winked at Annie and he didn't care who saw him do this. Annie knew that he was the chief architect of NewLight's constitution. In fact, he had actually led seminars for ministers on how to construct a church constitution that would stand up in a court of law. That is why her maneuver was not only on point, it was strategically brilliant. There was no doubt in his mind that the people were going to be shocked at what would happen next.

He looked at the congregation and spoke: "Ladies and Gentleman, as the Chair I have the parliamentary responsibility and authority to rule on matters just like this. What Miss Bryant has raised takes precedent over all other points of discussion. That means once I issue my ruling, any further formal discussion about this topic is prohibited until the Elders have re-convened and have met with Pastor Tim."

People started speaking to one another in hushed vocalizations of confusion. "Therefore, the chair rules that the motion to have a vote of confidence of Reverend Spenser is out of order and this meeting is adjourned."

Chaos erupted as soon as the prosecutor walked away from the pulpit. Some stood in shock asking each other what just happened. Others were whooping and shouting all types of positive affirmations. A few tried to corner Ralph and challenge him over points of order. But it was too late. Even Tony knew he had screwed up. But his wife refused to accept what had just occurred and was giving Ralph Mako the business by the left corner of the platform.

Dozens of supporters gathered around Tim and Kim. They showered the beleaguered couple with genuine affection and with words of encouragement. Kim was so overcome with the sense of love she felt from the church members that she sat down on a chair and cried. Tim sat beside her and put his arm around his bride.

Annie received many congratulations and some scowls for her parliamentary check-mate of the Phipps. She walked out into the parking lot and took a deep breath. It was hard for her to fathom all that had happened over the last few days. Nothing had been settled tonight, but at least Tim and Kim had a fighting chance.

As she conversed with a few people who were thanking her for what she did Bart pulled up in the pickup truck. It looked like both he and Frodo were happy to see her. She thanked the people that she was talking with for their support and hurried across the lot. When she opened the door Frodo greeted her with a wagging tail and a bark. She hopped in and said "Why don't you greet me like that?" Bart laughed and tried his best to wag his bottom.

When she got her seatbelt secure Bart asked, "So how did it go? Did they buy your argument from the church constitution?"

"Yes sir," she said with a bit of triumphal relief. "I don't know what is going to happen next. But a least we have a chance to let less prejudiced people have a say in this big mess."

That's great!" responded Bart. "I am really proud of you."

Annie grinned and said, "Thanks. Maybe now things will settle down a bit." For about ten seconds she felt relaxed. Then her cell phone pinged with an incoming text. It was from Kim and it read, "We need to talk. I'm pregnant."

CHAPTER 12

ANNIE HAD BART drive her home. When they pulled into her driveway she saw that Kim's car was parked on the left side of her garage. She had ridden with Kim, and the two of them had met Tim at the church parking lot before they entered for the church meeting. Evidently Kim came back as soon as they finished talking immediately following the meeting. Annie's head was swimming with all kinds of thoughts as a result of Kim's cryptic text. Bart knew something was up but was wise enough to not ask. Annie gave him a quick kiss and said, "I will call you tomorrow morning."

Kim met Annie at the door. She looked to Annie as if she had been given the death sentence and that she only had twelve hours to live. Despite Kim's harried appearance, the first thing Annie asked was "Where's Meagan?" Kim pointed towards the bedroom and then walked back towards the den. Annie followed her. They both sat down on the couch. Kim turned to Annie and said, "I don't know what I am going to do!"

"Who is the father Kim?" asked Annie in a somewhat blunt fashion.

Kim looked away and said, "That's it. I just don't know."

"Ok," replied Annie. "Then tell me this. How long have you known?"

"I had my suspicious for a while" said Kim. "But I took two pregnancy tests yesterday and the both came back positive."

"When was the last time you were with Darrell?" asked Annie trying her best to get to the bottom of this ever-expanding mess.

"Back in January," said Kim. "But I know what you are going to ask. I had a light period back in February. Since then I have felt kind of weird."

"I guess I shouldn't ask whether or not you used protection," said Annie in a somewhat condescending way.

"That was the only time Annie I swear!"

Annie got up from the couch and walked to the mantle over the fireplace. She was shaking her head. Things couldn't be any worse for Kim if she had made it her sole mission to screw up her life.

Kim interrupted Annie's train of thought. "I know what you are probably thinking and you are right to believe that about me," said Kim trying to keep herself from losing it. "But right now I need to know what to do. This could be Tim's baby. I am just not sure."

Annie looked at Kim and said, "Do you have any idea how Tim is going to take this? He has opened up his heart to trust you and now you are going to deliver this kind of news to him?"

Kim put her hands on her head and said, "I know, I know."

"No you don't know Kim!" barked Annie. "You have no clue what it feels like to be cheated on and then to trust once more only to have your heart broken all over again. If I was Tim I would kick your tail to the curb!"

Kim stared off towards the bay windows.

Annie didn't let up. "Do you have any idea how bad this is Kim?" asked Annie. "If Darrell is the father you will probably have to get a divorce and the people who backed you will look like idiots."

"You are right," said Kim. "That is why I might out of town and have an abortion. "Annie, would you go with me if I do this?" asked Kim.

"You know my answer to that question Kim" replied Annie incredulously. "How could you ask me to do such a thing? Your first thought should be to tell your husband."

"You are right," said Kim mournfully. "But if I do and it is not his child, Tim will put me out."

"You should have thought about that before you hooked up with Darrell Kim. My God, did you not listen to my description of his character after I broke it off with him? You of all people should have known better. It is like you totally ignored everything I told you about him."

Kim sat there looking as if she was in shock. Annie noticed this and sought to change her tactic to get her best friends attention. She moved over to Kim and squatted down beside her. "Kim, I love you. I know that deep down you regret all of this. But if you don't tell Tim what you are facing your marriage will implode on you. You owe Tim the courtesy of telling him the truth."

"I know, but things were just starting to get better."

"Do you want to live a lie?"

"No"

"Then you had better get your head straight about this,"

"But I am sure if I tell him this our marriage is over."

"If he ends the marriage Kim, at least he will be able to do it on his terms rather than being waylaid with a revelation when the child is nine years old that she doesn't belong to him. I mean, can you imagine how hard that would be?"

"No I can't."

"The please listen to me. As frustrated as I am with you right now, I am not going to turn away when you need me most. But I've got to tell you that if you are deceptive with Tim, my respect for you will be in the trash."

"You are right. I will do it tomorrow."

"Good!" said Annie. Then she plopped down on the floor with her back against the couch and sighed. Turing up towards Kim she asked, "Is there anything else you need to tell me while we are at it?"

"No Annie," replied Kim. "I am all confessed-out."

Tim had spoken briefly to Tony Phipps after the service on Wednesday night and arranged to meet with him early Thursday morning for coffee at Stardust. Tim wanted to find a way to resolve the situation peacefully. But he also wanted Tony and Ruth to know he wasn't going to just fade away into the night to fulfill their desires. Too much was at stake to simply give in and move away.

Tim arrived first at 6:55 a.m. and ordered a Sumatran coffee. He secured the same table that he and Ruth sat at not so long ago when she unloaded the devastating news that his wife had an affair with Darrell. He sat down and slowly sipped the rich hot brew. He gathered his thoughts about him and tried to figure out how he would start the conversation.

WALKER ARMSTRONG

After about fifteen minutes of waiting Tim refreshed his coffee and gave Tony a call. As soon as it rang it went straight to voicemail. Tim wondered if this was some kind of power-play on Tony's part to make Tim squirm a bit. If that were the case, it wasn't going to work because Tim's sights were set on some really important things. He decided he would wait about five more minutes and then head back home.

Tony showed up a few minutes later still wearing his neck brace in what seemed to be an agitated mood. In order to try to promote some semblance of respect Tim said, "Tony if this is not a good time for you we can reschedule."

"No," replied Tony in an exasperated fashion. "We might as well get this out of the way."

Tim could tell that this probably wasn't going to be that productive of a session, so he decided to lower his expectations and find some basic common ground about where to go from here.

"Well thanks for coming Tony," said a cautious Tim. "I first want to apologize for my behavior the other day. I had no idea that it was you who was behind me. If I had known that I would have responded differently. I hope you weren't hurt that badly."

"I appreciated the apology" replied Tony in a business-like way. "But my lawyer has advised me to not talk with you about these particular matters until some kind of resolution is reached."

Tim nodded. "I understand." Then he pulled the collar of his sport shirt away from his neck revealing some faint bruising. "This was a lot worse a few days ago. I had Kim take a picture of it when I was in the hospital. I guess I will have something myself to talk with a lawyer about."

Tony sat in shock. The look on his face appeared similar to a gambler who thought his full house was good enough to win, only to be bested by a royal flush.

"You do whatever you need to do Tony," continued Tim. "I really want to find a peaceful way through this that hopefully everyone can agree with."

"I think you know what our response is going to be," said a perturbed Tony. "It hasn't changed overnight."

"That makes sense," replied Tim. "But even if I chose to resign, we still would have to come to terms on a separation agreement."

"Oh, don't worry about that" said Tony in a condescending manner. "What we will offer you will be more than fair."

"I think you are missing the point here Tony," responded Tim. "The congregation expects us to meet and come back to them for with a recommendation."

Tony pulled out a sheet of folded paper from a folder in his briefcase and placed it in front of Tim. It was a separation agreement that was signed by all the Elders. It was dated from last week. Tim looked at it and then turned the paper towards Tony and slid it back to him. "I am not going to sign a document that I had nothing to do with, especially when it relates to my livelihood."

"No need to do any political maneuvering here Tim," said Tony. "I think we both know you need to leave. What we are offering is generous. If we have a vote of confidence and it doesn't go your way, then you are looking at getting nothing."

Tim sat back and looked straight at the man he once sought counsel from when it came to helping the church reach its potential. He now wondered why he trusted him in the first place.

"Well you need to understand something Tony. I am not going anywhere until I have at least one face-to-face meeting with the Elders."

Tony got red in the face. "It's your funeral Tim. But I promise you that in the end you will lose because we have right on our side. Who would support an adulterous wife and a pugilistic pastor anyway?"

Tim had to check himself. He looked Tony up and down and gave him the clear indication that he wasn't intimidated one bit.

Tony stood up and said, "It is obvious that you are not being respectful of the Elder Team or thankful for what we are offering you. I was talking to Barry before I got here and we guessed you would take this kind of position. You seem to not understand it is going to get a lot worse for you and Kim if you don't resign now."

"I will take my chances Tony."

The red-faced man nodded at Tim. As he was turning to walk away, a small grin slid appeared on his face and he said, "By the way, someone told me that they saw Kim buy two pregnancy tests at the drug store the other day. I sure hope if she is pregnant that it's your child."

Tim was wounded by this statement. He stood up and got right in Tony's face. "Listen you pompous ass. If you want to fight dirty I will get down in the mud with you."

Tony sneered at Tim with the kind of smugness that indicated he wasn't worried.

Tim got closer and whispered to Tony "For instance, maybe people would like to know that their Chairman of the Elder Team had a pornography problem a few years ago."

All the blood seemed to leave Tony's face with Tim's blunt threat. He did his best to recover from this heart-numbing counter punch. "Who would believe you at this point?" he quivered.

"It doesn't matter. There are enough people around here that dislike you and your wife that when they hear this hot little tidbit they will spread it around so much that it will burn down your little house of self-righteousness around you!"

Tony didn't say a thing but got out of the coffee shop as quickly as possible.

Tim stood there by himself in the back of the coffee shop for a minute, still trembling with anger. It took a few seconds for him to calm down. He then sat down and finished his coffee. When he gained a grip on the tempest in his mind he sent Kim a text that read: *Call me ASAP! There is something we need to talk about right now*!

Kim had just gotten out of the shower when she noticed Tim's message. Somehow she knew that he had become aware that she was pregnant. All of this, plus her morning sickness, caused her to spend a few minutes over the toilet.

When Kim rolling stomach settled down, she called Tim. He answered on the first ring. Kim swallowed a sip of juice and then said, "Hey I saw you wanted to talk. What is going on?"

Tim tried to give her the benefit of the doubt. "Uh, we need to meet somewhere private and talk. I don't even want to remotely discuss it over the phone. Can you be at Sawyer's Park in about thirty minutes?"

"Sure, I will see you then" said Kim. "Can you give me a hint about what has made you so fired up to talk?"

"No I can't" said Tim. "But I promise I will tell you as soon as I see you."

"Ok, well I will see you then. I love you." Kim waited for a response but all she heard was the beep from Tim hanging up.

The dread of what she was getting ready to go through seemed to be too much. She immediately called Annie at work and said, "Oh my God Annie, he knows, he knows! Tim knows that I am pregnant!"

"But how could he?" asked Annie. "You told me that you hadn't spoken to anyone about this but me."

Kim sat still for a second and then it occurred to her. "Oh no. That young girl that works for Ruth at the dress shop was in line behind me when I bought the pregnancy test kits. I am sure she saw it. What am I going to do?"

"Ok calm down a little," said Annie. She thought for a minute and said. "Tell him you feel in your heart that it is his kid. Then tell him that because of the circumstances you would understand if this was too much for him. You can let him know that regardless of his decision you will be ok."

"But Annie, I don't know that the baby is Tim's" said a shaky Kim.

"Well for now I think that you believe the best option. If it isn't true, you can deal with the fallout then. You are not lying to Tim. But if you automatically assume the worst, then things will probably deteriorate very rapidly."

"Ok, I think I can do that."

"Where are y'all meeting?" asked Annie.

"At the park" replied Kim.

"That's no good" said Annie. "Tell him to meet at my house. The atmosphere of a place has a lot more impact on people's moods than we realize. Tim will more likely be a bit calmer in my smaller place. Wide open spaces tend to stimulate wide open responses."

"How did you get so smart about this kind of stuff?" asked Kim.

"By trial and error girl" said Annie. "Call me when you are done."

Tim was aggravated that they he was had to go over to Annie's house to talk about a very private, potentially volatile issue. Lately he had felt that everyone was playing him for a fool. But this was a new day. No one, including Kim, would manipulate his any longer. He was determined to get to the bottom of the whole pregnancy thing, even if he had to get harsh with Kim.

Kim heard Tim drive up. She looked through the kitchen window and saw him get out of his car and walk up the sidewalk. He had the look of a serious man ready to confront somebody. Kim knew that any effort at being her normal bubbly self would be a bad tactic. If she didn't match his somber state it would get ugly fast. Kim went to the front door and opened it right before Tim rang the doorbell.

"Come in Tim," Kim said as she greeted him.

Tim nodded and walked in without saying a word. He moved past Kim without making eye contact and walked into the den. He picked the leather chair because it seemed to be the focal point of the room. He sat down and locked eyes with Kim as she sat on the far side of the sofa.

"How did you find out?" asked Kim.

Tim was a little shocked at first by his wife's forthrightness. He thought of being a little coy but was so worn thin that he moved to the heart of the matter. "I met with Tony this morning for coffee and he said that an undisclosed person saw you buying some pregnancy kits at the drug store."

Kim was almost distracted by the means through which discovered her secret. A deep sense of hatred for Ruth and Tony began to grow in her heart. But Kim was wise enough to realize that this wasn't the main thing at hand. She moved her focus back to her condition.

"I had my suspicions for a while and then I got two tests to make sure. I am pregnant."

Tim gripped the arms of the leather chair. Kim saw the veins bulge in his forearms. She knew Tim could snap her neck like a twig. Maybe Annie wasn't so smart after all. All she knew to do was to lower her head and look away.

"So," said Tim trying to get a grip on his building rage. "Who is the father Kim?"

"You are Tim." said Kim. As soon as she made the confession it felt right. She couldn't explain it but she knew it was true. "Based on my cycle and other factors it is you."

Tim didn't look convinced. He stared at Kim and said "By other factors you mean about the last time you and Darrell had sex, right?"

"Yes," said Kim in the most humble way she could muster.

"Kim, you had better not be lying to me. If you are I will not only divorce you, I will make your life a living hell." Tim's eyes were filled with the kind of fierce sadness that conveyed a man on the verge of erupting.

Kim recognized the sincerity of Tim's threat. "I know why you would say that. I would probably say the same or worse if I were in your shoes. I don't really expect anything from you. I will have get a test done as soon as I can to give you proof of fatherhood."

"So from your statement I assume you are keeping the child no matter what," replied Tim in a calmer fashion. "I think that this is the right decision regardless of who the father is."

"Yes, but I am sure the baby is yours."

Tim gazed downward. His lower lip was quivering. He looked like a little boy who had misplaced his parents in a large crowd. Kim prayed for the right words to say that would somehow convey genuine sorrow for the circumstances.

"I'm sorry seems so inadequate Tim," said Kim tenderly. "We have both wanted a child for so long, and for it to happen under these circumstances robs both of us the real joy we should be experiencing. If I could change any of this I would."

Tim didn't say a thing. He quickly wiped a tear from his cheek. He stood up cleared his throat twice in a loud enough and zipped up his windbreaker.

"Well, this changes everything. I know it would sound nice for me to tell you that I will take you back and we would then end up happily after. But that would be a lie right now. I really don't know what I am going to do."

With that statement he moved towards the door and exited without looking at Kim. She sat on the couch trying to form some semblance of a plan for her life, but heart felt like it was barely beating. All she could muster was a simple prayer: "Dear God, give me the grace to deal with all of this."

The following Saturday Tim walked into the conference room at NewLight Church. He had planned to have a short meeting. From the vibe he picked up on from the Elders he saw they probably felt the same way. Since he was the last person to arrive, he sat down on the opposite end of the long rectangular conference table from Tony Phipps.

"Tim, thanks for coming," said Tony. "We all want to arrive at a decision as quickly as possible. I am going to try to be brief"

"I think that would be good Tony," replied Tim in a stilted manner.

"Since you and I met last Monday, I have had some additional conversations with all of the Elders. That statement should not bother you. We just wanted to get the ball rolling so that we could help expedite this discussion. If you don't like anything we are going to propose, we can discuss it. Does that sound fair?"

"I think so Tony. What do you have for me?"

The Chairman of the Elders then handed out a one-page piece of paper to everyone at the meeting. It was a short proposal that presented Tim with the opportunity to take a two month leave of absence with full pay and benefits. At the end of that leave, it required Tim to have a follow-up meeting with the Elders to determine a permanent decision regarding his tenure as pastor. Tim gave it a careful examination.

"This looks very fair gentlemen" said Tim as he looked up from the proposal.

Ralph Mako was sitting to Tim's right looked right at Tim and said, "We wanted to keep this as simple as possible. You have been a good pastor and it was our desire to give you some time to pursue getting some help for the challenges that are before you."

"Well, I appreciate that," said Tim

"Now, we can't require you to get counseling" continued Ralph. "But I would strongly suggest that you talk to some kind of professional help about this. I know you are a private person Tim. So am I. But I am really worried, not only for your marriage but for you personally. I hope this is not too invasive of a remark."

"It isn't Ralph," said Tim showing the greatest respect he could muster for the District Attorney considering the circumstances. "I was planning on doing that very thing. But I appreciate your sincere concern. It is quite frankly refreshing after all of the things I have heard people say lately." Tim looked directly at Tony who avoided eye contact.

"So if there is no further discussion, snapped Tony, "let's have everyone sign this document. We will report back to the congregation in a letter with a copy of this document so as to comply with other requirements."

"Let's get this done fellas," said Tim nervously.

In a matter of seconds everyone signed two copies. Ralph Mako handed Tim a copy and Tim folded it and put it in the interior pocket of his leather jacket. He quickly stood and said "I want to thank you for your generosity and care during the most difficult time in our lives. I don't know what is going to happen. But when I do, I will let you men know, even if it is before our next scheduled meeting."

Barry Tompkins spoke up "Tim we will be praying for you and Kim and will hope for the best."

"Thanks Barry. I have only one request from this group."

"What is that, Tim?" asked Tony coldly.

"This is not an easy situation for you men to handle. I don't envy you a bit. But if you could keep the gossip to a minimum, I would appreciate it. All that innuendo does is to make a heartbreaking situation like this worse." Tim made a subtle form of eye contact with Tony. Tony returned a blatant look of contempt back towards Tim.

"I will promise you that I will not tolerate any kind of spiteful and salacious statements from anyone in this church Pastor," stated Ralph Mako. He looked directly at Tony and Barry to make sure that they knew he was ready to deal with any nonsense from the inquisitors who were spearheading the movement to immediately fire the embattled pastor.

"Thanks. I will be in touch." And with that brief statement Tim left the conference room.

"Well," said Tony in a cynical fashion. "He didn't give me a chance to have a closing prayer with him."

"I don't think his leaving will keep us from praying now, would it?" asked Ralph Mako.

"Uh, no I suppose not" shuddered the avowed enemy of the now almost defrocked minister.

Tim sat nervously in Dr. Marsha Allen's office. He had recommended her to dozens of people in his church. He also knew that Annie had been seeing her, but was unaware that Kim had been availing herself of Marsha's wisdom for several months. He felt like a failure and had considered leaving about three times while fumbling through some old magazines.

"Hey Tim!" announced Marsha from the bottom of the steps. She walked up to him and gave him a firm handshake. "It is so nice to finally meet you. You've been such a great supporter of what I do. I thought about sending you a Smithfield Ham or something as a way of thanking you."

Tim smiled and just said, "It is nice to meet you too."

"Come on upstairs to my office."

Tim followed looking around to see if there was anyone around who would recognize him. He walked into Marsha's earthy cocoon and sat down on the same spot his wife did.

"So, based on our conversation on the phone I assume you want to talk about how you are going to handle all the challenges in front of you. Is that right?"

"Yes."

"Marvelous. Now let me tell you upfront before we get started that my first session is normally free. But in your case, I am going to give you the first three for free because of how much business you sent my way. We will let that be our little secret, ok?"

"Uh, that is very nice of you. Sure."

"If you feel that this first session is helpful, I will have you fill out some paperwork and if you come more than three times, we will file the insurance."

"That sounds good."

"Good. Oh gosh, I forgot to ask you if you wanted some tea or water or coffee. Forgive my lack of hospitality."

"Don't worry about it. I am fine right now."

"Well, you let me know if you want something."

Tim nodded and looked around reading all of the pithy sayings hung on the walls.

"So, where do you want to start?"

"I guess Dr. Allen I want to figure out what I should do about my wife. I mentioned to you we are separated. But that's not all." Tim took a deep breath and looked up at the stucco ceiling.

"You are in a lot of pain aren't you?"

"Yeah," quietly replied Tim as if he was traveling aimlessly in a fogbank. Then he seemed to shake off the piercing ache of his grief, widened his eyes and sat straight up. "Anyway, she had an affair with a rake in our hometown and is pregnant. She claims the child is mine, but I am not sure."

"That is a really tough situation.

"You think?"

"So do you want to divorce her?"

"Some days."

"How about today?"

"Yes … Well, I don't know." Tim pressed both hands on top of his head and took another deep breath.

"Do you still love her?"

"I think so."

"Ok, so how can I help you with this?"

"I want you to tell me what to do, but I am guessing you won't do that will you?"

Marsha laughed. "No, but I want you to feel good about your decision. In my mind, you have two good options. You can forgive her and rebuild your marriage. Or, you can forgive her and end this marriage. The other options are not so good."

"What are those?"

"You can stay together out of some kind of shallow response to a religious ideal, putting both of you through a kind of agonizing existence that is empty of real love. Or you can divorce letting hate and hurt rule your life for years."

"Since you put it that way, I would like one of the good options."

"I thought you would. Since we have established that, let me ask you another question: Tell me about ways in which you failed your wife."

"Huh?"

"We both know that her adultery and possibly being pregnant with another man's wife is a train wreck, right?"

"Yes. It is a huge train wreck with lots of carnage all over the place."

"That's right. So why should we spend time beating up on your wife over something that is a no-brainer?"

"I understand what you are saying, but she has really hurt me and it is hard to let that go."

"Why would you say that letting it go is the same thing as acting like her affair is no big deal?"

"I don't remember saying that."

"Well it is what I heard. If I am wrong I apologize." Marsha sat still and waited on Tim to respond. He looked around for several seconds trying to speak but stopping twice in order to get a grip on his anger.

"Look. You don't know what it is like to be betrayed this way" he countered gritting his teeth.

"Who is assuming now Tim?"

"What? Has this ever happened to you?"

"Let's just say that I am happily married to my second husband."

"Ok, but I just can't forgive her and then go live together in some fantasy world."

"Is that what I said? Think about the good and bad options I just listed. Which option did you just represent?"

Tim sat on the couch for a moment and then replied "I guess the one where I don't forgive her and we just exist."

"Yes. Who in their right mind would want to do that?"

"No one. But I don't believe in divorce."

"I think I understand what you are saying. But can I share an observation I've made over the years about that perspective?"

"Sure. You're the expert."

Marsha smiled. "I'm not sure if you are being sarcastic, but I will move on and tell you anyway."

Tim dropped his head in embarrassment.

"Sincere Christians come into my office in this kind of situation and tell me that they can't stand their mates but that they don't believe in divorce. Do you see the dilemma in that position?"

"Yeah, they're damned if they do and damned if they don't!"

"You are right Tim. In my experience that never works. It is what we call a double bind in my business. That kind of thing disempowers people resulting in greater pain not less."

"So, are you saying that people should just divorce because they are going through problems?"

"Now Tim, you are too smart of a man to say something like that. Every marriage will have problems. It is built upon two imperfect people or as you would say sinners. But here is what Dr. John Gottman says are four things that sink marriages – contempt, criticism, defensiveness and stonewalling."

"Wow, that makes a lot of sense."

"It really does. Belief can be a shifting thing. But behavior is something that can be seen, described and adjusted."

"Are you saying belief is unimportant?"

"Boy, you are really loaded for bear aren't you? No. I am not saying that. Belief ... let me change that and say right belief is essential. But sometimes when we are hurting so badly we don't know what we believe. Have you ever seen that happen?"

"Sure. It is part of my struggle right now. It is hard to talk about because so much of my life has been about building up other's belief." Tim shook his head with great incredulity as he considered his own condition.

"That is why when we do things we know to be good, true and healthy we can boost our belief rather than wait around until we feel better or when we have figured everything out."

WALKER ARMSTRONG

"I think that is what I have been doing."

"What do you mean Tim?"

"I think sometimes I am relying on my feelings and other times I am trying to figure out why she would do such a thing?"

"Very good. Our feelings are great servants but terrible masters. If we did everything we felt like doing we would be in trouble."

"I have seen that a lot of times in my ministry," said Tim remembering multiple tragedies that were stimulated by individuals' impulsivity.

"I bet you have. And I am sure you have seen people stuck in the unbelief because they were looking for perfect explanations."

"Ok, I think I am beginning to understand a little Dr. Allen."

"I knew you would. By the way, I prefer Marsha. I am not that formal of a person."

"Ok Marsha."

"This is why I asked you my previous question about how you have failed your wife. You will never feel good about what she did because you shouldn't. And I have some news for you – people can be in therapy for years and not figure out their motivations for doing some crazy stuff."

"That is so true."

"Good. Now I want you to pick one of those four categories Gottman listed when you consider how you messed up in your marriage."

"What were they?"

"They were contempt, criticism, defensiveness and stonewalling."

"I would say stonewalling."

"And how would you say you stonewalled your wife?"

"If it is what I think it is I would say there were times when I shut down and didn't share with her what was going on with me."

"So, give me an example or a time when you shut her out."

"Well, I guess when we were trying to have a baby and we couldn't. We went to a fertility specialist and found out that there were things wrong with both of us."

"How did that make you feel?"

"I guess several things … probably insecure about my manhood because of my low sperm count. And then I guess mad because we couldn't get pregnant."

"Let's look at the first example. Why would you feel less of a man due to sperm count?"

"Isn't it obvious?"

"No. Enlighten me."

"Uh, if you are a real man you would have a lot of testosterone and with a lot of testosterone you would produce a lot of sperm."

"I want to challenge that assumption."

Tim laughed. "Of course you do."

"Did you know that sperm production is more complicated than just your level of testosterone, and in fact for most men, sperm counts can fluctuate a great deal from month to month? Based on that by your definition a guy could be a real man one month and a sissy the next."

"So you're saying that my definition of masculine is off?"

"Yes. For instance, I have a client that is about one hundred and thirty five pounds soaking wet and looks a little anemic. But he also happens to be the father of six children by three different women. I would bet you all the money in your wallet that if you saw him, you would never guess that he is that prolific."

Tim shook his head in amazement. "I bet you think I am pretty Cro-Magnon in my thinking huh?"

"I don't know. Are you?"

"I don't think so. Do you believe that this wrong way of thinking caused my problem with stonewalling?"

"Perhaps it did on some level. Give me another example of when you stonewalled."

Tim sat for a while and thought. He seemed relieved when he came up with another example. "There have been times when I was mad with people at church but I didn't want to share it with Kim."

"Why?"

"I'm not sure … maybe I didn't want her to think I wasn't a spiritual person."

"Ok. So based on the two examples you have listed, do you see any pattern here in why you have stonewalled?"

"Not really."

"Let me ask you this: Do you think you struggle with insecurity?"

"Yeah."

"Don't feel bad. I think we all do from time to time."

"So, I should figure out why I am so insecure?"

"I think that would be helpful, but for right now I want you to really focus on how stonewalling has had a really negative impact on your marriage."

"Ok."

"How do you think your stonewalling has been impacting your wife?"

"I would assume that it makes her feel alone."

"And how would that isolation make her more vulnerable to an affair?"

"Now hold on Marsha. Are you saying that I am responsible for her making this horrible choice?"

"Not really. Tell me the difference between the words contribute and cause.

"Contribute means you had a part in something and cause means, well you are responsible for it happening."

"Based on those definitions, do you think you contributed to her being vulnerable to having an affair or that you caused it?"

Tim seemed to get where the counselor was coming from. "I think I contributed to it."

"Very good Tim. And that is where I want us to start our work together. How does that sound to you?"

"Really good. Do you think that Kim can eventually come with me sometime?"

"I am glad you asked this question. I was planning on telling you something at the end of this session but now is as good a time as any -- As a matter of appropriate disclosure I need to tell you that I have been meeting with Kim for a while."

Tim was visibly confused a slightly stunned from that admission. He didn't know what to say.

"If you are uncomfortable with that I can refer you to some other good counselors in our region that could really be of help."

"Uh, I guess I am ok."

"Now, at this point I can't tell you what she has said to me without her permission and the same kind of confidentiality extends to you. But at some point, if there is a chance for any kind of permanent reconciliation it would be good for you to come together. How do you feel about all of that?"

"Can I just come and see you for at least those first three sessions by myself before making up my mind about that?"

"I think that would be a great idea. Why don't you fill out the paper work we were talking about earlier and then you can go downstairs and set up an appointment with our receptionist downstairs."

"That sounds good. Thanks."

"You are most welcome. Do you have any other questions of me at this point?"

"No."

"Well, I am looking forward to seeing you soon."

The next four weeks passed by quickly. Right after his first session with Marsha, Tim moved out his home and into the house of a fellow minister in Asheville. During those days he spent most of his time looking online for other job possibilities all over the United States and working out a lot at a local gym right up the street from his friend's house. He even grew a beard to give him the sense of beginning the process of totally reinventing himself. Because his pastor friend had talked him into seeing a lawyer Tim had also hired an attorney to begin to jumpstart the proceedings of establishing a separation agreement just in case things didn't improve with Kim.

Kim, on the other hand, had taken a more laidback approach to her healing. She had saved enough money from her work at the drugstore to live at home for a while until a more formal course of action had been taken. In the meantime, she had taken over the old guest bedroom and began to convert it into a nursery. When she wasn't busy building her little nest, she spent a lot of time with Annie, Meagan, Bart, Jake and Lola eating dinner, watching movies and finding the grace to laugh a lot more. Both she and Tim kept talking on the phone but hadn't seen each other for a month. They had individually decided to continue to meet with Marsha but only in one-one one counseling sessions. The final outcome of what was to happen in their marriage was still very much in the air.

Since Annie and Bart had reconnected, their relationship had taken on a deeper quality that provided them with the kind of momentum that was more and more leaning towards marriage. Meagan had decided to jump on board as a more enthusiastic supporter of her mom's romance with Bart, and had actually gotten a job at Angelo's as a waitress immediately following her fifteenth birthday and her mom's suspension of her chain gang servitude at The Center.

Exactly four weeks since Kim had told Annie about her predicament, Annie found herself at work trying to wrap up her day late Wednesday. She was seeking to finish a report on Medicare reimbursements for her boss when the power went out in the Center. When it didn't immediately kick back in she walked out into the hallway to find Abner Caudle the Maintenance Director. She chased him grabbed him as he was heading back towards the main mechanical room.

"Abner," asked a perturbed Annie, "what is going on?"

He looked in a hurry and turned back towards Annie saying "I think that a road crew cut through a line up the street. I am going to see why the emergency generator didn't kick on."

Annie tried to figure out what was she was going to do since her phone and computer were on the fritz. Before she had time to decide Sydney the head nurse came running up to Annie and said, "Come quick I think Pearl is having a stroke."

Annie didn't think. She just ran. When she got to Pearl's room, she saw the little old lady lying on the bed jabbering away. Dell Johnson a CNA was trying to get Pearl's blood pressure with little success because the feisty woman was waving her arms around like a conductor revving up the orchestra on a Beethoven tune. Sydney went to the bed and said

"Pearl this is Sydney, can you hear me?" Annie stood at the foot of the bed in shock. She had seen a lot of residents sick and die. But this was Momma Pearl. She was frozen in worry.

Sydney shouted for Annie to help restrain Pearl as she sought to administer a shot of some sort. Annie came out of her temporary paralysis and asked Sydney while holding Pearl's right arm down, "When is Dr. Gordon? Isn't he supposed to be here today?"

"Yes, but he got called in on an emergency at his office," said Jane.

"What are we going to do Syd?" asked Annie.

"We need to get the ambulance here," said the frustrated nurse.

"I keep getting an almost non-existent BP," said a frantic Dell.

Annie knew that this situation was really bad. She pulled her cellphone out of her pocket and dialed 911. She got a busy call and tried again. She got more of the same. "No!" she yelled.

"I think we are losing her!" shouted Dell.

Annie ran out of the room and in seconds came back with a wheelchair. She grabbed Sydney's arm who was trying to get a fix on Pearl's pupil with a little light. "Put her in this wheelchair" commanded Annie. "We are going to take her to the hospital in the Center's van."

Before Sydney could give an objection, Annie pushed her out of the way and lowered the bed rail. She said to the quivering woman "Hang in there, Momma Pearl, we are taking you to the hospital."

Pearl got a curious look on her face and said, "Why in the world would you do that? I am going on my honeymoon with Edgar."

"My God, she is reliving her wedding," said Annie.

Dell and Sydney scooped up the frail woman and gently placed her in the wheelchair. Annie ran out and grabbed the van key from the front desk. People who were already confused by the power outage now were wondering why Annie was in such an all-fire hurry. In about thirty seconds Annie had the van pulled up to the drop off. Dell and Sydney wheeled Pearl up to side door and placed her in the backseat behind the driver's side. They both jumped in and shut the door. All Annie could say at this point was "Hang on" as she gunned the accelerator.

Once they made their turn towards the hospital the van's worn-out shocks began to cause it to bounce violently with every minor bump in the road. As if on cue Pearl began to laugh and say "O sweet Jesus, you are quite the man Edgar! Woo-hoo!"

Annie looked back and made eye contact with Jane. They both knew that Pearl was re-living the consummation of her marriage with her deceased husband. Jane did her best to restrain Pearl, but the woman imagined herself clothed with the body of young bride. It seemed that the memory of that night of passion was enough to temporarily fill the weak body with the intense exertions that only wild love-making can bring.

In a matter of moments Annie wheeled right up to the Gordon Emergency Room. She jumped out and ran to find a doctor while Sydney and Dell extracted Pearl from the back seat and place her back into the wheelchair. Annie looked around and saw more people than usual in the Emergency Room than you would expect on a Friday morning. She saw several men dressed in lineman uniforms who looked pretty banged-up. She later found out that a texting teenager had run into the crew and the electricity pole that they were replacing. That was the reason they had lost power.

Annie saw Dr. Gordon standing by the front desk. It seems he had a patient that had a heart attack at his office and had followed the family to the hospital. She grabbed him even though he was in the midst of explaining to the triage nurse that the patient had expired. He quickly discovered why the normally self-assured woman was so frantic. He ran behind Annie and intercepted Pearl on her wheelchair. Dr. Gordon took charge and wheeled her back into an empty room saying "Miss Pearl this is Doctor Gordon. We are going to take care of you, ok?"

Pearl smiled and responded "Thank-you doctor. How is my baby boy? That was one stubborn child. I thought you would never get him out of me!"

Dr. Gordon didn't miss a beat. "He is a strapping boy. Just like his daddy!"

"Well Lord help us all then!' laughed Pearl.

Dr. Gordon whisked Pearl through the double doors leading to the curtain-framed rooms. Jane and Dell stayed behind but Annie followed her godmother into her room. Dr. Gordon yelled and got the assistance of a couple of nurses. Annie stood back and watched everyone work in syncopated fervor. She wasn't ready for this she thought to herself. "Please help her Dr. Gordon" Annie said in a hushed tone. "I can't lose her, not now!"

After a few minutes they got Pearl stabilized. Annie walked up to her bedside one the doctor and nurses temporarily left the room. She leaned close and stroked Pearls wiry white hair. "Momma Pearl I am here. It's Annie." A smile appeared on Pearl's wrinkled face. She opened her eyes slightly and said, "What is going on sweetie?"

Annie took a deep breath that was accompanied by a slight quiver. She looked down at Pearl and said, "You are sick and we are here to make sure you are ok."

"Oh, I don't feel so bad. Y'all need to help somebody that is really sick," said Pearl in a slightly haughty way.

Annie started laughing and then it turned to a low sob as she buried her face in her godmother's neck.

"Child, you need to settle down. Dying ain't so bad."

Annie jerked up and wiper her face with her hand. "You are not going to die Momma Pearl. You are so spunky that you will probably outlive all of us."

Pearl opened her eyes wider to reveal her stunning almond irises. She touched Annie on the cheek and said, "The Lord is calling me home baby. It is my time. I have had a great life and I am ready. Edgar has been calling on me every night for a while now. He misses me and I miss that old rascal too."

Annie wanted to accept this verdict but couldn't help saying "But I want you to be with me when I marry Bart."

"I will always be with you darling. I was the first face you saw when you came out of your mother's tummy. Besides, you are ready to launch out on your own without me. I got to be honest and tell you that all of your problems have aggravated old Pearl for a while. I have given you all the wisdom I have and then some. You just need to let me go little lady, that's all."

Annie nodded. Pearl was right once again. "You know I love you, don't you?"

WALKER ARMSTRONG

Pearl grinned and said "Of course. And I love you. Now, before I forget I have written down what I want said and what I want sung at my funeral and put it in my top drawer. Don't you let Rev. Booker say stuff about me that ain't true. I will come back and haunt all of you if you do."

Annie laughed and said, "Yes ma'am."

Pearl closed her eyes and said, "I am tired. Would you go and call my kids and let them know what is going on?"

Annie leaned down and kissed her godmother on the forehead and whispered "Consider it done. And save a place for me at that big reunion in the sky." Annie turned around, walked out and didn't look back.

CHAPTER 13

THE PARKING LOT of the Ebenezer Holiness Church was packed. Late-comers had to find places in the grass field behind the church or next door at the New Winds Shopping Center. The Lady's Auxiliary has already secured permission for overflow parking from the Harris-Teeter that was the anchor store of the almost new strip mall to park in marked off sections. Everything would be taken care of to insure that people felt at ease at this memorial service.

Middle-aged black men dressed in black suits with white gloves and red ties greeted mourners at the big cherry colored double doors of the white framed building. Over the doors was an oval-shaped stained glass window with a white dove holding a red rose under a sunlit cross. The caption at the bottom of the glass said "Welcome Holy Spirit."

Older folks, those needing assistance or women who were dropping off food for the fellowship meal following the service were let off behind the sanctuary at a multi-purpose building. This was added almost ten years ago to the original worship, office and educational space that were all built as part of the original 1939 site.

Because the church was somewhat land-locked a lot of alterations to the original plans were made to squeeze the new building into the left side of the property. This addition housed a gym, a huge kitchen and several educational rooms. There was a fairly tight semi-circular driveway that led to an overhang leading into the building. Other ushers dressed like those who were standing at the front door helped people through the side glass doors and guided them to the sanctuary.

When there were more than a few cars in line it could create a traffic jam of sorts. This happened several times due to the intermittent rain and the large glut of people that had not gotten there at least thirty minutes ahead of time. The massive conglomeration of cars, suits and dresses of every color made the gathering look like the funeral for a dignitary, and in a way it was. It was not every day you buried a woman who had helped hundreds of children come into the world.

Annie was sitting in the parlor with the family. She wore a sleeveless black dress with a simple strand of pearls draped around her neck. Her hair had gotten long enough to fit it under a white-laced bonnet that Momma Pearl had given her to wear at Edgar's funeral a few years back. Pearl used to say, "No decent church lady should be caught dead in church without a hat." Annie accentuated this classic Audrey Hepburn look with some pearl earrings that Bart had given her for her birthday.

Pearl's kids Mary-Marla and Teddy were there with their spouses, their adult children and twelve great grandchildren whom Pearl referred to as "the jewels in my crown." Others distant family members and friends were milling around speaking in hushed murmurs to the family. Annie knew most of them and tried to be as personable as possible when they said hello, but she was still a bundle of nerves. She kept rubbing Marla's back as the stately middle-aged woman dabbed her eyes with a tissue and made gentile gestures to each person that greeted her.

Marla was almost fourteen years older than Annie and helped to take care of her when she was an infant. After graduating from Gordon High, she went to Meredith College on an academic scholarship and double-majored in Music and Math. From there she got Master's in childhood education at UNC and then landed a job teaching elementary math for ten years in two schools in Lumberton.

Over that period, she found the time to have three children. Once the last child reached Junior High, she finished the work on her doctorate and eventually became principal of Jefferson Elementary. She had been involved in education for over thirty years and was presently considering whether or not she would take the Superintendent's job that had just been offered to her for the second time. Marla was a woman of grace that commanded everyone's respect because she called out the best in people. Annie thought that she was a taller and more urbane version of Pearl.

Edgar James Buford III (or Teddy as everyone from Gordon called him) was a man of mind-boggling accomplishments. He was one of the first African-Americans to play football for Bear Bryant at Alabama.

Teddy made All-Conference twice as an outside linebacker and was named Second Team All-American his senior year.

After a stellar career in football, he rejected offers to go pro and became a Marine Aviator. Teddy pulled two tours of duty in Vietnam before being assigned a squadron command at Cherry Point. From there he rose to the rank of Lt. General and retired after 35 years of service to his country.

Most people would have rested on their laurels, but not "Terrible Ted" (the moniker her earned for his fierce nature in combat given by his fellow pilots in Vietnam). He founded United Military Aircraft Design, an aerospace design and manufacturing firm based out of Wilmington. He started this company in order to get replacement parts of airplanes like the Harrier and the Warthog to the battlefield. In fifteen years, it rose from nothing to a Fortune 500 company. Ted now was in the process of winding down his second career at the tender age of seventy-two.

When speaking of their mother Marla would tell you that she got her passion for helping children from Pearl. Teddy would have said he learned about the value of hard work from his father and got his competitive nature from his mother. Both children felt that their mother's departure moved the mantle of modeling the pursuit excellence to their shoulders.

Pastor Melvin Booker made his way to the center of the parlor and spoke, "Folks, we are getting ready to go into the sanctuary. The first three rows on your left are reserved for family. The front row is for Sister Pearl's children and their spouses. Before we go in let's have a word of prayer."

"Lord Almighty, you are awesome in all you do. You made everything and everybody. We're here to today to celebrate the life of a remarkable woman. Although we rejoice that she is now home with you, all the saints and her husband Edgar we don't know quite what to do down here now that she is gone. Please speak comfort to the family. Make your name great in our midst in this service. We pray all of this in Jesus' name, Amen!"

Pastor Booker motioned toward the family guided Annie, Mary Marla and her husband Charles towards the left double doors that would bring them straight to where they needed to be seated. The rest of the family lined up behind them.

Reverend Booker walked in first and joined Sister Cecelia Hankins the Choir Director on Stage. Behind them stood the choir was decked out in purple and gold robes. To their left was Cecelia's youngest son Tony Hankins on the Bass, his cousin Marvin Hankins on drums and Cecelia's oldest daughter Torrance Hankins Livingston on the baby grand piano. Across from them on the other side was little Tonya Bishop standing adjacent to the choir in front of a mike stand. Beside her was Johnny Blevons on the electric guitar and in front of him was Sister Betty Taylor on the organ.

Two of the Byers Funeral Home attendants came forward and closed Pearl's casket. When they were finished, Melvin nodded at Sister Cecelia. She popped up and took a few quick steps to her musical lectern, which was saying something due to the fact that she was wearing four-inch spike heels. With unquestioned mastery of the moment, she had the choir rise and gave the old one, two, three countdown to Marvin to kick in a tuned-up version of "We Have Come into This House." The audience remained seated as the choir and the band played, but they didn't stay still. People swayed, raised their hands and shouted as the musicians did their thing.

When they finished to a flurry of "Amens" and "Praise the Lords" Rev. Booker then nodded at Sister Betty Taylor who transitioned keys to a more somber "We You There?" He had the congregation stand as he motioned to one of the ladies from the Women's Auxiliary to open the double doors and lead the family into the worship center.

Annie walked in first holding Marla's hand. They were both crying as they moved to the corner of the front pew. By the time the rest of the family filed in, they were barely able to fit into the last section, but eventually found a way to make it work, having smaller children sit in the laps of their parents. When the family was situated, Reverend Booker had everyone sit down and gave the initial greetings. He then recognized Mayor Thompson.

The Mayor walked up from the front pew on the right, acknowledged the fine job the choir did and gave his condolences to the family. Standing erect the his deep baritone voice switched from a comforting tone to a more oratorical timbre. "Because Annie Pearl Lawson Buford was such a significant citizen of this community" he bellowed, "it is only fitting that we formally honor her life in a way that symbolizes her lifelong commitment to the welfare of all of our children."

He was in his element. A few people visibly demonstrated their clear cynicism about his motivations because he was coming up on another election year. But most of the audience looked like that they were spellbound in his presence.

"Last Monday night," he continued with a bit more emotive seasoning, "upon hearing about her departure from the earthly bonds of this world, the City Council voted unanimously to designate the second Tuesday of every September as Pearl Bufford Day." He moved back from the pulpit mike a little, waiting for the appropriate amount of applause and affirmations to be dispensed.

As that subsided, he continued. "All city employees will be encouraged to use that day to do volunteer work at schools and hospitals to do something that would practically benefit our kids. Restaurants and other retail businesses will be asked to contribute at least ten percent of the gross receipts from that day to a matching fund set up by an anonymous donor to create a scholarship fund for an enterprising minority high school senior who is planning on going into the field of medicine."

This was too much for the former Marine. When Teddy heard the words of the mayor, he lowered his head and began to weep. His wife Joanne and his youngest son Nathaniel reached over to comfort the humbled leader. Others beamed with pride as the audience stood and gave the mayor a standing ovation. You might as well as gift-wrapped the mayor's gavel and gave it to him as a pre-announcement of his re-election. Anyone in the audience that Saturday morning who was toying with the idea of running or thinking about supporting another candidate for mayor now secretly genuflected to the consummate politician.

Pastor Booker settled the audience down and then introduced the next speaker, Mary Marla Buford Jones. The statuesque middle-aged woman oozed grace from the moment she left her seat till she spoke her first words.

"I want to thank all you for being here today. And thank you Mayor and City Council for honoring Momma in this way. She would have been very tickled for you doing this since she was all about the babies. I am sorry it has been so long that Teddy and I have been back to the church. This place holds a lot of memories for us, and we would not be the people we are today without you helping our parents keep us on the straight path."

In the midst of this expression of gratitude Marla paused, looked down at Annie and said: "Some of you might be wondering why a middle-aged white woman led the processional. If you are not part of our family, I could see why you would be a bit perplexed.

But let me enlighten you. Momma used to tell us that all the children she helped come into the world were 'a little bit hers.' But Annie was special. You see she was a breech baby. Some of you who know her aren't that surprised." Marla looked at Jake, Lola, Meagan and Bart and winked. They smiled back.

"Anyway, it was a complicated birth with lots of drama and confusion and fear. My mother helped to unwrap the umbilical cord no less than three times from around that child's neck." The audience whistled and gasped.

Finally, right before the doctor was going to perform an emergency C-section my momma sat back on her stool and said, "Little baby, I have had about all I am going to take from you. Quit this nonsense and come on out right now! And then Miss Lola's body relaxed and that baby slid on out. Isn't that right Lola?" Lola agreed with tears flooding her eyes.

"Well, Pearl picked that little girl up, wiped her face and said 'Why there you are sunshine. It is about time!' And do you know what that child did?" Nathaniel's little six-year son Derek busted out and said "What Aunt Marla?" Everyone chuckled at this unexpected question.

Marla grinned and said, "Well I will tell you buddy. That stubborn little girl opened those bright blue eyes and smiled as pretty as a picture.

My momma kissed that grinning child and showed Miss Lola that smile. It was then that Lola named her after my sweet mother. That's the gospel-truth isn't it Lola?" Lola nodded her head with pride and said "Absolutely!"

Marla then looked at certain friends she hadn't seen in a while and said, "Momma used to tell me that she knew that from that moment on the two of them would be forever connected." She then shifted her gaze back at Annie.

"Every Monday night when Momma and I used to have our talk on the phone she would tell me about her other daughter's visit. I would have gotten a little jealous if I didn't know what was really going on.

When Annie called me earlier this week and told me of Mom's home-going I was sad but happy. I was sad because my mentor was gone. But I was happy because if Teddy or I couldn't be with her when she greeted Jesus and Daddy at heaven's gate, then there was no other person I wanted to be there but my other favorite Annie Pearl!"

Marla walked down from the stage stylishly exhausted. Annie met her by the casket and hugged her neck. The two sat back down together and Reverend Booker stepped up to the pulpit wiping tears from his face. "Well glory to God," said the overcome pastor. "We are sure having some church up in here today, Amen? Now, Sister Pearl's oldest child General Edgar James Buford III is going to share a few words with us."

The pastor sat back down in his pulpit chair that resembled a throne more than a piece of simple Protestant furniture. Teddy moved quickly up the steps to the podium and pulled a sheet of paper from his suit pocket. His bullish stature and piercing almond-colored eyes portrayed a man who could command attention without speaking a word. In some ways, he was more like his mother than his sister. He could be disarmingly charming but in the blink of an eye he could change into an "in your eyeballs leader." Teddy put on a pair of bifocals, took a breath and began to speak.

"I am who I am by the grace of God and the compact right foot of my mother." The audience laughed. Anyone who knew Pearl and Teddy would heartily agree. "I don't know if it was because I had the rascal in me like my Daddy, or if it was pre-ordained by almighty God to make Annie Pearl my mother. Maybe it was a little bit of both. But regardless I am grateful.

I am grateful because I was gifted with two wonderful parents. My Pops was a hard-working, funny and even tender man. When I think of the word commitment, I see my Daddy pulling two shifts at the Gordon Mill to make sure I had some extra spending money before I went back to college at Tuscaloosa. There is not a day that goes by that I don't miss the sound of his strong voice or the sight of his mischievous smile.

But Momma had a different impact on me. Try as I may I could never charm her. She never let me slide, not because she was mean or difficult but because she knew I was a person capable of extremes. And this meant that I not only could soar to heights I could have never dreamed of but that I also could have become one of the sorriest souls that had even wore a pair of shoes."

The audience was both amused and surprised. Few people were as successful as Teddy, so it was hard to ever see him becoming a no-account such and such. The General definitely had their attention.

"Case and point. My parents were only able to come down a few times when I played for the Tide. One occasion was during my junior year when we were going to play Auburn. Momma and Pops got down early that week and came to our Thursday practice. I had the chance to introduce them to Coach Bryant before we cranked it up. That was a big deal.

Now some of you younger kids don't remember him. The best way I know how to describe Paul Bear Bryant is to say that if you combined Moses, John Wayne and the PE teacher that used to scare the stew out of you, you would be pretty close. He was the real deal. We both loved and feared the man.

That particular year I was doing pretty well. He praised me a few times in the locker room in front of the guys and that was better than winning a medal in combat. If I could please my parents and the Coach I kind of felt that I was on my way to being a successful person.

When I introduced him to my folks, he told them that I was 'one of the most gifted athletes he had ever coached' I almost cried. My Pops stood there with his chest sticking like he was saying 'yeah, chip off the old block.' But Momma was different. She wasn't impressed with Coach Bryant, or if she was, she wasn't showing it. She stood straight up on him and said, 'Coach, that boy of a mine has a long way to go before he becomes a decent man. I could care less about his abilities. I have done all I can to point him in the right direction. It is up to you to finish the job!' And then she walked off.

Teddy let that sink in for a second. "My five-foot nothing Momma did what her six-foot two, two-hundred-and-twenty-pound son would never have done. She straightened out a legend.

Well, during that practice he made sure that my character got worked on. I ran more in that practice than anyone on the field. My buddies on defense asked me 'What did you do to make coach mad?' I told them 'I don't want to talk about it.' My Pops later told me that one time when I was off to the side doing those awful drills Coach Bryant looked over to the stands and made eye contact with my mom and nodded. She nodded back."

That Saturday I had the best game of my career. I had twenty-one solo tackles, one fumble recovery and one interception that I returned for a touchdown. Every time I came off the field Coach didn't say a thing to me. He just shook his head at me and then looked away.

Near the end of the game our defense came off the field after a spectacular goal-line stand. The crowd was going crazy and I looked in the stands to find Momma and Pops. I saw them and my dad was going crazy. I could see he was pointing to me saying "That is my boy!" But when I looked over to Momma she wasn't smiling. She was pointing at the scoreboard."

Teddy stepped back from the pulpit. He looked around. Pastor Booker knew what was happening. He smiled and said "My my, my. You go on ahead and preach it brother!" Teddy then stepped back up and said "Did you hear that church?" Then the heart of his message started catching fire to in the minds of other congregants that started all kinds of spontaneous affirmations.

Teddy got a serious look on his face. "My Momma wasn't telling me that celebration was wrong in that situation, just premature. You see, there was an outside chance that Auburn could come back and steal

WALKER ARMSTRONG

that game from us. My Momma was saying 'Stay focused son. Don't quit playing hard until the horn sounds.'"

Then Sister Betty Taylor felt the move of the Spirit and started playing a rift on the organ. Pastor Booker stood up and shouted a long "Yes!" The Ladies Auxiliary followed his lead and stood in unison in their white dresses, purple and gold hats and white gloves waving their handkerchiefs in affirmation. The band joined in and soon the rest of the congregation was standing up and testifying.

Teddy spoke in loud booming voice, "I have done a lot of things in my life, some special things. I played football for a legend. I flew jets at twice the speed of sound. I have trained warriors and led them in battle. I have started a Fortune 500 company with nothing but a pen, paper and a pension. But whatever God has enabled me to do flows out of what happened that day on the sidelines over forty years ago. That day I became a man, not because of what I did but what I learned. The lesson that I learned from my Momma was this – never give up or give out until the task is done!"

The congregation erupted with even more fervor. It was so powerful that white people who were Presbyterians started raising their hands. The mayor was moved to the degree that he started hopping up and down. His wife Mary saw this and almost fainted.

But General Buford wasn't done. He leaned back and spoke more softly. "Some of you are in a bad place. Your marriage is on the rocks; your business is about to go under; your teenager has been caught on drugs again or you are feeling the pressure.

What happens next is what is really important. It is not about outcome. It is about stepping up and doing the right thing no matter what. If you do that, regardless of what transpires, you will live a successful life. If my Momma were here, she would tell you that. In fact, there are many people in this room that have heard that very message from Momma Pearl."

Terrible Ted then bowed his head and his broad shoulders shook a bit as he began to softly weep. He gathered himself and looked back at the congregation and said "And when the game was over and everybody else was running onto the field I looked up at my parents. I saw Momma with one arm around the love of her life jumping up and down screaming and crying and laughing and saying to me "I am proud of you baby!"

The congregation was quickly silenced by that powerful word picture. Teddy walked down the steps of the stage and stood at the head of Pearl's casket. He reached in the right coat pocket of his pinstripe suit and pulled out the Navy Cross. Next to the Medal of Honor, Sailors and Marines would tell you it is the highest one that could be bestowed upon a warrior.

Now Teddy was smiling. He looked around to his family who knew how much this symbol meant to him and they were crying. Teddy cleared his throat and said "I won this medal because I shot down four Migs on sunny day in the skies over Southeast Asia. The last one happened when my F-4 had one operational engine and no missiles. I knocked him out of the air with a well-placed burst of machine gun fire, just like the Tuskegee Airman did in those red-tailed P-51's over Germany twenty-five years earlier." The congregation shook their head in utter amazement and pride.

"That's why I thought it was only fitting to give it back to the person that taught me how to never slack off and never give up, no matter what." He bowed down and kissed the casket and then placed the medal carefully on the curved box.

Annie, Marla May and the rest of the family jumped up to embrace Teddy and the whole church clapped for a few minutes until Pastor Booker settled them down. He said smiling as broadly as he could, "Well some of you are going to be surprised by what I am going to say next. I was ready to preach a great message about the life of Annie Pearl. But I think enough has been said already. Momma Pearl used to tell me, 'Pastor, a good preacher knows when to shut up and sit down and let the Lord do the rest.' Then she would wink at me and a say, 'You are starting to get a little smarter.' I sure hope I am.

Now, we are going to end the service with Pearl's favorite hymn *Amazing Grace.* We will remain here until the last verse and then I will lead the casket and family out of the building. We will then proceed to the Gordon Memorial Park where we will lay her body to rest beside her beloved Edgar. I have been asked by the family to beseech everyone to come back after the brief graveside service to the fellowship hall and partake of the sumptuous meal the Ladies Auxiliary prepared for us."

With that being said Booker prayed a sweet prayer of gratitude not only for the life of Pearl but also for the special visitation of the Holy Spirit that they had experienced. When he said Amen, he let Sister Cecelia take the lead. The band, the choir and the congregation blended their voices in such an ethereal manner that everyone didn't want to leave. But they did.

About an hour later a lot of the folks that came to the funeral returned for the fellowship meal. There is something about delicious Southern cuisine that can bring comfort in the midst of grief. Fried Chicken, Salisbury Steak, Macaroni and Cheese, Fresh Greens, Potato Salad, Deviled Eggs, Baked Ham Bar-B-Que Ribs, Green Beans, Seven-layer Salad, about fourteen versions of Chicken Casserole, Mashed Potatoes, four different kinds of Cobbler Pies, Homemade Coconut Cake, Lemon Pound Cake, Chocolate Cake and even Pearls favorite Red Velvet Cake were just some of the notable highlighted dishes. No one went away hungry and a few were reaching for their antacids because of their unabashed gluttony.

People were gathered in pockets of smiling dialogues, sharing stories about Pearl. Dozens of kids ran in and out of the building oblivious of the real nature of the gathering. There was a sweet sense of relief and peace in the midst of all the sadness.

Annie walked up to Teddy and his family and gave him a tight hug. "That was the most inspiring message I have ever heard," said a beaming Annie. Teddy smiled and said, "Thanks. It was the most important one I have ever given in my life. Momma would have probably been mad at me for going on too much about her, but I am just as hard-headed as she ever was, so she would have just had to put up with my bragging. I am just glad it is over. This was more taxing than Paris Island."

Annie laughed. Teddy then put his arm on Annie's shoulder and spoke like the patriarch of the family. "Annie I can never adequately express how grateful we are for all you did for Momma. She really loved you and was proud of the woman you have become."

Annie tried to say something but couldn't. She still didn't know what she was going to do without Momma Pearl. If she was honest, she still felt like a teenager who needed to grow up a lot more before she felt that she could be called a full-fledged woman. And then there was the specter of her current challenges that had not been resolved. Meagan wasn't out of the woods by a long shot and Annie was still a novice in understanding how Ju-Ju really worked. She was just going to have to soldier on and figure it out on the way.

Bart walked up when she needed him to and shook Teddy's hand. "That was the finest eulogy I ever heard. I didn't know your mother well, but I thought she was the cat's meow. Oh, I'm sorry," he said recognizing his social misstep. "I am Bart St. Clair by the way."

Teddy grinned and winked at his wife "Oh, we know who you are. Momma talked about you quite a bit."

Bart looked at Annie with some slight panic. Annie saw his consternation and patted him on the back saying, "Don't worry sweetie. She was a huge fan. Walk with me while I fix you a plate of the best desserts." Bart smiled nervously and said goodbye to Teddy and his family.

The crowd didn't leave until almost seven o'clock that night, Most of the Caucasian folks left earlier because they didn't have the church stamina. Eight hours of all those wild swing in emotions and intense one-on-one interactions was the kind of activity that could wear out the most intense extrovert.

Bart, Annie, Lola and Jake stayed behind to help clean up. At one point Meagan took Annie aside and said, "Mom, I know that I have been a real pain over the last couple of years, but I want you to know that I am proud of you and I am trying to do better."

Annie squeezed her only child real tight. "Yes, you have been a real pain. But I do see that you are trying and think that is great. Momma Pearl always believed that you would get some of this 'rambunctiousness' as she used to call it out of your system early. And she thought that earlier is always better than later."

Gazing at her mom's serene countenance, Meg understood that Annie would always love her. She also knew that this love was so powerful that her mom wouldn't let Meg get away with stuff that could wreck her life. She tried to act nonchalant about what Annie said, endeavoring to not relinquish all power in the mother/daughter struggle for power. But her mom's blunt honesty gave the teen a sense of safety. She didn't understand it, but she liked the fact that Annie was so plugged into her life.

Annie patted her baby girl on the back of the head and took a deep breath as she looked around the Family Life Center. For the first time she realized that how much as she was going to miss Momma Pearl. She only hoped that she wouldn't screw things up too badly while she was ramping up her role as a person people could count on.

Tim gritted his teeth as he got out of his car. He knew he should have worn a jacket when he encountered the brisk spring air. He trotted through the parking lot to the church's front doors. Despite the cold, he stood in front of the building hesitating to pull open the door like he had done thousands of times before. He knew that this Elder's meeting would be difficult. He almost emailed Tony his letter of resignation so that he wouldn't have to darken the doors of the church again.

It was not like he was scared or clueless. He had already made a series of decisions that would grease the wheels of change he wanted to facilitate. First, he informally accepted the offer from his buddy to take a new job in Asheville at his business that did site planning and EPA work. Second, he gave Kim a very generous Separation Agreement, which included letting her stay in the house, to help her find some stability in the midst of a lot of stress. Third, he had strategically divested himself of assets in order to create a "moving fund." He sold all of his ministerial books to a minister friend in Asheville; some antique coins to a dealer in Black Mountain; and almost all of his gun collection to Jake. As far as Tim was concerned most people would find out he had moved after the fact.

Tucked under his arm were six copies of his letter of resignation. His simple plan was to short-circuit any nosy probing about personal issues by reading the letter at the start of the meeting. He had already decided that he would take whatever severance the church offered him. If he was pushed at points of privacy, he was also ready to do battle with anyone who didn't pick up on the more subtle hints to simply leave him alone.

All that was unresolved was the threat Tony had issued him about their altercation in the drug store. After talking with his lawyer, he was convinced that Tony and Ruth's discussion of the possibility of taking him to court was a tactic to intimidate him into resigning. They would be getting what they wanted so he figured that all of these ruminations were a moot point.

Tony leaned his weight forward and put his head down like a fullback banging ahead to cross the goal line. He turned left and walked through the darkened reception area of the office into an adjacent hallway. He took the first door to his right and stepped into a large conference room. Five of the elders were already present and seated. Tim noticed that Tony was the only member of the team that had not yet arrived. He said a generic hello to everyone and sat down.

Barry Tompkins noticed Tim's full beard and tried to make small talk by saying, "Wow, you look like Moses with that beard. Are those the Ten Commandments under your arm?"

Tim wasn't amused. He looked straight at Barry and said, "No something a lot less foreboding."

Ralph Mako could see that Tim was all business. He spoke up and said, "Tim, we appreciate you coming by tonight to talk with us. I can't imagine what you have been through over the last few weeks, but I want you to know that we care and have been praying for you."

Tim didn't even look at the DA. He considered Ralph's words a just a preliminary prelude to the lynching he was getting ready to experience. He was not angry. He was just determined to end this meeting as quickly as possible.

Ralph recognized Tim's unspoken message. He actually expected it. Unlike some of the other people who were more than ready to toss Tim and Kim into the trash heap of ministerial couples who didn't make it, Ralph's heart was truly heavy with an almost father-like concern for the younger man.

"Tim," replied Ralph in a very quiet manner. "You will notice that Tony is not here tonight. He has stepped down as the Chair of the

Elder Team due to a circumstance we will discuss in a few minutes. Is it alright if we pray before we get started?"

Tim really didn't care if they prayed or slugged it out in the parking lot. He was that far gone. He bowed his head and let Ralph do his thing. Ralph prayed a simple prayer that love and wisdom would rule the meeting. He asked God's help to allow imperfect people to come to a solution that would bless Tim and Kim and help the church move forward. For a split-second Tim felt strangely warmed by the prayer as if a little spark of hope had lit a small flame. But Tim stomped it out with the ferocity of the cynicism that now ruled his heart.

When Ralph finished, he passed out a sheet of paper that was addressed to the Elder Team. It was written on church stationery and Tim noticed that it was from Tony. A quick survey of the letter's contents revealed that Tony listed personal stress and legal issues were the key issues that moved him to "regretfully step down from his duties as Chair of the Elder Team." It was concluded with a lot of religious blather about how he and his wife were in prayer for the church and the leadership team and other stuff. Tim looked up at Ralph and said, "By this I suppose that he is going forward and pressing charges against me?"

"Yes," said Ralph. "I met with Tony and tried to dissuade him from this path, but he refused to listen. I think that he and Ruth's minds are made up"

Tim sat there for a moment. He could feel the anger rising up in his heart. He wondered why he couldn't be left alone; why Ruth and Tony seemed to be determined to ruin his and Kim's lives; and why in the world any lawyer worth their weight in salt would take on such a case.

"Well, that is just great" Tim sneered.

Before Tim could say anything that he would later regret Ralph interrupted him and said, "Tim, before we go any further can we tell you where we are in all of this. I think you might be surprised.

Tim reached into his folder to pull out his letter of resignation. He paused for a few seconds and then closed the folder. He had always respected Ralph and felt that it was in his best interest to listen. If Ralph stepped over the line, he would interrupt him and shut down further conversation with the blunt reality of his resignation.

Ralph could see from Tim's expression that he had a temporary reprieve. He knew in his gut that Tim was there to resign. But he wanted to apprise Tim of the full picture before such a serious decision was rendered.

"Since you have been gone, I have met one-on-one with all of the guys on this team at least twice. Other members of the church have come by the house and talked with Margie and me. The gist of these informal sessions was this: Apart from a few folks everyone felt very uneasy about how the whole thing went down."

Tim finally looked at Ralph. This was the first thing he had heard from a church leader in a long time that sounded reasonable. "Go on," he replied cautiously.

"Well," continued Ralph, "the idea was that if there was a concern about Kim's behavior she was never engaged in a personal manner. Secondly, the way in which Tony informed you was neither supportive nor compassionate. Third, because of the procedural snafu with calling meetings without involving you in the process, the entire Elder Team needed to repent and ask you, Kim and the church for forgiveness."

Tim was stunned. He was not ready for this approach. He was armed with a howitzer and was handed a daffodil. He tried to put some words together that would resemble a sound, intelligent answer, but couldn't pull it off. He just sat there with his mouth agape in utter disbelief.

John Baskin saw Tim's shock and tried to help. "Tim", he said, "I was one of those people who initially thought that we should get rid of you as soon as possible. But when Ralph pointed out the practical aspects of how we had missed the mark and the personal ways we let you and Kim down, I did a one-eighty. You have been such a good pastor and you have been a friend to me in some difficult days. Please forgive me Tim."

The befuddled pastor bowed his head trying to stay composed. He didn't dare look up because he still wasn't totally convinced that the iron fist clothed in a velvet glove wasn't coming his way.

Barry Tompkins spoke next. "I would echo John's statement. In fact, I wanted to ask for your resignation during the Church Business

Meeting at that terrible meeting several weeks back. But after meeting with Ralph and talking with my wife I really became convicted about how cold, harsh and unloving my heart had become." Then Barry drew in a quivering breath. "It was nothing like the heart of Christ. Please forgive me brother."

Tim tried to shake it off. He didn't like the feeling of being out of control. He reached into his folder to pull out the copies but his hand was shaking so hard he couldn't do it.

Lanny Knowles spoke next. He was the Owner/Operator of a Chick-Fil-A in Rockland. Chick-Fil-A was known for its strong evangelical stance about how to operate a For-Profit business by Christian principles. It was also famous for not being open on Sundays. But more than that, it had invested millions of dollars in providing college scholarships for teens who worked at their restaurants; helped build homes for Foster Parents; and participated in a host of worthy local charities that provided real help to hurting people.

"Truett Cathy, the founder of Chick-Fil-A spoke one time about a guy in one of his stores who had made a huge mistake," said Lanny. "He knew he probably should fire him and told his wife what he was going to do. She suggested that they pray about it and after that he changed his mind. He met with the guy and told him that his mistake could sink him or teach him an invaluable lesson. The guy took hold of that opportunity and today is one of the company's most important leaders. Tim you are too important to us to throw away. Please forgive me."

Now tears freely flowed from Tim's eyes. He was so overcome he didn't even try to wipe them away. They just fell one after the other splattering atop his folder.

Mike Fonville spoke next. He was the most introverted and somewhat shy leader in the bunch. A farmer by trade he usually let the more educated men speak and make recommendations. But his asset was his heart. He could change the whole tone of the meeting by asking a simple question like, "Will that decision show the love of God to our community?" All of the men respected Mike because he really didn't need to be a leader, but was willing to help people any way he could.

Mike got up from his chair and knelt by Tim's side. "Brother," he said. "I love you and I am sorry that I didn't speak up for you at the meeting. You are the best pastor I have ever had in my life. Me, Laurie and the kids have missed you and sweet Kim and we want y'all back if you are willing."

Mike then placed his burly left arm around Tim's neck and kissed him on the cheek. Tim then went from quietly weeping to bawling. He felt foolish but he couldn't stop. No one in the meeting had a dry eye. Once again Mike had led the way in portraying what true leadership was all about.

After a few moments of silence Ralph spoke. "Tim, I would be remiss if I didn't ask for you forgiveness too. I should have cut Tony short when all this nonsense started, but I was more preoccupied with how aggravating it was to deal with this problem than I was concerned about you and Kim's welfare. Please forgive me."

Tim nodded and said "I forgive all of you."

Ralph then sought to find a way to summarize what was going on. "Tonight's meeting is not about making a decision. It is about telling you that we are sorry and that we are willing to work with you and Kim at some kind of decision that would honor both of you and help the church. Is there anything you would like to say?"

Tim wiped his face with an old tissue he harvested from his back pocket. He found a way to gird up his emotions and then said, "Guys I really appreciate all that you have said tonight. I was expecting something totally different. God sure has touched my heart in an unexpected way and I praise His name for the gift of you support and friendship. I can't tell you what is going to happen next. I wish I could tell you that Kim and I are getting back together, but I just don't know. I don't even know if I am qualified or capable or both when it comes to being your pastor."

"Don't worry about any of that buddy," said Mike. "Just tell us how we can help you and Kim right now.'

Kim smiled at Mike. He always liked him and now he was convinced he was one of the finest persons he had ever met. "Thanks Mike, said a grinning Tim. "I guess just tell your wives to reach out and love on her. She doesn't need to be fixed or corrected. She is doing her best to pick up the pieces of her life. All that she really needs are true friends."

"We will pledge to do that very thing, right men?" asked Ralph. All the Elders said in unison "Amen!"

The meeting ended in a short prayer by Mike and several bear hugs. Ralph took Tim aside and said, "Can we meet together later this week. I want to share some more personal things that I think would be of encouragement to you."

"Sure," said Tim. "Just give me a call."

Tim said goodnight to everyone and then walked out of the building. The cold air didn't seem to bother him that much as he moved slowly to his car. He wondered what he was going to do as a result of what he had experienced. He opened the door and plopped down. It was then he noticed the voicemail indicator on his cell phone. It was Kim. He smiled and shook his head. "Boy, he said, "do I have a lot to tell her."

CHAPTER 14

TIM DECIDED TO call Kim rather than listen to his voicemail. She picked up on the second ring and said, "Hey Tim, thanks for returning my call."

"Sure," replied Tim. "What is going on?"

"Well I wanted to thank you for your generosity in the Separation Agreement. I really don't have anything to add. But the bigger reason why I called was that we need to talk about something that has come to my attention."

Tim rolled his eyes a bit. He felt a pain in his stomach as he tried to prepare himself for more bad news. "Ok," he said. "Sounds a bit ominous."

"I know, but don't worry, it is no new revelation from me," said Kim in the most reassuring way she could. "The deal is that I got the most recent version of *The Flaming Apostle* and you wouldn't believe who wrote the featured article and what it talked about."

The Flaming Apostle was a monthly newsletter from a non-denominational missions organization called Emerging Frontier Horizons World Missions that NewLight supported. It was the same group that sponsored Tony and Ruth when they went overseas after graduating from Bible College. It specialized in sending full time missionaries and short-term teams to places where there was little or no presence of Christian witness. Tony had been on the Board of Directors a few years back and now Ruth was wrapping up her second term.

This wasn't your average missions group. It has stringent qualifications, incredible state-of-the-art training centers and a sterling reputation in the Evangelical world. They were headquartered in Wheaton, Illinois which in many ways was the nexus of twentieth century Evangelicalism. Don Fanning, the Founder and Executive Director, was a career missionary in a remote part of Indonesia, and before that was a former Green Beret. He personally designed the one year training course that in many ways mirrored what soldiers underwent in Q-School. There was a language and general training school in Wheaton; survival schools situated across the United States and Central America; and a psychological assessment/placement center in Charlotte. To call EFHWM a hardcore organization would be an understatement.

Tim's mind was still buzzing from the Elder's Meeting so he lacked the energy to venture a guess. "Ok, I'll bite" he replied, "What and who?"

The title of the lead article is "Confronting Sin in a Leader's Life" and the author is Ruth Phipps.

"Oh no," groaned Tim. "What did she say?"

"Well, for starters let me quote this line" said an exasperated Kim. *When our Senior Pastor's wife had an affair that ultimately resulted in a pregnancy, key leaders in the church were faced with the unhappy duty of dealing with this terrible tragedy.*

"What?!" shouted Tim. He was so furious that he had to pull his car off the road and parked it at the McDonald's on Johnson Street. "She can't do that" he retorted. "That is libel, plain and simple."

"That is what I thought, said Kim. "But I wanted to talk with you. I called Judge Jake and set up an appointment with him tomorrow afternoon at four. Do you want to come?"

"You better believe it" replied Tim. "I will pick you up at 3:45 if that works for you?'"

"That's fine," said Kim. "Tim I am so sorry about all of this. I am willing to move away and let this go, but something inside of me tell me I should fight. I just don't want to make a bad situation worse. Does that make sense?"

"Don't worry about that Kim," said Tim in a firm manner. "There is a lot of stuff going on that Ruth and Tony have no clue about. There are fixing to step in their own trap they have laid for us and they don't even realize it. I will see you tomorrow. Get some rest, ok?"

"Ok Tim," said Kim in a calmer voice. "Goodnight."

She hung up and Tim pulled his car back onto Johnson Street. He was a little surprised at his current state of mind. In the span of a few hours he had changed his decision from getting the heck out of Dodge to taking a stand, even if it meant it would be his own personal Alamo. Tim knew that this battle was even bigger than he and Kim's deal. He was ready to face up to the religious bullies who wanted to make Kim and himself disappear.

Tim hit the accelerator as he took the exit towards Rockland. He felt like he did on Thursday nights when he was in High School before a big football game. Tim thought, *"Those two better have their A-game ready for the fight they started."*

Jake Sawyer's Law Office was located right off Main Street beside Stardust Coffee. If you blinked you could miss it. The small front door that faced the sidewalk had the street number 2408 etched in gold in the front glass pane. Once you opened the door you saw a wooden-framed directory on the left wall listing the current businesses that occupied the offices on the second floor. The steps were so narrow that it made you wonder if the width was up to code.

Sixteen gray colored concrete steps outfitted with rubber pads installed to prevent slipping led to the second floor. It had a marbled sixteen foot ceiling surrounded by twelve inch mahogany crown molding. Spaced perfectly across the white stone were three large paddle fans that helped to circulate the air during the summertime. Across from the landing another set of identical steps led to the back of the building which dumped you out in the back parking lot. Both the entrance and exit areas were encircled an ornate railing made of black metal and brass which gave it a nineteenth century feel.

There were three suites on the left and three on the right. Each suite had a door that was framed with ornate mahogany trim work. Encased within each of these beautiful frames were glass and metal doors. The transoms above each door were decorated with the stained-glass representation of a tobacco field at sunset. On the back left corner wall was a brass plate that read New Canaan Tobacco Emporium Est. 1904. Directly across from it on the far right were both state and national markers indicating that the building was a historic landmark. Evidently this floor was once the offices for the company that made The Country Gentleman Cigars.

Jake actually owned all of the second floor space. He bought it from the Gordon Family for a song twenty-three years ago and had everything refurbished according to its original specifications. His office took up two of the spaces to the left. Next to him was the Gordon Real Estate Office that was run by his first cousin Phillip Sawyers. Across from these suites was the Billings, Taylor and Johnson Eye Care Center. Jake had recruited them away from their former offices in Black Mountain five years back to start what he hoped would be a slow and steady restoration of the old downtown. These ophthalmologists took up that whole side with examination rooms, and a lobby that had quite an extensive array of spectacles.

When Tim and Kim Spenser arrived for their appointment Jane Sawyers, Jake's Administrative Assistant and the wife of his cousin Phillip, greeted them and asked them to be seated. The waiting room was neatly decorated in older leathers chairs and an old madras sofa, antique lamps and a large glass and wooden coffee table. All over the dark green wall were prints of what life was like in Gordon during its salad days.

Kim pointed out to Tim one of the pictures that was mounted on the wall behind the sofa they were occupying. It was two older men smoking a cigar and sitting in two Sawyers Mountain High Back Chairs. "Annie showed me a copy of this photo in her house" said Kim with a bit of nostalgia in her voice. "It is old man Gordon with Annie's Great-Grandfather William Sawyers. Mr. Sawyers was the primary tobacco provider for the New Canaan Tobacco Emporium. She told me that he also was the unofficial inventor of that special blend that made the cigar so good."

Tim was impressed. He never knew that the Sawyers family was that interwoven into the rich history of Gordon. None of them ever acted as if they were something special. In fact, everyone he had ever met that donned the Sawyers last name was a friendly, helpful person, no exceptions. The more he thought about it the more he now understood why Jake was so passionate about preserving what was good about this slowly dying town. It was practically woven into his DNA.

As Tim and Kim sat there admiring the picture, loud voices started emanating from behind the door that led to the offices. Jane pulled her sliding glass window back and apologized and told them not to worry. "Those boys are like brothers who have to tussle a bit now and then to make them feel tough!" When she closed her window, Jake and Larry Barber the midget walked through the door still continuing their argument. Jake was pointing at Larry saying. "Larry you got to quit chasing women. I am done representing you in court."

Jake then noticed the Spensers sitting right in front of him. Both he and Larry changed their countenances, put smiles on their faces and greeted the shocked couple. Larry pointed up at Jake and said to Tim "You need to counsel him Pastor. He has some real anger problems and like the Good Book says, a quick temper is the sign of a little mind."

Tim smiled at Larry and said "I'm not familiar with that version."

"Well," replied Jake still agitated. "I am sure that it says something about how an oversexed midget is a perversion of nature!"

"That is not what the ladies tell me old man!" countered Larry.

Kim couldn't help but laugh. That spontaneous giggle made both men frustrated that their mouths were spouting things that, upon reconsideration, they would not want ladies to hear. Larry said his farewells and Jake quickly ushered the couple back into his office.

Jake's office looked like a museum married a law office and had some offspring. It of course had the typical accoutrements you would expect of a barrister: a computer, laser printer, law books, filing cabinets and a huge desk with a burgundy leather chair behind it. But beyond these predictable props, there were paintings of Gordon, pictures of community events and even some Marine Corps paraphernalia including an actual WWII M-1 Garand rifle that hung between two book cases.

In the back right corner was a Sawyers Mountain High Back Chair that had once belonged to Jeremiah Gordon himself. It had a little brass stamp on the head rest indicating it was the 100th chair made. Who knew how much money that simple piece of furniture was worth, but Jake would never sell it because of its historical and sentimental value.

Kim noticed that on wall above that chair were an undergraduate diploma from Wake Forest University; a law degree from the University of Virginia; and a certification of Jake's completion of Marine Officer Candidate School. She wasn't surprised. She always suspected that Jake's homespun humor and country accent were a slick diversion a very incisive mind, and that his legendary toughness in the courtroom had something to do with his Marine Corps training.

The old Judge guided the couple to a small table that had three chairs. He placed a legal pad in front of him and sat down. "So Kim tells me that the Ruth Phipps is misbehaving" said Jake with a wry smile on his face. "How can I help you?"

"I am wondering what are our options here" said Tim. "Can we sue her for libel or slander or just being a hateful woman?"

Jake chuckled and said "I don't know about the hateful part, but you might grounds for a defamation suit." He pulled off a few papers from a file folder. "I have looked at the article and it obviously infers that the baby was a result of the affair. I am a little surprised that the organization published this because they have left the door open for them to be invited to the party. Basically the biggest thing to nail down is this - and I apologize ahead of time for being so abrupt – but who is the father of the baby?"

Kim sat up straight and looked right at Jake with confidence and said, "I believe it is Tim's baby." Tim didn't look so convinced.

Jake noticed the disparity in response to his question and sat back and in a parental tone said, "I think a lot of the both of you. I truly do. And I really don't like Ruth and Tony all that much. But you have to be willing to take this all the way, and that means being honest with me and with yourselves about this crucial question. Sometimes in situations like these it is better to just forgive and forget."

Kim didn't miss a beat. "I have done some research and I have found a DNA research company in Asheville that can take a sample of my blood and Tim's and see if there is a match. The results will stand up in a court of law." She looked at Tim and said, "I was going to tell you about this but all the stuff with Ruth got in the way."

Tim nodded and still didn't speak. Kim then turned back to Jake and said, "When we prove that Tim is the father, will that give us grounds to move ahead? I mean will it guarantee that we can nail Ruth for doing this to us?"

Jake leaned over and patted Kim on the hand. "Now let's not get ahead of ourselves. I don't like using the word guarantee and lawsuit in the same sentence. But if you get the results you are looking for, then yes, it that will go a long way to proving libel." Jake leaned forward and got really serious. "Let me ask you another question: Have you considered the consequences of finding out that Darrell is the father?"

Tim glanced over to Kim. He wondered the same thing. Kim paused for a second and then replied "That is not going to happen."

Jake raised his eyebrows and decided to press forward. "In that case, I suggest a course of action that prepares for battle but allows us to fire a warning shot across their bow before we commence to getting down to business."

"That sounds a little interesting," said Tim showing a little more animation than he had in a few minutes. "Tell us what you have got in mind."

"Well," said the seasoned counselor, "With your permission I would ask for Ruth and Tony to come to my office and I would lay out the situation for them in such a way that they would not only quit their nonsense, they would make a written apology for dragging you fine folks through the mud. If they ignore my warning, we will seek to sink their ship of straw."

Tim liked how Jake operated. He knew a man of wisdom when he saw one, and this grizzle barrister only picked a fight when he felt pretty sure he was going to win. And besides, Jake was trying to protect the community from further division and damage.

"I think that sounds good" said Tim spoken in more of an animated manner.

"Well alright then!" said Jake rubbing his hands together. "In the meantime if you decide to do the paternity test let me know, ok? When we get the results back that Tim is the father of the baby this will be our ace in the hole."

Jake got up and led the relieved couple to the front door. As Kim was exiting, she abruptly turned around and kissed the older gentleman

WALKER ARMSTRONG

on the cheek. "Thanks Papa Jake. This means more to me than you can ever imagine."

"Aw, shoot," said the blushing man. "It is my privilege. Besides, I ain't been in a good scrape in a while. Tony will remember that I am not the kind of adversary you want in a courtroom. Y'all just lay low and stay away from the Phipps'. We don't need to muddy the water any further." Tim and Kim agreed, waved goodbye and walked down the steps. Jake turned back towards his office and started whistling the Marine Corps Battle Hymn.

About a week later Ruth Phipps was standing out front of her store pacing back and forth on the sidewalk. Tony was running late. She had left him a message to meet here right at five. Jane Sawyers had called from Jake's law office asking the both of them to please come by at the end of the day to discuss a serious issue. Jake happened to own the building that Ruth used for her dress shop. Ruth had done some expansion without prior approval and a building permit. Tony just did the work on the slide, hoping Jake would not notice. Now Ruth was convinced that she was going to get kicked out.

Tony pulled up in front of the store and hopped out. "What is all the fuss about?" he asked Ruth.

"I don't know Tony, but I am worried he is going to kick us out," said a worried Ruth.

Tony grimaced. He didn't like that old man, and for good reason. Tony's father Raymond had been taken to court by a group of homeowners who lived in one of his developments. Evidently there were a bunch of faulty septic systems installed during construction that Raymond refused to repair. By the time Jake got a hold of him it cost Raymond a mint and almost sank his business. Since that time Jake's name was synonymous to a snake in the grass for the Phipps' clan.

When the Phipps arrived Jane escorted them into the large conference room at the back end of the office. Tony and Ruth sat down at the end of a long conference table. In a few minutes Jake came bouncing in wearing a broad grin. This confused Ruth and agitated Tony.

"I want to thank you two for coming by with so short of a notice" said Jake as he sat down adjacent to them. "I am sure we can straighten all of this out fairly quickly in time for all of us to get home for an early dinner."

"If this is about the renovations to the shop I will make sure that we get it inspected soon," said Tony in a rushed manner.

"Oh" said Jake. "I didn't know anything about that. Yeah, we will need to talk about that some other time I guess. What I wanted to discuss was something of a more personal nature regarding the Spensers."

"And what would that be?" asked Ruth defiantly.

"Well it has to do with the article you wrote for a recent edition of *The Flaming Apostle*" said Jake. He fumbled around and pulled out his glasses from his coat pocket and then pulled out a copy of the newsletter. "Er, let's see here … yes here is the quote that poses a problem: *When our Senior Pastor's wife had an affair that ultimately resulted in a pregnancy, key leaders in the church were faced with the unhappy duty of dealing with this terrible tragedy.* Yep, that's the one alright."

"What about it Mr. Sawyers?" responded Ruth.

"Well, Mrs. Phipps," said the spunky man in a little bit of a sarcastic way, "this is an almost textbook example of what we call in the legal profession as defamation of character – particularly libel."

Tim dropped his head. Ruth had no clue who she was dealing with. The old man had them dead to rights. Tony tried to warn Ruth that she shouldn't write the article but she was convinced that she was right to do so. As far as Tony was concerned they were as screwed as they could be.

"Well isn't that the truth?" asked Ruth.

"Oh yes. Mrs. Spenser is pregnant" said the wily lawyer. "But you clearly inferred that the pregnancy was caused by the affair. The problem is that Kim and Tim were recently tested by a company that specialized in this kind of thing. And do you know what? They proved beyond a shadow of a doubt that Tim is the Daddy. Isn't that great news?"

The color drained out of Ruth face and Tony looked away in disgust. Jake leaned forward and staring into Ruth's terrified eyes said, "I don't understand how all that fancy science stuff works. I just know that the results are defensible in a court of law."

Jake pulled out a piece of paper. It was a letter written on his law firm's letterhead. It was addressed to Mr. Don Fanning Executive Director of Frontier Horizons World Missions. Tim scanned the contents quickly and saw that Jake had informed the leader that they had printed a statement that was false and had put them in the crosshairs of a possible defamation suit. Jake had requested that Don contact him as soon as possible to see if a "God-honoring solution could be reached."

"I talked with that feller from up in Wheaton" said Jake. "He was very apologetic and promised to print a retraction. We had a little in common seeing we were both in the military. Did y'all know this guy was a former Green Beret? Whew! I sure would hate to make him mad. Oh, by the way, he told me to tell you that he will be in touch tonight."

Ruth wanted to say something, but was dumbfounded. Tony saw the opportunity to speak up and said, "What do we need to do to make this right Jake?"

"Well thank you for asking Tony!" said the triumphant lawyer. "I think that in order to avoid a costly and somewhat nasty legal battle you will need to make a public apology in church to the Spensers. It will need to be written and of course will need to be approved by both the Spensers and me before it is read."

Ruth understood what this meant. Not only would she have to humble herself and admit to being wrong in front of people who respected her, she would probably have to resign her teaching position as the leader of the "Digging into the Word" Bible study. Tony had already resigned his role as an Elder because of his procedural snafu with calling meetings without Tim's knowledge. This had turned into a nightmare for her.

She was feeling so nauseated that she suddenly got up and excused herself to go the restroom. Jake stood as any gentleman would as she rapidly departed the conference room. Tony rubbed his aching head and thought back to a time a few weeks ago when he felt on top of the world.

When Jake sat down he looked at Tony and said, "Now, about that thing with the building. I think you remember from our contract that you are prevented from making any renovations without my written approval."

"Yes sir, that is right. We were doing just a few changes and it got out of hand. I tried to tell my wife about this aspect of the contract but she felt that since we were such good tenants you wouldn't mind."

"Well, she was wrong. But I don't want this to get ugly. I reviewed your contract and the renewal of your lease is coming up in a few months. I think that it is in everybody's best interest for y'all to find a more suitable place to do business. I will give you an extra month to find somewhere to go if you need."

Tony didn't protest. He nodded and got up to check on his wife. He told Jake on his way out, "I will get you a copy of our apology in a couple of days."

Jake stood up and said to Tony before he left, "Thank you Tony and all the best to you and yours." Tony was so discouraged that he didn't have the energy to shoot Jake the bird like he wanted to.

The Worship Center of NewLight Church was packed for a Wednesday night meeting. The prior week all of the members had been sent emails and written notification about a specially-called Church Conference pertaining to Tim's role as Senior Pastor.

Tim and Kim were sitting on the front row. Sitting with them was Annie, Meagan, Lola, Jake and Bart. Surrounding this support group were all of the current Elders and their wives. The unspoken message people picked up on was that no matter what was going to be announced there was a spirit of unity among the leaders and their families that hadn't be present in a long time. The air was pregnant with nervous expectation.

The service opened with prayer from Elder Barry Tompkins. He was upbeat and full of gratitude for the hope and grace of the Gospel. When he finished the prayer people looked up and started to wonder aloud if something unexpected was going to occur.

The next person to take center stage was Ralph Mako. He reminded people of past events that led the church to the current state of affairs. He then asked Tony Phipps to come up and make a brief statement.

Tony walked up and kept his head down until he reached the pulpit. He pulled out a sheet of paper and began to read:

"On behalf of my wife Ruth and myself I want to apologize to Tim and Kim for how we have conducted ourselves during a very difficult time in their lives. We sought to do what we thought was right, but in the end our actions and words did more damage than good. Gossip and slander are never justifiable responses to brokenness, no matter what the circumstances. Both of us have spoken personally with the Spensers and have offered our resignations from all positions of leadership at NewLight. Fifteen years ago we helped to start this great church with the vision of offering our beloved community a Biblically-rooted and culturally relevant fellowship. We are grateful for our time here and ask that you pray for our family as we seek to discern God's will for us. Thank you."

With those words Tony stepped down from the stage, walked down the center aisle and quickly left the building without making eye contact with a single person. Everyone in the building sat quietly as Ralph Mako stepped back up to the pulpit. "I want to publically thank Tony and Ruth for their faithful service to the saints here at NewLight. This church would not be here, nor would it have been as successful as it has been without their tireless efforts. We will miss them and will continue to pray for God's blessings on their lives."

Ralph then paused. He then revealed that the Elder Team had met with both Tim and Kim on several times over the last few weeks to get a feel for where they were and how the church could minister to them. "As a result of these meetings, the Elder Team has a recommendation to offer to the church. I am going to ask the new Chairman of our Elders Mike Fonville to share with you this recommendation.

People grinned when they heard Mike's name. His reputation for being a common-sensed and humble man caused people to have an implicit trust in what he said. He was kind of the EF Hutton of NewLight. Mike didn't talk much but when he did it was worth hearing.

"Good evening my friends" said the shy farmer. "I am not really good at public speaking. I practiced what I am getting ready to share with y'all with my cows yesterday and they seemed to like it." People laughed and that laughter reduced the nervousness in the building.

"Before I speak I am going to ask Tim, Kim, the rest of the Elders and our family members to come up on this stage." No one was expecting this turn of events. Mike stood away from the microphone until he was sure everyone was on stage.

He looked around and then said, "Ok, we are a pretty big group here. It reminds me of my wife's family reunions. Her family reproduces like rabbits." Mike's wife Laurie covered her face in embarrassment as her twin sons asked their Mom what that meant.

"Anyway, Tim and Kim we love you guys and we respect you. None of us are perfect and so to pick on anyone who has made a mistake would be a stupid thing to do. There were more than a few Amens spoken from the crowd.

"This is true of me. Some of you who know me remember that when I was a young man I was a bit of a hell-raiser." People broke out in chuckles. "I probably shouldn't have said that in church should I?" Someone from the audience said "Don't worry about it. So was I brother!"

Mike laughed and replied "I know you were Billy. I did a lot of it with you!" People then erupted in more laughter.

"Anyway, what was I saying?" asked Mike. "Oh yeah, we love and respect these guys and the Elders wanted to do two things tonight. First, we wanted to publically apologize to both of you for letting you down when all this stuff first started."

Several members started clapping. Mike shook his head in agreement. "Yeah, we got carried away with trying to protect the church, which when you think about it is kind of crazy. I mean you guys didn't do anything to us. You made some mistakes and we left you out in the cold and that was wrong. So please accept our apology."

The next thing we want to do is to ask you to come back and be our Pastor. We know that you have a lot of things to work on personally, but we want you here with us. You are our family and we have missed you."

In the blink of an eye the whole congregation leapt to their feet and started cheering and applauding. Tim and Kim wrapped their arms around each other's sides and started crying. Mike started crying too. He looked back at them and asked "What do you say Tim and Kim?"

Tim walked up to the pulpit and tried to speak but people were so moved that they wouldn't stop rejoicing. He finally got them to calm down a bit and said, "We accept your gracious invitation to remain here in this fellowship." The crowd then went into another cycle of even more joyous celebration. Kim hugged Annie who was standing beside her and said "I can't believe that this is happening!"

Tim motioned for the folks to sit down. Slowly the folks settled a bit. When everyone was seated Tim spoke. "I really don't know what to say. The last few weeks have been the toughest and yet the most spiritually-stimulating of our lives. We both have been as low as people can be and have also experienced some incredibly miraculous things. Probably the greatest of all these occurrences is that Kim and I found out that we are expecting our first baby."

The congregation started cheering again. Someone in the audience said "Way to go Tim!" This made the pastor blush. "Thanks" he said. "This, along with many other incredible manifestations of God's grace, has brought me and my bride to this wonderful place of restoration. Many of the Elders said Amen to that statement.

"I am not going to speak a lot more. I just want to say that I love my wife and I am proud to be with her. She has shown more courage and character over the last few weeks than any person I have ever met and I am blessed to have her as my life-partner."

Kim walked up and placed her arm around her husband. She winked at him and spoke to the church. "Mike and I have a lot in common. Among these similarities is that I am not that great of public speaker. The only difference is that I haven't had the chance to practice with his cows."

People laughed and Mike pointed at Kim shaking his head in disbelief that she would kid him like that in church. Kim continued. "I want to thank you for the love and tenderness many of you have shown to me during the darkest days of my life."

A serene and strong look came over Kim's face as she spoke. "As strange as this might sound" she said with a smile in her voice. "My failures have brought me to a deeper place of faith than I have ever known. God is more real to me and my heart is fuller of compassion for hurting people in ways I could have never imagined. Thank you for everything. I promise that I will reinvest the love you have showered me with people in our community who need it."

Kim and Tim stepped away from the pulpit and gave each other a sweet kiss. The congregation stood again and applauded. Ralph Mako, who is normally a very reserved person walked up to the pulpit with tears all over his face. "Folks, he said, "we have had church here tonight, wouldn't you say?"

He then took on the role of Parliamentarian and asked, "Does anyone have a formal motion to offer?"

Larry Knowles stood up and said in a loud voice, "I move that we have Tim Spenser return to full-time duty as our Pastor!"

"Is there a second?" replied Judge Mako.

There were flurry of seconds peppered throughout the audience.

"Then all those in favor say Amen" replied Ralph.

The audience shouted in unison "Amen!"

"Those opposed to this motion please reply by saying "No." said the District Attorney. Not a squeak was heard. "Then the motion passes unanimously! As soon as he said this the crowd shouted and clapped even more.

Ralph pointed to the Worship Leader Charlie Downs and said, "Charlie, would you and the Band lead us in song that would appropriately dismiss us from this place?"

Charlie walked up and said, "You betcha!" Everyone took their place and they played a song that Charlie composed called *He's A Really Good God*. It was a song that employed every instrument they had on stage. It had a James Brown feel to it when the horn section played, and even the most conservative souls in the place couldn't help but move around and give God some raucous praise.

Jake was standing by Tim and said, "I didn't know you guys were Pentecostal!"

Tim laughed and replied "Neither did I but right now I don't mind a bit!"

CHAPTER 15

BART WALKED OUT the front of Angelo's. He turned left and started heading down Main Street to the old Gordon Furniture Factory. Jake had asked to meet with him there. Bart tried to figure out why Annie's Dad was so mysterious about the reason for their meeting. People who are haunted by their past have a constant nagging feeling that eventually someone will discover their secrets and open up old wounds with a sudden thrust of the sword of truth. Bart was no different.

People greeted him as he made his way to the building. He had lived in Gordon for a year and the town folk had started to treat him as a hometown boy. It wasn't easy to break into the close knit circle of friends, families and business partners, but Bart's efforts were starting to pay off. Business was solid at the restaurant and he was recently asked by the Mayor to be part of the Gordon Restoration Council.

Personally things couldn't be going better. His romance with Annie was continuing to flourish while Meagan had shifted her interactions with him from cold disdain to lukewarm acceptance. This spirit of endorsement was spreading all around him. Folks were constantly asking him when he and Annie were going to get married. It was a little hard for Bart to get used to the nosiness that is indicative of small town life. Still, everyone's friendliness seemed to unlock the mistrust that he had surrounding his heart.

After the controversy with the Spensers settled down Bart decided to join NewLight Church. This was a huge step because he hadn't been part of a local fellowship since he was a teenager. For the first time in years Bart felt at home in his own skin and around a group of people. He wondered if all of this was going to go up in smoke when Jake told him what was on his mind.

Bart was deep in thought about all of these things when he heard Jake's voice elicit a greeting. He looked up and saw the lawyer dressed in work boots, jeans, a Marine Corps tee shirt and a camouflaged baseball cap.

"Hey Doc," said the grungy-looking Judge, "thanks for coming by on so short of a notice." Jake jimmied the locked door open and motioned for Bart to join him.

As Bart stepped into he noticed the stale smell of old newspapers, turpentine and some other pungent aroma he didn't care to investigate. Jake slipped past him through the darkened hallway and disappeared into a room up the hallway to the right. Within a few seconds Bart heard the hum of a generator kicking in and saw long, fluorescent lights flickering to life throughout the building, illuminating the disheveled state of the old furniture factory.

Bart was now able to see old food wrappers, a spent Jim Beam bottle and a faded blue blanket were to his left in what appeared to be a reception area of sorts. "This place is barely passable for a homeless person," Bart mumbled to himself. He could only venture a guess at why the old man brought him to this dungy place. Maybe Jake was going to get rid of him and chop up his body with some of the old furniture-making equipment. Stranger things have happened.

Jake popped out of the room he entered earlier with the nervous energy of a teenage boy on his first genuine date. "I know it ain't much, but just use that world-class mind of yours and picture this place in its heyday." Jake grabbed Bart by his right shoulder and ushered him through an ante room that was still dark, and straight out into a brightly lit trash infested factory floor.

The ceilings were about twenty five feet high with huge round duct pipes snaking from one end to another. Thirty tables made up of three rows of tens were still neatly spaced in the kind of configuration that indicated some type of assembly process. Above the tables was a sub-stratum of smaller pipes that had two hoses that ran down to the tables. In the back right corner was a ladder configuration that ran straight up through about a four-by-four hole in the ceiling.

Jake noticed Bart doing his mental math and offered a little assistance. "This was once the finishing room for the M-1 stocks the factory made during WWII. Here they put the last coat of lacquer on the stocks and then placed them on that ladder contraption over yonder."

"Yonder?" Bart bemused to himself. He wasn't fooled. Jake liked using country phrases but Bart had already been warned by Annie not to underestimate her Dad's intelligence.

"From there," he continued with the focus of a museum guide, "the workers took the stocks to a quick-dry room and then they went down another ladder over there for final inspection and shipping."

Bart nodded and then pointed to a bigger room that looked like it was equipped with large lathes and sanding equipment. "Yeah, I was going to show you that" said Jake. He briskly moved ahead of Bart who was starting to be a little intrigued with all the history in the building.

When they entered the room Bart immediately noticed that some of the equipment to the far left side looked like it had either been replaced or retrofitted. Sitting between two newer looking machines were some shiny tools and some sort of engine that had been taken apart and was lying on a large piece of cardboard.

"This is where they used to make both the finished cuts, sanded the stocks" said Jake in an almost hushed tone of respect. "In that room in front people sprayed on a mixture of stain and primer lacquer." Jake shook his head as he was calling back old memories. "My Papaw, Daddy, uncles, aunts and cousins all worked in this place since it was built. People made a good living here Bart, and Old Man Gordon was good to all of his employees. Even his boys continued on the tradition by retrofitting this place from making rockers to stocks for the M-1."

"What happened?" ask Bart.

"Well, they tried to re-tool to make chairs again after the war, but it was too expensive. Because the Gordon's were patriotic people they didn't charge the government enough for the production of the M-1 stocks. The company almost went into bankruptcy three different times."

"How long did the company stay afloat?" queried Bart.

"It hung in there until about the late 1980's. The last of Gordon's sons Will made a valiant push to bring it back. He even picked up a contract for production of the M-14 stocks in the early 60's, and things were pretty good again. But by then polycarbonate steel, plastic and other materials replaced wood, and so pretty soon the M-16 replaced the M-14."

Jake reached behind into a box behind an older lathe and tossed Bart a stock of an M-14. Bart liked the solid feel and the wood and wondered if the same hands that saved countless lives could have taken lives if he had not ended up as a surgeon.

The wayward surgeon pointed his imaginary rifle towards the ceiling and squeezed off a couple of imaginary rounds. Jake smiled at Bart and grunted out a clear "OooRah!" and then continued his historical lecture.

"The company was then bought by a group of foreign investors and they tried to make it into an antique reproduction factory. They cut the production force in half and it did ok for a little while. But when it became cheaper to make furniture overseas the company eventually folded into what you see here today."

"What a shame," said Bart.

"Exactly" replied Jake. "That is why I brought you here today."

"I don't understand," said Bart.

"Follow me" said the sly man with a devilish grin on his face. They walked through the large production area into a darkened area. Jake threw the wall switch and in the middle of the room were two rocking chairs. One sat atop a large table and looked finished, while the other was hanging upside down on four suspended wires.

"Bart my boy, do you know what these are right 'chere?" inquired the somewhat sarcastic man.

"What are Sawyers Mountain High Back Rocking Chairs?" replied Bart as if he was answering a question posed by Alex Trebec.

"That is correct for a thousand!" countered Jake in the spirit of Bart's response. "Come to think of it," mused Jake, "that is what I would like to sell them for. Would you like to buy them?"

Bart didn't know what to think. They were lovely chairs indeed, and he could see them on the front porch at the old farmhouse he was restoring. But he knew there was something more to this offer. "I am not sure. I think you need to tell me more," said the younger man in his best bartering manner.

"Ah, you are picking up on all of this" smiled Jake. "Ok, let me elucidate. I did some background checks on you. You left your medical practice after you made a mistake on a patient and he died. But from what I can surmise the mistake could have easily been made by any surgeon. According to one of my colleagues there was really no gross negligence on your part."

Somewhat irritated by the man's invasiveness Bart asked, "And how did you find out about all of this?"

"Don't worry about that," said Jake in a reassuring way. "If you have been practicing law as long as I have you can call in a few favors now and then."

Bart realized that Jake was within his rights to check on him since he had fallen madly in love with Annie. "Go on," he said to Jake, hoping there would not be any more embarrassing revelations.

"Thank you!" said the judge. "Anyway, since my daughter loves you to pieces I wanted to make sure you were not going to be one of those fellers who shows up on some Friday night TV program that investigates unsolved murders and such."

Bart nodded. He could see how a protective Father would be wary of a man with his background.

"What I discovered was something very different. I found out that the death of your wife and daughter about took you down. You became a living ghost who sought to first drown his problems with alcohol. When that didn't work you tried to change your identity by becoming a chef and using your middle name. Is all that correct?"

Bart looked down at the ground and nodded yes.

"I am sorry about your former wife and daughter. But you have to know at some level by now that with her history of mental illness that this really wasn't your fault," said Jake as gently he put his on Bart's shoulder.

"Sure feels like it is Jake," said Bart taking a deep sigh.

"I could see that" replied Jake. "But you are a good and decent man Bart, and I am an excellent judge of character. Well, except for my partner Larry. But he is family and you are just plain stuck with family."

Bart smiled. Jake's compliment was like money in the bank. "Thanks Jake. That means a lot coming from you."

"So, all that being said, the first big question I need to ask you about your future is this: Have you stopped running?"

Bart was shocked by the question. But he knew he had to answer and do it with all the honesty he could muster. "Yes, Jake. I am."

"Outstanding!" shouted Jake

"That leads me to my second question" said the seasoned lawyer as if he was making his final argument in a really big case. Looking Bart straight in the eye he asked him, "Are you going to marry my Annie?"

Bart shook his head in humorous disbelief. If he didn't adore Annie he would have felt like that this conversation was a prelude to a shotgun wedding. "I was going to ask you for her hand in marriage very soon," said the blushing bachelor.

"Good," said Jake. "Then why don't you buy these two chairs to put up at the farmhouse? Think of them as a wedding gift to Annie."

"Ok," said Bart. But what does me marrying Annie have to do with the furniture factory?"

"I am glad you asked that question my boy," said Jake as he pulled two cigars from the back of his britches. He took out a clipper from his front pocket and quickly snipped off both ends of the stogies.

Giving one to Bart he explained his idea. "I have put together some plans to re-open this factory. The idea is practical elegance. We will make furniture that is high quality but low cost. Phase I we will make rocking chairs and kitchen tables. Phase II we will branch out to creating kitchen hutches for smaller kitchens. This will be the kind of stuff a young couple can afford. And if they take care of could hand down to their kids."

Jake pulled out some papers from a small briefcase that had been leaning against the back of the table. "I have all the legalities neatly tied in a bow and enough operating capital raised to cover us for a year. So, my third and final question is this: Would you be interested in investing in my plans to bring life back to this wonderful old town?"

Bart stood there in shock. This was the last thing he expected. He was both honored and scared. "I really am not a business man Jake," said Bart trying to dissuade the stealthy entrepreneur.

"Oh I would disagree with that Bart" said Jake as he pulled out a small blow torch lighter shaped like a 1911 .45 pistol and lit his cigar. "You built one of the most successful medical practices in the southeast in a short period of time and I got a suspicion that Angelo's is doing pretty well too!"

Jake had done his homework. Bart bowed his head in defeat, took the lighter from Jake, lit up and then asked, "So tell me more about your plans."

"Oh" said the judge blowing a large plume of smoke into the stale factory air, "they are audacious my lad, utterly audacious!"

Annie felt on edge as her Mini-Cooper zipped down the road. Bart had left what sounded like an anxious voicemail on her phone and asked if she could come by the farmhouse during her lunch break. Deep down she knew she shouldn't be worried. Their relationship was going great and they had started making some initial plans about their future. Still, anytime Bart got distant or acted nervous she wondered if the rabbit that lurked in his subconscious mind was not playing tricks on him again.

Bart waved at Annie from the front porch as she drove up to the circular driveway. It had been over a week since she last visited and she immediately noticed several changes in the exterior of the house. First the cobblestone walkway had already been installed. It perfectly matched the cobblestone foundation and chimney that wrapped around the old home like frosting on a piece of pound cake. Bart also had the grungy yellow paint that once covered the exterior replaced with a brilliant white and had all the shutters trimmed out in a very traditional black. When Annie looked up she saw that the old deteriorated slate roof had been replace with some gray-tinted shingles. The somewhat rundown farmhouse now looked almost brand new.

She got out of the car and said "Wow! This looks great!"

Bart wiped his brow in relief. "Whew, he said. "I was hoping you would like it. Come on inside. I have some things I want to get your opinion on!" Bart walked down the steps and picked Annie off the ground and gave her a passionate kiss.

"My goodness Sir Bart!" she squealed. "I think I will plan to come see you every day at lunch if I am greeted like that!" He wiggled his eyebrows in a mischievous fashion and picked her up and carried her inside.

When they walked into the living room she saw that Bart had finally finished restoring the walnut floors. Their rich hue and marbled appearance gave Annie an immediate sense of warmth. Pointing to them she said, "These look great babe!"

"I followed the color pattern you suggested" he said with pride. "Look at the dental mold around the ceiling. Do you think I should stain it the same color as the floor or go with a different color?" She looked for a moment at the small sections he had stained and painted. Pressing her finger to her lips she paused and then said "Let me think about that some more."

From the living room they went into the kitchen and she was even more impressed. Bart had taken out all of the old appliances and installed a stainless steel gas stove, huge sink, and refrigerator. He continued the same rich colored flooring from the living room and added a new countertop that was black, gray and had a hint of the mahogany color embedded into the stone. All the cabinets were brand new and had hardware that Annie loved. Bart had several pain swatches on the walls and pointed to them asking Annie, "Which color would look good in here?"

"My initial thought is to go with the light coffee color here" she said pointing to a sample. "Get a little of that and paint it on this wall here and I will have a better idea."

Bart nodded and said "Yes Ma'am" and led her to the left into what used to be a dingy storage room. He had put rubber tile floor down, installed a sink and on the opposite side put a new washer and dryer in with brand new cabinets above for convenient storage.

"Oh sweetie, this is exactly how I suggested you do it!" This is perfectly spaced for doing wash. You can close it off with that new door and if you ever put a garage to the left of the house you can make this an easy entryway into the house!"

Bart was relieved that Annie liked all that he had done so far. "Come with me" he said excitedly. "I want to show you what I have done with the back porch!"

The walked out of the kitchen and turned left down a hallway. Before you reached the Master Bedroom there was a small bathroom on the left and a small bedroom on the right that Bart had turned into a study. A few paces further down was another hallway that ran perpendicular to the other. If you turned right you would go back towards the steps at the front door that led to the second floor. If you turned left it led you straight out the back door. They turned left.

As soon as Annie walked out she noticed that Bart had the porch floor re-done and had extended it out several feet. It had also been framed up to make it a screened in porch. Although incomplete, the view of the rolling hills behind Bart's property and the fact that Bart had taken her suggestion to heart took Annie's breath away. She stood there thinking about how this house was starting to resemble what she dreamed of as a little girl.

Bart interrupted her fantasy by saying "Hey look over here." Annie shook herself loose from her romantic thoughts long enough to see two brand new Sawyers Mountain High Back Rockers in front of her. "Are those what I think they are?"

"Yep" replied Bart. "Your Dad built them and I bought them from him."

Annie rushed over and sat down. She leaned back and began to rock ever so slightly. Closing her eyes dozens of memories swept over her. She remembered her Nanna rocking her back and forth and telling her stories about her Daddy. She thought of rocking in that same chair the day of her Nanna's funeral. She couldn't help but shed a small tear of sweet remembrance.

"Do you like them sweetheart?" asked Bart, already knowing the answer.

"Uh, huh." said Annie in an almost childlike way.

"Annie, would you look at me a second?" Annie opened her eyes and found Bart knelling in front of her. She gasped.

"Annie," Bart said gathering a deep breath, "a lot has happened to me lately. All of it has been good, but I hadn't had the time to sit down with you and tell you all about it. I promise that tonight after closing I will come by your house and give you all of the details."

Annie was about to interrupt Bart and he gently placed two fingers on her lips. "But all of this has shown me how far I have come and how much God had healed this wondering broken heart of mine."

Annie started crying. Bart wiped away a few tears with his handkerchief. Now tears were welling up in his eyes. "I wouldn't have ever learned how to trust again or how to love again if it wasn't for you. You have given me a reason to stop my running and plant my life in a place where it can bloom and grow.

Annie nodded her head and said, "I feel the same way darling. I had given up hope that I would ever meet someone that would make me feel wanted and appreciated until I met you."

Bart took Annie's right hand and placed it over his heart. He got the most sincere, earnest look upon his face and told her, "I feel like a man who after having a transplant re-discovered what it was like to be healthy again."

Annie touched her own heart and said, "Oh Bart that is the most loving thing anyone has ever said to me in my entire life. I love you so much!"

Bart kissed Annie and said "I love you more!" Bart looked over to the chair beside them and then looked back at Annie. "You know," commented Bart with a wide smile on his face, "I got two of these chairs because there is no one on the earth I would rather rock and grow old with than you. Annie Pearl, will you marry me?"

Annie grabbed her face with both hands out of shock. She was speechless. All that she could muster was the rapid gesture of her head quickly moving up in down in total agreement.

Bart laughed and said "Great! Now I can get off this knee. I didn't know how much longer I could stay down here." He slowly moved up and then sat down in the chair beside Annie happy and relieved. They grabbed hands and then Annie said, "Kim and I have been talking and we have come up with some plans at where to do the ceremony, the reception and what kind of foods we want to serve."

The ebullient look on Bart's face quickly turned into an expression of confusion. He wasn't sure how Annie could so speedily change from shock to planning mode in a matter of seconds. Annie noticed Bart's expression and giggled. "Oh you silly man" she sweetly chastised, "surely you didn't think that this was the first time such a thought crossed my mind did you?"

Bart slumped back in his chair and shook his head. Once again he was reminded that there were very few things in life that he was truly in control of, especially when it came to the romance department. "Anything you want babe," he said admiring the energetic woman as he listened to her master plan for the wedding.

Tim Spenser sat holding Kim's hand as the sonographer moved the wand over her greased, swollen belly. For the first six months everything in the pregnancy had gone picture perfect. In fact, Kim never seemed to miss a beat and had a lot of energy to take care of all of her duties at church and at home. That's why when initially asked if they wanted to have an ultrasound done they opted out because their health insurance only covered this procedure when there was a problem in the pregnancy.

But over the last week she began to feel really strange. Her blood pressure had spiked several times and she had started taking on a lot of water-weight. Her obstetrician Dr. Sampson suggested that they take a closer look and see what was going on with the baby. Both Kim and Tim acted like it was a routine process, but secretly were worried that a more serious problem was lurking around in Kim's body ready to reach out and break their hearts with unexpected bad news.

As soon as the technician finished, Dr. Sampson walked in and took a quick review of the images. He smiled and then told the couple, "We have recently installed a video projector to put larger images on this screen on the far wall so parents could get a clearer picture of what we are dealing with. Look right there I will show you what we are seeing."

The doctor clicked the mouse and the projector kicked on. At first what appeared on the screen looked a large mass of indistinguishable features. Kim looked at Tim frightened by the sight trying to figure out what was wrong with their baby. Suddenly the mystery unraveled and the blob became two distinct entities. Tim blinked to re-focus his eyes, but the initial picture he saw stayed the same. He looked at Dr. Sampson and asked, "Is that what I think it is?"

Dr. Sampson smiled and said "If you mean twins then yes."

"Oh dear Lord, O dear Lord" responded Kim in an almost catatonic tone.

Tim did what any red-blooded man would do in that kind of situation – he fainted. This was not some kind of dainty crumpling of the body into a neat pile in the floor. Tim fell backwards into the computer and other machinery disabling it to the point that the screen went blue. The sonographer helped to soften his fall a bit, but Tim still hit the concrete tiles pretty hard.

When Tim collapsed, Kim and the sonographer screamed at the same time as if on cue. The doctor rushed over checking his head for lacerations or lumps. Fortunately he was no seriously hurt, and in a couple of minutes Dr. Sampson had Tim sitting up sipping on some juice while she explained to the shocked couple the adjustments that needed to be made in Kim's diet and physical activity. She ordered Kim to immediate bed rest and warned them that if the edema and blood pressure issues weren't resolved soon she could be stuck in the bed until the twins arrived.

As the couple was leaving Tim stopped in mid-stride and said, "Oh my gosh, I forgot to ask … what are the sexes of the babies?"

Dr. Sampson smiled and said "It looks like a boy and a girl. I have sent some images to the front desk to have some copies made for both of you to take home and show to family and friends."

By the time they checked out Kim was back on mission and was running through a list of changes that they needed to make to the baby's room to accommodate having both a boy and a girl. Tim walked along nodding his head and mumbling something under his breath. When Kim assessed that her husband was still woozy to drive, she opened the passenger's door and helped him get in. Kim quickly walked around the car, squeezed herself into the driver's seat and started back home.

About half-way back Tim came back to life. "Oh my Lord Kim, he said as if he had just heard the news, "we are having twins!"

Kim laughed and said "That is right sweetie we are. How does you head feel?"

"It hurts really bad but I think I will be ok," said Tim, forgetting that his wife had her own problems to deal with.

"How about I get you a milkshake from the Dairy Barn while we are out" said his wife in a consoling way.

"That would be great. I want the cherry pineapple if that is ok?" said Tim sounding almost like a little boy. He then looked out the window and said with a sigh, "I sure hope I can handle all this pressure of having twins!"

Kim rolled her eyes and replied, "I am sure you will honey. But don't worry about me, I will be fine."

"Yeah, I know you will" said Tim. "You are a pretty tough lady."

Kim turned down Lofton Drive mumbling to herself "Well, at least one of us has to be."

Meagan sat outside on the front porch waiting for her mom to arrive. Annie had told her daughter to study for her year-end exams ahead of time because they were going out to eat at Angelo's. Meagan noticed that her mom sounded nervous and she wondered why they would go out to eat on a Thursday night. They typically ate takeout barbeque from The Singing Pig while Meagan finished up her homework. She knew Annie well enough to believe that something was up.

Annie pulled up and Meagan jumped in. "So what's all the fuss about Mom?" asked the anxious teen. Annie put the car in reverse and said "We will talk about it once we get to the restaurant. How did exams go today?"

Meagan looked frustrated and bored. "Fine" she said as she fiddled with the radio dial looking for something other than the romantic junk her Mom believed was good music. "I think I aced my two exams today. I will be happy when I am done."

"That's great sweetie!" said Annie turning off the blaring rap music that was reverberating in her little car. Annie recalled that a few months back she wondered if Meagan would make it through high school. Perhaps her daughter had really begun to turn the corner. Annie breathed a silent prayer that this glimmer of hope would be an expanding reality.

They drove a little further in silence and pulled up behind Angelo's parking right beside Bart's truck. Annie opened up the door and Meagan walked past her to Bart's office. She found Frodo in the office chair that he normally occupied when his master was busy cooking. Meagan's usually disinterested demeanor changed when she saw the dog.

"Hey buddy!" said the girl. Meagan and Frodo had built quite the relationship over the last couple of months. The dog seemed to make her mom's sickening romance more palatable. His thumping stub of a tail indicated that he enjoyed the way Meagan rubbed his head.

Annie walked in and said "Hey Frodo." Annie tapped her daughter on the shoulder and said "Let's go Meg. Bart has reserved a table for us." Meagan rolled her eyes and followed her Mom to the kitchen.

Everyone greeted the pair as they strolled in. Bart stopped what he was doing and walked up to Annie and gave her a big kiss. Meagan made the universal sign of wanting to vomit and the whole staff laughed at her predictable teenage antics.

"Well," said the flabbergasted woman. "That is a lot different greeting than the one I got the first time I came into your sacred kitchen."

"I didn't know back then what a great kisser you were," said Bart winking at Meagan.

Meagan shook her head and said "I am going to find our seats. Is it the same booth we usually use?" Meagan asked Bart.

"Yes Mademoiselle," replied offering the teen a slight bow.

"Whatever" said Meg as she waved off the gesture and walked through the double doors.

"She isn't going to make this easy for me is she," stated Bart as he gazed into his lover's face.

"Of course not!" said Annie. She gave Bart a kiss on the cheek and told everyone "See y'all later." The staff really liked Annie because Bart's dictatorial ways almost evaporated when she appeared.

Annie found her seat in the booth. She looked at Meagan and said "You know, I didn't raise you to be rude. I suggest you find a way to put that sassy attitude aside or I promise that this summer your social life will be seriously curtailed. Understood?"

"Yes ma'am," said Meagan.

Billy Lampkin, a senior at Gordon High, appeared at their table. Meagan thought he was the most gorgeous boy in the school. She froze as he flashed his million dollar smile.

"Good evening ladies!" said the charming young man. "May I get your beverages?"

"Hello Billy," said Annie. "Are you ready for graduation?"

"I sure am!" replied Billy. "Me and my pals are going down to Wrightsville Beach as soon as the formal stuff is over."

"Please be careful" said Annie in a parental tone. "You do remember that the legal drinking age is twenty-one, don't you?"

"Mom!" said Meagan embarrassed by Annie's direct nature.

"Oh don't worry, we will be extra-careful Miss Bryant I promise" said Billy while winking at Meagan. "So what will it be?"

"I will start out with water, how about you Meagan?" said Annie.

Meagan didn't reply. She was trying to imagine what Billy looked like with a tan. Annie recognized her daughter's far away gaze and told Billy "She will have a Coke."

"He is a very handsome young man isn't he?" Annie asked Meagan.

"I guess so, I really didn't notice" said Meagan trying to act nonchalant.

Annie didn't buy the act, but knew that forcing conversations about the birds and the bees was usually not successful with her strong-willed daughter. "Well I know that you are dying to know what is going on and why we are eating tonight."

"Yeah, that has crossed my mind," said Meagan. "What is the big freaking deal?"

"It is all good news," said Annie. "First, Kim and Tim went to the doctor and found out that they are having twins! It is going to be a boy and a girl. Isn't that great?"

Meagan wasn't moved by the news as much as Annie thought she would be. "Sure," said the detached teen.

"And that is not all," said Annie ignoring her daughter's less than stellar attitude. "She and Tim already had a boy's name picked out. They want to call him Michael. But they wanted to know if it was alright with you if they called the girl Meagan. What do you think?"

This announcement caught Meagan off guard. Despite all of her efforts at being seen as an aloof person this statement touched her. She really liked Kim because Kim treated her like a young adult. "So I guess they are going to be ok. I mean do you think that their marriage is going to survive?"

"Yeah, it looks that way" said Annie.

"That's good," said Meagan. "They are like my favorite couple in this town."

"There is a challenge," said Annie. "Kim is going to have to stay in the bed for most or all of the remainder of her pregnancy. She wanted to know if you could help her out around the house this summer. She said she would pay you."

"Yeah, I could do that," said Meagan with a little more animation.

"Good," said Annie. "I will let her know."

"You mentioned telling me something else?" asked Meagan reminding her sometimes forgetful Mom.

"Just wait a moment," said Annie looking back towards the kitchen. She motioned to Billy to go back into the kitchen. In a matter of seconds Bart came out with a bottle of wine. He sauntered up to the table, uncorked the bottle and poured some wine in the three glasses that had already been placed there before Annie and Meagan arrived, with one glass that had a little more than a sip inside.

"Meagan," said Annie grabbing Bart's hand. "Bart has asked me to marry him and we wanted to tell you here. We know that this is going to bring some big changes in all of our lives and hoped that you would really be on board."

Meagan didn't look a bit shocked or even perturbed. "I can't say that I didn't see this coming," said the young girl like a seasoned adult. "I know mom really loves you, Bart." Annie smiled and leaned her head against Bart's. "But I just want you to know that you are not going to be my boss or something like that."

"Don't want to be," said Bart.

"Ok," said Meagan. She sat and thought for a second. "I would want Frodo to sleep in my room."

"I think that he would like that a lot," said Bart.

"Well then," said Meagan raising her wine glass. "I guess all that I can say is here's to family." Bart and Annie raised their glasses and clicked them with Meg's and said in agreement "To family."

Megan gulped down her small sip and said "This stuff tastes really good. Can I get another glass?"

Annie and Bart looked at each other and said in unison "No!"

CHAPTER 16

DOWNTOWN GORDON WAS packed full of people. The annual Fall Festival had attracted a larger than normal crowd, probably due to the city-wide sales incentives that merchants had been advertising for over a month in papers from Asheville to Charlotte.

It also didn't hurt that the New Canaan Furniture Factory had recently opened the same week as the start of the International Furniture Market in High Point. Jake had hired two seasoned sales associates to man their exhibit at the Market. This has stimulated enough interest to get several potential buyers to travel up to Gordon to talk about doing business with the revived company.

Instead of being the eyesore that everyone saw when then entered on the eastern side of downtown, Jake had made sure that the newer version was a landmark that people would be proud of. He removed the most of the bricks on the front of the building and replaced it on one side with glass displays of their two current products: the Sawyers Mountain High Back Rocking Chair and the New Canaan Kitchen Table. On the opposite side he had two other displays that chronicled the history of Gordon and the furniture company.

When you entered the building you immediately walked into a small showroom. Here both retail and wholesale customers could view the products and make purchases. Beyond the showroom were offices and behind the offices were the manufacturing and shipping spaces. Everything about the new facility reflected efficiency and quality. If you didn't know any better, you would have thought that this facility was brand new.

The new company employed one hundred and seventeen people with a plan to double that number over the next two years. Jake had done his homework when it came to advertising. He had several newspapers and TV stations cover the Grand Opening. He was able to get Senators, several congressmen and the Governor to attend the ceremony. Even the Wall Street Journal™ wrote a cover article entitled "The Re-Birth of a Manufacturing Legend."

But on this particular Saturday night most of the activity was on the backside of the factory where some of the older storage buildings were located. The parking lot was jammed, not with employees cars, but with party attendees. Jake and Lola had spent a good bit of money and time decorating the old building and lining the back lot with colored lights. Their family was throwing a big shindig celebrating the marriage of their daughter Annie Pearl Sawyers to the heart surgeon/restaurateur Ian Bartlett St. Claire.

The two got married at NewLight Community Church. Tim Spenser performed the ceremony and anybody who was somebody in Gordon made sure that they came. The only obvious omission was the Phipps clan. Ruth had closed down her dress shop and rumor had the whole family had been attending a smaller church in Black Mountain. Almost all of her onetime supporters at NewLight had either left the church or had quietly re-assimilated back into other Bible studies. In some ways, it was like they never existed except for the fact that their names appeared on a plague in the lobby of the church commemorating the founding of the fellowship.

Jake and Lola stood at the front door of the former storage building welcoming their guests. On the right of the entrance was a makeshift coatrack made of old pipes from the factory. Beside the coatrack were three tables pushed up against the wall reserved for wedding gifts. Past those tables was the line for food. Lola got ladies form Sawyers Mountain Methodist and NewLight Community Church to chip in and bring every kind of finger food you could imagine. The line then flowed into a series of tables that were scattered over half the area of the large room. The tables were decorated with white linen cloths and a small pumpkin/flower/candle configuration that Annie came up with for the centerpieces.

Beyond the tables to the far left side of the storage facility was an area designated for dancing. The entertainment for that night was none other than Big Wayne and the Gordonettes. Big Wayne was Wayne

Chapman who ran a tire and automotive shop north of town and played rhythm guitar. The Gordonettes were made up of Wayne's wife Cordelia (who also played keyboard); her sister Suzy Byers; and Anne Sawyers a distant cousin of Jake's. The band was comprised of Wayne's son Tommy on the drums; NewLight's Worship Leader Charlie Downs on the Sax; Mayor Nolan Thompson on the trumpet; Elder John Baskin on the trombone; Earl Knowles on the trumpet; the reformed drug dealer Tommy Blankenship on the bass; and none other than Pastor Melvin Booker on lead guitar.

Big Wayne had put together some version of this band since he was in high school back in the seventies. Now they occasionally played for clients like the Moose Lodge or Grand Openings of shopping centers and such. Their repertoire was as diverse as their band. They played anything from Lynyrd Skynyrd to Cole Porter. They had their own website and Wayne often joked that they had some groupies "but most of them had faded away because they had started to become grandmothers."

Tonight they were really cooking. Several people were on the dance floor shaking their groove thing to the band's version of "25 or Six to Four," including little Larry who had brought his latest romantic conquest to the party. There is nothing quite like the sight of a midget bumping and grinding with a three hundred pound lady.

Annie and Bart were walking around greeting their guests at each table and thanking them for their support. When they arrived at Mary Marla's table Marla stood up and gave both Bart and Annie big hugs. For Annie it was like embracing Mamma Pearl.

"Teddy sends his love and wants to say how sorry he was he couldn't come to the wedding" said a grinning Marla.

"Oh that is so sweet!" replied Annie. "Tell him that we missed him but understand that he needed to be in Washington."

"I've got something for you baby sister," said Marla as she opened up her purse and pulled out a card. "This is a note that Momma wrote you. I found it while going through her things. If you look on the back of it is says to be opened at your wedding."

Annie shook her head in disbelief. She thought about opening it right there but was worried that she might get too emotional. She gave Marla a kiss and thanked the rest of her family for coming. Then she excused herself and walked out the main doors into the cool October evening. She looked around to see if anyone was watching and opened the letter. It read:

My dearest Annie,

If you are reading this I am in Glory with Jesus, my darling Edgar, and all my loved ones that have gone on before me. I know you miss me. I miss you too. But today is a day of celebration, not mourning. So dry those eyes of yours right now!

At this point of my letter is only fitting for me to say this very important thing: "I told you so!" You can't deny Ju-Ju baby. I knew that both you and Bart had some old ghosts to get rid of before you could finally get together, but I was certain that it would happen. I only wish I was there for you to give me a public apology for doubting Mamma Pearl!

Don't worry about Meagan. If you and Bart nurture the kind of relationship you should have, that sweet darling will find her way through life ok. I mean you found your way, and you were more of a pain in the ass than that child every thought about being. I ought to know because I was there.

I think you and Bart make a great couple. Tell him I said to quit the charade of being a chef and go back to being a doctor. He has done enough penance for his past mistakes. Oh, and tell him he is still wrong because Joe Montana is the best quarterback to have ever played the game.

I leave you with this: If you have Ju-Ju, don't think for a second that you can't lose it. It is magic that requires work.

But if you and Bart never slack off you will reap blessings that you could never have imagined. If it was true for me it can be true for you.

Please tell Teddy, Mary Marla and all my grandchildren and great grandchildren that I couldn't be prouder of who they are. And the same goes for you my darling little Pearl. I knew you would be part of my heart the first time you smiled at me, and I was right (as I normally am). I will be saving a place for you at the big homecoming dinner in the sky.

Much love,
Me

Annie placed the letter on over her heart and quietly wept tears of deep gratitude. As she was thinking about all that had happened to her life over the past year Bart came up from behind her and kissed her on the cheek. "Are you ok?" he tenderly asked his new bride.

"Oh, better than ok" said Annie as she turned and gave him a long passionate kiss. "By the way" she said after disengaging from the soulful connection. "Momma Pearl says that you were wrong and that Joe Montana is the best that ever played."

Bart laughed and said "Ok, Ok I give in." He grabbed Annie by the waist and said why don't we rejoin the party?" She agreed and the waltzed in just in time to join the dance train as the band played the old Motown standard "I'll Be Around."

Annie and Bart joined in and were shuffling along, seeking to match rhythms with the syncopated snake of people Bart whispered in her ear, "Do you think that the rest of our lives will be this zany?" Annie leaned her head back and then just plain smiled.

But as the music and laughter swirled upwards dissipating into crisp Fall air, a solitary figure sat on the side of a hill, embedded into the landscape of Mountain Laurel and White Oaks, looking for an opportune time to descend.

WALKER ARMSTRONG

CPSIA information can be obtained
at www.ICGtesting.com
Printed in the USA
BVHW071018261221
624843BV00005B/81

9 781669 800538